Death BEFORE Daylight

By: Shannon A. Thompson

Death Before Daylight
Copyright ©2015 Shannon Thompson
All rights reserved.

ISBN:978-1-63422-088-0
Cover Design by: Marya Heiman
Typography by: Courtney Nuckels
Editing by: Kelly Risser

For more information about our content disclosure, please utilize the QR code above with your smart phone or visit us at

www.CleanTeenPublishing.com.

To Alex – for dreaming up daylight in a dark place.

ONE

Jessica

"**I**'M LEAVING," I SHOUTED OVER MY SHOULDER AND OPENED THE front door, but I stopped before stepping outside.

"No, you are not," my mother responded while running out of the kitchen. Her blonde hair was piled on top of her head, and the frizzy strands were as crazy as her bewildered expression. "It's too dangerous right now."

It had been two weeks since the battle, two weeks since we lost so many, and two weeks since the news called it a mass suicide. The rumor said it was a cult of some sort. I hated the gossip. I hated how people assumed Teresa Young—or Camille—was a part of it. But I couldn't tell anyone the truth. No one would know she was a hero.

"It's fine, Mom." I was officially a professional at faking a believable smile. "No one is in trouble—"

"We don't know that." The frown lines around her eyes deepened. "I don't believe the news any more than the next person."

My smile was almost impossible to keep. Luthicer, the only half-breed elder capable of mass illusion, created the news. So far, Hayworth hadn't questioned it. Not once. But my mother was.

I shut the door, and the lock clicked into place. "I won't leave," I said, but I wasn't listening to myself. My mind was too busy racing. Luthicer's illusion was failing. It never failed.

1

"Okay," she breathed, leaning her back against the wall. "Don't you have homework?"

Winter break didn't end until tomorrow, but I still responded "Yeah" because something was definitely wrong. "I'll be upstairs."

"Okay, Jessie."

I didn't look at her again as I raced upstairs. I couldn't. I had to focus on getting to the shelter. The elders had been in meetings nonstop, and I promised Eric I would be there. I was over two hours late.

When I pushed my bedroom door open, my heart slowed. I felt his presence before I saw him, but I didn't recognize it. My hands sprang up, and my knees bent. I spun around, ready to kick, but he leapt back and hissed, "It's me."

I froze.

His electric green eyes were like his name. They pierced through me.

"Pierce." I cursed and my muscles relaxed. My chest rose as I sucked in a breath. "Sorry," I muttered. "You could've told me you were here."

"I tried," he admitted, tapping his temple to signal his telepathy. "It isn't working."

I searched my mind, dipping in and out of all the connections I had gained over the past year. They felt like light switches, flipped off and stuck. My connection with Pierce—my guard—had sizzled away overnight. "I didn't hear a thing."

"Like I said, it isn't working," he repeated, his eyes searching my expression. "Are any of your other powers changing?"

I stilled. I knew what was happening because the elders hadn't stopped talking about it. The powers were shifting. While most of the Dark were weakening, one shade couldn't even transform anymore. The Light hadn't even been around, but if Luthicer's illusion was dwindling, then we knew their powers were ceasing as well. Neither side won the battle, but the battle had beaten us all.

"What's going on?" I asked without knowing if I was asking him or myself. "This isn't right."

Nothing was.

"We have to go," Pierce said, reaching out. His palm faced me. "I have to admit," he said. "I thought you might have gotten in trouble when you didn't show."

I didn't have the heart to tell him why I was late. My memories were still restoring, and they paralyzed me any time they did. One day, I remembered something, and the next, I forgot it, but when a memory came back, I relived it as if it were happening in real-time. This morning, I remembered how I had told Eric I hated him. The realization made me sick. I hadn't put on my engagement ring since, but I was going to see Eric for the first time in days.

"Hold on," I said, stepping over to my desk. I opened the drawer and pulled out the jewelry. When I slipped it on my finger, I sensed Pierce's stare. "Don't tell him," I managed. "Please."

"My duty is to you, Jess," he said, but his words were quiet.

Even worse, the telepathic communications changed. A line in my mind shifted, but only one buzzed, quiet and unused. Eric. Anytime I wore the ring, I could feel him. I had yet to ask if it was the same for him.

"Let's go," I said, taking Pierce's cold palm as our molecules disintegrated into the darkness I called home.

———◆———

Camille's grave was the first thing I saw when we transported into the underground shelter. I barely noticed how cold the hallway was. I could only stare at the black room I had yet to visit. Her funeral was the day after Eric gave me his mother's ring. My guilt had kept me away. Eric encouraged me to grieve how I needed to, but he didn't tell me how he was grieving. He hadn't even mentioned her to me.

"He hasn't gone yet either," Pierce spoke as his hand slipped from mine.

I stared at my guard, trying to piece his shade features into his human identity. It was impossible. Pierce's heightened cheekbones and slanted eyes were anything but close to the artful and half-blind Jonathon Stone. But his grand smile was the same.

"Has he said anything to you?" I asked.

Pierce didn't have to shake his head. We both knew Eric was in denial. Since the Marking of Change, he hardly left the shelter. He practically lived there. But he hadn't visited the one room I thought he would spend his time in—especially since the elders' meeting room was across the hallway.

Before Pierce and I continued speaking, the meeting room's door cracked open. A boy slipped out, and his black hair flickered in and out of the shadows, even though his blue eyes burned through them. "Jessica." His voice was unforgettable.

I sprang forward, and Eric wrapped his arms around my torso. His usual earthy scent was gone. He smelled like the shelter's cold, hard stone. As his fingers drew circles on my lower back, he spoke to Pierce, "How is everything?"

"Not good."

I moved closer to Eric's side. "My mom started questioning the news."

Eric's back tensed. "Not her, too." There had been others.

"What did Luthicer say?"

"Not much." The circles beneath Eric's eyes showed how little he had slept. "He's weaker than usual, so that is making it difficult for him to run experiments, but he can still run individual illusions."

He could make my parents forget.

"He can't do that to the whole town," Pierce said.

"That's the problem."

"So, we haven't gotten anywhere," Pierce always said what everyone was thinking. The Dark was weak. The Light was weak. The prophecy hadn't done anything. We were losing our powers again—at least, most of us were.

"*Are you weak?*" Eric asked through our telepathic line.

I glanced at him. "*No.*"

"*Me neither.*"

Unlike the others, our powers were intact. The descendants were fine.

4

"What's going on?" Pierce spoke up.

Eric stepped away from me as if our touch changed our conversation. "Nothing."

Pierce's jaw locked.

"We can't talk right now—" Eric began, but Pierce interrupted him.

"Camille isn't here anymore," he said her name like a curse. "If we don't stick together, she won't be the only guard to disappear." His sharpened tone dropped to a harsh hiss, but his eyes softened. "You two are all I have."

I couldn't breathe, but I could move. I stepped toward my guard. "He's right, Eric," I said, squeezing Pierce's arm.

I waited for Eric to say something, to explain how our powers were intact, but his gaze focused on my hand. "We'll talk later." He opened the meeting room's door. "For now, we have to talk to them."

Behind him was a large table, an elongated desk meant to hold ten elders, but only three chairs were regularly used. Luthicer sat on the end, and Bracke sat next to him. Urte stood by the far wall as if there was a window to look out. None of the men glanced up at us. We might as well have not been there. We couldn't do anything either.

TWO

Jessica

"I CAN'T DO THIS." ERIC'S CHEST SANK AS HE GRIPPED THE BRICK wall. "I just can't."

"You can." I held myself back from yelling at him. Ever since the meeting in the shelter, Eric hadn't spoken to anyone. Even when the elders asked for his opinion, he kept his lips pressed together. He acted like he had nothing to say. I knew him well enough to know that meant he had everything to say. Still, he remained silent.

"Come on." I tried to pull him toward our high school, but he dug his heels into the ground like a toddler would.

"It's not a good idea—"

"We can't keep hiding," I interrupted him. "That's not an option."

But it was. Eric's green eyes said it before he did. "They know who we are, Jessica."

I knew it. We all did. The Light was aware of our identities, and we didn't have one inkling about who their soldiers were—not even Darthon. Unlike Eric, I was safe. According to the Light, my death would bring Darthon's. Hurting me was the last thing on their list of priorities, but hurting Eric was at the top.

"If you hide, they will think you're scared," I spoke to him without touching him. *"And they know where the shelter is."*

"I know I told you I would, but—" he started.

6

"You promised me you would," I corrected.

We spent our entire winter break discussing whether we would return to Hayworth High. At first, the elders were against it, but they changed their minds. Everyone knew our names. The Light knew where we lived. They knew the shelter's location. They even knew where we slept. But Eric stared at Hayworth High like it would be the place of the attack.

His eyelid twitched, but he never looked at me. He focused on our school, the one place where he never had to be a shade, but that time was gone. He couldn't hide. Not even at home.

"If anything happens—" I started, but his voice entered my mind.

"Nothing will happen." It wasn't until he rested his right hand on his ringed finger that he smiled at me. My ring heated up on my hand. "Let's go." He started walking before I realized he had come to a decision.

I had to jog to catch up with him. "Try not to look like you're going into battle."

He shook his arms to loosen up. "It's a constant state with me." He paused as we neared the doorway, but his gaze flickered around the students flooding in for their first day. No one gave us any more attention than usual. It was...normal.

As Eric opened the door, he glanced back at me. "It's January, isn't it?"

"Yeah, why?"

Before answering, he leaned in and placed a kiss on my lips. When he pulled back, a flush spread over his cheeks. "It's been one year since we met."

It had been. We had met at the river, and then, we met in school—two people, disguised as other identities, yet we found one another in both lives. Fate was tricky like that. It consumed us when we thought we were free, and it freed us when we thought we were captured. Our love was a river, always changing under the mercy of nature's elements, but we continued to flow, even when we trickled.

"Happy anniversary," I said as he took my hand in his, and

we walked into Hayworth High together.

———◆———

I dropped Eric's hand as we entered our homeroom. "I was not expecting this."

Zac and Linda were standing by the far wall, talking to Robb, while Crystal was sitting by herself at her usual table. In all the chaos, I had forgotten how the siblings had transferred in. I hadn't even told Eric, and Crystal didn't know Eric and I were dating—or engaged.

When she looked up, her eyes lit up only to dim when she saw Eric standing by my side. She pursed her lips, and I forced a smile. Over the break, we had spoken over the phone, but not enough.

"Come on," I said to Eric, and he didn't argue. He followed me over to Crystal.

"Hey, Jess," Crystal's voice strained against her throat before she coughed. "Sorry," she muttered. "Recovering from a cold."

My leg leaned against her desk. "Well, at least you're better."

She rolled her eyes. Her signature move. "Please," she started. "I wasn't going to miss the first day. The school newspaper would be at a loss without me." Pen marks already littered her hands, but her usual notebook was nowhere in sight.

"Where have you been?" she asked, glancing over at Eric. "Uh—"

Eric tensed. "Hey, Crystal."

I fanned a hand at him. "You guys have met," I stumbled over my words, unsure of where to go from here. The way Crystal's mouth hung open wasn't helping. "Eric—he's—um—Eric is—" When I looked at Eric, his grin looked like it would break into a laugh. He was enjoying my nerves.

"I'm her boyfriend," he finished my sentence. If I hadn't known he was freaking out only a few minutes before, I wouldn't have believed it. He was calm now.

"Boyfriend," Crystal repeated, glancing between us. I recognized the look. She expected us to say we were kidding, but we weren't. "Boyfriend?" Her palms slapped the desk as she stood up. "Since when?"

The entire classroom stared. Heat crawled up my neck, but Eric laid a hand on my shoulder like drama was his element. "December," he answered as I said, "July."

Our widened eyes met. Our lies didn't match.

"January," we both sighed the truth.

Crystal gaped. "Like this January?" I couldn't hide my face from her. She read it with the precision only a best friend could have. "Last January?" she squeaked as her expression crumbled. "Why didn't you tell me?"

Because I had my memory wiped wasn't exactly an answer I could explain.

Instead, I settled on, "It was complicated."

Crystal bit her pierced lip. If I didn't know better, I would've thought she was mad, but she wasn't. She was falling apart.

Eric tiptoed backward. "I'm guessing this is one of those girl talk moments?"

"Girl talk is a must," Crystal agreed without looking at him.

Eric ducked away before I could stop him. He placed his headphones on his ears and cranked the music high enough that I could hear it as he walked to our table. As much as I hated to admit it, I didn't know if the Light would attack us at the school, and having him near me was the only comfort I had.

My fingers twitched at my sides. "I'm sorry," I whispered and dipped into the chair next to her. When she didn't sit, I pulled her down next to me. Our knees touched. It was the closest we had been in weeks.

"Why didn't you say anything?" She had perfected the melodramatic whine. Her appearance only added to it. Her white hair frizzed at the staggered tips, and her dark roots peeked through more than usual. She was a mess, and I hadn't even realized it.

"What's going on?" I ignored her question. "What's

wrong?"

"Since when have you even liked Welborn?" She ignored my questions, too. "I mean, I figured as much when you danced at prom, but—" She squinted at Eric from across the room as if he were an apparition. "Eric Welborn? I can't believe it."

"What about Welborn?"

I knew the voice.

Robb was standing behind us, but he was close enough. Goose bumps traveled over my neck. He had attacked me weeks ago. The bruises were long gone, but the pain remained. My fist curled.

Crystal laid her hand on my arm. "She's dating Eric," she whispered, oblivious to the fact that Eric could hear a conversation from across the room. Even with his music cranked, he had perfected his abilities, and he would be listening since Robb was close. But that's not what bothered me.

Crystal was talking to Robb like nothing happened last semester.

"What?" Robb's eyebrows squished together. He didn't seem uncomfortable at all. He seemed like Robb McLain, the boy I met after he almost threw a coffee on me. "Since when?"

"January," Crystal answered. "Last January."

Robb chuckled. "Knew it." He sat on the desk next to us and propped his foot on Crystal's chair, but he looked at me. "You always talked about him."

But I hadn't. Not unless it had to do with the project. I fought the urge to look at Eric. Instead, I looked behind Robb. Zac and Linda remained at the back of the room. They hadn't even come over to say hi.

"Oh," Robb pointed behind his shoulder. "I've been meaning to introduce you to my friends. They just transferred in."

"What?" Stomach acid rose up my esophagus. "I already met them—"

"Really?" Robb glanced over his shoulder, but his friends never looked back. "Well, that saves me an awkward introduction."

"*Are you okay?*" Eric's voice crashed into me.

My hand shot to my neckline, and my racing heart burned through my sternum. Every beat was fiercer than the last. Every breath was harder to grasp. I couldn't move.

"Jess," Crystal's heightened voice shattered my panic. Before I knew it, her cold fingers wrapped around my hand, and she yanked my hand so hard I fell forward. My left hand was in her grasp, and my ring sparkled under the florescent lights.

I pulled away, but it was too late.

"Is that—" Robb started. "Is that from Welborn?" All the amusement in his voice was gone.

"It's not an engagement ring," I half-lied as I focused on my telepathy with Eric, "*Help.*"

Eric was there before I even mustered the strength to stand up. As soon as his hand wrapped around my arm, my knees stopped shaking. I leaned against him.

"Are you okay?" he asked, playing the part of a concerned boyfriend instead of who he was: my concerned fiancé, the first descendant of the Dark.

"I feel sick."

"Sorry, guys," Eric said and turned toward the teacher. "Ms. Hinkel, I'm taking her to the nurse's office."

My vision blurred, but I heard Ms. Hinkel ask, "Already?" Her question was replaced in seconds. "Okay, then. Just get a note before you come back."

"Thanks." Eric shuffled us to the doorway. "We'll be back," he finished with a familiar tone. It was the way he ended his sentences that always gave him away. The last word dropped off, quieter than the rest. He was lying.

We weren't coming back, and I knew he was right. We shouldn't have come at all.

THREE

I DIDN'T TAKE HER TO THE NURSE'S OFFICE, BECAUSE THE NURSE couldn't do anything. We sat by the willow tree instead. I waited for her to speak, my arms propped on my knees, but Jessica only pulled her legs up to her chest. I expected her to press her nails into her palm—something she always did when she was nervous—but she didn't do it this time. She just breathed, her back rising and falling as her eyes moved over the school.

I leaned forward to skim my fingers across her arm. She acted like I hadn't even touched her. "It's been happening a lot," I guessed, thinking more of her memories had slid back into focus. "Hasn't it?"

Luthicer's spell to wipe Jessica's memories had worked in some places and failed in others. Even though Camille had broken most of it, effects remained, bouncing around in Jessica's mind. Over break, I had witnessed at least five panic attacks as she regained the moments she had forgotten. Strangely, most of those memories were human ones. But Jessica said something I didn't expect. Something I couldn't have guessed.

"That's not what happened," she said before shivering. The snow was gone, but the air felt like it was filled with ice. When she didn't explain further, I studied her face, paler than usual, only flushed at the cheeks. She didn't move, but I knew her mind was racing.

"What happened then?" I was starting to think I should've taken her to the nurse. "Was it Robb?"

"No—yes," she stuttered. "Not exactly." Her forefinger curled around her hair. "I remember." She hadn't forgotten what had happened between Robb and her, but her eyes glossed over. "Don't I?" she squeaked. "What happened—" She struggled to say it out loud. "Robb did that, didn't he?"

My fist tightened just thinking about that night. When I had seen Robb and Jessica, I hadn't realized it was them at first. My windshield was covered in water, but I saw enough to know what was happening. A guy was attacking a girl, and that was enough of a reason to pull over. It wasn't until Robb pulled away and yelled at me that I saw Jessica's face.

"Of course it happened," I struggled to keep a calm tone. "I was there—"

"Then, why don't they remember?"

Her words froze my anger. "What do you mean?"

"They acted like nothing happened." Her hold tightened on her legs. "All of them."

Her words didn't compute. "What?"

She threw her hands up in the air, but her legs remained propped up. "Crystal wasn't mad at Robb at all."

"Are you sure they don't think you forgave him?" I worded my question with care.

She shook her head. "Crystal wouldn't do that without talking to me first, and Robb was going to introduce me to Zac and Linda."

Jessica knew them, but why didn't Robb remember? At one point, she had even doodled Zac's name in her notebook. I didn't remember they were transferring—not so quickly anyway—but it was our last semester. We would graduate in May. If they were going to transfer from St. Lucia's, then they were going to do it now, but I hadn't prepared myself. Jessica hadn't either. Our lives had become too chaotic outside of school to pay attention to our peers. The events slipped right past both of us.

"Robb thinks I don't know them," she continued, "but I

told him I did, and he didn't remember anything. Not one thing. He thinks we're strangers."

"That doesn't make sense."

"I know," she agreed, "but I recognized the feeling, the power. It was an illusion," she explained. "That's why I got dizzy. It triggered mine." A shaking breath escaped her. "I know it was."

I wanted to argue, to tell her Luthicer wouldn't have done it, but I couldn't because I believed her. Jessica didn't lie, not to me anyway, but I spoke anyway. "Luthicer wouldn't do that."

"Someone did."

Her eyes started to water, so I stood up and offered her my hand. She looked up at me, and I felt like I was looking at the nameless shade she was before—disconnected and lost.

"Come on." I leaned down to grab her hand.

As I pulled her to her feet, she asked, "Where are we going?" Her hand landed on my arm like it was an automatic part of her nature, something she didn't even notice, but my insides twisted with recognition. Her touch affected me more than I liked to admit.

"Do you seriously have to ask that?" I tugged my car keys out of my back pocket. We couldn't transport in the middle of the morning unless we wanted to risk hurting ourselves. "The elders might know something."

———◆———

When we arrived at the park, we got out of my car in silence. I didn't bother hiding my car anymore. Even though I spent eighteen years hiding who I was, everyone knew now. I had to get used to it. Being myself all the time was new to me, and anything new was uncomfortable.

We walked across the grass, past the river, and ducked into the crowd of trees. Across two trails and down a riverbed, the opening of a small cave hid behind fallen branches and old logs. It used to have a protection spell around it. If someone trespassed and found it, they would see a rocky wall, but the powers were fading, and the opening flickered. I pulled the branches back so Jessica could enter without her curls snagging on the twigs, but she had already tied her hair up.

When she ducked under the brush, I followed her, watching her ponytail as it swung back and forth. She had calmed, but not enough. Even with others walking about, her anxiety escaped in staggered breaths.

"Almost no one is here," she said, noting the few people passing by.

On an average day, a couple dozen shades would be in the shelter, but today there were only six. They were only able to transform because of the underground darkness and the extra powers pumped through the walls by the elders.

"Shades have human lives, too, you know," I reminded her. It was only nine in the morning. People were at their day jobs, continuing life as if it were normal, as if we hadn't lost a war weeks ago, as if I hadn't lost my battle.

"Pierce," Jessica straightened and called before I saw him.

The black-haired boy jogged across the room and hugged her. "Are you all right?" He was quiet enough that a human wouldn't hear, but loud enough that I could.

Jessica nodded as she pressed her head against his shoulder. He patted the top of her head as if she were his sister. I had never seen him get close to anyone, not even his family.

"Jonathon." His human name slipped out of my mouth.

The two of them stepped apart and blinked as if they forgot I was standing there.

"What are you doing here?" I asked.

He ran a hand through his hair, and the black threads stuck up. "Something was wrong." He gestured to Jessica. "I felt it." He was her guard. Of course he had sensed it. Guards had unexplainable connections with their warriors. I knew because my own connection was severed.

"Yeah," Jessica spoke up, and then explained to Pierce what had happened. This time was much faster than she had told me.

He listened as if he were expecting it and didn't even flinch. "I had a feeling something was up," he admitted. "I saw

Crystal and Robb hanging out in the parking lot this morning." Even he knew Crystal wouldn't have done that without talking to Jessica first.

I walked past them. "Are the elders here?"

"Only Luthicer and Bracke," Pierce said, but I already knew by the time he answered.

Luthicer and my father were standing outside the meeting room, the door propped open behind them. "We heard," my father said, waving us inside. We followed, and Luthicer shut the door behind us.

"I didn't do it," Luthicer spoke before anyone could sit down, but no one sat anyway. "It must have been the Light."

"But why?" Jessica asked. "There's no reason to do that."

"There is. They know who you are," Luthicer said, as if we could forget.

"What does that have to do with anything?" I leaned against the wall. "They're just her friends."

"Exactly," Luthicer said. "They can't hurt her. They don't want to hurt her. Not physically anyway."

Jessica sucked in a breath. "What is that supposed to mean?"

Bracke—my father—messed with his shirt as if he were searching for the glasses he didn't need as a shade. "It means they want to confuse you."

"Don't soften it," Luthicer bit back, and his pitch-black eyes focused on Jessica. "They know what we did to you, and they want you to think we gave you false memories. They want you to distrust us." He didn't have to say the last part, but he did anyway, "The Light wants you to go to them."

FOUR

Jessica

"I WON'T," I REPEATED FOR THE UMPTEENTH TIME AS ERIC DROVE IN silence. I hated the silence more than I hated the memories coming back. The silence made me feel like we wouldn't make new memories. It felt like the end. "I won't go to them. I trust the Dark—"

"I know that," Eric interrupted harshly. His jaw swung like he was preventing it from locking. "I'm sorry." The Charger's engine roared as he took the last corner, but trembled when he parked. His hands remained on the steering wheel. "It doesn't make sense."

He didn't have to tell me that. Luthicer's theory was only an educated guess, but it was all we had.

"Can Luthicer create false memories?" I asked.

"That's how the illusion works," he explained as his fingers tightened on the wheel. "Didn't you have false ones when your memory was gone? You couldn't have thought six months never happened."

Eric was right. When I didn't have my memory, I had an array of summer memories spent with Crystal, Robb, Zac, and Linda. I still didn't know which ones were real.

"But he didn't do it this time," Eric clarified. "They might not know Robb did what he did, but I do. Urte does. Camille—" He stopped. It was the first time I heard him mention her name out loud. "Luthicer wouldn't have done it without telling us."

17

I reached over to touch his shoulder, and a shock spread through my fingers and into him. He jumped and would've jumped out of his seat if it weren't for his seatbelt. Air seethed between his teeth, and I stared at my hands as purple sparks flew out of them. I closed my fist, but it was too late. Eric saw it, and his green eyes were wide.

"That hurt," he said and rubbed his shoulder.

"I—I didn't mean to," I apologized, staring at my reddened palm. It wasn't dark out. Not even close. It was still morning. We had left the shelter right after the meeting. My powers shouldn't have worked, even if I wanted them to. "I don't know what happened."

"It's okay," Eric said, but his voice was strained. "My powers have been strange, too. I almost transformed in front of Noah the other night." A smile spread across his lips only to fade.

The hairs on the nape of my neck stood up. I knew the feeling. The first time I had felt it was the day my identity was revealed. *"Lights,"* I spoke to Eric telepathically. It was the only power we could use during the day.

"One light," Eric responded, barely moving.

One really powerful light.

Darthon.

Eric started reaching for his keys, but I grabbed his arm to stop him. "My parents."

I didn't have to explain further. Eric leapt out of his car, and I followed him. We ran toward my house, and we didn't stop running until we were on the front steps. I fumbled with my keys, cursing to myself when I dropped them, but the door burst open before I could pick them up.

When I looked up, I saw blonde hair, and my esophagus squeezed the air out of me. I gasped before I realized I wasn't looking at Darthon at all. It was my mother.

"Jessie," she said my name like a scorn, but I reached up and wrapped my arms around her neck.

"Hey, Mom."

Her hands landed on my shoulders, and she pulled away

slowly, her brown eyes searching my face. "Are you okay?" Her palm went to my forehead. "The school called and said you were sick, but you never showed up at the nurse's office. I've been calling your cell—"

"It's upstairs." I had left it at home. Again. "Sorry."

"Mrs. Taylor?" Eric spoke up, and my mom's eyes darted to him. "It's my fault. I should've had her call. I thought she would be better at home."

"It's been an hour."

"I sat in the hallway for a while," I explained. "I asked Eric to bring me home."

Her brow wrinkled as she leaned over to see the Charger on the street. "Eric?" she repeated. "Eric Welborn?" She knew the name. Everyone in Hayworth did.

"Yes, ma'am," he responded with a polite tone I had never heard him use before. He sounded years older than he was. "I'm Jessica's lab partner in homeroom."

"Jessica?" she repeated. He was the only one who called me that.

I squeezed my mom's arm. "I'm okay. I just need to lie down." I tried to distract her. They hadn't even met yet. "Are you okay?"

The Light's energy had dissolved as fast as it had come. If it was Darthon—and I was sure it was—he was gone.

"Okay?" my mother repeated everything we said like she hadn't heard it. "Of course I'm okay. I was worried about you."

"Is Dad at work?"

She nodded. "Why wouldn't he be?"

"I don't know," I muttered, turning back to Eric. "You should get back to school, huh?"

He flinched. "Yeah." Inside my head, he spoke something else, "*I don't want to leave you alone here.*"

"*I'm okay,*" I promised.

He nodded at me before focusing on my mother. "Sorry for getting her back late," he said, "but it was nice to meet you."

She smiled. "Nice to have a face with a name."

"Talk to you later, Jessica," he dismissed himself only to

linger. Then, his hand rose in a wave, and he stepped off the porch. He didn't look back. He focused on his car, and I waited until he got inside it to drive away before I shut the door. I locked it as his Charger roared down the street.

"He seems…nice," my mother finally spoke.

"He is." I moved toward the stairs. "I'm going to lie down—"

"Are you two dating?"

I wasn't prepared for the question.

I gripped the railing of the stairs. "What?"

She pointed at the door like he was still there. "Is Eric your boyfriend?"

"Why would you think that?" I managed, unable to answer her. Eric and I had yet to discuss how we would tell my parents. We hadn't had time to.

Her arms folded around her middle, as if she were hugging herself. When her hip cocked to the side, she blew her bangs out of her face. "Jessie," she spoke as if she were going to scorn me. "You can tell me anything, you know."

"I know that."

"So—"

"We're dating."

She didn't seem surprised. "Did he give you the ring?"

My hand curled like I could hide it.

The side of her lip pulled up. "You thought we wouldn't notice?" My father knew, too. "That looks quite expensive."

"Mom—" I paused. "Can we talk about this later?"

For a millisecond, I thought she would argue, but she didn't. "Sure, honey. Just get some rest."

I started to leave again only for her to call after me, "Jessie?"

When I stopped, the window at the top of the stairs caught my attention. The sky was blue for once. It would be one of those rare warmer days in winter when afternoon hit. It might even be sunny. "Yes?"

"Be careful, sweetheart."

I looked downstairs. From where I stood, she seemed short and young, like a woman I had never met. "Why do you say that?"

She smiled. "I know what it's like to be young and in love," she said, but she stumbled over the L-word. "You're only seventeen."

"I know."

"And Eric is, too."

"He's eighteen," I corrected, somehow feeling like his age justified what I knew about him. He had been through more than anyone I knew. He was straightforward and delicate at the same time. Both of his identities—Shoman and Eric—were unique, but he knew who he was in both. When I first met him, he was everything I wanted to be. Over time, he showed me how I wanted to be myself, and that was how I fell in love with him. Sometime between the river and the sky, my identities had grown into me in the same way his words had grown into my soul.

"Eighteen, seventeen, twenty-five," she listed ages for the simple numbers they should've been. "You're still children, and he has a reputation—"

"Mom," I interrupted, knowing what she must have thought about the reckless, rich kid. I had heard enough rumors to understand her thoughts. "He's a good person. You'll like him. I promise."

Her eyes never moved from mine. "Have him over for dinner soon."

I didn't fight her request. "I'll ask him when he's available."

"That would be nice."

I nodded in agreement, but it was difficult to feel like I was being honest. Between training and the failed war, I wondered if Eric and I could hang out together like a normal couple. Normal didn't seem like a possibility. It never was.

FIVE

"I DIDN'T EXACTLY WANT TO LEAVE YOU THERE," I SPOKE THROUGH gritted teeth as sweat dripped down my brow.

"I was fine," Jessica responded, attempting to hit me with her powers again, but I blocked her with one arm.

For weeks, we had trained together, but it was different today. For once, Urte didn't hover nearby, taking notes or bellowing instructions. We were alone.

"He never showed up." Jessica refused to say Darthon's name.

As my hand rose, she disappeared into a cloud of smoke, reappearing from the wall behind me. She tackled me to the ground and pinned my shoulders against the floor before I sensed her. She was a fast learner. She always had been.

"That's not exactly the point," I retorted, trying to roll out from under her, but she shoved her knee against my shin. I winced. "Do you have to be so forceful about it?"

When she laughed, the pressure released. "I said I wasn't going to go easy on you, and I don't want you to go easy on me either."

"I wasn't," I admitted as I shoved her off and leapt to my feet.

"You're cheating." Her body moved into position, shoulders straight, knees bent. Even in the fluorescent lighting, her purple eyes flashed.

"You shouldn't have relaxed."

She didn't respond with words. This time, her fingers flicked, and a shadow spewed across the floor. Before I could pull away, it latched onto my legs and flipped me into the air. My back hit the ground, and air burst out of my lungs. Her foot landed on my chest in milliseconds.

"You should stop talking," she said, breaking her own rule.

I grabbed her ankle, but my hand went through her. I was pinned.

"If you were a human, this would be a different story," I grumbled, knowing we were far from it. She was as strong as I was when we were shades. It didn't matter that she was smaller or even a girl. Her strength was equal to mine, and she was faster, too. Planning was the only advantage I had. Urte had years to teach me strategies. Jessica had weeks. And my favorite move was already in process.

Use everything around you that you can.

Earlier that day, we had practiced with targets, and one disk wasn't in complete shards. "I guess you win this round." I started concentrating on my senses and threw them out. The air I controlled grasped the disk, lifting it into the air to soar toward her back.

Spinning around, she caught it with one hand. "Please." She broke it in half before tossing it to the ground. "I can feel your senses."

I took the moment to grab her leg, the one she had forgotten about. It solidified under my hold, and I yanked her down before rolling on top of her. When she tried to disappear, I grasped the shadows to keep them whole. Her arms were beneath mine, and her face was pressed against my chest. She squirmed for a second before she gave up. "Not fair."

"I know," I said, "but fights aren't fair."

She moved again, barely, but she moved. "I can handle myself in a fight."

"You're okay in a fight," I teased, watching the aggravation flicker over her gaze.

She squirmed again, trying to kick my leg with her boot.

"Okay?" she repeated. "Just okay? I do better than okay." She wasn't lying. "You would be nothing without my help."

"Oh, low blows," I sang, forcing her shadows to solidify again. "You are mad."

"I'm determined," she corrected.

"I never argued with you," I pointed out. "You make me who I am. I wouldn't be anything without you."

"Aw," she cooed, smiling at my words, but right when I thought she was enjoying our time together, she swung her leg over and knocked my torso off her. This time, she was the one on top. "I win."

I winced, stretching my neck to breathe. "You know, most girlfriends would have thought that was romantic."

"We're training," she said. "How romantic can we get?"

"Pretty romantic." I propped myself up to kiss her.

She tensed, half-expecting me to take control again, but I whispered, "You win," and she relaxed against me. Her hand curled through my hair, and her mouth pressed against mine, deepening the first kiss we shared all day. When my hands landed on her hips, she leaned away, and her black hair fell between us. She pushed it back, and her face flushed.

"Okay, so that was a little romantic," she admitted as she rolled off me. She plopped down next to me, but her warmth radiated beneath my skin.

Her arm pressed against mine, and our heavy breathing echoed around the room. The ceiling seemed endless, stretching for miles above us, but we both knew it wasn't. Luthicer had placed an illusion on it when he created the training room with Urte. It only appeared to go on forever. In reality, it went up ten feet.

"What are we going to do about Darthon?" Jessica finally said his name.

We had school in the morning. We had to go back, and Jessica had already decided to pretend things were normal with her friends. She didn't want the Light to believe they had disturbed her, but her voice shook when she spoke, "He must be at Hayworth."

"We can't do anything until he does," I spoke the truth. "We just have to be ready when he makes a move."

Her fingers dragged across the back of my hand. "That's not exactly what I meant."

I refused to look at her. "What did you mean?" I asked, even though I already knew what she would say.

"Why wouldn't he just kill you?" she asked. "If he knows who you are, why would school stop him from killing you there?"

It was a question the elders had considered a million times, but I hated the only theory we had.

"If he's waiting to absorb me—" she said the last words I wanted to hear.

"We don't even know what that means, Jessica," I interrupted, "and it isn't going to happen."

Her clothes crinkled as she flipped onto her side. From my peripherals, I could see her eyes staring up at me, how her black hair drifted over her forehead in a slick wave. "We're going to have to talk about it eventually," she said. "Ignoring the possibility isn't going to make it go away."

"Who knows?" I wished the ceiling were real, how it stretched on forever with no end. "Maybe it will."

"Darthon isn't going to die randomly."

"He could get hit by a bus," I joked, but she didn't laugh.

"I'm serious, Shoman."

I glanced over, staring at the crinkle that had formed above her nose. "You know, you're kind of cute when you're aggravated."

"Eric," she grumbled in protest, but a smile pulled at her lips.

I rolled onto my side to face her. "I know." I pushed a strand of hair out of her face. "But there's nothing we can do but wait."

"I don't like waiting."

"I've noticed."

Before I could continue, the training room shifted, and the illusion ripped apart. The ceiling was stone, and the floor became rocky. Jessica's eyes widened, and we sat up as the door burst open.

"Hey," a young boy shouted as he ran in.

Jessica and I leapt to our feet, but I enjoyed the blush that crossed her face as Brenthan stopped a few feet away from us.

"Are you two okay?" he asked as his older brother, Pierce, followed him inside.

"We're great," I dismissed the fact that we had been seen lying on the floor. Jessica stepped behind me like she could hide herself. "What are you two here for?"

Pierce laughed, but his hand moved over his face like he could shove his chuckle back into his chest.

"I learned a new spell today," Brenthan beamed. He only had his powers for a year, but he was growing quickly, and his excitement reminded me of my stepbrother, Noah.

My hands clapped together. "Let's see it, then."

"Okay." Brenthan stepped back, raised his hand, and his palm began to glow green. Sparks shot out from his fingertips before a tiny ball of electricity exploded from his touch. It dipped, twisted, and flew around the room. Everyone ducked as it hit the nearby wall. The stone cracked.

Brenthan's mouth hung open. "Oops."

I laid my hand on his head. "You did good," I said, staring at the charred pieces that landed on the floor. Urte would throw a fit. "Every shade has to do a little damage to the shelter."

Brenthan leapt up. "Really?"

"Just work on your aim."

"And work on that with the other fourteen-year-olds," Pierce said, pointing to the door. "Come on."

"Yeah. Yeah." Brenthan's head hung low as he slumped toward the door, only turning around to wave. "See you later, Shoman. Bye, Jess." Then, he was gone.

Pierce shook his head as the door shut. "I swear," he muttered. "That kid will never stop idolizing you."

I smirked. "What's wrong with that?"

"It's impossible to compete as a big brother when your best friend is the first descendant," Pierce joked, but his face relaxed. "We have another meeting."

"Of course we do." I looked at Jessica. "Are you coming?"

She shook her head. "I can't. My parents are watching me a little more closely than usual," she explained. "I should go home in case they check on me. Again." The elders would understand.

"All right." I picked up two water bottles and handed her one. "Get home safe."

She took a drink before responding, "I will."

Pierce started for the door, and I followed him, but Jessica grabbed my arm. I twisted around, and she let go, but didn't speak. Her bottom lip hung open, and she stared at me like I would disappear.

"You okay?" I asked.

"I just—" she paused. "Can you meet my parents?"

I had to repeat the words in my own head to come close to comprehending what she asked. "What?"

Her face went scarlet. "Can you meet them?"

"Sure. I'll schedule them in-between arguing with Luthicer and rebelling against my father's rules," I joked.

She slapped my shoulder. "I'm being serious," she said, but she laughed. "My mom wants to have you over for dinner."

I thought of the blonde woman who looked less than pleased when she heard my human name. Eric Welborn wasn't exactly someone parents wanted their kids to hang out with. I had figured Jessica dismissed us as lab partners, nothing more, but she obviously hadn't.

"I can meet them." I tried to control my voice, but Jessica heard my hesitation.

Her nose twitched. "You don't seem very excited."

I touched her arm, trying to ignore the fact that Pierce was listening to every word. "Don't take this the wrong way," I stated. "I'm not."

Her body tensed, and I ran my thumb over her arm. "Not because I don't want to meet them. I do," I clarified. "I just don't feel right meeting them yet."

"Why?"

I raised my brow and forced a strange voice, "Hi, Mr. Taylor. I showed your daughter a dangerous world in which she almost got killed—twice. Thanks for approving of our relationship."

She slapped my arm again, but we both laughed.

"I'll meet them, Jessica." I made the promise anyway. If it was important to her, it was important to me.

"When?"

"Tomorrow if you want."

Her shoulders relaxed. "Tomorrow, then."

"What are you telling them?" I asked. This time, I was the tense one.

"What do you mean?"

I reached down, grabbed her left hand, and showed her the ring I had given her one month ago. "Am I your boyfriend or—?"

"That would probably be best for now." She pulled away. "We can figure out the rest later."

I nodded, gesturing to Pierce. "I'll call you after the meeting." Telling her I was going to call her was the only way she would answer her phone.

"Sounds good," she agreed before leaning over to wave at her guard. "Keep him out of trouble."

"I'm normally the trouble," Pierce joked back, but Jessica was already gone. She had disappeared into her transportation. Only her purple smoke remained.

I took a sip out of my water bottle as I watched the smoke disappear, too. When it was gone, I walked over to Pierce.

He didn't move. "Trouble in paradise?"

"This isn't exactly paradise." I opened the door to lead the way.

"It will be," Pierce spoke at my back as he followed me into the corridor. "When everything is done, we'll all be good."

"I sure hope so," I muttered back, truly hoping it would be.

SIX

Jessica

I LEANED AGAINST CRYSTAL'S SEDAN AS SHE THREW HER NOTEBOOKS into her bag. She had yet to look at me since picking me up for school, but I was waiting for her interrogation. I was waiting for anything, but she acted as if nothing had happened, even though her hair couldn't have been more out of place. She didn't even have her usual lip ring in, and her punk clothes had been replaced with sweatpants and a pink hoody. We had forty minutes before school started.

"Did you have any plans this weekend?" I asked, desperate to talk to her, but she shrugged. I sighed. "Crystal, I am sorry."

"I know." She shut her car door. "We don't have to talk about it."

"But—" This wasn't her. She would've never refused an opportunity to hear information. Whoever she was now was affected by the memory loss. I was practically staring at myself a few weeks ago. "I want to talk to you about it."

She shifted her bag to her left shoulder. "What's there to talk about?"

"What do you remember about last semester?" The question escaped me.

Her dark eyebrows squeezed together. "Everything," she said. "Why? Is this about Eric?"

"No," I said, but I needed an excuse to ask such bizarre questions, so I changed my mind, "Kind of, actually. Yeah."

"I mean, I knew you liked him. That's why we got a gift for his birthday," she said, revealing something she remembered, "but engagement? Seriously? You can't get engaged to someone in high school."

My hand fell behind me. I couldn't tell her the truth. Eric and I were destined, no matter how fickle our destiny had become, and I did love him. But the ring was a shock, even to me. When I thought of how he found my biological parents' grave, I succumbed to the feeling of relief—the precious calm of a storm I had lived with my entire life—and I found that serenity in Eric.

Crystal's hip cocked to the side. "I want to be supportive, I do," she continued, "but I think you're making a mistake. It's too soon. Way too soon."

Any explanation I gave wouldn't be enough. "It's not like we're planning a wedding." In fact, we hadn't even discussed it. We were too focused on defeating Darthon. A wedding would have to wait. A future would, too. But the others didn't see that. They only saw two teenagers, blindly embracing one another in the hallways.

"Planning one or not, it's too soon," Crystal repeated. Even though she lost her memory, she hadn't lost her ability to be honest. "I'll give him a chance," she added, but her voice rose. "Only because of you."

"Thanks," I muttered, but Crystal wasn't listening anymore. Her eyes fixed behind me, and she propped herself up on her tiptoes as she waved. "Zac! Hey, we're over here."

His name sent chills down my spine, but I looked his way. The black-haired boy strode across the parking lot, raising one palm to signal he had seen her wave. Among even the slickest cars, he shone. His pressed clothes didn't look like a student's wardrobe. In his black jacket and slacks, he could've been a teacher.

"He's cute, isn't he?" Crystal whispered out of the side of her mouth.

I only stared, wondering how she didn't recall how she obsessed over him. She probably didn't even know he had kissed her in my driveway before—once, while looking at me.

"Hey." His gaze lowered to Crystal. "Shouldn't you head to the newspaper room?"

She blinked. "Why?"

"The desk lady quit," he said it like she should know.

"What?" we both screeched, but he nodded as if we had whispered it.

"What do you mean she quit?" Crystal asked.

"I don't know." Zac shrugged. "She walked out yesterday."

"I have to go," Crystal said, already jogging toward the school. "Thanks for the heads up."

I started to follow her, but Zac grabbed my arm. His fingers dug into my bicep, and I whipped around to face his grin.

"Where are you going?" he asked. "I thought we could talk."

I pulled away. "I'm busy."

His grin slipped off his face, but his teeth remained visible, perfectly white. "You remember?"

My heart slammed into my rib cage. "What do you mean?"

"Crystal's acting like she doesn't know me, and Robb—" He paused. "Well, we know about Robb." His hand ran through his hair, but every strand fell back in place. "I thought everyone was playing a prank on me, but you—you're not. You remember me, right?" His rushed voice was as desperate as his widened eyes. It was an expression I hadn't seen on his face before.

I stepped back and almost tripped over myself. If he remembered, the Light hadn't touched him, but they should've if they were targeting my friends. I remembered what Luthicer said. If the Light was trying to trick me, they were doing a good job at it. I was as confused as Zac was.

He stepped toward me. "Jess?"

"Why do you think I remember?"

His cheek cocked up into a smile. "Because you hate me." He pointed over my shoulder. "And so does he."

I looked over my shoulder as Eric appeared, walking faster than normal. A scowl consumed his face. His headphones were strung over his shoulders, but he didn't grab them as he

got close enough to speak, "Hey." His hardened tone was louder than it should've been.

"Morning, Welborn." Zac folded his arms. "I guess we're
classmates now."

Eric's hand landed on my shoulder. "I guess so."

"We're just talking," I muttered.

Zac chuckled over me. "We're talking about how everyone's lost their minds." He didn't even try to hide it. "Except for
you two. You two seem fine."

Eric's fingers dug into my shoulder. "I have no idea what
you're talking about."

"Sure, you don't," Zac sang, his voice dropping and rising
like a tempting string of notes. "I don't care if you want to admit to it or not," he continued, "I know something is up with
you two, and I'll figure it out."

Right when I thought he would shift into Darthon himself,
he spoke like a human would. He spoke like he didn't know
about the Light or the Dark. He spoke like he hadn't heard of
the descendants or the war. He seemed oblivious, and I didn't
believe a second of it.

Eric's grip didn't loosen. "You might need to get your
head checked." He didn't believe it either. "You're starting to
sound a little insane."

"Whatever," Zac responded as he walked away, throwing
his hand over his shoulder in a half-wave. "Congrats on the
engagement," he called back at us. "I expect an invitation."

I shot forward to hit him, but Eric grabbed my arm.
"Don't."

"He knows something, Eric," I said beneath my breath.
"He's not like the others. He's—"

"If he were Darthon, he would've done something," Eric
said, but his words were quiet. "Wouldn't he?"

My attention diverted to Zac. I tried to match his walk
with Darthon's, but everyone was different as a human. Other
than their attitudes, I couldn't see a correlation. I couldn't see
a correlation in anyone.

My hand curled into a fist. "I don't know," I grumbled,

"but there's something not right about that guy."

"I don't like him either," Eric agreed, "but that doesn't give us the right to kill him."

"I don't like him." I said it like it did give me the right. "I don't like him at all."

Zac's black hair bobbed against the snowy backdrop of our school like an outlined target. If I could transform, I could hit Zac from where he stood yards away, but I couldn't. In daylight, I was a human.

"We can't hurt him if we don't know," Eric reminded me of the Dark and all of their rules. Rules we didn't normally follow. In this case, Zac's death would be useless if he were innocent. It would probably make Darthon laugh.

"As much as I hate to defend the guy, he could be innocent," Eric said, but he sounded far away.

"Maybe the Light isn't only trying to confuse me," I managed.

Eric leaned back to catch my eyes. "What are you thinking?"

It was the way Eric defended Zac, a guy he had hated from the start. It was the fact that the Light hadn't attacked yet. It was the sudden change in Eric's demeanor, how he was suddenly willing to follow the rules of the Dark, but it was the reason Eric was holding back that stopped me the most. The Light could absorb me, and if they were waiting for that, they needed Eric to remember the possibility. After all, it was that reason Eric was holding back. It was what stopped him from believing Zac could be Darthon. He was being too careful. He was too willing for the Light to make the first move, out of fear that our first move would hurt me.

I swallowed my nerves. "Maybe the Light is trying to confuse you, too," I expressed my thoughts. "Maybe they want both of us."

SEVEN

THE FLYING TARGET SHATTERED INTO PIECES AND DISSIPATED BE-
fore hitting the floor. After school ended, I had rushed to
the training room. I didn't want to linger in the parking
lot only to run into Zac or Robb or anyone associated with Jessica. The morning had been anything but comforting, and the
afternoon wasn't any better. Jessica and I had barely spoken in
class, and it took everything in me to ignore Zac at the back of
the room. Even then, I could feel his eyes on my back. Maybe Jessica was right. Maybe she wasn't. Either way, I couldn't
guess, but the paranoia consumed me. The single bit of relief I
had rested on Linda, of all people. She was in a different class
and lunch period. At least, I didn't have to deal with her. Now,
my relief came through training.

Even though I had been training for two hours, I didn't
feel tired. My adrenaline grew as if my energy was preparing
for a battle I couldn't sense yet. I was supposed to be at Jessica's house for dinner in thirty minutes, yet my concentration
struggled. I was too focused on Darthon—on who he might
be and how I would defeat him.

Another target flew into the air, and I shot at it, only for
the training room to buzz. The blue cloud of my Dark powers
shook as the room spun into the rocky walls it truly had. The
training session was over, but not by my choice. Someone was
coming in.

When the door creaked open, I didn't bother looking. "About time, Urte." I hadn't received instruction for days.

"Not Urte," a boy's voice spoke up.

I spun around to face Pierce as he shut the door behind him. He leaned over, picked one of the water bottles off the floor, and tossed it to me. I caught it, opened it, and took a drink before I spoke again. "What's up?" I asked. "You don't come here often." Aside from the day before, his appearances were becoming a rarity.

He rubbed the back of his neck. "I haven't had time to."

"Guard duties?"

Pierce slumped. "That's what I came here to talk to you about."

"You sound like a girlfriend."

A smirk appeared on his face. For a brief moment, he looked like the guy I had grown up with—ready to laugh at a reckless plan we had concocted—but his carefree demeanor disappeared when he folded his arms. "There's really no other way to say this except bluntly." As he spoke, my chest tightened. "I know you don't like how Jess and I have been acting."

"I don't know what you're talking about," I responded too fast. Even I heard how convoluted my voice had become. No one would believe I told the truth, but I didn't correct myself, even though the images flew through my head—the way she touched him, the way he responded so casually. Even if I didn't want to admit it, it bothered me. It drove me mad.

Pierce chuckled like I had confessed telepathically. "I've known you my entire life, Shoman." He didn't use my human name, even though everyone else had since it had been revealed. "I wouldn't like it either."

"Then, why do it?" The question fell out of me.

He straightened. "You remember Camille." Her name sounded far away, like a whisper over the rush of a river. "You remember how easy it was to lean on her, to talk to her, to watch her paint her toes—"

"What's the point?" I snapped as my guard's life flashed in front of me, only as a memory.

Pierce's expression dropped. "You know how it is between a guard and a warrior. It's a tie, a connection," he explained everything I knew. "You know how a warrior feels, but you don't know how a guard feels."

I stretched my arm over my head, counting out each breath as I measured the stretch. I didn't speak, but I was listening.

"It feels different," he said, but the explanation twisted through my veins. "I'm not even used to it."

I dropped my arm. "Do you like her, Jonathon?"

His jaw hung open before he collected himself, snapping his mouth shut only to open it again. "Not like that," he said. "Not at all like that," he promised. "That's what I came here to clarify."

I tried to fight the smile that took over my face, but I couldn't. I even chuckled. "Okay, man," I managed. "Thanks."

"Glad that's over with," he mirrored my laugh. "Want to go for a flight?"

"I can't." I was already picking up my things. "I have dinner, remember?"

Pierce's face twisted as he recalled yesterday's conversation. "Is that today?" He stared at the wall like a calendar hung on it. "Any chance you two can reschedule?"

"Why?"

"There's a new breed of shades coming out." He didn't pause long enough for his words to sink in. "A half-breed's daughter developed powers. Urte's been working with her all day, and I would have to bet she's not the only one."

"Wait," I interrupted. "What? A half-breed's kid doesn't have powers."

"That's the problem," Pierce agreed. "She does, and we don't know why, especially since ours are dwindling."

Jessica and I had yet to tell him the truth about our powers. Ours were stronger. I wanted to tell him right then and there, but Jessica wanted to tell him, too. I would have to wait.

"When did you hear this?" I asked.

"This morning," Pierce said it like it was an apology. "I've been trying to meet the girl myself, but Urte won't have it."

"Well, that explains where he's been," I muttered. "What's the plan?"

His grin was too wide for his angular face, a piece of Jonathon poking out from under his shade form. "I found a way to send her a message," he said. "She's meeting us at the river."

My adrenaline returned. "When?"

Pierce looked at his wrist as if he had a watch on it, but his wrist was bare. "Well, let's see," he drew out his words. "Tonight," he said. "She'll be at the river at midnight."

EIGHT

Jessica

"I DON'T LIKE IT, JESSIE," MY MOTHER SPOKE UP FIRST. FOR ONCE, she had curled her hair and worn something other than sweatpants. Still, she looked like she was asleep somewhere else in the house. "I've never even heard you mention going on a date before now."

"It does seem soon," my dad added, his voice deeper than usual. Unlike my mother, he looked focused, ready to meet the boy who gave me a ring.

"Just give him a chance." I glanced at the clock above the kitchen sink. "He'll be here soon." And I wanted to prevent him eavesdropping on their disapproval.

"Of course we'll give him a chance, Jessie." My mother said my name in every sentence she spoke. "It's just—worrisome. It's a lot."

"And that ring is too much," my father agreed.

"It's not an engagement," I tried to convince them, but I felt like I was also trying to convince myself. "It's a promise ring." It was the only excuse I could come up with, the one I thought would settle their nerves. I was failing.

"That's a mighty expensive promise," my dad muttered.

"It looks like an engagement ring," my mother added.

"It was my mother's."

His voice broke through the conversation before I even sensed him entering the room.

Eric stood in the doorway, dressed in black slacks and a nice shirt. He almost looked like he had on prom night. I could practically see him beneath the willow tree, pushing the branches away as his eyes met mine. The only difference was, this time, he held a bouquet of flowers.

"Sorry for letting myself in." With his free hand, he pointed over his shoulder. "I rang the doorbell and knocked, but no one answered." He stepped forward and held the bouquet out toward my mother. "These are for you."

Her cheeks burned red as she grabbed them. "Oh, um. These are lovely." She didn't even bother hiding her glance at my father.

His eyebrows rose to his receding hairline, and he rubbed his forehead like he could erase his previous expression. "I've been meaning to fix that doorbell," he excused, stepping forward to shake Eric's hand. "Nice to meet you."

"Nice to meet you, too, sir," Eric responded as they shook hands. Afterward, Eric glanced over at me. "You look nice."

My stomach twisted. "Thanks," I managed. "You, too."

His shoulders rose as if he had taken his first breath since arriving, but he didn't speak. The silence in the room was drowning us.

"I'm going to get water for these," my mother spoke up, walking to the sink. In seconds, she had a vase filled and the flowers placed inside. "They'll make for a great centerpiece." Once they were placed on the table, she waved at the seats, and Eric took the cue.

He crossed the kitchen and sat down. I sat next to him, and my parents sat on opposite ends. For once, our four-person dining table was full, and we were eating dinner together. Tonight we were having pot roast and salad. Normally, we had whatever pizza my dad picked up on his way home from work.

"So, Eric," my dad started as he filled his plate with food. "Tell us about yourself."

Eric hadn't moved since sitting down. He hadn't even looked at me. He just smiled at my parents. "I like music and running, but I want to travel when I'm older," he explained, taking a moment to place salad on his plate. "I think the world has a lot to offer, but I haven't had many opportunities to see it yet. Jessica's told me how you all have moved around a lot. That must have been exciting."

My mother stared, but my father wasn't fazed. "Are you planning on going to college after graduation?"

Graduation. College. I had forgotten. Everything else had consumed me, but Eric nodded. "I'm not sure where yet, though."

"It's getting close, you know," my dad said. "Jessie filled out a few applications yesterday."

"No, I didn't," I said.

My father's eyes landed on me. "I put some in your bedroom."

"I'll get around to it," I mumbled.

"She's a great artist." Eric's voice rushed with excitement. "Have you seen her paintings?"

My hand curled beneath the table. I hadn't shown my parents anything.

"An artist?" my mother asked. I could feel her eyes on me. "I didn't know you painted."

"In school," I clarified, hoping Eric would get the hint.

When Eric looked at me, he tilted his head to the side. "They're good." He didn't get the hint. "She would do really well in an art school."

"An art school?" my dad repeated.

I hit Eric's knee under the table. "*Don't,*" I said telepathically. "*I haven't told them yet.*"

He didn't even flinch. He acted like I hadn't done anything. "I think studying different cultures would be interesting." He changed the subject to focus on himself.

I sighed.

"I've been reading about African history recently," he continued. "Did you know Pablo Picasso's paintings were inspired by African sculptures? Modern viewers think he was bizarre, but in reality, he was part of a European movement in his time. He—" Eric stopped.

My parents' jaws were hanging open.

Eric fiddled with his shirt. "I get carried away sometimes."

"No, no, it's okay," my mother said, taking a moment to eat her food. "We were just—" She looked at my dad, but he didn't look back at her. He was too focused on Eric. "Surprised." Her sentence finished with a polite smile. "Most children—I mean, teenagers—don't study outside of school."

Eric glanced at his plate. "I like to read." It was the only thing he did outside of training. He may not have been interested in school, but he did have interests. It was one of the things I appreciated about him. But even I didn't know he was reading about Pablo Picasso.

"Eric also likes classic cars, Dad," I eased the conversation away from art. "He drives a Charger."

"I thought you crashed that." My dad didn't hesitate.

Eric choked on his food and coughed until he took a sip of water. "Yeah," his voice dropped. "I was being reckless," he said. "It won't happen again. I learned my lesson."

"I expect you won't drive like that with my daughter in the car."

"Dad," I interrupted, but Eric laid a hand on my knee, keeping his focus on my dad.

"Of course not, sir," he promised. "Your daughter means a lot to me."

My dad's darkened eyes softened. "And what are your intentions?"

The cliché question I dreaded. I knew he would ask it. I only hoped he wouldn't. It sounded like something out of a Lifetime movie, a chick flick that I would never watch.

"We're just dating," I clarified, but Eric spoke up at the same time.

"If I can be honest," he started, his gaze flickering over to me. "I intend to keep my promise."

He didn't have to say it out loud. He had told my parents he wanted to marry me.

I almost fell out of my chair.

My mother practically did. She started to stand up only to

force herself to sit back down. The only noise was the tapping of her nails as they moved across the table. My father wasn't even moving. He hadn't paled. He just stared.

Eric cleared his throat and placed his silverware down. "I know it seems serious," he said. "Because it is," he added. "But I have good intentions." His hand squeezed my knee as if he were telling me it was fine. "Jessica reminded me what it means to have good intentions, and that's no small thing."

My father leaned back in his chair. "That's why you gave her your mother's ring?"

Eric nodded.

"Your mother is…" my dad paused. "Your mother passed, right?"

Eric tensed. "Yes, sir," he said. "She died when I was five."

"And your father?"

"He's alive."

My dad shook his head, signaling that wasn't what he meant. "Does he know you gave away your mother's ring?"

"Yes, sir," Eric said, reaching into his shirt pocket. He revealed a business card, and he slid it over the table to my dad. "My father knows about Jessica and me," Eric explained. "He says you can call him anytime."

A gasp escaped my mother's mouth, but she covered her face as though hiding it. Eric acted like she was successful anyway.

"I understand your hesitations," Eric said, sounding more like an adult than I ever expected him to. "But I hope you'll give me a chance." He looked at me, but he spoke to them. "I also understand you don't have to, and if that's your decision, I'll respect it."

"Eric." His name broke out of me in the same way his words broke me. "*Why would you say that?*"

"Relax, Jessie," my dad said before I could continue ranting to Eric telepathically. "It's okay." He slid Mr. Welborn's card into his front pocket. "You're kids. We don't need to be so serious." His tone shifted as he adjusted in his seat. "Just be—safe."

My embarrassment moved up my neck and over my face.

42

"Dad—"

"And enjoy this food." He lifted his fork, pointing it at the plates. "I would like to see your car up close after dinner, too."

"You can drive it if you want," Eric said. He never offered his keys to anyone. Not even Pierce.

"See, dear?" my dad lightened up as he faced my mother. "I told you Jessie could pick a good one."

My mother laughed, her giggle bouncing more than usual. "I guess you're right," she said, taking a moment to eat her pot roast. "Thanks for coming over, Eric."

"Thanks for having me over," he said, removing his hand from my leg. "*And thanks for letting me be honest,*" he said to me.

"*You could've warned me,*" I retorted, focusing on my plate. I hadn't even touched my food, and I couldn't tear my eyes off the smirk on the side of Eric's lips.

"*Warn you?*" he spoke back. "*Where's the fun in that?*"

———◆———

"I cannot believe you," I spoke to Eric as my father revved the Charger's engine. Once the car pulled away from the curb and took off, I found myself leaning against Eric's arm. His eyes followed the black car as it sped down the neighborhood street.

"What?" Eric's tone was as childish as his toothy grin. "I think they like me."

"Don't get cocky."

"I'll try to keep myself in check." Eric's arm rested across my shoulders.

The sun was setting, but even in winter, the orange glow drifted across his tanned skin. If he were a shade, the light would've looked like shimmering water on his pale complexion, but I would never see him as a shade during sunset. We always had to wait until darkness fell. Unless he was being reckless.

"Why didn't you ask them?" I spoke up.

"Ask them what?"

When it came down to Eric giving me his mother's ring, he had found my biological parents—their grave—and he had spoken to them. But he hadn't even met my parents, the ones who had adopted me shortly after I was born. The question had been rattling inside of me for weeks, but I only recently found the words.

"Why did you ask my biological parents for permission, but not them?" I reworded my question.

Eric's arm moved away from me, but he faced me. His green gaze was a forest of protective trees with the same feel that surrounded the shelter. "I should've, Jessica, and I know that," he started, "but I didn't think we'd tell them we were even dating for a while."

The explanation he had given me in the training room echoed inside of me. Even our peaceful moments were outlined in chaos. He didn't want to start his relationship with my family during a war.

"I wasn't going to tell them the truth tonight either," he said, "but I don't want to lie to them any more than we have to."

They wouldn't know I was a shade, not now, and possibly ever. That part of my life wouldn't include them. I understood that. But Mindy knew, and she was human. Eric's reality was crashing with mine.

"How is Mindy dealing with it?" I asked.

Eric's palm landed on my head. "She's—learning," he said, "and your parents will, too."

"What?"

His eyes widened. "You didn't want to tell them?"

I hadn't even considered it a possibility. My expression must have told him that because he kissed my forehead.

"In time," he started, "this will be as normal as everything else."

My fingers curled against his shirt as the Charger's headlights flickered toward us. My father was returning.

"It's getting dark," Eric whispered against my hair.

"Are you going out with Jonathon?" I asked.

Eric's arm twitched next to mine. "I meant to tell you," he said. "We're supposed to meet him by the river at midnight."

"What?"

"There's a new shade," he explained as we watched the car park against the curb. "She wants to meet us."

"A new shade?" I asked. My father was getting out of the car.

"We'll have to talk later," Eric muttered, raising his hand in a wave. "Can you be there?"

"Of course."

"Great," he said, suddenly raising his voice into a shout, "How was it, Mr. Taylor?"

"That is some ride you have." My dad tossed the keys across the front lawn.

The silver was a silhouette against the sky, but Eric caught them without even looking up. "You can drive it anytime."

"Oh, that was enough for me," my dad said, walking over to stand next to us. "Thanks for coming over." He had said the phrase one hundred times since dinner.

Eric nodded. "Dinner was great, but I should get going." He gestured to the clouds. "It's getting late, and we have school in the morning."

My dad tapped my arm. "Responsible, too."

"Yeah," I began, staring at Eric. "Responsible."

Eric didn't bother hiding his grin. "See you later," he said and started walking to his car, not even bothering to kiss me goodbye. Not in front of my dad. Not when we would see each other in a few hours.

"Have a good night," I called after him.

He waved over his shoulder. "You, too."

"See you in a few."

NINE

FIFTEEN MINUTES BEFORE MIDNIGHT, I ARRIVED. MY BODY PULLED out of the shadows, and I formed right in front of Pierce and Jessica. Her hand was on his arm, but she dropped it when I arrived. I had to remember the conversation Pierce and I had. Guards were close to their warrior shades. It was a connection. Not a romance.

"About time," Pierce said it like I was late instead of early.

I scratched the back of my head. "How long have you guys been here?"

"Two minutes," Jessica said.

"She's been here for two minutes," Pierce clarified. "I've been here for thirty."

"Well, you did say midnight," I pointed out.

"Midnight is when she arrives," Pierce argued. "I thought we had to explain things to Jess."

"And I'm waiting for that explanation," she said, and as if she had given an order, Pierce explained everything.

A new breed of shades had appeared—or a new breed of lights. She was a half-breed's daughter. We didn't know how it was possible, and we definitely didn't know who she was. But if we could figure it out, we might be able to understand why our powers were shifting.

"Isn't that the elders' job?" Jessica asked, sweetly naïve.

Pierce and I laughed in unison. "The elders aren't exactly

good at their job," I said, ready to hear what else Pierce had to say, but he didn't elaborate.

"We've been meaning to tell you what's going on, too," Jessica spoke to her guard.

His shoulders rose, and a silence barrier streamed out from him as if anyone could be listening from the shadowy forest behind us. We had as much privacy as we were going to get. "What's going on?" he asked.

"Our powers are stronger," Jessica explained, sharing how her powers had worked in the middle of the morning. "And then, we sensed him."

"Him, being?" Pierce didn't want to believe it any more than we did.

"Darthon," Jessica confirmed, "but he left when we got there."

Pierce looked at me. "And you left her there?"

"Don't judge me." I lifted my hands. "You're the guard, and I didn't see you anywhere."

"That's because I was busy trying to meet the new shade," he retorted, and his expression twisted. "She's here."

He didn't have to say it. We had sensed her energy. It was wavering in pieces, an odd combination of sparks of the Light and shadows of the Dark. She didn't feel like a half-breed. She was something else entirely—and she was walking on the sidewalk. Like a human.

From a distance, I could make out how tiny she was. She was shorter than anyone else I knew, but her curves were dramatic. I didn't realize she was our age until she was only a yard away. Even then, I doubted she looked anything like she did as a human. If she did, we didn't know her.

Her hair was as long as Luthicer's, stretching to her waist, but it was pitch black. Two strands in the back were white, but she had severed them off, leaving stubs to spike out above her head like a second set of ears. But that wasn't what caught my attention the most. Her eyes did. They were like Pierce's—electric green—but tan swirls confiscated the edges of her irises. Her pale skin contrasted against them, and her lips did the same, as white as the moon.

She stopped and looked us over like she had seen us a million times. The sight of shades was nothing new to her. "I'm assuming one of you gave me this." She raised a ripped piece of paper. Her voice was as harsh as her glare, the sound of scraping glass. "You do realize you could get me in a lot of trouble, right?" She knew the Dark's rules, too.

"I gave you that." Pierce laid a hand on his chest. "I'm Urte's son."

"I'm assuming Urte doesn't know about this," she said.

Pierce opened his mouth, but I stepped in front of him. "I don't know what the elders told you," I started, "but their rules aren't everything, and you have the right to know us."

Her hand lowered as her multicolored gaze darted over me. "I came, didn't I?" As she went to put the paper in her pocket, her hand flickered in and out of the shadows, and she lost her grasp. The paper fluttered to the ground, and I picked it up before she could.

"You'll get used to it," I said, knowing she didn't have a grasp on her powers. Newbies never did. Not unless they were Jessica.

"I'm not exactly supposed to transform. Not until they figure out what's going on," she revealed a set of rules the elders had given her. "Is that what this is about? Do you guys know what's going on?"

I cringed. "No—"

She started to walk away, but Jessica grabbed the girl's arm. "Wait," she said. "We just want to talk to you." Jessica dropped her hold. "We might be able to figure it out."

"Isn't that the elders' job?" the girl asked exactly what Jessica did.

"We don't like waiting on them," Jessica explained, "and I bet you don't want to either."

The new shade folded her petite arms. "They sure like to take their time."

"How long have you known about this?" Pierce asked.

The girl faced him. "A while, but I'd rather not get into specifics," she said. "I don't enjoy opening up to just any stranger in the middle of the night."

"At least she has attitude," Pierce spoke to me. *"She'll make for a good comrade."*

"Worry about that later," I responded.

"What do you know?" I asked, trying to find common ground.

Her lips pushed to the side. "How about you tell me what you know first?"

Jessica took the lead. "Do you know who the descendants are?"

Her odd eyes squinted. "They explained the prophecy to me," she said, "but it doesn't sound like that worked out."

I flinched. "I'm Shoman."

The girl's neck whipped around, and her bottom lip hung open. "You," she said, pointing at me. "You're the first descendant?"

Jessica nodded. "And I'm the third."

"And I'm just the guard," Pierce explained, "so you can trust us to handle it if the elders find out we spoke."

She didn't calm like I expected her to. She stepped back, and the white parts of her hair wavered as her energy grew. I recognized the emotion. She was panicking.

"You—you guys can't be the descendants. Like, *the* descendants," she stuttered, but we kept nodding. "That would mean—" Her eyes focused on Jess. "You're Jess? Jess Taylor?"

Jessica flinched. "Yeah," she said, but her nails dug into her palm. "I guess I can't be mad they told you." Everyone else knew anyway.

"And that makes you," she pointed at me, but she didn't get a chance to finish.

"I'm Eric," I said, hoping she would explain who she was, even though she knew the rules. Never give up your identity. Ever. Jessica and I had lost that opportunity.

"Eric Welborn," she added my last name, looking between Jessica and me. Her hands went up to her face. "This is too weird."

Jessica voiced it before I could, "So, you know us?"

The girl's hands dropped as she attempted to steady her shaky expression. "Yeah," she revealed. "I know you. I mean, I know you who are. I've seen you at school."

She went to Hayworth. We knew that much.

"This is weird," she said, turning away from Jessica like she could forget her. She only focused on Pierce. "Who are you, then?"

He raised his hands in front of him. "I'm the mystery."

"Right," she said. "Me, too." She wasn't about to tell us who she was in her human life. "But they Named me Jada, so I guess you can call me that."

Jessica squeaked, but when I looked over at her, she was smiling. "Nice to meet you, Jada."

Jada nodded, but she kept her distance. "I suppose Darthon isn't going to be at this meet-and-greet."

"No," I sounded harsher than I wanted to. "He's an enemy, not a friend, and if you ever see him, you run."

The girl stroked her hair in the same way Luthicer touched his ever-changing beard. "Do you know who he is?"

"No."

Jada didn't respond this time. Jessica did. She laid her hand on my arm, but didn't look at me when she said, "I'm going to go."

I grabbed her hand, and my fingers intertwined with hers. *"Are you okay?"*

"I will be."

I wanted to question her, to figure out what was going on, but I had an inkling I already knew. Jada had a name. Jessica had never received one. She would talk to me when we weren't around the new girl who had no idea how important her name could be to Jessica.

"Get home safe," I whispered. We always said it to one another.

"I will," she said, and then, she was gone. The blackened smoke from her transportation was cold against my skin, but it disappeared faster than usual. She hadn't even said goodbye to Jada.

The new shade stepped back as if the smoke could harm her. "Sorry," she muttered. "I'm still getting used to it—to that."

"It'll be normal before you know it," I said, wondering if the truth was a good or bad thing.

"Where did she go?" Jada asked.

"Home," I answered, but she didn't hear me.

"It makes sense now," she spoke up, looking at the space where Jessica once stood. "Why they Named me Jada."

"What do you mean?" I asked.

"They Named me after the third descendant. They wanted us to sound alike," she explained. "The elders think we're connected."

My fist curled as I thought about the Naming room, the ceremony that changed my life forever. If they had just Named Jada, she had only been a part of the Dark for two weeks. This year, I had missed it, but it was the first year no one complained about my absence. If the ceremony was the same, the ancient ones—whoever they were—felt a connection between Jada and Jessica. In Jada's eyes, it was innocent. In mine, it was everything but innocent. It was a bad sign.

Jessica was the third descendant, someone who existed by accident, and Jada was a new breed of shade, someone who existed, but shouldn't. If Jessica had something to do with it, the prophecy did, too, and if the prophecy didn't work, this girl's powers weren't going to either. Not how they should anyway.

"Are there others like you?" I asked, trying to avert the conversation away from Jessica. "Are there others that were Named after her?"

"Slow down," Jada gave orders like she was born to do so. "There are more like me—new shades—but I'm the only one Named after Jess." It was the only response Jada had given that relaxed me. "That we know of anyway."

"Listen," I said and sighed, "I know you're not supposed to say a lot—"

"I'm not supposed to be having this conversation," she corrected, "but I'm here, and I want to know what you want from me."

Pierce cleared his throat. "You understand you're different, right? That you shouldn't have powers at all?"

"That I was human?" She nodded. "I've known that."

"Known?" Pierce repeated.

Jada's lips pressed together in a thin line, but it was too late to take back the singular word we had latched onto.

"You knew about the Dark before you had powers?" Pierce guessed.

Jada's gaze moved to the forest like she could run into it and escape, but her feet dug into the ground like she was forced to stay. The expression told us everything we needed to know. She knew before she had powers. Her parents had broken the Dark's law.

"This is fantastic." Pierce straightened up like it was, indeed, fantastic. "She could have powers because she knew about the Dark," he theorized. "It might be a good test to tell another child of a half-breed and see what happens."

"We can't do that," I snapped.

"What?" Pierce defended. "We're already crossing a line. Don't tell me that's where you want to follow the rules."

"We can't affect people's lives like that," I said. Telling someone they were born into a paranormal world was not something I took lightly, especially since the paranormal world was crumbling.

"For all we know, someone's already told their kids," Pierce continued to argue. "We'd just have to check—"

"*Pierce,*" I screamed in my friend's head. He even stepped back. "*You can theorize all you want—just not in front of her.*"

"*Got it, boss.*" In all the chaos, Pierce found the strength to be humorous.

"My dad didn't tell me by choice," Jada's defense split between our telepathic communications. "I caught him once—in his transformation. I thought I lost my mind." Her rambling was almost too fast to follow. "But don't tell anyone. He told me how much trouble he could get in. I don't want him to get in trouble. He's been in too much trouble before. He almost got killed by those Light people, and I don't want to be ostracized—"

"Relax," Pierce interrupted. "We aren't going to tell anyone."

Jada bit her lip, but her eyes were already watering. "I really shouldn't have come."

"Yes, yes, you should've," Pierce said. "This is good. This is going to help us. We just need to know who your dad is."

Jada pushed her tears back. "I can't do that."

"You don't have to." My words fell out of me, but I wouldn't let her know the truth.

"*I know who her dad is,*" I told Pierce so he wouldn't keep pressuring her.

Pierce faced me, but I focused on the girl. I had recognized the unusual length of her hair for a reason. Her nuances were familiar, just as her story reminded me of the one I was told a few months ago by the only half-breed I knew. He worked for the Light until they wanted to use his human daughter in battle. He killed lights to leave. The scars covered his arms. I would never forget the marks. I would never forget him.

"*Luthicer,*" I said. "*He's her dad.*"

TEN

Jessica

WHEN I FELL OUT OF MY TRANSPORTATION, I WAS TWO BLOCKS away from my house. I had aimed for home, but I hadn't even gotten close. It was only when I remembered Eric's training I figured out what had happened.

"You have to truly want to go where you're transporting to, or you'll end up somewhere else." He had explained while setting up blocks in the training room. "It might be easy when you have a goal, but it's difficult if you let your emotions take over. You might end up in school or in a car or somewhere else you enjoy. You don't want that to happen. You want to focus."

I was yards away because I wanted to be yards away. I wanted to walk. I wanted time to think.

My stomach squeezed when I thought about it. The Dark hadn't Named me. They said they would, but no one had gotten around to it. They didn't have time. But they had time for her.

Jada was beautiful. She was one of those rare girls that were both petite and curvy, the kind of girl society pressured us all to be, and she was nice. And scared. As much as I hated to admit it, her confusion reminded me of myself when I met Eric for the first time.

He was a dream, translucent, yet whole, and the way he touched my face was the only way I could believe he was real. Even now, one year later, I found my hand on the cheek he touched all those months ago. I had to touch Jada, too. That was why I grabbed her arm.

She hadn't been cold like Eric had been. She was warm, and she sizzled beneath my palm. Her powers tempted me like sin did. Every desire I had focused on her. I wanted to know her, to figure out who she was, to harness whatever power she had. I wanted to rip her apart.

Her name wasn't even half of it. It was mostly her powers, and they had reminded me of one thing. The Light realm. The fire burning. The stone. The red room Camille had died in.

I hadn't wanted to leave Camille, because I didn't want her to die. The memory of how her skin had flickered away like pieces of metal was my worst memory, yet I held it close now. Maybe I didn't want to leave because of Camille, but maybe there was more to it. Maybe I didn't want to leave the Light realm for another reason altogether. Maybe I wanted to stay for the same reasons I wanted to keep my hold on Jada. I recognized the Light power the way I cherished my Dark powers.

They felt the same.

My head screamed, and I grabbed my hair, wishing I could tear the thoughts out of my mind.

The Light was not the Dark. If it were, I would've wanted the powers when I met Camille for the first time, the night of prom, but I didn't. Camille's powers had nauseated me. Fudicia's Light powers had torn me apart. They had burned. The feeling was torturous. Yet, it felt different now. Something had changed.

I dipped back into the shadows, letting the blackness cool my skin, and I sank into the darkness of the night. I remained there, floating in nothingness, levitating in a pool of molecules until I fell out.

My knees hit the lawn with such force that blades of grass waved out in front of me. I stared at the frostbitten tips, sparkling an iridescent purple beneath the winter moonlight. A rain of my violet power fell from the cloudless sky, but it never touched my body. It bounced off me as if it didn't belong to me, and it flickered red before soaking into the ground. The water became yellow when he arrived.

Darthon.

He was standing in front of me. He was on my front lawn.

I leapt to my feet, tearing my sword out of my arm, but it flickered like a hologram.

Darthon never took his blade out. He only smiled.

"What do you want?" I growled, clenching my fist, begging for my weapon to work, but nothing changed. It even flickered on and off.

The black pits he called his eyes followed the hologram's shaky appearance. "It'll only work if you want it to work." Just like the transportation. "You don't want to kill me."

His entrancing voice broke what little concentration I had on my sword. It zipped back into my arm, searing my bones, and breath seethed between my teeth. The only hope I had was the energy it had put out. Eric would sense it. He would know I was in trouble. He would come.

Darthon laid out his arms as if he were asking for a hug. "You're the one that called me, Jess," he said. "If you want to bring Eric into this, fine. Do it." His voice dropped. "Go ahead."

"I already did." My knees bent, but I didn't survey my surroundings like training had taught me to do. This was the real world. There was no time for looking away from the target.

"Great." His grin stretched. "We share the same goals."

Eric. Darthon wanted him to come. He wanted us both. I was right. The Light had always wanted us both.

"*Don't come,*" I tried to warn Eric, but it was too late.

"We've got company," Darthon said it just as two shadows split the front yard in half.

Pierce appeared, and so did Eric as Shoman, his sword in full view. But he didn't last long.

Darthon flicked his hand, and the yellow rain splattered over us as if a bubble had been placed over our heads. Pierce smacked against the outside, pounding on the force field as he screamed. I couldn't hear him. Shoman, though, was on the inside, and his sword was gone. He wasn't even standing. He was on the ground, screaming, and I could hear him. The screech pierced my ears.

I rushed over, falling down next to him as the Light energy prickled against my arms. Darthon had us trapped in a room full of his energy, the same energy that hurt shades, the energy that was torturing Shoman. Not me.

"Eric," I tried to get his attention, but his eyelids squeezed shut. His screams didn't stop. He never stopped squirming. Pierce never stopped pounding on the walls. I never felt a thing.

I looked up at Pierce, and my guard's green eyes met mine. His pupils widened, his hair wild, his expression dropped with every millisecond. Burnt flesh curled off his knuckles. The blackness behind him began to open up, and I knew the elders were coming. Everyone was coming, and I stood, knowing I would have to face Darthon until they did.

"You don't have to worry," Darthon said before I could speak to him. "You won't be the dead one."

A bright light shattered from the ground, filling the bubble, and it blanketed us in a fire I had only felt a few times. It was the fire in Jada's veins. It was the burning sensation of my desires. It was the Light realm.

"You're coming with me." Darthon's voice was all I heard. "Both of you."

ELEVEN

THE FLOOR WAS HARD, UNEVEN AND COLD. My SHOULDER DUG into the ground, and my skin grated against the concrete. When my eyes opened, I expected a flood of light, but murky shadows met me. In the corner, a single candle flickered, and a miniscule wave of illumination darted across my jeans.

I was human.

"About time." The voice was the only sound in the small room, but it didn't echo like it should've. It came and disappeared like it had never existed at all.

My neck stung as I arched my back, trying to find the source. It didn't take me long. He was sitting right next to me—except he was in a chair, and I was on the floor.

Darthon.

His blond hair was the brightest part of the room, but he was untouched by the candlelight. His dark eyes sucked it all in like a black hole, and his grin showed how much he enjoyed it.

"I've watched you die four times now," he continued to speak, "and each time, you wake right back up."

Only then did my memories return. I was with Jada when Pierce and I sensed Darthon. We transported to Jessica, and it was over. We were taken to the Light realm, and I couldn't handle it as Shoman. Shades died in the Light realm, but so did humans. I had already lost consciousness a dozen times. I expected to die. I even waited for it. But I kept waking back up. This wasn't the first time, and it wouldn't be the last, but it was my first time seeing Darthon.

"Humans can't exist here," he continued, standing from his chair only to kneel down next to me. He reached down, twisted his fingers through my hair, and yanked my head up off the ground. "So, tell me how you can." His hot breath skimmed my cheek.

I couldn't answer, because I didn't know. He was right. I should've been dead a long time ago. I shouldn't have existed. But I did. Shoman was obsolete in the Light realm, but Eric Welborn remained. My only hope resided in how our powers had shifted.

"Where's Jessica?" I managed, ignoring his question.

When he removed his grip, my cheek slammed against the floor.

"Jessica," he repeated her name like it was a dirty thing. "She's alive," he said. "No thanks to you—her hero."

Of course she was alive. If she weren't, Darthon would be dead, too. The question wasn't about her life. It was about her location because she wasn't with me. I had no clue where she was, or how alive she was. She might have even been in the same state as I was.

"She's the one who called me, you know," Darthon's words halted my thoughts as his hand rose, and glitter rain fell from his palm. Aside from the golden coloring, it looked exactly like the power Jessica used—the only power I didn't recognize, the only power I didn't have control of.

When the rain disappeared, Darthon's face appeared in front of mine. "I just didn't take her as the type to call on two men at once."

I reached up to choke him, to grab him—anything—but he disappeared only to reappear on the other side of my torso. He kicked my face, and my jaw cracked. My neck sizzled. My spine was melting.

But a scream didn't escape me. Not this time. I had been expecting it.

His knees popped as he kneeled down again. "You're used to pain, aren't you, Welborn?"

"I've had training," I spat, removing my mental state from my body. I had felt this pain too many times to count—thanks to Urte's torture machine. I would have to thank his foresight if I ever saw him again.

"Look how much good that's done you," he mocked, but he focused too much on his words.

My fingers latched onto his ankle, and I yanked as hard as I could manage. My bicep ripped, but he fell backward, slamming onto the ground. He was up before I could do anything else, and he had kicked me again. This time, my ribs were breaking, and I felt my car wreck all over again.

As I curled up, he cursed. "I would think twice before starting a fight in this realm, Welborn," he spoke as his foot pushed against my side. "You're nothing but a human here."

But my human side lived. Despite all the rules we abided by, I could live in the Light realm, and he couldn't hide the truth.

"I don't have to fight you," I spat back, knowing I could only overcome him with words. "You can't kill me, not even in your own realm."

His boney face hardened. "Oh, I can kill you," he said. "I already have."

"Then, why am I alive?"

"Because she's protecting you," he spoke through gritted teeth.

For a millisecond, I saw Jessica, but the knowledge stayed with me longer. I was safe. For now.

Darthon's foot dug against my side, and my lungs squeezed. "She won't protect you forever," he threatened. "She'll stop. She'll run out of energy, and I'll be here when she does," he continued. "You will die—permanently—but until then, I'll enjoy watching you die again."

With that, his foot flicked from my ribs to my head, and it slammed against the side of my skull. The crack was the last thing I heard before I drew one last breath and succumbed to darkness.

TWELVE

Jessica

"**P**IERCE," I CALLED FOR MY GUARD ONE HUNDRED TIMES, BUT I never received a response. "*Urte—Bracke—Luthicer— anyone!*" My mind sizzled out with a deafening static, and my attempted connection broke.

Still, I planted my feet on the ground and laid my hands on the far wall. The concrete room was a prison with one door—a locked door I had tried to break too many times to count. The only thing I succeeded in breaking was the skin on my knuckles, and I had been awake for thirty minutes.

The room looked nothing like the one I had previously seen in the Light realm, but I knew I was there. The lack of temperature gave it away. I would never forget the heatless fire, and it was impossible to forget Camille—the woman who died to get me out of the same realm I found myself in again. This time, I would get out on my own, and I would find Eric, too.

"*Shoman,*" I called for him, and unlike the others, his connection didn't sizzle out. Still, he didn't respond. He was alive, but he wasn't conscious. Or he wasn't able to use his powers. Why mine worked, I didn't know. I didn't even feel pain. I hadn't the first time, and this time wasn't any different.

According to the Dark, the Light realm killed shades. It tortured them. But I was a shade, and the realm blended into me. The waving energy sank against my skin, and pleasant goose bumps trailed up my spine.

I had to fight a smile as I called out to him again, "*Sho-man.*"

"That won't work here."

I spun around with my hands in front of my torso. My fighting stance was automatic. Urte had taught me that much. But he hadn't taught me what to do when my predator wasn't prepared to attack me.

She stood in the doorway, but her hands were full with a set of clothes. When she tossed them across the room, they landed on the ground near my feet. A sandwich wrapped in plastic sat on top. "Those should fit you," she said. "I hope you like cold grilled cheese."

I didn't take my eyes off of her face. The boney cheekbones and crimson lips were all too familiar. Her gaze was the worst part about her. It lingered like the first time I met her.

Fudicia.

"You tried to kill me," I said, remembering how she had tossed me down a hill, unintentionally exposing my human identity to Eric. It hadn't even been one year.

Fudicia's eyebrows rose to her hairline. "If I knew who you were, I never would've laid a hand on you."

"You killed Abby—Hannah—you killed her." I knew that much.

Her crimson lips moved from side to side as she contemplated her words. A minute seemed to pass before she spoke, "It was necessary." The Light wanted to convince the Dark that they intended to kill the third descendant, and they had succeeded. "I won't hurt you again," she continued. "Consider me your guard as well."

So, she was Darthon's guard. The Dark suspected it, but it was a fact now.

"I have a guard," I said, thinking of Pierce, although I no longer felt his connection.

"That half-breed?" The words hissed out of her. She wasn't speaking of Pierce. She didn't even care he existed. She was focused on Eric's guard.

"Camille," I corrected as heat rushed over my face.

"She's useless to you now."

My fist curled. "She's dead."

She leaned back as if she had developed blurry vision and couldn't see me. But her face quickly contorted into a smile. "Sure." Her voice was drawn out. "You can call it that."

"I watched her die." I saw the pain, and Fudicia was acting like Camille was nothing. Like her death wasn't even relevant to my life, to everyone's life.

"We don't value half-breeds here," Fudicia said. "You shouldn't either."

I studied her stance, searching for a single weak point—a straightened knee, a relaxed arm, a bend in her ankle—but she disappeared.

When she reappeared, she was sitting on a chair in the corner of the room. Her hair hadn't moved an inch. It didn't wave or react to her fast movements. It was perfectly still, seamlessly in place. An illusion. She had been sitting there for a while. She couldn't move fast. She could only appear as if she had. If I paid enough attention to the sound of her voice, I would know where she actually was, and I could attack. But I forced my eyes to widen, and I stepped back. I wanted to seem surprised. I didn't want her to know.

"I wouldn't try to fight me just yet," Fudicia said, but her voice was close to me. "I'm not here to fight you." She stood to my left.

"I don't trust you," I managed, wanting her to speak again.

"I don't expect you to," she said, but her next sentence was a contradiction, "I'm here to answer your questions, Jess."

My name should've never left her lips.

I reached out, and my fingers wrapped around her bicep. As soon as I touched her, she appeared where I knew she actually was. Her illusion melted away, but I couldn't guess her next movements. She bent down, twisted her torso, and tore her arm out of my hand. Even then, she never hit me, but her bottom lip hung open.

I kept my hands up. "Don't think you can trick me."

"I didn't think I could," she said, but she stepped back only to step back again. Her back was practically against the door. "I just wanted to see."

"See what?" I snapped, fighting the urge to slap the grin off her face. She hadn't been testing me. She couldn't have been. She only wanted to seem that way. "Everything is an illusion to you people."

"You people?" she repeated, her voice rising. "Is that how you define yourself? You people?"

Myself. Like I was a part of them.

I ignored her mind games. "Where's Eric?"

"Please." Her eyes rolled. "You saw how pathetic he was in battle. How could you see value in that?"

"Everyone is valuable."

"That," she pointed to me, "is a contradiction."

I didn't respond.

She raised her hands to mimic a traditional scale. "If everything has equal value, it diminishes the value of everything else." She waited only to meet my silence. "I'm guessing you've never taken Economics."

"I'm not here for class," I retorted, "and if you hadn't kidnapped us, maybe I'd be learning about that right now."

Fudicia folded her hands. "Let's try this again." The words escaped with her exhaling breath. "Ask a valuable question." The harshened tone was as much a threat as her glaring eyes.

"Is he alive?"

Fudicia's palm hit the wall, and the sudden noise made me jump back.

"How do you expect to save us all when you're focused on a stupid boy?" she screamed, her tanned face reddening.

Save them all? I was about to ask what she meant, but I couldn't keep my concentration for long because Fudicia spoke again.

"What are we? Where do we come from?" she used the questions as an example. "Who killed your parents?"

My heart leapt into my throat. "My parents?"

"Finally," Fudicia said as she sat down in the chair. "We're getting somewhere."

"Who killed them?" I demanded an answer.

She pointed at the pile of clothes on the floor. "Eat half of the sandwich, and I'll tell you."

I glanced down at the plastic wrapped sandwich, but I didn't pick it up. It had to be a trick. The Light had no reason to change my clothes, feed me, or make me comfortable. They had left me on the floor, after all, and Eric was unconscious. I knew he was alive. I could feel his heartbeat residing in my own, but it was slower than it should've been. He was weak. I wasn't. I wanted to hear he was alive, and I wanted to know who killed my parents. Every part of me wanted to know everything, but no part of me trusted the woman who had killed Hannah Blake, Eric's previous girlfriend.

"It's not poisoned, Jess," Fudicia spoke as if she guessed my thoughts.

"Why are you feeding me, then?"

"Well, we can't exactly let you starve." She reminded me of what Darthon had said.

If I died, he died. Would he also go hungry if I did? Would he get sick? Would he go mad? The possibilities filled my mind, but all I wanted to do was tell the elders of the Dark. The thought of the Dark grounded me.

"You can't keep us here forever," I said, refusing to pick up the food. "Someone will know we're missing. My parents, my friends, the school—"

"The Dark already covered it up," she said. "You took a trip with Eric's family. Your parents, too." Her tone turned harsh. "I suppose it had to do with your sudden engagement."

The lie didn't even require a massive illusion. The Dark only had to put one on my parents—the ones that hadn't died in a car wreck, the ones who hadn't been murdered fleeing town. The Dark suspected the Light had something to do with it, but there was no proof. Not until now.

"Eat," she ordered again.

This time, I obeyed.

I picked up the sandwich, sat down in the other chair, and took a few bites. The grilled cheese was greasy, and every bite made me thirstier than the bite before it. I struggled to swallow as I ate, and Fudicia watched, making sure every bite was consumed. My stomach twisted as if I would throw up, and it didn't stop twisting even when I finished. I dropped the plastic on the floor, and I grabbed the sides of my seat. "Tell me."

Her lips arched like her brow did. "Tell you what?"

"Who killed my parents?"

"My parents killed your parents."

Her answer threatened my nauseous stomach.

Fudicia leaned back. "Their legacy is how I became Darthon's guard."

This time, her words made me vomit. I bent over, and the liquid fell out of me like it had been waiting to escape all along. My throat burned. My head spun. I couldn't breathe.

"Fantastic," Fudicia muttered as her heels clicked across the ground. She had stood up, and she was heading for the door. "Darthon isn't as patient as I am," she spoke as she opened the door. "Remember that when he comes to see you."

I managed to look up so I could see the hallway. The walls were red velvet, the floors were wood, the lighting was golden, and everything was as bright as fire would be.

"Oh," she continued, leaning back in one last second before she left. "I suggest you clean yourself up."

THIRTEEN

THE UNBEARABLE PAIN WAS ONLY BEARABLE BECAUSE URTE HAD taught me to ignore it. When I woke up, my arm was split, my leg shattered, my stomach ripped, my skin torn into nothing but shreds. I grew used to the taste of my own blood—it was impossible not to. It was the closest thing I had to water in a day. Maybe two. Maybe three. I didn't know how long I had been in the Light realm, but I didn't think I would leave soon. The breaking floor had grown into me, or I had grown into the cracks. I didn't know. But my body smothered into the destruction of it all. It was the destruction of me.

Just as I began to move, I stopped myself.

The door opened, flooding the once dim prison with a blinding light. My reflexes closed my eyes, but I only kept them shut because I didn't want them to know I was awake. I would stay unconscious in their eyes for as long as possible. I didn't want to die again. But with every beat of my heart came a pounding footstep, closer and closer, until the person stood next to me. I heard their clothes shift as they bent down, but their knees didn't pop. It wasn't Darthon.

"You awake yet, useless?" the boy asked.

I didn't respond, but I felt his fingertips brush against my eyelashes.

When my eyes flinched, I knew it was coming. He kicked me, and a groan escaped my lungs. I couldn't hide it anymore.

My eyes opened to a boy standing above me. His different colored irises were the first thing I recognized. He was the half-breed Fudicia toted around like a handbag.

When he kicked me across the face, he spoke again, "That's for the time you broke my jaw."

To keep my mind off the pain, I focused on that night. It was when I found out Jessica's identity. Fudicia hadn't cared I attacked him at all.

"I didn't break your jaw," I managed. "I dislocated it."

His foot collided with my stomach. I curled up, but he didn't stop. His attacks escalated, one after the other, no stopping for air or rest. My arm, my leg, my shoulder, my head. That's when I lost count of what was happening to me. The injuries that once burned like wildfire now fogged over one another.

I didn't have time to count the amount of times the teenager kicked me, breaking ribs or other parts of me, but I didn't need to. Every time I woke up, I was healing—slowly, like a shade would—only I was human. The difference was how my body felt every bit of the healing as it happened. I stopped counting the injuries a long time ago. I only waited to die.

"Stop it, half-breed." Another voice shattered through the attacks. At some point, the door must have opened, because the room was bright.

The kicking halted, and the half-breed exhaled as if he had forgotten to breathe. "He deserved it."

"Don't justify yourself." The other man was Darthon. "I'll take over from here."

The half-breed nodded. "Yes, sir." With that, he left without another word or so much as a glance, but his shoes left blood on the floor as he walked away. My blood. I stared at the spots until the door shut, leaving Darthon and I alone.

"Stupid mutt." He dropped a piece of bread on the ground, and the crust soaked up the blood I had lost. "Do you know why we don't Name our half-breeds? Because half of them aren't worth a life." He chuckled like he had made a "this guy walked into a bar" joke, but the information was news to me.

It explained why Fudicia didn't care if I hurt the half-breed the day she attacked Jessica and me. She didn't care if he died. Half-breeds weren't a loss to them. They were simply another body to clean up. Just like how Luthicer's daughter would've been.

The Dark didn't share that belief with the Light. Half-breeds were among the thirteen-year-olds at the Naming like the full-blooded shades. It was something that separated us from them. Everyone was a person to the Dark—even half-breeds, even humans. The Light only cared for their own.

"Aren't you going to eat?" Darthon asked, like we were two buddies grabbing a sandwich after soccer practice.

I didn't see the point, so I ignored the food by rolling onto my back. I half-expected to see an endless ceiling—like the one Luthicer created for the training room—but the ceiling was short. My eyes tore away from the sight only to land on Darthon. He stared back, and I knew he wasn't here to hurt me, or he already would've.

"What do you want?" I asked.

Darthon sat down in the chair. "I want to talk to you."

"I doubt you kidnapped us to have a chat."

"Actually," Darthon rested his chin on his hands. "I did."

I couldn't prevent the laugh from escaping me. "You're joking."

"Well, I technically took you to kill you," he admitted, "but there's a hole in that plan."

"You think?"

"I did take Jess to talk to her," he said it like he hadn't done so yet.

I watched the boy—someone who wasn't much older than me, someone I had been raised to kill, someone whose blood was already supposed to be on my hands. I never thought I would actually talk to him.

"What do you want with her?" I concentrated on my words to clear my thoughts about the pain of healing. My skin was inching itself together.

"I have lots of plans for her." As he spoke, his expression illuminated only to dim as he lowered his face to study me. "But I want to know what you know first."

The look in his eyes was one I had seen before. It was the same look I held after the Naming. After I learned who I was and what it meant, I returned home. My father didn't speak to me about it. He didn't even come out to greet me, so I ostracized myself in the bathroom. The mirror was the first thing I broke. It was the reflection I hated—the widened pupils, the pale cheeks, the shaky lip. I hated myself. Apparently, it was something Darthon had in common with my thirteen-year-old self.

"You don't want to kill me," I stated.

Darthon didn't nod, but he didn't have to. Being destined to kill wasn't easy to accept. It was a curse.

"This has never been about you, Welborn." My name slipped off his tongue as if he had said it a million times. Of course he knew me. We probably went to the same school. "It's always been about Jess."

I knew that. She was my weakness, but she was his, too. We shared it in different ways—with my love, and his demise—but we shared it nonetheless.

"I only need to get you out of the way to move forward," he said, his eyes flickering over me, "and I will once I figure out how you're surviving." My life had a deadline. "Once your connection is severed, her power will drive the Light to succeed."

"And you're telling me this because?"

"Because, Welborn," he hesitated, "we're going to make a deal."

"What kind of deal?"

"Not yet." Everything was on his terms.

When he didn't speak, I found the strength to succumb to my only hope for survival—understanding. I cleared my throat. "So, what do you want to know?"

His hands moved to his mouth, and his fingers tapped his lips. Even Darthon had nervous habits. "Where does your bloodline come from?"

"You know that—"

"I do," he agreed, "but you don't."

"My father—"

"Jim?" he chuckled. "You still believe he was the first descendant's bloodline?"

My chest squeezed, and I wheezed out a shaky breath. "He is—"

"Your mother was."

The woman flashed before my eyes even though I didn't want her to. I tried not to think about her. I fought the urge to remember her face, but it was impossible. Her short, black hair framed her round cheeks like a disfigured China doll. The whiteness of her skin had been blinding, and I knew I inherited her intense gaze. That was her shade form—Evaline—but I couldn't see her human face. I only saw the time she took me to the woods to witness the bats. She was a shade then, and she was dead shortly after.

"She was the head of your bloodline," Darthon finished with a hardened stare. His silence waited for my response, but I didn't have one. "You didn't know, right?"

"You're lying."

Darthon grabbed his chin like he could force his expression to relax. "Let me guess." He ignored my accusations. "Your father already told you not to have a kid."

He had warned me. The morning after I lost to Darthon, he had spoken against it to Jessica and me, but I only saw it as a thing of embarrassment. "Every parent says something like that—"

"Your dad had other intentions," he interrupted. "Your mother lost her powers when you were born, and when you have a child, you will, too."

The memory of the bats flooded through me, the night sky melting away with the pastel colors of the sunrise, the silhouettes of the scurrying creatures I visited. My mother had been a shade, but I was a human. I was five years old. I knew that much.

"You're wrong," I argued. "She was transformed—"

"And any shade can transform since birth. Full powers are

71

given later," he pointed it out like the Light shared our Naming ritual. "Tell me, did you ever see her use her powers? Did she ever protect you or teach you how to fight or—"

"I was five," I spat, managing to sit up. My spine snapped into place like it had been broken. "She couldn't have taught me yet."

Darthon leaned back. "Perhaps."

"There's no 'perhaps' to it."

His brow straightened out in the same way Luthicer's did when he confessed to his past. "Maybe you should ask your father why she killed herself."

"Since you seem to know everything, why don't you?" My voice ripped against my throat.

Darthon didn't flinch. "I won't keep you here forever," he said. "You can ask your father when you return." He wasn't going to tell me any more than he already had.

"So, why tell me this at all?" I wanted to punch him, but I didn't have the strength.

Darthon stood, but he sat back down like he didn't have the strength to leave either. "As much as I hate to admit this, Welborn, you and I are the same—"

"We are not the same."

He stared at the wall as if he hadn't heard me. "You might die by my hands, but the least I can do is guarantee you don't go to your grave with lies in your head." His words silenced me. "I want you to understand your death when it comes. You'll find peace in it then."

FOURTEEN

Jessica

Darthon didn't come that night. No one did. But I found myself immune to sleep. My eyes propped open like I had taped my eyelids to the arches of my eyebrows. I stared at the door, and it wavered over my lack of sleep. When it clicked open, I thought I was hallucinating, but Fudicia was as solid as the overbearing walls.

"Get up," she said, but she didn't look at me.

It took me a minute to realize I was curled up on the floor. At some point, I had fallen asleep.

When I didn't move, Fudicia stomped across the room, and her hand wrapped around my bicep. "Come on."

My knees wobbled as I stood to walk. I didn't ask her where she was taking me as she yanked me out of the dungeon and into the hallway. The red walls might as well have been painted with blood, and I was relieved when she directed me into another room.

A bathroom.

The golden light reflected off the granite countertops and marble steps. A shower sat at the top of the small stairs, already running hot water, and the steam glimmered as a bright mist.

"Get cleaned up." Fudicia let me go to leave the room. When she exited, a lock clicked outside of the room. I was taken out of one dungeon to be put in another one, but this one had a shower.

My skin itched, and my clothes were heavy in the humidity. I waited, anticipating she might enter again, but she didn't. Instead, she spoke through the door, "If you don't get in, I'll treat you like a child and bathe you myself."

"Fine," I snapped back, tearing off my T-shirt. I dropped my pants and peeled off my socks before stepping into the open stream of water. The hot water met my skin, and air hissed out of me. The dirt trailed off my body in dark rivers. Light hues of red spiraled into it, and I shivered. I was bleeding somewhere, but I couldn't find the source. The injury was gone. Or it wasn't mine at all.

Eric.

My hand slammed over my mouth to prevent me from crying out. I couldn't stop fighting now. I had to be strong, and I had to do what they said if I wanted to get both of us out alive.

I forced my mouth open, and the shower's steam filled my lungs. The dust and grime that had suffocated me cleared out, and I coughed. My eyes closed as I lifted my face into the hot water, letting it stream down my hair, my cheeks, my collarbone, and my shoulders. I lost track of my body after that.

The shower was warm, refreshing, and perfect. It was serenity, and I almost forgot I was a prisoner.

My heart slammed against my chest as my eyes popped open. Before I submitted to the comfort, I grabbed the faucet and turned the water off. Cold air swirled in with the steam as I stepped out. My toes curled against the marble floor.

"You done?" Fudicia spoke as she opened the door. Her eyes moved over my naked body before she threw a towel at my head.

I caught it, covering myself before she could continue to look. If the shower made me forget, her stare forced me to remember. But she didn't give me a chance to get dressed. She grabbed my old clothes and left me standing in the miniature sauna.

"You have new clothes out here," she called over her shoulder.

I followed because I didn't have any other choice.

The bathroom was attached to a bedroom that hadn't been there before. The Light realm shifted as fast as my thoughts did, but the room existed now. It was small, but it had everything a bedroom needed—a bed, a nightstand, a lamp. A pile of clothes sat on the end of the mattress.

My eyes focused on Fudicia, but my nails dug into my towel. I didn't want to move. I was positive she would kill me at any moment.

Fudicia groaned as she turned her back to me. "I'm not here to hurt you," she grumbled, "so get dressed." Even though her back was to me, she would attack if I did. I could hear it in her voice.

I walked to the pile of clothes only to touch the silky fabric. The color was as rich as a sunset over the Midwest. Golden threads stitched the pieces together, and designs spiraled down the sides of the dress. It was long-sleeved, thin, but bearable.

"Why is it so nice?" I asked. It wasn't everyday a prisoner was forced to dress up like royalty.

"Just put them on," Fudicia said. "You're already late."

"Late?"

"It's dinnertime," Fudicia explained, but I wondered if it was the same time in the Light realm as it was in the human world. If it was, that meant they had just returned from school—from Hayworth—from the place I yearned to be.

I forced myself to get dressed because it meant I was one step closer to returning to my family, to the Dark, to my loved ones.

As if she could sense I was dressed, she turned around. This time, her stare didn't move over me. "Ready?"

"Who will be there?" I asked, hopeful they were feeding Eric, too, but her frown told me otherwise.

"Just come," she said, opening the door. She didn't drag me this time. I followed anyway.

I tried to keep up with the tall woman. "Is he okay?"

She was silent; the only sounds were our footsteps as we walked down the corridor.

"Is he?"

"No."

That one word was enough to kill me.

"But, if you must know," Fudicia continued, "Darthon is keeping him alive." The side of her lips twitched up. "But I doubt he will do it for much longer." She didn't have to tell me to obey. Her orders hovered in her tone.

The rest of our walk was silent. Neither of us spoke or dared to look at one another. As much as she said she wouldn't hurt me, I didn't believe her, and I knew she figured I wanted to hurt her. I only needed good timing. We both understood it.

Two wide doors sat at the end of the hallway, and my heart pounded to the rhythm of my approaching footsteps. The wooden design reminded me of the doors in the Dark's shelter. The familiarity was chilling. I half-expected to see a library when she opened the door, but I didn't.

She stuck a key in the handles and pushed the oak doors open in one movement. The red room stole my breath. Like my clothes, the walls were crimson. In the Light realm, everything was lined with red, and this wasn't an exception. Even the decorations had scarlet edges, including the black horns sticking out of the walls. Antique furniture circled the room, and thick candles cast a glow over the long table in front of us. The place resembled where Camille died, but it wasn't the same room. A heatless fire was missing.

Fudicia grabbed my arm and pulled me over to a chair. "Sit."

I grabbed the table in front of me, feeling as if I could break the wood in half, but it tingled under my fingertips. It wasn't real. It was all an illusion.

"Enjoy your dinner," she said right before she left.

I was alone now, but I didn't dare stand up from the table. I wasn't as alone as I originally thought. I could feel him—his energy. He was the heatless fire that was missing.

"Darthon."

He appeared like a flame that lit itself.

The tips of his blond hair were gelled up, and his black eyes were holes of darkness. His complexion shimmered over his high cheeks bones and defined jawline, but his smile held no light. His teeth were like razors, sharpened into spikes, but his expression was full of delight.

"You continue to impress me." His voice sounded closer than his body was, but—unlike Fudicia—I believed he sat where he sat. The energy was too strong for him not to be where he was. His entire presence was like gravity, impossible to forget, possible to believe in, a theory merged into a law.

My fingers uncurled from the table. "What do you want?"

He waved his palm over the table, and food appeared. "You must be hungry."

As the smells of freshly cooked food met my nose, my stomach growled.

His grinned stretched. "Don't hold back," he said. "We'll talk once you've eaten."

I hesitated, and then reached over and grabbed a piece of bread. Instead of eating it, I threw it at his face. It smacked his forehead, only to fall into his lap.

The confident smile slipped off his face. His upper lip twitched. "What's the problem, Jess?"

He said my name like he knew me.

"Where's Eric?" I asked.

His sigh was as loud as a thunderclap. "Do we always have to make everything about him?"

I glared back.

"Fine, then." His elbows propped on top of the table. Veins pushed against his tan skin. "He's alive, and I'll keep him alive if you listen to me."

"I'm already listening." Anything to save the Dark.

Darthon's gaze dragged over the silk I wore. As if he had touched me, goose bumps trailed over my collarbone. When his eyes snapped up to my face, he spoke, "I don't plan on hurting either of you if you comply."

If you comply. His threats were harsher than Fudicia's worst tone.

"I thought your entire life's purpose was to kill Eric," I spat back.

He flinched.

"Unless you can't," I added, realizing it as I spoke. Shades weren't supposed to live in the Light realm. Darthon should've already killed him. It was the only reason to bring Eric with me, but Eric was alive. Somehow, in some way, I could feel his heartbeat in my own veins.

Darthon's fingertips curled around his chin. "You're quite intuitive." He smiled like he was proud, but I smiled because I couldn't fight it. I was right. Darthon couldn't kill Eric. He was safe.

"You're impressive," Darthon continued, laying his head on his open palm. Candlelight flicked over his face, and he glittered like an angel would. "But that's to be expected from a Light member."

Eric's heartbeat disappeared beneath my pounding one. "I'm not one of you."

He nodded. "Not completely anyway." He straightened up only to lay his hand on his chest. His fingertips spread over his sternum. "You must feel it, the Light power coursing through your veins, the sizzle of desire, the sickening lack of satisfaction you have with the Dark." His words sounded far away. "It's in you. It's only been awakened recently."

"I'm not one of you," I repeated.

Darthon's bottom lip snapped shut. When he leaned back, his shoulders slumped. Right when I thought he had relaxed, he shot up, and his metal chair crashed against the cement floor. The air rushed through the room, brushing past me, and he disappeared, only to reappear to my left. He grabbed my arm and yanked me up like I was a doll.

"You are," he shouted as he latched onto both of my shoulders. His thumbs dug into my skin. "You're one of us."

I kicked his knee, and we broke apart. I had to grab my chair to prevent myself from falling, but Darthon didn't grab anything. He remained standing, right in front of me, and I reached over for anything I could use as a weapon. The table disappeared.

"I own this place," he said, but his voice wavered.

My skin tingled where he had touched me. I wanted it to burn, but it didn't. It felt like an energy boost. My muscles ached for it again.

"You can feel it, can't you?" he asked, quieter this time. He hadn't grabbed me to hurt me. He grabbed me to show me, but I could already feel the bruises forming.

I wanted to close my eyes, but I didn't dare to. I would not look away from him. It had to be an illusion. I only had to find the source of it.

Darthon's crumbled brow straightened out. "The Marking of Change was never about Welborn." His name hurt. "It was about you—you changed."

"I didn't—"

"When Camille gave you her powers, they never left." His words shot out. "She activated you."

Camille. The Light realm. She had been here before, and so had I. Even I couldn't deny how she had been in pain, and I hadn't felt a thing. The Light realm had felt familiar from the start.

"She began the absorption process. Not me," he continued to rant. "I never forced you."

Until now.

"Absorption," I repeated the word I had heard too many times, the word the Dark knew nothing about. The prophecy always said the Light could absorb the third descendant, but it never explained what it meant. It only proved I was Eric's weakness. "What do you mean—the process has started?"

Darthon sat down in the nearest chair. His hands landed in his lap, opening and closing over and over again. "Think about it," he began, "Just think." He tapped his forehead like he meant to break it. "Your bloodline was created when the Dark and the Light separated. There are two of you and one of me."

So, I was still a shade.

"You're the reason we're unbalanced," he said. "You can't just be a shade. You have to be both." Breath shot out of his lips in a hiss. "You are both."

"I'm not—"

"Shut up," he growled, laying his head in his hands. "Just shut up."

I stepped back, glancing around the room as it shifted. The doors were gone. The horns were gone. The furniture remained. I couldn't escape, but Darthon didn't seem to notice I was looking for a way out. He was too busy rocking back and forth.

"How brainwashed are you?" His whisper broke the space between us. He stared at me through his fingers. "What did those dimwits convince you of? That Eric would win and you'd ride off into the sunset together?" His tone rose. "Life doesn't work that way, Jess. Only movies do."

I couldn't fathom a response.

He grabbed his seat. "Let's say they told you the truth," he spoke. "Let's pretend you're only a shade. Let's say Eric wins," he stuttered over the last part. "Why would balance mean only one side survives? Why would balance result in the Dark having complete control?"

That wasn't balance at all.

"It doesn't," he was the only one who could say it out loud. "That's why your bloodline exists. You're supposed to lead the new Light—as the light you already are—and you know what happens then?" His pause was deafening. "They'll kill you, too."

"The Dark would never kill me." My words manifested on their own.

"I," Darthon pointed to his chest, "I would never kill you. My people would never hurt you. The Dark? They will."

"You're wrong—"

He slapped his chair like he had to hit something. His knuckles were white. "Your death would mean the end of the Light forever, and that's all the Dark wants."

When I didn't respond, he stood up, and I stepped back.

His body froze feet away from me, but I could feel his energy seeping into me. My veins were vibrating. "Stop it," I hissed, knowing he was the cause of it.

He didn't stop. "You feel that because you're connected with me." The electricity inside of me grew. "Your death will cause the Light to die, and that's why your death would kill me," he repeated the worst sentence he had ever spoken during the Marking of Change.

"That was a lie."

"No, it wasn't." Darthon took a step forward. "Don't you remember the first time we fought?"

I did. It was a memory that returned with a vengeance. My powers were new to me, but I had broken Darthon's neck. I had killed him, and then, he had stood back up—alive—revealing only Eric could kill him. Unless I died. Then, I could kill Darthon.

"I ran because I didn't want to hurt you," his voice dropped to a whisper. "I would've been killing myself if I took your life."

My powers. The faulty prophecy. The absorption. The bloodlines. It all made sense now.

"You're Eric's weakness because protecting you guarantees the Light's life," he continued, taking another step toward me. With every step, the energy grew deeper. The gravity became heavier. "That's why he is weak. That's why he doesn't deserve to live."

Darthon's hand grazed my arm, and I slapped him away. Hot air sizzled down my throat. "This isn't about Eric," I said, but couldn't step away. "The Dark deserves to live."

His lip stretched up one of his cheeks. "If I live, the Dark can live through you. You'll be a shade, then." When Eric dies. "Or you can let me die and wait for them to kill you afterward."

I didn't understand what he was saying. I only stared at him as his expression slipped into one I had never seen before. His bottom lip trembled for a moment, but it froze as if it never had, and then, he was in front of me. His hand grazed my cheek. It was only then that I realized what happened. I had slid to the floor.

"You'll be all right," he said, his touch pulling away from my face. "You'll be able to handle the truth with my help. We'll even give you a Name." A real Name, something the Dark never gave me.

His words were as warm as my shower had been. They

moved over me as if they had cleansed a disease deep inside of me. But I didn't want it. I didn't want to feel the Light energy inside of me, but it was there—and it was inviting me to dive deeper.

I closed my eyes to stare at my memories, to remind myself of Eric by the river, to feel the first kiss we shared, to believe in the Dark and only in the Dark. As the Dark cloud consumed me, the Light popped and strained against my insides. I collected it and forced it out.

It shattered across the floor, and the marble cracked in half.

Darthon didn't flinch. He only sat next to me, placing his hand on my back as I wheezed. I couldn't even push him away. My energy was gone.

"It's only going to hurt you more if you keep fighting it," he said, knowing exactly what I had done. I rejected the Light energy. "Shades can't survive in here. The only reason you can is because you're one of us. Once you accept it, you'll be better—"

"Don't touch me."

He moved away, but he didn't move far. He maneuvered his way in front of me, facing me so that our toes pressed together. It reminded me of how Eric helped me stretch in the training room.

I stared at his feet like I could pretend I was back in the Dark's shelter—like I could forget the reality in front of me, like I could force Darthon's words out of me—and then, I looked at his face.

It was rounder than I originally thought, but his sharp cheekbones created an illusion of age. He had a widow's peak and a scar on his brow. When his eyes widened, his face tilted to one side while his smile moved to the other. If Pierce had similarities with his human form, maybe Darthon did, too. Maybe we all did.

"What are you looking for, Jess?" he asked, but didn't try to hide his face. He wanted me to see it. But I heard it. He called me Jess. Not Jessie. Not Jessica. Not an assortment of names someone could be called by. He knew me as Jess.

"You know me," I said, "outside of all this."

His expression didn't change. It was neutral. "I knew you were the third descendant for a long time," he admitted, "but even I didn't want to believe it."

"Why not?"

"Our weakness," he said. "It's the only thing Eric and I have in common." His toes pressed harder against mine. "You."

"I'm only your weakness because I kill you—"

"Not entirely."

I yanked my feet up and hugged my knees to my chest. Every muscle inside of me burned. I hadn't eaten, and I had expelled any influence the Light had on me. For once, I felt human and weak, but I wasn't either one if I had the willpower to believe it.

"You don't love me," I argued what he had insinuated, but his eyebrows shot up.

"Of course I don't," he said, but his face dropped. "But I do desire you."

It was his tone. It was the way he looked at me.

I pulled the Light energy back and leapt up to my feet. The power sparked a flame inside of my veins, and I put my hands in front of me. I wanted to kill him, even though he would come back to life, but he didn't move.

He stayed on the ground and looked up at me in the same way a child would. "Prom gave you away."

My hands dropped. "Prom?" That was months ago, way before I thought he knew who I was. He had held a knife to my throat. He could've taken me then, but Eric convinced him I was an innocent human. Evidently, he hadn't been entirely convinced.

"I saw him protect you, and I knew he'd already fallen for you," Darthon said as he stared at the wall. "I only had to watch you to figure out who he was." His lip curled. "But that pesky half-breed." He cursed. "Your memory loss made it tricky."

Luthicer. He knew that Luthicer was the one to remove my memories. He knew everything.

"How long did you know about Eric?" I managed.

Darthon sneered. "We would've known earlier if it weren't for that fake mother."

Ida. The elders had already told me everything I had missed. The woman had yet to meet me. She was mourning Eu. His death affected the shelter as much as Camille's had. Eric hadn't attended either of their funerals.

"If she wasn't there when we declared war—" His voice drifted off. "We did that for you, by the way. Everyone in the Light was willing to sacrifice themselves to a war just for you," he said it like he was proud. "What did the Dark do? Shun you with confusion?"

"That was my choice," I bit back.

"Are you still proud of that choice?"

His question broke me.

I jumped forward, ready to tackle him, but he shot up and grabbed my arms. I kicked him in the leg, but he didn't kick me back. Instead, he twisted my arm behind my back and slammed me against the wall.

"Don't fight me here," he spoke against my neck. "You'll only regret it."

I struggled, trying to escape his grasp, but he leaned against my back until my face crushed against the wall. I could barely breathe, but I kept fighting. He shoved his knee into the back of mine, and my muscles tore. Air hissed out of my lungs.

"Stop," he sounded like he was begging. "Just stop fighting."

"I won't."

And he was gone.

I spun around only to see him standing by the door. It had reappeared with the table full of food. "You aren't a prisoner here, Jess," he said, opening the door to reveal the hallway. "Walk around. See it for yourself. You'll see how much you belong here."

I didn't hesitate. I lunged for the table, grabbed the nearest knife, and threw it at him. He leapt to the left, and the blade bounced off the wall, clanking across the ground.

Darthon didn't leave or lock me inside like I thought he would. He walked across the room, picked up the knife, and placed it on the table—only inches away from me. "Work on your aim," he said, disappearing in a beam of light before I could fathom what I had seen.

Darthon was limping. His arm was red, and bruises formed around his shoulders in the same places he had hurt me. My injuries appeared on him. We were connected.

He wasn't lying.

Fifteen

I DREAMT OF MY MOTHER THAT NIGHT. THE BATS CIRCLED OVER-
head, and she pointed up while kneeling down. Her other
hand was on top of my head, and her fingernails scratched
against my scalp. Her voice shook.

"Even the scariest animals can be beautiful," she said.
"You're beautiful."

"Boys aren't beautiful, Mom."

As she took my hand, I didn't look at her face. I only stared
at her ring, the one that was on Jessica's finger now, and then,
I woke up.

The Light realm was as dark as that night was, and for a
moment, my dream melted over my reality. I saw the forest as
she walked toward it without me, but the memory disappeared
against the stone walls. I was awake.

I laid a hand on my sternum to make sure my body was
intact. Darthon hadn't hurt me recently. No one had. But I
could already sense his presence.

"You're awake," he spoke like he had been waiting for
hours.

"Do you enjoy watching me sleep?" I rolled over to face
him.

He was already grinning. "You look like a princess."

His words made me sick, but his movements were worse.
He walked over and knelt inches away from my face. "Can you

sit up?"

"I'd rather not," I said, but he didn't give me a choice.

A bright light burned my skin, and despite my will to lie on the ground, my body lifted until I leaned against the wall. My back contorted, and my stomach clenched like my teeth.

"Good morning," he said, but the red skin around his eyes said something else. He hadn't slept. "I wanted to have a little chat with you."

"Why is that not a surprise?"

His smirk melted, but his powers grew, and the air sizzled. It was hard to breathe, but I forced myself not to gasp. I didn't want him to see my pain. I wouldn't give him the satisfaction. When I didn't budge, he hit me across the face and laughed.

I spit out the blood before wiping my mouth. It wasn't even torture anymore. It was as meaningless as a handshake.

"What's so great about you anyway?" he ranted. "You've never even killed someone."

"Most of us don't rate a person's worth on how many murders they've committed." I waited for Darthon to hit me again, but he didn't. He only stared at the wall. "I'm guessing your talk with Jessica didn't go well."

Darthon didn't look over as he pulled the collar of his shirt down. Four bruises scattered across his shoulder. "You could say that."

"She hurt you." The words escaped me.

"Indirectly."

My heart lunged into my throat. He had hurt her. The bruises on him were hers.

"What did you do?" I growled.

His eyes snapped over to me. "You worried?"

I didn't speak. I couldn't. Jessica could handle herself. She always could, and I couldn't lose my mind over a few bruises. I had to stay in control.

"I could do a lot," Darthon continued as I tried to fight my anger, the same emotion Luthicer told me the Light would use against me. "She's not as strong here," he said, "and I kind of like the pain."

I snapped and grabbed him. He shoved me back, and my spine hit the wall. The breath in my lungs pushed out, and I couldn't conceal my gasp this time. "Leave her alone," I managed.

"Then, be my slave," he spat.

My violence cooled. "What?"

"You heard me." It was his deal, the one he hadn't explained yet. "Follow my orders, do everything I say, kiss my toes," he elaborated. "That sort of thing."

I stared at the blond boy in front of me, the exact opposite of my Dark appearance, but I was the only one to flinch. "You're sick."

He smiled like I complimented him. "That's why I understand your mother better than you do."

This time, I hit him. He didn't see it coming, and my fist collided with his cheek. His face snapped to the side, and he leapt up before I could hit him again. His wild-eyed stare resembled a child's. He wasn't even mad. He was amazed. It was as if no one had hit him before, and he chuckled like he enjoyed it.

He took the time to rock his jaw back and forth before he spoke. "Both of you are so violent."

Both. Like Jessica was as physical as I was.

"I meant your mother, Welborn," he ranted as if he knew my thoughts were always on the third descendant. "Can you, at least, attempt to stay focused?"

"I don't care what you know about her." This time, I was talking about my mother. She was dead. There was nothing I could do for her. Jessica, on the other hand, was alive, and so were hundreds of Dark members who were relying on us. If I could do something for them, I would. Worrying about the past wouldn't help the future.

"Don't worry about Jess," he said, sitting down again. This time, he was further away and definitely out of reach. "It's not like I could kill her."

But he could hurt her. Even if it hurt him, he was used to pain like I was. Jessica didn't have as much training as we did.

Not even close.

"You handle physical pain too well," Darthon spoke what I was thinking. "Torturing you doesn't satisfy me." His words explained why he had finally stopped.

"What's that supposed to mean?"

Right when I thought he would threaten to hurt Jessica, he changed his stance. "I guarantee you don't handle emotional pain well," he said it like he knew me.

"Too bad I'm not emotional."

Darthon's eyebrows rose until they disappeared beneath his bangs. "About your mother? Hannah? Teresa?" The human names for Abby and Camille sounded strange coming from him.

"They're dead," I interrupted before he could continue his hit list. The Dark didn't concentrate on death. We were raised to ignore it, to suppress the care for life. If I had been taught to think about life, I would've hesitated to kill Darthon even more than I already had. It was the single reason I wouldn't think about Camille. I wouldn't. She would be disappointed if I did.

Darthon allowed the silence to linger like he could sense my brain moving.

I shoved my thoughts away and snapped again, "They're dead."

"Jess isn't."

If a soul could darken, mine did.

Darthon must have seen the evil in my glare because he grinned, "I thought so."

"If you kill her, you die," I reminded him.

He leaned back on his hands. "If I'm going to die anyway, I don't see it as a loss."

"You're bluffing."

"Not really." The light in his eyes brightened. "We killed Hannah for this. I killed my parents for this," he said. "What makes you think I wouldn't kill Jess if it came down to it?"

I didn't even hear his last words. "You—you killed your parents?"

"They raised me to be a murderer. They had me kill my first dog." Darthon lifted his hand to stare at his fingernails. "They're proud I practiced on them after that."

Darthon didn't just have blood on his hands. He had his own bloodline on his hands. As blond and bright as his outward appearance was, he was complete darkness on the inside, and we were in his realm.

"But—" Darthon's voice shivered up my spine. "If I can save her, I will."

My focus stuck onto his deal, the only way we could get out. "And you're going to save her by making me your slave?"

"Now, we're talking." He clapped his hands together, and his fingers threaded into a grasp. His knuckles were white. "Once you work for me, I can separate you two."

"So you can kill me," I finished.

"Precisely." He nodded like we were making a million-dollar business deal. "So, yes, I believe that's the deal we want."

We—like I wanted it, too.

My mouth wouldn't move. The agreement was too heavy to say. It was impossible to even ask for clarification.

Darthon's brow crumbled at my hesitation. "It's you or Jess," he said. "Which do you prefer?"

"We don't have to die," I argued. "You do."

"She's one of you, Eric," he said. "If you want to achieve balance, what makes you think two shades can live? Where is the balance in that?" His voice wavered over his stutter. He never stuttered.

"The balance is between you and me, not her," I reminded him.

"And why do you think her bloodline was created?" he asked. "She'll take the place of the Light if I die, and she'll take the place of the Dark if you die." Even though he admitted I didn't have to die, his words drowned me. "She's half of each of us—a new breed—and a part of her will die no matter what we do."

Jessica wasn't a shade. She was a light, too. She was both without being a half-breed, and her powers were different because she was different. The signs were right in front of me, yet I hadn't seen them. I didn't want to see them. I hadn't seen her from the beginning.

I closed my eyes, fighting the images of Jessica's purple rain only for it to be replaced by my mother's ring—the one I gave Jessica, the one I made a promise with. "You're wrong," I managed. Darthon couldn't separate us. He couldn't.

"I'm not wrong," he growled, "and that's precisely why I'm more equipped to survive with her."

I opened my eyes as he stood up, signaling our conversation was nearing the end. "And I'm sure I can get her to see that when you're not around."

He had already told her she was a part of the Light. He thought my presence was the only thing holding her back, but he was wrong.

"It's not about me, Darthon," I shouted at his back as he walked away. "She won't abandon the Dark."

He spun around on his heel to face me, but his expression hadn't budged. "She doesn't need to abandon the Dark," he said, one step ahead of me. "She only needs to abandon you, and if you truly love her like the ancient ones say you do, you'll let her leave you. She'd be better off with me. She'll thrive. She'll take the Dark to new levels, and she'll govern a new state with her power, far beyond yours or mine."

I couldn't speak. It was as if he had cut my tongue out and slit my throat. The information had to be lies, but it was backed up with facts, with memories I didn't even understand, with information the Dark never shared.

"You have one day to think this over," he said. "I'll be back to make that deal." Whatever that entailed. "And then, you can enjoy a few weeks of life before I come to kill you."

"How gracious of you."

He stepped away, but his expression was stoic. "Just think it over."

SIXTEEN

Jessica

I PICKED UP THE KNIFE DARTHON DISCARDED AND TOOK IT WITH ME as I walked around. As far as I could tell, the realm was empty, but I didn't trust it. I never would. Even though my heart was warm, I cooled it with my thoughts.

Darthon wanted me to be in the Light, and he wanted me to govern a new Dark—after Eric was dead. The fact that Darthon believed I would even consider it proved how insane he was. I wouldn't let Eric die. I would get him out. I only had to find him first.

The hallways shifted as I walked down them. When I opened one door, the red carpet curved into a new direction, revealing a room I hadn't seen before. It was a maze of madness, but I relied on my instincts.

I pushed open the first door my eyes locked on.

The first thing I saw was four sets of black horns sticking out from the floor. The heatless fire in the corner was too familiar. Camille. She had died here. I could picture her face in the corner.

"You won't find him."

I knew it was Darthon before I turned around.

He was soundless as he walked up to me, stopping only a yard away. His black shirt made his skin glow like an angel in the paintings I studied, but his smile was unlike anything I had seen in art. It was unnatural. His pointed teeth were more like an animal's than a person's, and his frozen demeanor was that of a statue.

I found the words. "I wasn't looking for him."

When he tilted his head, every inch of movement seemed deliberate. "Have you thought about what I said?"

It had only been hours, three, at most. Knowing what he wanted was impossible to comprehend, let alone contemplate. Even he had to know that, but Fudicia's words flooded through me. Darthon wasn't as patient as she was. He didn't have time. He should've been dead, after all, and his empty gaze made him look like he already had died. I wondered what his eyes looked like when he was a human, if I would recognize the expression if I had the chance again.

My silence was enough of an answer for him.

Before I could react, his hand snapped up and smacked me across the face. I hit the ground. His fingers wrapped around my hair by the time I started fighting back. I tried to stab him, but his free hand took my only weapon.

"What don't you understand?" he hissed against my throat, the same piece of flesh he held a knife to during prom. "I have more power here than you—than him—but you could be better if you just listened to me."

I reeled back, kicking at his knees, but it wasn't enough.

He slammed me against the wall. "I have other ways of convincing you to give him up."

Eric.

"It isn't about him," I screeched as my cheek scraped the wall.

Darthon's grip loosened, but only for a moment. "You love the Dark that much?"

Bracke's face was the first one I remembered, how his expression had softened over time. When I first met him, he was cold, skeptical about how I wanted to be Eric's friend, and then, he had smiled at me in the hospital after Eric's car wreck, and I knew he loved his son more than anyone.

Pierce's face was next, and Camille's followed. I had to fight the image of her death, skin tearing off her bones.

I twisted, trying to escape Darthon, but he pushed my arm against my back. "If that's how you're going to be—" His voice trailed off, but he yanked me off the wall. He hadn't dragged me three feet before Fudicia came out of a door.

"Darthon?" Even her eyes were wide. "What are you doing? You can't hurt her—"

"I'm not," he growled, dodging Fudicia as she attempted to pull him off me. "I'm just giving her a new prison."

I dug my heels into the ground, but it wasn't enough. Darthon pulled my hair, and I fell forward. He had his hand wrapped around my wrists in seconds. My skin burned.

"Let me go," I screamed, but no amount of fighting stopped him. I was too human.

He dragged me down the hallway in minutes and kicked open a door as it appeared. He lifted me up only to toss me to the floor. My legs scraped against the ground, so I raised my arms to block him from hitting me, but he didn't.

I only moved my arm when his footsteps echoed away. He slammed his fist against the wall. "I'll kill him, Jess."

"You can't—"

"I already have."

The words slammed against my chest like he had hit me instead of the concrete.

"See this wall?" His forefinger was white when he pressed the wall. "He's one wall away from you." Eric was right next door. "And you will be able to hear him tonight when I kill him again. And again when he comes back to life. And again after that."

Eric. He was dying. That was why his heartbeat kept fading and returning. Darthon wasn't lying. He couldn't kill him, even when he could.

"Wait—"

"I will wait when you become one of us."

"I don't know how," I shouted back, every part of me burning.

"Maybe you'll figure it out," he said and marched over to the doorway, flicking the knife out so I could see it. "The screaming might help you think."

I stood up to chase him, but it was too late. Darthon slammed the door, and I slammed against it, hitting it with all the force I had left. Nothing happened. Nothing but my desperation.

"Fudicia!" It was the first time I wanted her help. "Darthon!" I shouted their names over and over, but no one responded.

I ran over to the wall Darthon had hit and hit it myself. "Darthon, stop!"

A shout was the only response I had.

Eric's shout.

My blood went cold in my veins, and any heat the realm gave me left. Even though he wasn't speaking, I recognized Eric's voice as he screamed. The screams were constant, more alive than my breathing.

I hit the wall until I couldn't anymore.

Another scream followed the shattering of what I could only guess was bone. He didn't scream after that. My tears might as well have been acid rain.

That was how I remembered the rain, a power that came naturally to me, but one Eric couldn't control. It was the sign I had been different all along.

I squeezed my hand and drowned out my breath as I laid my palm out. I waited, urged for it to come, and slowly, just as Eric's heartbeat began to return, the rain flickered from my fingertips. The purple color didn't stay purple for long. It burned red and splatted against the ground like blood.

The door opened.

Darthon stood there, his hair as wild as his eyes, but I stared at his hands. Eric's blood was on his fingertips.

"You called?" he snarled. "Or are you just distracting me?"

The red power I had was theirs—the Light's—and it was also mine. I knew how to become one of them, and it rested in my veins. The purple powers would have to die, but I clutched onto it.

"If you leave him alone, I'll—"

Darthon marched over. "I didn't come to bargain, Jess." He spat on my face when he grabbed me, but this time, his grip slipped. From the blood.

My stomach twisted before I threw up again.

Darthon didn't even notice. He dragged me straight through it, and my vision blurred as he pulled me down the hallway and into the room. Eric's room.

Darthon let go of me then.

"This is your fault," he said.

Eric's body was mangled, torn and bloody. His muscles were shredded, his skin was ripped, and his limbs were shattered. The only sign of life he had was the sickening wheezing that escaped his lungs. His chest inched up as he breathed.

"Eric." I scrambled across the room on my knees until I was by his side.

His face was barely recognizable. I lifted my hands to touch him only to move away. "Eric." *"Can you hear me?"*

"Get away from him," Darthon ordered.

I didn't move. I only searched Eric's body, struck by how his injuries healed, how his human body reconnected, how the slice on his abdomen was closing. He was coming back to life only for Darthon to kill him again, only for Darthon to continue to torture the both of us—until one of us broke and the Dark died. I couldn't let the Dark die.

The knife lay by Eric's ribcage.

I grabbed it.

Darthon chuckled. "We already know how bad your aim is."

"I'm not aiming for you," I spat.

"Don't," Darthon screamed as he shot forward, but it was too late.

I plunged it into my chest.

SEVENTEEN

W HEN I WOKE UP, DARTHON WAS WAITING, BUT HE WAS QUI-
et. He was never quiet.

I glanced around the room, half-expecting the half-
breed to be ready to attack me, but no one was there. We were
alone, and Darthon lingered in silence. When I looked at him,
his eyes focused on the ground near me. My blood had dried
against it, a reminder of how much I hadn't healed. I had only
just come back to life. My chest was cut. As I moved, I sensed
my ribs were broken. I stopped moving out of the fear of punc-
turing a lung.

"The deal," Darthon finally spoke, "I want you to take it,
and I want you to take it today."

Be my slave. I remembered his proposition, even though
I wanted to forget it.

Darthon looked at me, but it was the first time I had seen
his complexion so pale. "If you take it, I'll let you both go right
now."

Jessica.

In my delirium, I had heard her speak my name. But her
voice hadn't sounded peaceful. She had screamed. It was worse
than the death I succumbed to.

I stared at the ceiling. "How is she?"

"Alive."

His tone made my veins twist.

I only looked back at him to search his face, expecting to see a threatening glare escape him, but nothing came. He was frozen. But he didn't have an injury on his skin. If he had hurt her, he would've been hurt, but he wasn't, even though he talked like they both were.

"Just take the deal, Welborn."

"I'm not going to be your slave—"

"If you don't take the deal, she'll die."

"You can't hurt her."

"She'll die."

It was the look in his face—the way his jaw popped into place as he locked it, the way his eyes wrinkled with his brow, the way he didn't look away from me.

"I don't see how it will work—"

He shifted as if he had to move to loosen his jaw. "It's a spell."

"An illusion," I corrected, knowing how their powers worked. "And if that's the case, I can break it."

"Then, take that chance," Darthon said.

My fingertips pushed against the ground as I forced myself to sit up. "Why would you want to control me?"

He laid his chin on his hands. "Because I need you to leave her."

"What?"

"You heard me, Welborn," he said. "Stay away from her, and she'll be just fine, and if you break the illusion, then, fine. I just need time, and as long as she has you, she'll believe in the Dark—"

"You don't get it, do you?" I snapped. "She isn't fighting for me. She's fighting for the Dark. It doesn't matter if I leave her—"

"Then, take the deal."

I was silenced.

Darthon's hands dropped to his knees, and he leaned forward. "If you're that confident in her, then, listen to me, and do as I say," his growl echoed. "Take the deal."

I had to look away.

Leave Jessica? Stay away from her all over again? I had done it before and failed. I had failed everything, giving up when I thought she was dead. But she hadn't given up on the Dark or me. She came through, and she fought. She always would. I knew that. And if it meant our escape, I would have to rely on that. Our destiny was only a shadow of the bigger picture. Even if our destiny died, the Dark wouldn't. The Dark was what mattered. Jessica had proven that to me when I told her I gave up. It was my chance to do the same for her.

"I still don't see how this will work," I managed, unable to tell him I agreed.

"I'll put the spell—"

"The illusion," I corrected again, "that I will break."

"Fine." Darthon still agreed.

Something was wrong.

"I'll put the illusion on you," he said, "and you will listen to my orders when I come to you," he explained. "You won't be able to tell her about our little deal either. You won't be able to tell anyone anything."

So, it was a sensory spell. Luthicer had explained them in training. The Light couldn't physically control someone's movements, but they could control parts of the mind, trick them into thinking they couldn't speak or hear or see certain things. It was how they could attack in broad daylight without anyone seeing.

As much as I hated it, it was a relief. I was expecting something more powerful, something that wouldn't be easy to break, but I reminded myself it was Darthon's illusion. He wouldn't make it simple to destroy.

"Why wait for me to agree to it?" I asked, trying to understand as much as I could so I could relay it to Luthicer in the future. He would know what to do. "Why not just do it?"

Darthon's eyes searched mine like he knew what I was thinking. "It's more powerful if you agree." Darthon might have been the most honest person I had ever met, and I hated him for it as much as it fascinated me. "It also means that you will live—Jess will live—and if you don't agree, one of you won't," he paused. "By that, I mean Jess."

"Is the only rule to stay away from her?" I interrupted, refusing to talk about her death. It wouldn't happen. I wouldn't lose anyone else.

Darthon's lip twitched like he wanted to smile. "Of course not."

"What are the others?"

"You can't talk to her, touch her, telepathically communicate, or anything like that. It's forbidden." With every statement, my stomach churned. "But, most of all, I can change the rules whenever I want to."

"So, you control me."

"Like a pawn."

"This isn't a game, Darthon."

"I never said it was," he retorted, "but you're stuck with me for now."

I forced a smile back at him, wanting him to see that I could remain positive despite his conditions. If he were like me, mental torture would be the best way to fight him. "Being stuck with you hasn't been that bad."

He flinched.

"If I agree—"

"Which you should if you want to leave here alive," he added.

"Sure. Sure. Life and all that." I waved him away. "How do I know you'll free Jessica?"

"You don't."

I swallowed and focused on my face, refusing to let the muscles budge a centimeter. He wouldn't get the satisfaction of seeing my hesitation. I didn't know what he would do, but I knew what Jessica would do. Even if he kept her, she would escape and be loyal to the Dark no matter what. She could handle herself, and our relationship was only a slice of the Dark's power. We weren't the only ones fighting Darthon, but he had forgotten that. There was only one problem.

"How will I know who you are?" I asked, knowing he couldn't order me around in the human realm in his light form.

Someone would sense him, probably Pierce.

Darthon's smile stretched. "You'll know my identity soon enough."

It was the last thing I expected to hear.

"And you won't be able to tell anyone about that either."

"I could kill you," I pointed out.

"You won't be able to attack me."

My stomach sank. "Another rule?"

He nodded.

"You can't control my physical movements."

"Not unless you have reason to hold back," he said and tapped his head. "Don't forget, the Light knows who Jess is."

He didn't have to explain. If I attacked him, they would attack her. I understood his upper hand now.

"Unless you don't care about her life," he continued, "then, by all means, come after me."

"I'll find a loophole," I promised.

He raised his brow. "Are you really threatening me right now? When I'm giving you a chance to escape, to go talk to your father, to learn about your bloodline?"

"You're only letting me go because you can't kill me here," I snapped, refusing to let his words mess with my memories again.

"That's a part of it," he agreed, "but I need to sever your connection with her first. Then, I'll kill you."

"I could find a loophole before then."

"I doubt it."

"You don't know Jessica or me," I said. "We aren't as vulnerable in the human world as we are here."

His face hardened. "Is it a deal or not?"

"Deal."

It wasn't like I had a choice, but that wasn't new to me. I never had choices. It was how I lived my life, and I was perfectly comfortable finding a way around it.

"Great," Darthon said as he stood up, crossed the room, and knelt by my side. He grabbed my neck, and my skin scorched like it was on fire. When I squirmed, he held me down, and my vision blurred. The only part I could make out was Dar-thon's face as the skin peeled over, as his black eyes lightened to brown, as his skin washed out and his hair thickened.

"When you wake up, you'll be home—safe and sound." Robb McLain promised right before I blacked out.

EIGHTEEN

MY EYELIDS WERE AS HEAVY AS THE REST OF MY BODY. WHEN I woke up, I struggled to move anything, but I had woken up. I was alive.

The breath that filled my lungs felt foreign, a momentum of destruction as my heartbeat slammed into my ribs over and over again. My sternum hurt. That was the first thing I felt with my fingertips. It was hot and bumpy. When I looked down, I saw the scar.

"How are you feeling?"

Darthon's voice was the last thing I wanted to hear, but it was the first thing I computed.

"How—" I couldn't finish my sentence.

"I don't know." He was sitting at the edge of the bed in a room I had never seen before. Unlike the rest of the red rooms, this one was black, only lit from the single flame on top of a lampstand. Kerosene. I could smell it.

I touched my chest, the place where I had plunged the knife. It had healed, not completely, not like I was a shade, but it had healed. Eric wasn't alone. I couldn't die either. But now, I couldn't kill Darthon in the same way Darthon couldn't kill Eric. Whatever was happening was beyond any theory I could fathom.

"Why'd you do it?"

His question was the only thing I heard. When I looked

at him, his fingers were tangled in his hair, his shoulders were slumped, and his eyes—for once—weren't on me. He stared at the bed sheets instead, and his whisper was barely audible when he repeated the question. His fingers tightened in his hair.

"It wasn't for him." I thought of Bracke and Pierce and Luthicer, but I mainly thought of Camille and Eu, the two who had died for my sake. Even when I did it, I knew it wasn't for Eric. It was never for Eric. It was for the Dark, for the people who finally explained my identity and protected it with their lives. My life was the only way I could give them back theirs, and I had failed. I was alive, and so was Darthon.

"You don't want to be one of us that badly?" Darthon's hiss was more of a whimper.

I searched his neck, the only part of his body that was exposed. I yearned to grab his collared shirt and pull it down. I wanted to see if he was scarred, too.

"I'll never be one of you," I said. Even if I had to die, I wouldn't become a light. Especially if it meant the Dark's bloodline had to die. The Light wasn't my family. Even if my biological family had been born into it, they had died trying to escape, and so would I. They ran for a reason. They died for a reason. I knew that now.

"Don't do that again," Darthon said.

I bit my lip, refusing to speak.

"It's not worth it," he said, opening his mouth to close it, to open it again. "Do you know what Eric would think?"

"It wasn't for him," I snapped, but Darthon's silence brought on the thoughts.

Eric's mother had killed herself. He told me how Camille had accused him of trying the same, how it had torn him apart, how much he was against suicide. But mine was different. It wasn't out of depression. It was out of desperation. Mine was different.

"I don't care what it was for," Darthon said. "It's not worth it. If you want to kill me—"

"I do."

Darthon's face flushed. "Then, do it in the human realm."

Realm—like everything was separated.

"Just don't kill yourself," he struggled with his words, choking on them as he spit them out, one by one. "You can't die anyway."

"That doesn't make sense—"

"It will," he said it like he didn't understand it either, but he promised that he would figure it out.

"And when it does?"

"I'll kill Eric."

I swallowed.

"Until then," he paused as he stood up, "I'll send you back, but only if you promise."

I knew what he was saying. He wanted me to promise to stay alive. "I can't do that."

"I'll let Eric go, too," he said, spinning around to face me. His angular face softened, and for a moment, I wondered what he looked like as a child. "I'll send you both back—alive."

Eric.

The images of his bloody body flooded my mind, crushed my insides, reminded me of how alive I actually was, how alive he was.

"You'll let him go?"

Darthon nodded without hesitation. "If you change your mind about becoming a full light," he began, "come back to me."

Before I could ask what he meant, the door opened, and Fudicia walked in. The half-breed followed. He was carrying Eric, and when he dropped Eric on the ground, I leapt from the bed only to land by Eric's side.

"Eric," I gasped his name.

His shallow breathing was unnerving. While most of his injuries were half-healed, dried blood stained his skin. Like paint, separated shades of browns and reds mixed with his bluish bruises. I doubted I would ever be able to paint again.

"He's not dead, Jess—"

"That doesn't make it better," I snapped, digging my nails

into the pieces of his shirt that had remained intact. "What the hell is your problem?"

If I had lost my energy before, it was back now. I was ready to fight again.

Fudicia and the half-breed stepped between us like they knew what I was thinking.

I looked over their faces, young, yet old at the same time. The indentions of their expressions, the determination imbedded in their skin, told me they weren't afraid of hurting me anymore. They would if I tried anything again. Darthon was better off hurt than dead.

"We'll continue protecting you," Fudicia said.

"You've done enough." I wanted to scream, but my words were calm. I was too focused on Eric.

"*Wake up,*" I coaxed, attempting to reach his unconscious mind. "*Wake up.*"

His eyelashes didn't even flutter.

"So, Jess," Darthon was next to me when he spoke, somehow moving past his guards without a fight. "Are you ready to go home?"

I glared at him. "I don't see why you're doing this."

"I have my reasons."

When he laid his hand on my shoulder, I tried to move away, but his fingers dug into my skin. "You can't get away from this," he whispered, only inches away from me. "Trust me," he paused, "I tried."

And then, I was gone.

———◆———

I was wrapped in the flames of the sudden hell Darthon created. The heat tore at my skin, my face, my hair, and my breath was stolen by the wind. As soon as I believed I would burn to death, the flames flipped into frigid water.

My fingers tightened, and cloth ripped beneath my touch. Eric. His faint heartbeat flickered, and I reached out until I grasped his shirt again. It didn't tear this time. I pulled, yanking myself more toward him than him toward me, and we spun.

I gasped as my head broke the surface of the river, and my hair tangled around my neck. I tried to scream, but the air escaped as a whimper. My telepathic line was my only hope. *"Eric."* Every section of my mind screeched. If he didn't wake up, he would drown, and I would drown with him if I didn't get him up. The Dark needed him.

I dove back down. When my feet skimmed the river-bed, I kicked to prevent my ankles from sinking into the mud. Grasping Eric's shirt, I attempted to swim up, but I couldn't tell if we had budged. The water was moving too fast.

With one last shove, I broke the surface as thunder crashed above us. Even the surface was drowning with rain. "Eric," I shouted again, but the wind shouted over me.

Another wave smashed into my ribs, and I dropped into the river again, my body crushing into the muddy ground below. My hands searched the bottom, my eyes opened without need, and my body shook with panic. After everything we survived, we were going to drown. But I wouldn't accept it until we did.

I pushed my way through the water and latched onto a branch. Before I could pull, it pulled me.

"Jess." The sudden voice came from the branch before I realized it wasn't a branch at all. It was a person—a boy—and Darthon flashed in front of my vision.

I shoved him away. "Let me go."

But he didn't. He grabbed me again. "It's me," he said. "Jess, it's me."

The boy's green eyes pierced through the brilliant lightning, and my fingers dug into his arms. "Jonathon." Even though he was a shade, his human name came first.

"You're okay," he said as I spun toward the river.

Three men lunged into the water.

Urte and Bracke's hair melted into the blackness, but Luthicer was the glowing angel who yanked Eric's body out of the water. As soon as the elder picked Eric up, Luthicer laid him on the shore. Eric wasn't breathing. Urte knelt down, breathed air into his lungs, and pushed on his chest. Bracke barked orders, but I couldn't hear anything except for Pierce.

"You're okay now," he kept repeating. "You both are."

Nineteen

I T WAS A FAMILIAR SCENE. BRIGHT, BUZZING, FLORESCENT LIGHTS.
Feet tapping the ground. Heavy words masked with low
whispers. Even before I opened my eyes, I knew I was in a
hospital. I only prayed it was in the shelter instead of a human
one.

I shuddered as my eyes adjusted to the brightness. The
moist air was cold, and the bed beneath me was warm from
my body heat. It was soft. I had almost forgotten what it was
like to wake up on a mattress instead of a stone floor.

"Eric." The man's voice was as familiar as his ice-blue eyes.
"You're awake."

The last time I had heard that phrase my enemy had spoken it. This time, it was my father.

"Hey," I croaked out the word.

My elbows propped the rest of my body up. That's when
I saw myself. My arms were torn, and even though my chest
was wrapped, blue bruises pushed over the sides. The only difference from the Light realm was the rest of my skin. It wasn't
covered in dried blood. Someone had cleaned me.

"How are you feeling?" The nurse spoke this time. I hadn't
even noticed her, but I did notice the old walls. We were underground. The Dark's shelter was my hospital this time.

"I feel—" I paused as I moved, my sore muscles inching
around, "better."

My father waved her away, and she obeyed because she had to. He held the authority now. Not Darthon.

"You'll heal faster now than you did from your car wreck," he said as she left the room. "We found you before any humans did."

I sighed. If humans had found me, I would've been in the hospital for days. Now, I would be fully healed in that time.

My mind spun, but I drowned out my thoughts and leaned back, tracing the dark ceiling before I closed my eyes. I breathed in the scent of the shelter, the thick musk of the earth we took safety in. I had never noticed the smell until now. Correction—I had never taken the time to notice it.

"You can tell we are underground," I whispered.

My father didn't respond.

I opened my eyes to make sure he was still there, and he was, sitting in a chair by my bedside. "I wonder—" I stopped myself from telling him what I was thinking. What else hadn't I noticed? What else had brushed past me during my training days? Were there other parts I hadn't smelled, or touched, or felt? I couldn't believe I had ever been alive at all.

When my dad finally spoke, he said the last thing I thought he would say, "It's going to be hard returning to your normal life." He leaned forward, placing his elbows on his knees. "It always is after something catastrophic. Take your time."

"Catastrophic?" I repeated the word like I had never heard it before. Was the Light realm catastrophic? It soaked into me just like my own blood had. But that wasn't the worst part.

A memory. A problem. Something that had been said. A thing that had happened. I wasn't sure I could remember, but it lingered like my injuries, pushed against my skull like a migraine.

I shivered.

"Jess is all right," my father guessed what I was thinking.

Jessica.

Her name struck me.

Stay away from Jessica. It was Darthon's deal—his orders—his face was melding right in front of me, but it tore apart when I breathed her name, "Jessica." I sat up, looking around the room for her, but we were alone. "Where is she? What did Darthon do to her?"

"Relax." It sounded like an order. "There was barely a scratch on her."

"What?" I couldn't believe it. "She wasn't hurt?"

"She was a little delirious when we found you," he admitted. "Other than that, she was the same as she was when you were kidnapped."

The same. Darthon hadn't hurt her at all. Not a single bit. He had kept his word, and now, I had to keep mine.

It couldn't be true.

Darthon's deal had to be a dream, a fluke in my memories, an illusion brought on by torture. After all, I had been killed—hadn't I?—and I was unconscious. I didn't even know how long I had been out.

"What day is it?"

"You were gone for three days." That was it.

My father's face twisted into a wrinkled frown. "We tried so hard—so, so hard—to get you both out, but we couldn't even reach you. It was impossible."

"Dad." I stopped him. "This isn't your fault."

"We should've been able to do something—"

I shook my head. "I couldn't even do anything." Not there. Not in that realm.

"How are you alive?" he asked, but his words stuttered out.

He knew what I did. Shades died in the Light realm. Even Camille—a half-breed—succumbed to their power. I shouldn't have stood a chance. I knew that when Darthon took us.

"I—I don't know."

Before he could ask another question, a knocking broke through our conversation. A teenage boy walked in, and his green eyes locked onto mine. His grin almost broke his face.

"You're all right," Pierce said it like he would rush across the room, but he leaned against the wall. "You looked horrible last night."

"Thanks."

"Well, you did." Pierce's voice cracked, only calming when he faced my father. "My dad wants to talk to you, Bracke."

My father stood up. "Where is he?"

"The meeting room."

He walked to the exit, only to turn around and look at me once more. "I'm glad you're safe."

"I know."

When he spun away, it wasn't quick enough. I saw the mist in his eyes, the deepening of his wrinkles as he fought back his tears. My dad—the man I had only seen cry once— was about to cry again.

My chest tightened.

"You'll get to go home tonight," Pierce said and broke up my thoughts. "The nurses said you're healing faster than any shade they've seen before."

"But—" I gestured to myself. "I'm human."

He pointed to my arm. An I.V. was in my vein. "It pumps Dark energy into your bloodstream," he said. "Only the latest and greatest by Luthicer."

The elder I once hated had somehow become a friend. "That guy is a genius." But I remembered his daughter, Jada, and how she came to us the night we left. All my memories were slowly creeping in with the medicine.

"So, how was it?" Pierce didn't hold back. "What was the realm like?"

"I don't know." I raised my hand to rub my head, but I stopped when the I.V. pulled. It stung. "I was unconscious most of the time."

"You and Jess both." Her name. "Neither one of you will tell me."

"Where is she?" I asked, fighting the urge to pull out the medicine so I could check on her myself. "Is she okay? What did she say?"

"Nothing." Pierce frowned for the first time since entering the room. "She's pretty upset about the whole thing. Had to fight just to keep her out of here. She wouldn't even let the nurses look at her."

"But she's okay?" I half-expected them to be lying. "She's not hurt at all?"

"Not like you. Just a few scrapes," Pierce seconded my father's story. "But it doesn't seem right."

"As long as she's okay," I interrupted.

"But why would Darthon hurt you and not touch her—"

Darthon.

His face formed in my memory. As clear as Pierce sat in front of me, I saw him. The brown hair and eyes to match. Robb McLain.

"I know—" *who Darthon is.*

The last words didn't slide off my tongue. I choked on them. My throat burned where Robb had grabbed me, where Darthon had placed the illusion on my skin, the one I had agreed to.

"I know—" I tried to speak again. *Robb McLain is Darthon. Robb is Darthon. Darthon. I know who he is.*

Not a single word came out.

The illusion was real. I couldn't tell them. I couldn't speak.

"Eric?"

"Jonathon." I only used his human name to warn him. "Something—" *isn't right with me.*

There it was again. The burning on my throat, the spell in my blood. The medicine was acid. I yanked it out.

Pierce leapt up. "Eric—"

"I'm fine," I stuttered, unable to look at him as I realized the truth. A lie had escaped me, but the truth was impossible to explain. Darthon was controlling me.

"Eric?"

Her voice was the only reason I didn't panic.

Jessica stood in the doorway. Her curly hair was pulled back, causing her blue eyes to look wider than usual, and her cheeks flushed when I met her gaze. She rushed across the room before I could muster a word.

Unlike the others, she wasn't afraid of my injuries. She touched me like she always had, dug her nails against her palm like I always hated. I grabbed her hand to stop her from doing it. Her skin was soft.

"Sorry," she muttered, knowing what she had done, but her face lit up. "How are you? Are you okay? Have you eaten yet?"

I laid my palm on her face and dragged my thumb over her cheekbone. "Stop worrying about me," I said. "How are you?"

She bit her lip before she said, "I'm really happy you're okay." She was still worrying about me, still refusing to listen to me. As much as it bothered me, it reminded me of the reasons I loved her. And she was right in front of me again.

"I'm fine, if anyone was wondering," Pierce spoke up. "Other than being ignored, of course."

Jessica laughed, and it was the sweetest sound I had ever heard.

"Shut up, Jonathon," she spoke through her giggles, but she wiped away the tears that escaped her eyes. I wondered if she was crying out of happiness, relief, or fear. I wanted to know.

"Scorn me for worrying about you two," Pierce continued sarcastically. "It's not like I'm your guard or best friend or anything like that."

She stuck her tongue out at him, and he stuck his tongue out back. Like children, they giggled. Like an adult, I watched. But Jessica's focus was back to me, and I knew she heard my silence over Pierce's voice.

"Eric—"

"I'm okay," I said before she could question me, and I pulled her against my chest before she could look at my face and know I had lied. "I'm glad you're okay," I whispered against her forehead before I kissed it. She tensed against me.

I tensed, too, but for a different reason. *Stay away.* I knew Darthon's first rule.

"*Jessica,*" I spoke to her in silence. "*Can you hear me?*"

Instead of pushing against my chest, she pulled herself away, so she could see me. "Of course I can."

"*I have to tell you—*"

114

My brain singed when I tried to tell her who Darthon was. I grabbed my scalp.

"Eric." Her nails were against my arm. "Eric, are you okay? What happened? Did I hurt you?" She moved away again, and I was cold.

I shook my head. "You didn't hurt me."

"What is it, man?" Pierce spoke up. "What's going on?"

I opened my mouth, and nothing came out. Not a single sound.

I felt myself pale.

Jessica said my name again.

"Do you have a pen?" I asked.

Pierce leaned over to the nurse's station and grabbed one without question. "Want some paper, too?"

I glared at him.

He chuckled like our lives weren't at stake. "Here." He handed me both.

I gripped the pen, but it froze in my fingers. I couldn't even write it down. I dropped it.

"What is going on?" Jessica's high-pitched voice rose. "What's wrong?"

I couldn't speak. I couldn't tell them. The only thing that happened was the burning in my throat, the touch of Darthon's fingers on my neck. He was controlling me, and I had agreed to it. There was nothing I could do about it. I couldn't warn Jessica or confess to Pierce, and I definitely couldn't fight it. I didn't have free will anymore—not until I broke the illusion—and that meant one thing.

I had to break up with Jessica.

TWENTY

Jessica

"ERIC'S ACTING WEIRD," I SPOKE TO JONATHON AFTER ART CLASS. Eric had avoided me all morning, but he also avoided Jonathon. He hadn't spoken to anyone that I knew of, but he couldn't avoid me in homeroom.

Jonathon scratched the paint off his fingernails. "You two went through a lot." When I didn't respond, Jonathon adjusted his glasses. "Just give him time."

Time—it was the last thing we had, but Eric was acting as if it existed. After he woke up at the shelter, he paced the room like his father often did, and then, he left. He didn't even say goodbye. Jonathon was the only reason I didn't follow. My guard took me home instead, and he kept repeating how Eric needed time. It reminded me of how much time Jonathon had with Eric. They had known one another since birth. I had only been around for one year—a year that felt much longer than it should have.

"Just stay focused," Jonathon said before I could walk away. *Darthon could come back.*

"*I know.*" He didn't have to remind me. "I'll see you after school."

Jonathon nodded, and with that, he was gone, off to his other courses with the crowd of students he disappeared into. I joined the crowd and walked into my homeroom, knowing Eric wouldn't arrive until the bell rang.

Crystal was the first one to approach me. "Welcome back."
It didn't sound welcoming at all.

I laid my bag on my table. "Hey."

Eric's seat was empty until Crystal sat in it. "How was
your trip?"

"It was okay," I said, waiting for the interrogation to continue.

Crystal had the right to be upset. She was my best friend,
and I hadn't told her anything. It wasn't like I could, but she
didn't know that. I would've been upset with her, too.

She folded her arms, but a smile finally broke her lips.
"Tell me about it at lunch?"

"Sure."

When she got up and left, I knew Eric was behind me.
I could feel his heartbeat in my veins. Even though we were
back from the realm, the sensation hadn't left, but it was different now, stronger and pounding. Like he was scared.

I watched as he took his seat, and I didn't stop when I sat
next to him. He refused to make eye contact with me, and if
I tried to catch his eyes, he focused on his bandages. He had
three—one wrapped around his torso, and two circled his
wrists—but I could only see one that encased his hand. His
long sleeves hid the rest. They would be off before tonight.

"Are you okay?" I whispered.

"Class is going to start," he said, just as Ms. Hinkel came in
and demanded our attention.

Homeroom passed, and when the bell rang, he gathered
his things without talking to me. Sweat collected on his brow.
His heartbeat increased.

I grabbed his arm before he could walk away. "What's up
with you?"

"Huh?" His sunken eyes made him look asleep, like he was
stuck in a dreamland far away from me.

"You've been quiet all morning." I walked by his side as he
headed for the lunchroom. "Are you tired?"

He didn't respond.

"Do you have a headache?" I searched his face for any sign

of response, but his expression was stoic. "If it's from your concussion, you should relax—"

"I'm fine, Jessica," he snapped.

When I stopped, he did, too.

His green eyes widened as he searched my face, and then, his arm shot out and wrapped around my shoulders. "I'm sorry." His breath was against my forehead, and he breathed twice before he spoke again. "Everything is going to be okay," he said it like it wasn't going to be.

My palm landed on his chest just as he stepped away from me. "Eric?"

He smiled, but I knew it was forced. It was the way his upper lip extended to the right instead of the left, the way his shoulders fell, the way he adjusted his backpack to distract himself. Even if we had only known one another for a year, I knew him well enough to know when he was lying.

"It's nothing," he said again before I could ask him what was wrong. He ran a hand through his hair, and his bangs stuck together like he hadn't showered. "We should probably get to lunch. You have to talk to Crystal, don't you?" This time, his smile was sincere.

I shot one back, and we walked together, but didn't hold hands. He kept his on his bag, and I stuck mine in my pockets. It was cold outside, but it was warm enough for the students to sit there. Everyone was desperate for fresh air.

"Want my jacket?" he asked as we approached the elongated bench where everyone always sat, but Crystal was the only one who had arrived.

"I'm fine."

Eric dropped his bag by the table and shook off his coat. Before I could continue arguing, he handed it over, and I slipped it on.

Crystal watched, and a grin broke her lips. "Aren't you two adorable?"

"Yeah. Yeah." I sat down next to her and pulled out my lunch. Eric sat on my other side.

Crystal had to lean over to get his attention. "So, where'd

you two go?" Unlike the previous times she had spoken to Eric, she didn't stutter this time. Whatever horrible past they had was starting to melt away. "Aruba? The Caribbean?" She rolled her eyes. "Please, tell me it wasn't somewhere lame like Seattle. It just rains there. I need some sunshine."

"Georgia," Eric answered.

"My extended family still lives there." I seconded the lie the Dark created.

"Didn't realize you had extended family," Zac spoke before I saw him, and he kissed Crystal on the cheek before I could stop him. His dark eyes were on me the entire time, but I didn't hold his gaze for long. Robb and Linda had joined us. She was in the lunch period before ours, so she would have to leave soon.

"Hey, guys," Robb spoke for both of them.

Crystal chirped a reply, but I didn't hear it. I was too busy remembering what he had done, how he didn't remember, how only Zac remembered.

"You were saying?" Zac pressed as he put his coffee on the table. He must have stolen it from the teacher's room.

"My dad's family lives in Atlanta," I managed. It wasn't a complete lie. My uncle lived there, but my dad hadn't spoken to his brother in years. As far as I knew, they had never forgiven one another over their mother's will. It was one of the reasons my dad was happy to move to Kansas when he got the chance. We didn't talk about it any more than that.

"Isn't that where you moved from?" Zac asked.

I nodded. "But we moved around a lot for his job."

"What does he do anyway?"

"Enough questions," Eric snapped.

I jumped at his tone, but when I looked at him, I froze. Aside from his flushed cheeks, his complexion had paled. "Eric—"

"Can I talk to you for a minute?" Robb interrupted.

I glanced over, expecting him to be looking at Linda, but his eyes were on the last person I expected. He was talking to Eric.

Eric shifted away from me.

"About that thing we were talking about earlier," Robb continued.

When they were silent, I looked between the two, twisting my neck to the left to see Eric, turning it to the right to see Robb. They never broke eye contact.

"You two were talking earlier?" Crystal giggled. "What a reunion."

Robb smiled. "It's good to be friends again."

"So, talk here," Linda spoke up.

Robb waved her away. "It's guy stuff."

"Guys don't have stuff." Crystal took Linda's side of all people. Apparently, everyone had made up while we were gone. I wondered if they had lost more memories than the bar, if the illusion was affecting more than just their thoughts, but it wasn't like I could ask.

Eric stood up. "We can talk."

Robb mirrored his movements. "We'll be right back," he spoke to Linda instead of anyone else. She didn't even look at him as they left. I had to pull my eyes off the blonde to watch Eric walk away with Robb, forcing myself to remember how they had fought in the hallway only a few months prior.

Crystal leaned over to steal my chips. "That's the weirdest thing I've seen all day."

"Not really," Zac joined in. "They have a lot to work through."

Hannah Blake. Even if Robb had forgotten the bar and the fights, he had to remember Hannah's death. Everyone did. Her memorial was displayed in the school, right outside of the principal's office. The only other girl Eric had loved was someone I would never meet, but Robb knew her. As far as Crystal had told me, they had all been best friends. It was just another world I would never know. The only unique part I did know was her Dark name—Abby. Eric never called her Hannah.

My hands curled against my legs, but I only noticed when Crystal bumped her shoulder against mine. "Lighten up, Taylor," she said, but she covered her giggle when it escaped her. "I guess you'll be a Welborn eventually."

"I guess so," I muttered through my embarrassment, but my breath caught when I saw my ring.

The piece of jewelry that bound Eric and I together was glowing, but it was doing more than that. The metal was warm against my cooling skin. Even in the January weather, it pressed against my finger as if it yearned to be inside of me. The warmth coursed through my veins like blood, like it was alive, but I hid it in my pocket like I had to make it stay.

TWENTY-ONE

ROBB LEANED AGAINST THE BRICK WALL SO HE COULD FACE THE bench. It was yards away, too far for even Jessica to hear, and he wanted it that way. But it was close enough for others to see us, and I wanted it that way. Even if Robb put up an illusion to hurt me, Jessica would know. Her senses were strong enough for that. To keep calm, I imagined half of the student body was in the Dark, but it also meant the other half was in the Light—when, in reality, they could've all been humans. Mindy was the first one I thought of before Robb's smirk appeared.

"So, who's going to talk first?" he pondered aloud.

"Looks like you just did."

He chuckled, raising his finger to point at me. "That's what I always liked about you, Eric—your wit."

I wanted to punch the smile off his face.

"I miss that about you."

"I don't miss you at all," I growled.

Robb's eye twitched. "We used to be friends, Welborn."

"Good thing we aren't anymore." After all, I was destined to kill him. It was that reason I gave up all my friends in the first place, including him. But I remembered how he fought it, how he came to Abby's funeral, how he showed up at my house and tried to convince my father to let him in. I counted how many times he came.

"Sixteen," Robb said as he looked at the sky. "Sixteen times I came to your house, and sixteen times you ignored me."

Apparently, he was thinking the same thing.

"I suppose you were right to."

"You killed her," I spat.

Robb's brown eyes shot down to me, but he wasn't glaring. "Fudicia did it." Even I had seen her peek inside the car. "But that's not what matters," he paused to fiddle with his shirt. Cigarettes poked out from his pocket, but he didn't take one out. It wasn't allowed on campus. It would only bring more attention to us.

"Go ahead," I coaxed, hoping he would fall for it, but he was smarter than that.

"I'm not an idiot." He pushed them back into his shirt. "I was afraid you'd forget."

He knew it would take me a while to remember it all, and I was the one who had fallen for his plan. I had admitted to my memory when I blamed him for Abby. It was all a game for him.

"Did you even try to break up with Jess?" he asked.

"I'm not leaving her."

"Then, our deal isn't going to work out." After he spoke, he hissed and waved his hand. A shallow burn reddened his skin.

I spun around. Jessica waved her hand as she stood up. Zac was already apologizing. He had spilled his coffee on her, and her injury appeared on Robb, too. When I tried to go to her, Robb gripped my shoulder. My neck burned.

"You said you wouldn't hurt her," I snapped.

"Not if you follow the deal."

My jaw ached.

"That includes you hurting me," Robb reminded me.

"She's my fiancée." I pulled away from his grip. "She won't accept a breakup without question."

"That's your problem, Welborn," Robb said, "but I suggest you figure it out fast."

I stared at Zac, knowing he was in on it. Jessica had been right from the beginning, and I defended him when I should've trusted her instinct. "Who's he? The half-breed?"

Robb didn't respond.

"That makes Linda Fudicia," I told him everything I knew. "Half-siblings, after all." The reason for their sudden transfer was starting to make sense. Robb needed his henchmen, and if I had to guess, Crystal was one of them, too. I just didn't know who.

Robb walked past me and shrugged like he didn't care. "Do what you want to them." He didn't care about anything but himself, the Light, and Jessica. "They can defend themselves."

He walked away, but I followed him like the shadow I was. "My people can defend themselves, too," I threatened. Jessica and Jonathon were stronger than he thought. "You just wait."

"Use your actions instead of your words, Welborn," Robb whispered. As we approached, he lightened his stance, even grinning as he waved at the others. "I leave for two minutes and you guys get in a fight."

"It was an accident." Crystal wiped her sweater with napkins. Zac had gotten her, too. "We're fine, other than my clothes."

"I'll buy you new ones," Zac promised.

Crystal was glowing. "Today?"

"Sure thing."

"What do you say, Jess?" Crystal's hands were on Jessica's shoulders like she was about to hug her. "It'd be fun."

"It wasn't my clothes that got ruined," she laughed, but it strained against her throat. She was trying to clean my jacket.

I touched her arm to get her attention. "It's fine."

"I'm sorry," she started to speak, but she stopped when she saw my face. I hated to think about what she saw. She knew me well enough to know something was wrong. Her eyes darted between Robb and I, and I hoped she would see what he was, but she turned back to me. Her focus wasn't on him. "Are you okay—?"

"Can we talk?"

Her face flushed. "Sure."

"Alone."

She looked back at her friends, the people that were truly her enemies, but she nodded. "We'll be right back." She followed me without question until I headed for the willow tree. "Why are we going way up here?"

It was our tree. I had to give her any sign I could that I didn't mean what I was about to say, and I needed to find any comfort I could in order to lie. As I stared at the tree, at its base where I almost died, I almost wished I had.

"My memories are coming back," I muttered as I tore my eyes off the grass. "All of them."

She waited, as I knew she would. After all, she knew how horrible memory loss was, and it sickened me to use it against her.

"What did Darthon tell you?" I asked.

She glanced over her shoulder.

"No one can hear us," I promised.

When she faced me, she brushed her hair out of her face. She only did that when she was nervous. "Why are you asking that?"

"Did he tell you that you were like him?"

Her shoulders lifted.

"Because he told me that."

"What—"

"I know it's true," I forced the words out, but couldn't force myself to look at her. If I pretended I was talking to someone else, I could do it. I could convince myself it was the act it was, the script Darthon—Robb McLain—had forced on me. If I didn't do it, he would hurt her again, and I couldn't have that. Not until I could figure out a way for us to fight back.

"So, what?" Jessica spoke up, and it was the last thing I thought she would say. "So, what if I'm like him?"

I blinked. "So, you are a light."

"And a shade," she pointed out. "We can find a way to tell the elders, and they'll understand just like you—" She tried to touch me.

"I don't understand." I stepped back. "I don't like this. I don't like lights."

Her hand froze in the air where she had reached for me. Her ring sparkled. "What are you saying?"

"I don't like you."

"You need to calm down," her voice shook, but the rest of her body went rigid. "I know a lot happened, Eric."

"I'm not Eric." I wanted to tell her I was Darthon's pawn, but I knew the words would never come.

Her eyes flickered over my face. "You are."

"I'm not," I snapped. "I went in there as Eric and came out as someone else."

She wrapped her arms around her torso. "You're not making any sense."

I closed my eyes as I said the part I dreaded the most, "Eric loved you, and I don't." My heart was too loud in my ears for me to hear myself say, "I'm breaking up with you, Jess."

Silence.

I expected her to slap me, to beat me with her fists, to take her ring off and chuck it over the hill. But nothing happened.

When I opened my eyes, she was staring at me. Her face wasn't flushed. Her fingernails didn't dig into her palms. She wasn't even crying. A small smile pulled at her lips. "Jess?" she repeated the name. "You never call me that."

She was seeing the signs.

Every bit of me felt like it was breaking. "Do you understand?" I asked.

For the first time, she looked away, her gaze shooting over my shoulder and toward the field so many had died on. The last thing Eu probably saw was the willow tree we stood under. It was still alive because he fought, because he died.

"I understand—" Jessica's throat moved. "I understand you're not being yourself, but you're crossing a line, Eric." This time, she glared at me. "A big one."

I could breathe again. "The first part is more important."

Her eyebrows pushed together. "We can talk about this, okay? Whatever you're going through—whatever happened— we'll get through it—"

"We can't," I stopped her from dismissing what I had said.

"We're over."

She flipped her hand up, but it wasn't to slap me. My mother's ring shone in my face. "We're engaged."

"Not anymore." I shook my head. "Not right now." I didn't deserve it. "Keep the ring if you want."

When I started to walk away, she grabbed my arm. "You can't be serious."

I only touched her to remove her hands from me. "I am."

"*I don't believe you.*" Her voice was in my head.

I shut off our connection, and it sizzled out.

That was when her eyes watered, and I couldn't stop myself from hugging her one last time. She shook against my chest as I kissed her forehead. "Take care of yourself, okay?" I said it expecting a response, but she never gave me one.

I pushed myself away, spun around, and walked down the hill. I had obeyed Darthon and left Jessica, but I wouldn't obey him for long. I would find a way to break the illusion, and my first stop was the shelter.

The Dark would have to save me again.

TWENTY-TWO

Jessica

H E SAID IT LIKE IT DIDN'T MATTER, LIKE HIS EMOTIONS WERE buried, like he was the Eric I had met, not the one I had grown with. But he hadn't sounded like he was lying.

I could barely breathe as I watched him walk toward the student parking lot. He wasn't returning to class. He was leaving, and I knew where he would go.

I spun around on my heel and ran down the other side of the hill, pushing my tears back. He couldn't mean it. He couldn't. If anything were impossible, it was Eric's breakup, and I wouldn't let him push me away when he was hurting. Whatever Darthon had done to him had taken a toll, and there was one person I knew who could help.

"Jonathon." My mind throbbed from Eric shoving me out, but I found the strength to call my guard. *"Jonathon!"*

He didn't respond, but I could feel the trickle of his powers. Even though his abilities had shifted, mine hadn't. I would get through to him if I had to march into his classroom.

"Jess." Crystal was in front of me before I realized she had been chasing me, and she was gripping me before I could stop her. "Where are you going? Are you okay?"

I almost didn't hear her. "What?"

"Robb told us," Crystal informed me.

I looked over, realizing the others were only a foot away. I glared at Robb. "What did you say to him?"

His hands were up like my glare was a gun. "We talked about Hannah," he promised. "That's it."

I ignored him because he was useless. "I'm leaving," I told Crystal.

"I'll tell Ms. Hinkel."

I walked away before she could continue our conversation, but she called after me, "Call me if you need to."

I ignored her to focus all of my energy on Jonathon. *"Where are you?"*

It was a scream, and his connection leapt. *"Jess?"*

"Come to the front," I ordered. *"It's an emergency."*

Even though he didn't respond, I walked straight for our meeting place, making sure to avoid the office as I left the building. If they questioned it, I would lie. *I have a doctor's appointment. My mom is picking me up. She'll tell you about it when she gets here. I promise.* Luthicer would put up an illusion later, and we would figure out what was wrong with Eric. My plan would work. It had to.

"Jess?"

Robb, again. He had followed me, and his hair stuck up like he had messed with it the entire way. His shirt was even wrinkled. But he didn't mess with any of it when he stopped a few feet away from me. "Are you all right?"

"Perfectly fine." I searched the entryway for Jonathon's face.

"Is it true?" he asked. "Did he leave you?"

"Why do you care?" I snapped.

Robb's brown eyes widened.

"Sorry," I muttered, my hands shooting up to my temples. I rubbed them, hoping to ease the pain Eric had caused. "It's just a lot—"

Robb's palm landed on my shoulder before I realized he had walked closer. "It's okay, you know." He spoke like he knew I would believe him. For once, I didn't feel the urge to push him away. I felt warm.

"Just breathe," he coaxed. "Go home if you need to."

The warmth was familiar, like the ring I wore. I took a

breath, and the fog melted away. The crisp air was fresh and natural, a soothing reminder that spring was nearing. When my heartbeat calmed, I realized it had been racing before. I wrapped my arms around Eric's jacket. It smelled like him.

Tears pushed against my eyes, so I closed them. "I'm okay." I stepped away from Robb's touch. "I will be." Once Jonathon comes.

"Jess?" Right on time.

I looked over as Jonathon approached, stumbling like it was his natural way of walking. His glasses fell down his nose when he stopped by my side, and for a moment, I swore his blind eye even saw me. They both widened. "What's wrong?"

"I'll tell you in the car," I said, knowing his car was in the parking lot. "Can you drive?"

"You two are friends?" Robb interrupted.

I looked over. "Yeah."

Jonathon didn't bother defending our friendship. "We can leave right now." He was already walking toward the parking lot.

"I'll call you later," I lied to Robb, only to tell him the truth after, "Thanks for calming me down."

He nodded, but he looked far from calm. His expression made him look like he was the one who was broken up with. I looked away before I saw myself in him.

"What's going on?" Jonathon muttered as we walked out of earshot. "I haven't heard you that panicked since—"

"We need to go to the shelter," I directed, picking up speed as we neared the parking lot. "Now."

Jonathon grabbed my arm, nearly losing his stance. "Wait." He forced me to face him. "Tell me what's going on."

"Eric—" I stumbled over his name, and I had to close my eyes and take a breath before I could speak again. "Eric isn't Eric anymore. Something's wrong with him."

"I told you," Jonathon began, "he just needs space."

"Too much space," I interrupted. "He just broke up with me."

Jonathon's hands dropped from my arms. His bottom lip

hung open, and his breath escaped him in a fog. "What?"

"Don't make me repeat it," I muttered, leaning against his car—the same one Camille drove before she died.

"Jess, wait." Jonathon took off his glasses and cleaned them with his shirt. "You're probably overreacting—"

"He said he was serious," I sputtered out the words. Eric's emotionless voice was hardly audible. If it weren't for my powers, I doubted I would've heard him at all. "He said he doesn't love me anymore."

"What the hell are you talking about?" Jonathon's face reddened with an anger I wanted to snatch from him. "Eric loves you. He always has, and he always will."

"I know," I interrupted, "but he said it anyway. He—"

"He gave you a ring, Jess."

"His jacket, too." A laugh escaped me, and guilt consumed me for it. The coffee stained the clothing. "I shouldn't be laughing." As I said it, I knew I wasn't. My escaped tears were freezing against my cheeks.

"Jess," Jonathon's voice was as soft as his embrace. "It's okay. We'll figure this out."

I nodded against his sternum.

"You won't lose him." Jonathon only let me go to open the passenger door. "And I won't either." His grin was wide, like the one he had when he was Pierce. "Let's go to the shelter."

I agreed, jumping into his car before he joined me. As we sped out of the parking lot, I remembered the first time I got into Eric's car, how I learned his middle name, how he questioned why I wanted to get to know him more than anyone else. I hadn't been able to explain it back then because I didn't know, but I knew it now.

I loved him, and I wasn't going to allow him to be alone anymore.

TWENTY-THREE

"Y**OU'RE FINE, SHOMAN.**" L**UTHICER STEPPED AWAY TO FILL OUT** the clipboard he brought with him.

"Are you sure?" I leapt off the examiner's table to stand by his side. "You didn't find anything? Not at all?"

Luthicer's beard practically hit me when he whipped around. "Not a single spell." The edges of his eyes radiated as they formed slits. "Should I have found one?"

Yes. I wanted to say it, but I couldn't. "Did you check my neck?"

"You were there, weren't you?"

He had. Luthicer had checked every part of me, even the parts I wished he would stay away from.

I hit the wall.

Luthicer jumped back. "Shoman—"

"I'm fine." My knuckles burned. The injury would take more time to heal now, but it didn't matter. Darthon's spell wasn't detectable because I agreed to it. The illusion was everything he wanted it to be.

Luthicer stared at the cracked wall. "Your father won't be happy to hear about that."

My dad. Mindy. Noah. My family. They were relying on me just as much as the Dark was, yet I had barely seen them in the past few weeks.

"I'm going home," I muttered. "Thanks for your help."

"Try not to further your injuries," he called after me, but I almost didn't hear him.

I was in the hallway, and I wasn't alone. Jonathon stood in front of me, and Jessica stood behind him. They had followed me.

I tried to walk past them, but Jonathon grabbed my arm. "Wait—"

"Let me go," I snarled.

Jonathon didn't listen. He transformed, and his strength dug into me. If I were going to fight him, it would have to be in our shade forms.

"You're going to explain yourself," Jonathon as Pierce spoke as his grip tightened, "and we're going to help you—"

"You can't," I snapped.

"What's going on here?" Luthicer's voice bellowed over us as he entered the hallway. "You guys should be at school. All of you."

"We would be if Eric hadn't dumped Jess," Pierce said to the elder, but he was glaring at me. "Now, tell us why."

"What?" Luthicer interrupted Pierce's anger. "What are you talking about?"

"That's enough, guys," Jessica interrupted the elder as she tried to pull Pierce off me. "Let him go."

Pierce yanked his arm away from Jessica, and she stumbled back. My anger boiled. Pierce glared because he could sense it. *Stop fighting us.*

I shut him out—just like I had shut Jessica out—and everything burned. It only got worse when Pierce's hand collided with my jaw. I hit the ground before I realized he had hit me.

"Pierce," Jessica screamed as Pierce latched onto my shirt.

His green eyes bore into me as he spoke, inches from my face. "I'm tired of your shit, Eric," he growled. "I know you've been through a lot. We all have. We all lost Eu. Camille died for this—"

I punched him.

Pierce flipped back into his human form when he slammed against the ground.

"It's not like that." My scream tore against my throat.

Jonathon wiped his mouth, and blood smeared across his hand. Blood I had drawn out of my best friend.

I stepped back.

Luthicer was staring. Jessica was, too. The entire hallway was creeping into chaos as shades poked their heads out from various rooms. Two young kids huddled behind someone who was probably their dad. Their blue eyes were like mine.

"It's—it's not like that," I stuttered again.

"Then, what is it like?" Jonathon asked as he pushed himself off the floor. He was already transforming again.

Luthicer stood between us with his arms raised at each of us. "That's enough, boys."

"Are you going to explain yourself or not?" Pierce pushed his chest against Luthicer's hand. "Or are you going to continue shutting us all out? We'll just die that way." I had never heard Pierce scream before. "And we would've already if Jess hadn't saved you."

I backed against the wall.

"Leave," Jessica spoke to me as she moved to the side, revealing the open hallway. "Go."

"Don't you run away," Pierce was fighting Luthicer in an attempt to get to me. "Face something for once. Face it."

"Pierce," Luthicer was yelling back at him. "Calm down."

"I'm not calming down over this," Pierce spat, and blood flew off his torn lip. "You're destroying everything. You're letting her die in vain—"

Camille. She died to save Jessica, and she wasn't coming back. She would never be trained by Luthicer, or laugh at Pierce's jokes, or help me stretch again. She was gone.

"Eric." Jessica's hand wrapped around mine before she pulled me toward the exit. "Go." She practically shoved me away. "Go home."

"I'm sorry," I muttered, hoping she would grab me again, force me to stay, but she pushed again.

"I know," she said against my back before she shoved one more time. "Just leave."

And I did. I ran and never looked back.

TWENTY-FOUR

Jessica

"I SCREWED UP BACK THERE, DIDN'T I?" JONATHON'S HEAD HUNG low as he muttered a curse at himself. He was finally human again.

I grabbed his chin to force him to look up. "You think?" I dabbed his sliced lip with a rag.

He winced, but he didn't pull away. His lip wasn't healing like it normally would've. Everyone's powers were weaker, aside from Eric and me.

"He could've hurt you worse, you know," I said and set the rag on the countertop. The water had mixed with his blood, but the red color only reminded me of one thing—how my purple rain had shifted in the Light realm.

"I know that," Jonathon admitted, leaning over to open the curtain of the nurse's room. Luthicer was standing a foot away, grumbling on a phone. I couldn't remember the last time I saw a Dark member use a phone, let alone an elder. Their telepathy was shaky.

Jonathon closed the curtain. "I can't believe he's calling my father," he said. "I'm not a child."

"You sure acted like one." Even I hadn't seen it coming. Jonathon never attacked anyone. Aside from the battle, I hadn't witnessed him throw a punch. I had only seen him paint.

"Doesn't mean my dad should be called." Jonathon continued to rub his temples, but his veins pounded against his forehead. He had to adjust his glasses. Fifteen minutes passed, and Jonathon's hands were still shaking.

"Is he at work?" I changed the focus to Urte, Jonathon's father and Eric's trainer. The elder wouldn't be happy when he arrived.

Jonathon nodded.

"What does Urte do anyway?"

My guard let out a half-laugh, but he hesitated to answer. "Cupcakes."

"What?"

Jonathon nodded again, and we both broke out into mild laugher. "Don't tell him I told you that," he said between chuckles. "It's a very profitable business, especially during the holidays."

I tried to picture George Stone baking, but I could only imagine him drinking. "I didn't even know Hayworth had a cupcake shop."

"We don't. He runs it right out of our house," Jonathon continued, his mouth turned down. "My mom started it."

I stopped laughing when he mentioned his mother, the woman who had left her family behind when Eric was Named Shoman. She wanted to abandon the Dark, and Urte refused. Eric had told me how the moment had brought Jonathon and him closer. They had both lost their mothers at a young age. Camille had been a fill-in for both of them. The fact that Jonathon had thrown her in Eric's face stayed with me.

I found something to say. "I didn't know."

"It's okay." He fought his frown. "It's good to laugh at something."

"Why'd you hit him anyway?" I couldn't prevent my next words, not when I thought about Camille. I had barely known her, but she gave her life up for mine. In that sense, she didn't feel like a stranger at all.

Jonathon looked away from me as if I were a stranger. "He shut me out."

Eric. The shaky telepathy they shared was completely severed, and I recalled my own slicing pain when he shoved me out.

"Me, too," I confessed, trying not to obsess over the time at the willow tree, but it consumed me. Eric's eyes were darker, quieter than usual, just like his voice was, and he winced when he shoved me out. I knew enough about our powers to know he had forced it. When someone wanted to do it, they didn't wince at all. Whatever Eric's reasoning was, it wasn't me, and it wasn't Pierce either.

Jonathon wove his fingers through his hair as if he could read my thoughts. "He should've hit me harder." He cursed for the umpteenth time. "Camille would kill me for throwing her in his face—"

"We're all a little tense," I interrupted as I laid my hand on Jonathon's shoulder. "Eric will be fine."

"Will he?" Jonathon's glasses slipped to the bottom of his nose only for him to push them back up. "I can't—" He practically hit his thigh when he dropped his hands into his lap. "I can't believe I did that."

"I can't believe I didn't slap him myself," I tried to comfort my guard, to protect him from his own actions, but he stared at the floor like he didn't hear me.

"I know you're right," he said. "Something is wrong with him. Eric would never act that way. He'd never hit me, but he sure as hell wouldn't run away from fighting me."

"He ran so he didn't have to hit you again."

Jonathon shook his head. "He ran because you told him to." His words crushed me. "Eric would rather fight than run. Even if it were against me, he was born to fight. My dad taught him to fight. He only taught him to run from one person."

Darthon. I knew the rules. Eric was taught to run only if he encountered Darthon before the battle. The Marking of Change had already happened. There was no reason to run anymore.

"You're right, Jess," Jonathon emphasized my name. "Something is wrong with him."

I wanted to continue to talk to Jonathon about it, but Luthicer entered the room. The dark pits of his eyes moved between us. As he leaned against the wall, he fiddled with his beard, and it seemed to grow from his touch.

"Urte will be here in twenty."

"What?" Jonathon huffed. "No express transport?"

"Don't take our powers so lightly." Luthicer's voice was as tight as his grip on his beard. "Now, which one of you is going to explain that little fiasco?"

"It's my fault," I started, but Jonathon stood up.

"Eric broke up with Jess."

"Jonathon." I almost cursed at my guard.

"What?" He kept his back to me and focused on the half-breed elder. "It's true."

Luthicer looked over Jonathon's shoulder to meet my eyes. "Is it?"

I couldn't deny it any longer. I nodded.

Luthicer didn't budge. "You seem extremely calm, Ms. Taylor."

"Because I know it isn't me." My fingernails curled into my palm. "It isn't us."

"It's him," Luthicer agreed, but didn't elaborate as he walked past Jonathon to take a seat at the nurse's station. I stared at him, waiting for him to speak, but he only picked up a clipboard to read it.

"You know something," I accused.

Luthicer glanced up. "As an elder, I'm supposed to hold meetings before I talk to warriors such as yourselves, but—" He pointed to the chair Jonathon was near, and Jonathon followed the man's silent order. He sat down again. Luthicer drew in a long breath before he continued to speak at Jonathon, "I'm not sure I even see you as a warrior anymore."

"Well, I'm technically a guard," Jonathon tried to joke, but Luthicer didn't laugh. Jonathon's shoulders slumped. "That's a little harsh."

"Think about that the next time you attack Shoman."

Jonathon folded his arms and glared at the wall, but he nodded.

Luthicer watched the boy with a parental glare, but his

brow softened when his attention turned to me. "And I owe you for breaking the fight up."

"You're the one who held him back—"

"And you're the one who got Eric to leave," Luthicer interrupted. "Don't discredit your actions. You did well, Jess."

My cheeks burned. "I didn't want anyone getting hurt."

"And no one did." Luthicer gestured to Jonathon. "Not much anyway."

"It was a good punch," Jonathon said.

Luthicer ignored him and held the clipboard toward me. "I owe you." He shook the wood until I grabbed it. "Before you two got here, Eric came in, demanding to see me. Pulled me right out of my office with his yelling."

I wondered what job Luthicer had that allowed him to stay in the shelter during the day, but my thoughts were brushed aside when I looked down at the clipboard. A single paper sat on top with Eric's name etched onto it.

"He wanted me to check him for spells, illusions brought on by your time in the realm," he explained as I read over the report.

Everything was negative. "I don't understand."

"He's clean," Luthicer confirmed.

"Well, that wasn't very helpful," Jonathon said.

Luthicer's glare silenced him. "Do you ever think of anything but joking around?" When Jonathon didn't respond, Luthicer sighed. "Although I'm an elder, I don't have unlimited powers." He raised his hands as if to expose his chest. "I'm not as magnificent as people think I am."

"*Magnificent,*" Jonathon's voice was in my head. "*Right.*"

"But I do know when someone is talking silently," Luthicer said and continued to glare at Jonathon. "Really. I taught you better than that."

"What are you saying?" I interrupted their bickering.

Luthicer leaned over to tap Eric's report. "I'm saying there are other types of illusions—kinds I can't detect—powers Darthon has above everyone else, even me or a full-breed elder."

My heart pounded. "How do we break it?"

Luthicer's long lips folded. "If he put an illusion on Eric, I wouldn't be able to break it."

I almost dropped the clipboard. "But you did before."

"At the Marking of Change?" Luthicer asked for clarification.

I nodded, but I also mentioned the time after prom, when Eric had been strapped to a table the night I sacrificed my memory.

"That was different," the elder explained. "Those are physical strains of an illusion. There are also sensory illusions—a type that affects the way you see or hear things."

The slice of information was just a reminder of how much I hadn't learned in my first seventeen years of life, before I found the Dark.

"They're small but effective," Luthicer continued as if he knew I needed him to. "They can be powerful under one condition," he paused as if I could guess. When I remained silent, he finished, "If Eric agreed to it."

"Agreed?" My breath squeaked out of me. "He'd never do that."

"He wouldn't be able to say it if he did."

"But—"

"What I'm saying, Ms. Taylor, is this: if he did agree, there's a reason, and that reason is the key to breaking the illusion down." Luthicer leaned forward, placing his elbows on his knees as his eyes dragged over my face. "If you're not telling us something about the realm, now is the time to do it because Eric can't."

I swallowed. We were separated for the three days we spent there aside from one moment, the single event I had yet to confess. When we got back to the shelter, the nurse wanted to check me, and I had practically attacked her to get her off me. Her touch felt like a burn, and I knew what the burn was: Dark energy. It was reacting to the energy of the Light in my veins. The powers weren't complete, but they simmered with the same warmth the knife had when it entered me. To admit to my attempt would be confessing to the truth: I was also a light. I wanted to tell the Dark more than anything, but I was failing to find my words when Eric's sentence repeated through my memory.

I don't like lights.

Maybe Darthon was right. Maybe they wouldn't trust me. Maybe they would kill me. I didn't know, and I didn't want to risk any more than I already had.

"They tortured him," I choked out, trying to make a decision in the seconds Luthicer had given me. He was a half-breed, and the Dark loved him, but my situation was different. Too different.

"That's all I know," I finished.

Luthicer was silent as he continued to stare at me, but he cracked his bottom lip open. "And you?" His voice was a whisper, harsh and dark. "What did they do to you?"

Eric knew. He knew I was one of the lights, but he obviously hadn't told anyone. Not yet. The fact that he didn't tell them told me that my hesitation was correct. The Dark had lied to us, but they had especially lied to Eric. He didn't trust them, and I knew I shouldn't either. Not until I could figure it out. Not until I could figure out what Eric was thinking. Even if he left me, we were a team, and our connection was the only thing I trusted to get us through it.

We had hope left.

"Jess?"

Luthicer was still in front of me, but he had to repeat my name for me to realize it.

"They left me alone," I lied.

Luthicer's chest rose as he took in a breath. "Okay, then," he said as he stood up. "If we learn anything else, I'll let you two know."

"Thank you," I managed, hoping to have a chance to talk to Jonathon before Urte came. In my mind, Jonathon was always a part of the team. Even if he hurt Eric, I trusted him, too. Somehow, in some way, I would tell him.

"Oh, and Jonathon," Luthicer spoke up as he left the room.

"Your dad is here."

"Fantastic."

When Jonathon stood up to leave, I grabbed his arm. "Wait—"

"I should go, Jess," he said it without looking at me. "I've done enough damage for the day."

My grip dropped from his arm. "Can you talk later?"

"It'd be better if we waited for the meeting." Jonathon moved away, but he flashed a grin. "You're a strong person, Jess. Thanks for helping me."

I bit my lip, but I nodded before he left me alone to my thoughts.

TWENTY-FIVE

"I NEED TO CHANGE MY SCHEDULE," I SPOKE BEFORE I REALIZED who I was speaking to.

The blonde behind the counter smiled when I finally met her brown eyes.

I gripped the counter. "Linda." She had to be Fudicia. Her or Crystal. Either way, they were both guilty.

Linda tapped her nails across the keyboard, but her smile never faltered. Apparently, in her transfer to our school, she had signed up to be an office student, a duty offered only to seniors. It was just my luck she was the one I had to speak to if I wanted to switch homerooms and get away from Jessica.

I stared at the girl who had dated Robb for as long as I could remember, and I tried to place Fudicia's face on her. Linda's was soft, her cheeks as round as her eyes. But her lipstick was as red as Fudicia's lips were. For once, I could see the light in the human, the innocent version of the sadistic woman who had killed my first girlfriend.

"What class do you want to switch?" Linda spoke as she flipped her hair over her shoulder.

"Homeroom."

She peered up at me. "I can't do that."

"Why not?"

Her hand flicked up as she placed a form on the counter separating us. "I need a parent's signature."

I didn't hesitate. I leaned over the counter and snatched the pen right off of her ear. A gasp escaped her as I scratched my father's name on the form and threw both the pen and the form back at her. "There you go," I spat. "A parent's signature."

"I can't accept that," she said as her eyes darted down the paper. "Mr. Welborn."

"Don't bullshit me right now."

Her thin eyebrows rose. "You are so lucky I'm not a real secretary." Her words didn't make sense until she picked up her pen and checked the approval box. She was letting me transfer.

I lost my breath.

"There's only one class open," she continued as she glanced at her computer screen. "You won't be in the same lunch."

"Even better," I muttered. "Are we done here?"

"Not yet." She stood from her desk only to lean against the countertop. She stuck her hand out toward me. "I'm Linda, by the way."

I stared at her palm, forcing myself not to hit her. The teachers would see Eric hit Linda, not Shoman hit Fudicia, the murderer. "I know who you are."

Her attempted handshake curled up. "I know." She didn't even deny it. "Maybe we should eat lunch sometime." Her voice was like liquid, lucid and smooth. It was the same tone she used when I first met her as Fudicia, tied up in the shelter after she had killed more shades. How much blood she had shed was beyond me, but a drop was enough.

When I didn't respond, she stepped back to put gum in her mouth, breaking one of the rules our teachers enforced like it was a drug. "You should be in homeroom right now."

I picked up my bag. "While you're at it, you can mark me as absent."

I started for the door, but she called after me, "Would you mind straightening out Hannah Blake's memorial?"

Abby. My palm coated with sweat as I grabbed the doorknob.

Linda giggled behind me. "Someone might have knocked into it this morning," she continued. "I was just about to do it, but since you're leaving—"

"Fuck off, Fudicia." The curse escaped me as I left the room.

My body was on fire before the door slammed behind me. I didn't do as she said. I didn't straighten out Abby's memorial. I grabbed it instead, plucking it off the wall to take it with me. Fudicia wouldn't get the satisfaction of torturing me, but I would get the satisfaction of knowing she would have to explain it to the office. The attention was another way I could signal to the Dark that something was wrong. I hadn't talked about Abby since she died, let alone touched her memorial, but if she were watching, I knew she would laugh.

Abby was like that. She always laughed, and I found myself laughing for the first time as I left the school with her photo in my hands.

Even the dead could help me more than the living Dark could, and there were two more deaths I had to confront before I could cause another. I knew that the second Jonathon threw Camille's death in my face. It was the only way I could fight back. I would kill Darthon. I just had to resolve the past first.

TWENTY-SIX

Jessica

HIS SEAT WAS EMPTY. THAT WAS THE FIRST THING I NOTICED when homeroom began. Eric wasn't in class, and there wasn't a single sign he was coming. My attempt to talk to him about how I was a light and a shade was put off again. I would have to wait. But the second thing I noticed took over my worry.

Our teacher never asked me to move away from Robb or Crystal. Even though I wasn't supposed to sit at their table, Ms. Hinkel didn't question it. She never even looked at me—unlike the rest of the class. Their eyes had been on me since I arrived at Hayworth High.

Everyone knew. The rumor was too loud to ignore, even when it was whispered. Eric had broken up with me, and I was the desperate girl who hadn't taken off his ring yet. I stared at it until class ended.

"Here." Crystal's voice caught my attention before I realized what she had done. A silver necklace sat on the lunch table in front of me. When I looked at her, she forced a small smile. "So you can hide it."

She was giving me a necklace to keep his ring on.

I pushed the necklace back. "I don't want to hide it—"

She picked the chain up, grabbed my hand, and forced the jewelry into my palm. "You don't want to listen to the rumors either," she pointed out. "Don't give them a reason to talk."

The silver burned against my palm, but my heart leapt. She was right. I took off the ring only to string it around the necklace. Crystal helped me clip it on, blocking the view of anyone who was watching. The ring pounded against my sternum as I put it inside my sweater.

Crystal plopped down next to me and kicked her feet up on the table. "You okay?"

I stared at the willow tree, half-expecting Eric to be there, even though I knew he wouldn't be. "Where'd he go?" If anyone knew, Crystal would.

"You don't want to know—"

"I do."

Crystal fiddled with the ends of her hair. "He transferred out, Jess."

"What?"

"That's why Ms. Hinkel didn't make you move," she explained. "She's probably trying to figure out where she's going to put you."

I waved away her secondary information. "How do you know he transferred out?" I couldn't bring myself to say Eric's name.

When she bit her lip, her lip ring sparkled. It was purple today. "Linda told me about it this morning," she explained. "She works in the office now. Handled his paperwork herself."

Eric wasn't going to come to class ever again. He was distancing himself. Even I couldn't deny it.

"I didn't know Linda and you were so close," I muttered.

"She's my boyfriend's sister." Zac was Crystal's boyfriend now. "What do you expect? She's going through a hard time, needed a girl to talk to—"

I stopped her. "Hard time?"

"You didn't hear?" Crystal straightened up. "Robb dumped her."

I huffed. "What's new about that?" All the drama seemed so mundane now.

"True." Crystal laughed. "But it's hard for her." She leaned against me. "You'll both get through it."

"I know," I managed to reply, knowing I didn't have to get through it at all.

Eric and I were not Linda and Robb. We were descendants with a destiny, one we had to fight for, even if we weren't fighting together.

"You don't have to worry about me," I spoke again, but my voice came out in a whisper.

"Yes, I do." Crystal grabbed my hand like we were children. "Don't tell me you forgot." She beamed, only inches away from my face. "We're best friends. Lean on me all you want. You don't have to pretend to be strong in front of me. Just be Jess."

Her words were the first to reach me. I cried. But it wasn't from Crystal's friendship. It was how white her hair was, how it reminded me of the snowfall on the day I almost lost everything. It was her purple lip ring, how the color told me I would lose my own purple powers. If I were going to fight back, my powers would be red.

It was only a matter of time before my powers were the same color as Fudicia's smile, or the blood Darthon had taken out of Eric. It had only been three days since our escape—the same amount of time we had been held captive. Three—the amount of descendants that existed until one of us fell. It was then that I realized why Darthon wanted me to come back. He wasn't any different from Eric or me. We were just three people who hadn't asked for anything but a chance to live.

TWENTY-SEVEN

WHEN I RETURNED HOME, I FELT HER—JESSICA'S HEARTBEAT. Even though I had severed our connection, the feeling hadn't left my veins. Until now. When it disappeared, I almost fell over. It returned in seconds, and it was the only reason I could stand again.

My breath stabilized, but I fought the urge to call her to see if something had happened to her. When the Dark didn't panic, I knew she was fine. It killed my own panic, but I still had things to worry about.

I stared at Abby's portrait, placing it in my desk. Her auburn hair was all I could remember now. Her voice was slowly fading. My memories were escaping me, or they were burying inside of me. The feeling was foreign. Perhaps it was what Urte called coping. I didn't know, because I shut the drawer at the thought of my trainer.

Jonathon had to have told Urte what I had done. By now, the Dark had to know, including my father, but I hadn't faced my family yet. I had barely seen them. But I could smell dinner cooking. It was ready, and Mindy was calling my name before I could think of an excuse to stay in my room.

I walked into the hallway, kept my eyes down, and sat at the table. I might have been able to avoid Jessica at school, but I couldn't avoid my family. I had to face something, and I would, just like Jonathon had screamed. I lifted my eyes to see my dad staring at me.

Mindy and Noah were quiet when he spoke. "Your teacher called today." His fork scraped against his plate. "She said you skipped."

"I did."

Mindy leaned over to lay a hand on my shoulder. "I'm sure he has a reason, dear."

"I don't," I said.

Mindy's hand dropped, mirroring her bottom lip. If I didn't know better, her red hair frizzed with her confusion. Unlike her son, she knew about the Dark, but we had yet to speak about it. Noah would be told when he was older. That was what my father decided, and he was continuing to dictate everything as he said, "So, come up with one."

"I don't have one," I repeated, knowing if I tried to tell him the truth, Darthon's spell would stop me. For once, not bothering to lie would be my only way to signal something was wrong.

"Eric." My dad glared. "It's school. You're supposed to go."

"Do I not have to go?" Noah chirped.

I stared at my stepbrother, the preteen who was bordering on growing up. He was around the same age I was when I learned about who I was, but he had years to figure out who he was. For once, I envied his pudgy face.

"Go to school, Noah," I said. "It's important."

"Which is why you should go," my dad interrupted.

"I will," I snapped. "I'm just adjusting—"

"To your new schedule?"

He already knew.

"Why did you transfer out of your homeroom?" he asked. Even he knew it was the only class I had with Jessica. It was the only time we felt normal. I used to cherish it.

"I don't like the teacher," I mumbled, unable to explain.

"Ms. Hinkel?" My dad's eyebrows shot up to his receding hairline. "You've never complained about her before."

I shrugged, hoping he didn't focus on Ms. Hinkel too much. It would be counterproductive if my dad started suspecting her.

"So—" Mindy's preppy voice slid between ours. "Did anything happy happen to anyone today?" She didn't want us to fight more than we had already been forced to. As far as I understood, she had been a mess when Jessica and I were taken. When I finally came home, she hugged me tighter than she ever had before. Noah made fun of her. He had the same illusion put on him everyone else had. He thought I had gone on a trip with Jessica's parents. It made me sick.

"Anything exciting?" she pressed.

"I didn't get any homework," Noah offered.

Mindy clapped. "That's great." Her eyebrows pushed together. "I think."

"I transferred out of homeroom successfully," I said it like it was a good thing. "That was pretty exciting."

My dad hit the table. "What has gotten into you?"

I wanted to scream Darthon's name, tell him my enemy was controlling me, but all I could tell him were minor facts that didn't matter. "Someone stole Hannah's portrait." I never called Abby by her human name.

My dad's face paled.

"It might have been me," I added.

"Isn't Hannah dead?" Noah asked before Mindy hushed him.

"Let's talk about something else," she offered. "Something nice."

"Jess is nice," Noah said Jessica's name when I least expected to hear it.

I stared at the boy, fighting my words as they came out. "We broke up, Noah."

My stepbrother dropped his fork, and the clanging was the loudest noise in the room. I glanced at my dad, expecting him to yell again, but he didn't. His lips were a thin line against his wrinkled face. Mindy was the last person I looked at. Her face was as red as her curls.

"You're just fighting, right?" Even she knew I wouldn't break up with Jessica.

"No," I responded. "We broke up. We're through—done—for good."

"Eric—"

"Well, I'll be in my room," I interrupted her before she could question it. Out of all the people to interrogate my actions, I didn't want to see my human stepmother understanding me more than my shade father.

I left before any of them could speak again and shut my bedroom door, even though I knew I would have to open it again. If my calculations were correct, my dad would knock in thirty seconds. When he got in, he would put up a silence barrier before he screamed at me like he was a banshee instead of a shade. Noah would remain oblivious, but so would my father. No one would know Darthon was Robb McLain.

The knocking was ten seconds late.

"Come right in," I said and opened the door.

I was wrong again. My father hadn't chased me. Noah had.

He fiddled with his pockets, lingering in the hallway. "Are you sure I can come in?"

I couldn't say no. I gestured to my room, and he stepped inside, his brown eyes moving over my walls. Unlike him, I didn't have decorations up. I kept everything organized. My room was the only thing I ever had control over.

"You can sit," I said.

Noah sat on my bed like I had ordered him to do it, but he looked around like a stranger. He had been in my room before, and a part of me wondered if the illusion had affected parts of him it shouldn't have. Jessica had gone through the same thing, but she was older. Noah was just a kid.

I sat on my desk chair. "You okay?"

"Are you?"

I stared at the preteen, the one I used to fight to keep out of my life, the boy whose dad had ditched him after Mindy's divorce, the kid who referred to me as his brother. Not stepbrother. And he reminded me of Jonathon when his mother left his family. He had sat in the same place when he told me. That night was the first time we took a flight against the rules, and for the first time, I wished Noah were a shade, so I could take him out, too.

"I'm okay," I started, but Noah stopped me.

"Did you guys really break up?" His hands curled into fists against his khakis, reminding me that Mindy still chose the clothes he wore. "You two seemed good for each other."

He was upset, but I didn't know why, because I hadn't taken the chance to get to know him. "Things change," I managed. "It doesn't mean that it's a bad thing."

Noah glared at the carpet. "That's what happened to my dad and mom." The divorce. "I—I don't think you're like that."

"I'm not," I said it before I could stop myself.

Noah's brown eyes were glistening when he finally looked up at me.

I swallowed my nerves. "Look, Noah," I paused. "Jessica and I are teenagers. Teenagers break up—"

"Not you two." He shook his head. "You look at Jess like Jim looks at mom." His face flushed as he finished his rant, "If you leave her, Jim will leave mom."

"That isn't going to happen, Noah."

My stepbrother wiped his nose. "I like it here."

"I know." I moved across the room to sit on the bed next to him. "You're never going to have to leave here." I brought my hand up to lay it on his head, but I couldn't bring myself to touch him. "You're my brother, okay?"

Noah glanced up, but our eyes only met for a minute. He wrapped his arms around my torso before he tore himself away. When he leapt from the bed, a grin broke his lips. "If you tell anyone I cried, I'll tell everyone you have a nightlight."

A chuckled escaped me. "Fair deal."

He nodded, but the beam left his face when my dad entered the room. The door had been open the entire time. I didn't even know how long he had been standing there.

"Noah," he said. "Can I talk to Eric alone?"

He glanced at me like he was willing to fight my dad if I wanted him to. "Get out of here," I said, and he did.

My father shut the door, and a silence barrier was up just

as I had predicted, but he didn't scream when he spoke. "Tell me what's going on."

"I can't—"

"What happened between Jess and you?"

"Nothing." For once, the truth came out without a fight. "We broke up. That's it."

"What do you mean, 'that's it?'" His voice rose and dropped like he was fighting himself, not me. "Eric, as much as I hate to admit this as your father, I know how much you love Jess—"

"I—I—" I couldn't say I didn't love her. Not again. Once was enough. All I could manage was four words. "The prophecy is wrong."

He glowered. "The prophecy might be cryptic, but it was never wrong."

"Then, Darthon would be dead."

"Stop dwelling on that," he snapped. "The prophecy is not wrong about your feelings for Jess. I witnessed it myself. Don't tell me I imagined it."

"You might have."

He pointed to my hands. "Then, why are you wearing your ring?"

I stared at the jewelry my late mother left behind, the single gift she had given me, but it hardly seemed like a gift now. It was a reminder of what Darthon had told me about my bloodline. If I were going to ask my dad about it, this was the time to, but I opened my mouth only to shut it again.

My mother's death was one I had to face, but I wanted to deal with Camille's first. She had raised me more than anyone. She deserved the attention. I would have to ask my father after I visited Camille's grave. I only hoped I had enough time to do both.

"I guess I am wearing it," I muttered.

"You guess?"

I didn't respond.

"Are you going to take it off?"

I shook my head.

My father groaned, and my bedroom door squeaked as he

leaned against it. "This is why Jonathon and you fought, huh?"

I cringed. "Urte told you, then."

"Of course."

"If it means anything, Jonathon punched me first."

"And you punched him back," he pointed out.

"I only did it to defend myself." I couldn't tell him about Camille. I cursed instead. "Jonathon is an idiot."

"Right now, Eric, I don't think you have the right to call anyone an idiot." His words were harsh because they were true. "Why'd you break up with Jess?"

Because I'm under Darthon's control. The words were so easy to think but impossible to say. My neck felt like it was on fire. I had to grab it to calm down. I already had a plan in place, one I had thought over carefully, one I had obsessed over since I dumped Jessica, but taking action was another thing entirely.

"Her death causes Darthon's," I struggled to start.

"Is that what this is about?"

"It's true."

"So, what if it is?"

I despised how calm his voice was. I yearned for him to yell at me. I missed how he was when I was a kid, when my mom had died, when he blamed me for everything.

"You know it's true?" I pressed, considering my plan.

I listened to my father's breath as he hesitated. "We believe it is."

"And you don't want to kill her?"

"Of course not."

"Never?"

"Never, Eric."

It was everything I needed to hear. "Then, you should know why I left her."

My dad waited, and in his silence, I wondered how much Jessica would hate me when she found out what I would say.

"She's one of them, Dad." I couldn't stop my next move any longer. I had to fight back. "Jessica is a light, too."

TWENTY-EIGHT

Jessica

THE MEETING WAS CALLED SHORTLY AFTER MIDNIGHT, BUT I waited for Pierce to come to my house. He had to reach me over my phone, and for once, I had the ringtone on. It only took him fifteen minutes to arrive, but it took us thirty minutes to get to the shelter. We walked in complete silence. Meetings were never a good thing, and when we arrived, all of the faces confirmed my hesitations.

The remaining elders—Bracke, Urte, and Luthicer—were present, and Eric stood against the wall. The only face that surprised me was Jada's. She stood in the far corner. I didn't have a chance to say anything, though. Before I could, Urte announced, "Everyone's here."

"Great." Bracke sat at the head of the table. His blue eyes and black hair mirrored Eric's as Shoman. Everyone was transformed like we were facing a battle instead of holding a discussion. "Shut the door, Eu."

Luthicer cleared his throat. "Bracke—"

Eu was dead. In all of the commotion, the leader of the Dark had somehow forgotten. He was more like Eric than I realized.

"Right." Bracke cursed. "Urte."

Pierce's father had already closed the door before the order came, and he lingered near his son in a way I hadn't seen him do before. The other father-son duo—Shoman and Bracke—

couldn't have been further apart. In fact, Shoman was closer to me, and I couldn't help but stare. Somehow, his shade appearance seemed different, like Eric was peeking through his own skin.

"I've asked you all to come here to discuss an important change, but I would like to clarify one thing first—a rule above all other rules." Bracke's voice tore my concentration away from Shoman. "Nothing we speak about today leaves this room."

My guard chuckled. "That's very *Fight Club* of you, Bracke."

"Pierce." This time, the warning came from Urte instead of Luthicer. Pierce's jokes were no longer welcome, and by the silence of everyone else, I didn't feel welcome either.

I swallowed before I asked, "What's this about?"

"You should know more than anyone else." Bracke leaned his elbows on the table, and for a minute, I remembered how Darthon had looked sitting across from me. "Isn't there something you want to tell us?"

My heart skipped. "No."

"About the Light realm?" His eyes said it all. I recognized the look only because Eric had the same one. This was my last chance.

I glanced over the room, skipping from face to face until I landed on Jada. Her white and black hair exposed her as a new breed of shades, but it mainly reminded me of how she, a brand-new member, had a name, and I didn't. I was always going to be Jess. Shoman even called me that now. Darthon was the only one to offer me a Name, but my identity was in the Dark. Although my enemy had tried to tear it apart, I held it close to my heart—the same one I had tried to stab.

I fought the urge to touch my scar.

"Jess?"

My name was spoken by Luthicer, the only man in the room who had eyes like Darthon.

I bit my lip, unable to tell them anything yet. My pain was mine. Protecting the Dark was the only thing that mattered. My other half, the part the Light claimed, didn't matter until the Dark was safe. I would find a way to save myself after.

"I have nothing to say," I managed.

Bracke brought his fingertips up to the bridge of his nose, as if he were adjusting glasses that were no longer there. "Is it true that you're also a light?"

My neck snapped as I looked at Shoman. He was the only person who could've told. "Eric."

He focused on the ground.

"Look at me," I demanded.

"This isn't about me, Jess," he emphasized my name, but his eyes didn't rise. I could only see the blue eyes in his father's face.

"Shoman told me," Bracke confirmed, placing emphasis on the first descendant's name in the same way Eric had focused on my nickname instead of my full one. "We wanted to confirm it with you first."

I had lost my chance. My lie was exposed for everyone to see.

My back pressed against the wall when I stepped back.

"They won't hurt you," Shoman spoke as quietly as he did when he broke up with me, only reminding me of how the Dark hadn't hurt me, but how he had.

My fingers curled into a fist as I confessed the words I didn't want to say, "It's true." I was half-light. Not a half-breed. But a full-breed, depending on who lived. I saw it in the red rain.

"What?" Pierce stepped away from his father to lay a hand on my shoulder. His green eyes searched my face in a way his human eyes never did. They were focused, and his expression fell when he looked at me. He turned around to face the elders. "Come on," he groaned. "This is just more shit Darthon is trying to confuse us with."

"It's not," I stopped him before he got yelled at again.

Pierce laid a hand on my shoulder like he didn't mind if he was scorned. "Jess—"

"It's true," I promised.

I half-expected his hand to drop, but it didn't. He didn't move. He didn't speak either.

"So, are you absorbed, then?" Luthicer's monotone voice broke the tension.

"No." My head shook. "Not entirely," I clarified, thinking of Darthon's words. "He asked me to come back if I wanted to be absorbed, if I accepted it."

Shoman choked, but before I could see his expression, he had covered it with the unreadable face he had when I first met him—when he insisted on being called Welborn instead of Eric.

"I won't," I spoke more to him than anyone else. "But Darthon wants me to." I turned back to the others. "He thinks I'll love the Light power now that I've felt it." The words escaped before I realized I had told them more than I intended.

I covered my mouth, only to drop my hand to my side. I couldn't undo what had been done. If I could, I wouldn't have a scar on my chest.

"What are you saying?" Urte asked.

My eyes landed on Shoman because I could feel his powers. They vibrated through the room like the chilly wind on his birthday. For once, he looked back at me, but his stare was one I had never seen before. It wasn't warm like the time I had met him on the river's railing. It wasn't the confusion I had seen in his car when he told me his middle name—James, after his father. It was the sharp sting of a glare from one enemy to another.

I stepped behind Pierce as if instinct had taken over. The uncontrollable need for comfort consumed me.

"It's okay." My guard finally let me go. "No one is going to hurt you. Right, guys?"

Everyone nodded. "You're on our side, Jess," Urte said.

"No matter what," Luthicer seconded.

Jada was smiling. It was that reason I stepped to Pierce's side, the side furthest away from Shoman. I couldn't worry about him anymore. I had to take action for myself.

"Darthon—" My voice shook as I swallowed my decision. "Darthon said Camille started the process when she gave me her powers in the Light realm."

Luthicer snatched his beard like it would fall off.

"Absorption started because I felt it," I continued, knowing I had done everything to protect the people in front of me, and they would do anything to protect me back. That was what made us a team. Darthon had always been wrong about them, but he had been right about one thing. Me.

I raised my tingling hands. "I can feel it, not as much now that we're out, but it's there," I said. "Darthon's telling the truth about everything. We're connected." I thought of the bruises we had shared. "My powers will shift over to the Light if he dies."

I couldn't say the other part, but Luthicer did. "And you'll stay a shade if he dies?" His forehead pointed toward Shoman, but I couldn't look at him. Not again.

I nodded.

"How do you know this?" Bracke asked.

I stared at my hand as it fell to my side. "I used the powers."

"What?" Pierce's voice squeaked like he was a human.

"I had to," I stumbled over the three little words. "I didn't have a choice. Darthon was blackmailing me, and—" Eric's screams repeated over and over in my mind. I couldn't speak.

"Use them again," Luthicer ordered.

I focused on his black eyes. "I can't," I said before I corrected myself, "I don't want to."

"Use them," he repeated.

Bracke stood up. "Don't force the girl."

"With all due respect." Luthicer kept his stare on me. "I want to know she isn't lying again."

"Luthicer." Urte's tone sounded more like a curse than a name.

"If we're going to be a team—a real team—then we have to stop lying," Luthicer's bellow echoed around the meeting room, and he stood, towering over us all. "That includes the elders." He took two steps toward me, only to stay a foot away. "I'll help you if something goes wrong," he promised, "but you have to use them. Burying an ability doesn't help anyone."

"I don't want to," I repeated, but my hands were already

warm. Just like the red color, the Light powers felt like exposed blood.

"We all have to do things we don't like." Luthicer's voice dropped into a husky tone I hadn't heard before, and I wondered if he had used the same voice when he trained Camille. "That's war." He reminded me of the battle we hadn't won yet. "And if you want any chance at winning this—at getting him back." His head swung to the left toward Shoman again. "You'll show us."

I only looked away to glance at Shoman. He wasn't arguing, but his jaw bulged out.

I raised my hand toward Luthicer before I tore my gaze away from the guy I had kissed too many times to count. I couldn't look at him if I had to remind myself of his screams, the sounds of his torture that had tortured me, too. The Light had forced me by using Eric against me, and now, the Dark was, too.

"For the record," I managed to speak as the memory flooded me. "Darthon used the same tactic to get me to use them."

It was in that instant, Shoman finally stepped toward me, but it was too late. Red. It fell from my fingertips, and the dark room glowed with the fire I created. The color melted across the shades' faces, and they grimaced as I curled my fist. I wanted it to stop, but my heartbeat raced, and my body warmed as if I had been chilled before. I had to suck in a breath to shut it out. Everything inside of me felt like it had frozen.

I shivered and wrapped my arms around my torso as if I could hide it from the others. "He might know I used it," I whispered, knowing it was the only way I could call him.

Luthicer's black eyes had widened into large pits. "Your hair."

I glanced down, but the black strands were the same as they had always been when I transformed into a shade, straight and sleek. "What about it?"

"It was white," Pierce explained. He was standing further away from me than he had been before.

I touched my face. It felt the same, too, but I wondered

if anything else had changed. Were my eyes black? Only the others knew what I couldn't see, including Shoman. He was the only one who hadn't stepped away.

"Well, now we know." Bracke coughed as he sat back down only to stand again. I waited for him to pace, but he didn't. He smiled at me. "You don't have to worry. We'll figure this out."

"Until then," Urte interrupted, "you are both to live here under observation."

"Both?" Shoman asked.

"Don't act like you are any better," his father snapped. "We know you're under an illusion."

Shoman's shoulders fell like he had expelled a breath he had been holding. Whatever Darthon had done to him, Shoman had confirmed it without arguing.

"But we can't take it off of you," Luthicer added.

Shoman's face dropped, and his hair covered his eyes. He only did this when he didn't want anyone to see them. I knew him well enough to understand that, but I also knew him well enough that I wanted to fight it. If he were under an illusion, then Darthon had the power. It meant Darthon was winning. It meant my powers were the only way we could fight back.

Bracke finally began to pace. "We'll just have to observe you two until we can figure out our next steps."

"I can't live here," I interrupted.

Bracke's neck snapped up at my argument. "You'll be allowed to leave, go to school, and see friends. With permission, of course," he said it like it was a comfort. "We don't need you two getting kidnapped again."

"That was my fault," I argued.

Bracke inhaled a large breath. "We don't need to risk anything right now."

"So, why allow us to go to school?"

"We can't create that big of an illusion," Luthicer explained. The elders had thought about the situation before speaking with us. "It's for your own good."

"You're imprisoning us," I snapped.

Everyone gasped, like I had accused them of treating us

like the Light had, but they were. The concept of being forced to live in the shelter was no different from Darthon keeping us in the Light realm without our permission. Torture or not, the Dark couldn't tell us where to be, especially given the circumstances it would have to fall under. My parents would have an illusion placed on them again. Everyone would succumb to the pain of confusion I had to deal with, but I had chosen it. My parents hadn't.

"I'm sorry you feel that way." Bracke was the first to break the silence. "But this is different."

"How?"

"Darthon obviously wants you, and he's done something to my son, so we need to know everything we can if we're going to fight him back, if you are going to fight him back." He knew I had to fight, too. "It's also better for you two to have a place you can rest without the concern of being attacked."

"And my parents?"

"We'll have to use another spell," Luthicer confirmed my biggest concern.

"It didn't even work last time," I pointed out, remembering how my mother hadn't believed the news any more than anyone else. The only successful one we knew about was the one on my friends, and even they were acting strange. "Who knows what will happen with our powers acting weird. You could hurt them."

Luthicer's face dropped, and for a moment, I saw brown eyes peek out from his black gaze. His cheeks had even softened. "I won't hurt your parents."

I turned to Eric. "What about Noah?"

His eyebrows shot up at the name of his stepbrother. Even I knew the Dark had decided to keep the preteen oblivious. He would have to be controlled, too.

"Aren't you worried about him?" I asked.

"Of course I am," Shoman snapped, but a rumble escaped his throat. He stared at the wall before he spoke again, "I think it's a good idea, Jessica."

My full name. He hadn't used it in days, and the sound of

it felt more like a promise than anything else. If he was under an illusion, I wondered if it were his way of telling me to trust him again, even if he were telling me to do something I dreaded. Even if we weren't together, he was on my side, but I had to listen more if I were going to understand him.

"Fine," I agreed, unable to take my eyes off him. I wanted him to look at me, to flat out say what he was thinking, but his jaw locked, and I knew he wouldn't speak. Not again.

"Then, it's settled." Bracke clapped his hands together once. "Go home and pack. We'll pick you two up tomorrow."

Luthicer and Jada left in a beam of light as if they had been waiting for the signal all along. Urte grabbed Pierce's arm and dragged him out as if he knew he would have to force his son to leave, and Bracke followed the two as if he understood Shoman and I needed to be alone. But Shoman started to leave like he didn't want to be alone with me.

I slammed my left hand on the doorframe to block the exit. Shoman nearly hit my arm as he came to stop.

"How could you tell them without talking to me?" I hissed.

Shoman lowered his face so he was inches from me. "Why didn't you tell me Darthon forced you?"

Eric's torture. He knew that part now. He just didn't know the rest of it. I had kept more secrets than he did, and I still was.

My hand curled against the wood, and Shoman's eyes moved over to my grasp. His chest dropped. "You took off your ring."

I hadn't. It was strung on my necklace, nestled right against the scar that burned my flesh, but when I opened my mouth to tell him, I couldn't find the words. He wasn't the only one who couldn't speak. We were both being controlled in one way or another.

"I guess that makes us even," I said and dropped my hand so he would stop staring at my empty finger.

As I walked away, I grabbed the necklace and pulled it out of my shirt. Mine was on, but I had seen Shoman's hand. His ring was on, too. We were the same, even when Darthon didn't want us to be. We were still together, but we would have to fight separately.

TWENTY-NINE

NEITHER OF US HAD TO GO TO SCHOOL THE NEXT DAY. JESSICA was packing. I only knew because Urte told me after I moved in. Jonathon was staying with her, and the day passed comfortably. The opportunity gave me a chance to avoid Robb, but more importantly, it gave Jessica time to avoid Darthon, too. But I spent my time differently than Jessica did. After I finished moving, I forced myself to walk to the front of the shelter to the one place I had been avoiding.

Camille's grave.

The marble room was coated with diamond dust, and it glittered against the rows of candlelight that lit up the wide space. Candles were colored the various shades of the Dark—green for guards, blue for warriors, white for elders. Only one purple candle existed, and I wondered if the Dark would change it to red if they ever learned about Jessica's other powers.

A stone larger than any memorial I had ever seen towered against the back wall. Shadows curled up the sides, but the golden candlelight licked the front. Cursive letters spelled out her inscription.

Teresa Young.
Guard of the first descendant and protector of the third.
She has saved us all.

As I read the last sentence, my kneecaps slammed against the floor, and the noise ricocheted through the room. Saved. She had saved us by giving Jessica her powers, and Darthon had tortured them out of her by torturing me. Why she hadn't told me wasn't the question. I knew why. I had pushed her away like Darthon had ordered me. Despite that, she fought for me like Camille had. Still, Jessica was alive, and Camille wasn't. I was the reason she was dead.

"Camille." My hand shook as I touched her gravestone. When I stared at it, my own face reflected back. My human face. I couldn't bring myself to transform after the night before, but my brown hair looked black in the shadows. My reflection was melting into my other half.

I closed my eyes. *"I need you."* I used our telepathic line even though it no longer had another side. It buzzed with white noise.

I wanted to hear a scorning, a lecture followed by her sweet laugher, but silence met me. I wanted to see her long hair as half-breed and her short hair as a human. I wanted to point out she looked like a shade as a human. I wanted her to flip me off before she painted her nails again. This time of the year, she usually chose pink. For spring. It was her favorite season, and she was always too eager for its arrival.

My fist slammed against her grave. Usually, she would tell me to get my anger in check, but she couldn't now. I was alone. The first time she ever told me I wasn't alone was at my mother's funeral. It was that moment she became my friend instead of a guard.

Now, my friend was dead.

I hit her grave again, only to fall backward.

When my back hit the ground, I saw him. Even though my position made him look like he was upside down, I recognized Luthicer. He was standing in the entryway.

I sat back up before I said anything. "What are you doing here?"

Luthicer's footsteps echoed as he approached. "I thought I would ask you that." He sat down next to me, and I met his eyes in the reflection of his greatest student's grave. "But I think we both know the answer to that."

I was finally accepting it.

"Coping is a complicated thing, Eric," he continued to speak, "I would ask you to stop hitting it, but—" He paused. "I think Camille would have a great laugh at that."

A chuckle escaped me, but I had to rub my burning eyes. "She'd be glad I was venting this way instead of crashing another car."

"We both would be."

I stretched out my legs and pressed my feet against the stone in the same way we had when we practiced stretches. "How'd you know I was here?"

"As quiet as this place is, the sounds break into my office." He pointed at the left wall. "I was just glad it wasn't screaming for once."

"Screaming?"

"Pierce. Urte, too." Luthicer shrugged. "Your father practically lived here last week." He didn't have to clarify that it was when Jessica and I were in the Light realm. "The other half-breeds come here, too. They looked up to her a lot."

I hadn't even thought about all the other lives Camille touched. She was Luthicer's student, but he had dozens, and she had helped them just as much.

"She was a remarkable person," Luthicer said.

I nodded. "Camille was stronger than anyone else I knew." Including me. I remembered every time I had pushed her away, too many times to count throughout childhood. "I didn't deserve her as a guard."

Luthicer drew in a breath. "Do you know who chose her to be your guard?"

"No." My throat hurt, but for once, it wasn't from Darthon's spell. I was still fighting my pain. "But I'm guessing you do."

"Do you want to know?"

I stared at my reflection as I nodded.

"Your mother."

When I turned to the elder, he shifted back. His elongated nails scratched the floor when he moved, and goosebumps traveled up my arms as I folded them across my chest. My voice vibrated against my sternum when I asked, "She did?" I didn't have a singular memory of my mother with Camille.

The elder removed his nails from the floor only to comb his beard. "I had just arrived myself." His knuckles went white when he gripped his facial hair. "A part of me wonders if her parents didn't abandon her at all."

My chest tightened. I knew Luthicer's story. He left the Light to protect his daughter, but he had killed a dozen lights in order to do it. If his sleeves hadn't been long, I would've been able to see his scars. "You killed her parents."

The skin around Luthicer's cheeks crinkled. "I can't be certain," he said, "but I was going to tell her when everything was over." He only let go of his beard to touch her stone. "I suppose a lot of things went unsaid."

"Like what?"

He hung his head. "When she arrived at the shelter, I was one of the elders who voted for her abandonment."

Ostracization. It was rarely performed, but it did happen. Before I could question why he wanted to decide that fate for Camille, he continued, "Your mother was the only one to vote against it." The side of his face lifted. "Evaline was a very persuasive person when she wanted to be."

Evaline. It was her Dark name. She was born Kimberly Smith, and she was reborn Evaline when she was thirteen at the Naming. Those two facts were among the only things I knew about her.

"I don't remember her very well," I confessed, knowing I could count my memories of her on one hand. The time she showed me the bats was the most prominent one.

"You were kids when she died," Luthicer said it without the singular word I expected to hear. Suicide. She shot herself in the head. Died instantly, according to the autopsy report. I had a copy stashed in my desk, and now, it rested under Abby's portrait. Two of the three women I had lost.

"She took Camille in herself," he said, but his voice rose

and dropped as his tone shook. "We tried to tell her not to, but she didn't believe in abandoning children."

I huffed. "Aside from me."

"Maybe she didn't."

My mouth snapped open to yell at him, to scream, to accuse him of crossing a line, but the expression that clouded his vision halted me. His eyes weren't light eyes. They were flickering to brown. His human side was peeking through, and he laid a hand on his forehead to cover his irises.

"Do you remember the necklace Camille gave you?" His whisper was only audible due to the marble. It hissed into an undeniable echo.

He didn't have to ask me. The elixir in the willow tree pendant had saved Jessica's life after Fudicia had attacked her. "How could I forget?" A chuckle escaped me when I recalled how I had dropped it during a flight. Luthicer accused me of breaking the rules. I had hated him back then.

"That jewelry was special," he said. "That power was special."

"I know." Being able to imbed a spell in liquid was unique. That was the singular reason Luthicer had caught us. He knew Camille was the only one who could've made it, and he figured out she would only give it to me. "You nearly terrorized me because of it."

Luthicer wasn't laughing. "Your mother taught Camille how to do that."

My breath caught itself.

"Your mother taught Camille more than I did," he continued, "and if I had to bet, she had enchanted more pieces than just a necklace." His fingers flicked over, but it was enough. He was pointing to my ring. "This isn't the first time you've had it, you know."

I searched my memories, but nothing came.

"Your mother gave you hers the night she died."

My hand stretched out in front of me, but I couldn't picture it in my hands as a child. I only remembered the night she showed me the bats, and the memory was clouded by the time

I took Jessica to see them.

"She always wanted you to have them," he said. "Your father only held them for you until you were old enough."

The elders knew about the rings just like they had known about the prophecy. It was the singular rule the prophecy had proven to be true. My love for the third descendant, for Jessica, was unbreakable.

"Maybe waiting was a mistake," he finished.

The sapphires had once glowed, but now they were dim, even in the candlelight. My ring seemed to be an ordinary jewel—nothing more than a family heirloom—but every person I knew appeared to be human until they transformed. My necklace had been ordinary until it wasn't. Everything around me was special. My ring wasn't an exception to the rule.

"Maybe that jewelry," Luthicer said and hesitated. "Maybe it's the only reason you are alive."

I leapt to my feet, and Luthicer mirrored me. It was only then that I realized I was in a fighting stance. My body had taken over. Luthicer's sleeves had fallen when he raised his arms, and his white scars radiated in the darkness. I dropped my hands, and so did he.

"I'm sorry," I muttered as my mind raced. The information was overwhelming.

Luthicer's breath was loud as it expelled from his lungs, but he calmed down as he rolled his sleeves down. When he leaned forward, he used the cloth to clean Camille's grave. I had left smudges where I had hit it.

His eyes met mine in the clean reflection. "You died in the Light realm, didn't you?"

I stepped back. "I never said that."

"You didn't have to." He spun around, his height towering over me. "Shades cannot live there, and half-breeds only can when Darthon allows it." That was why Camille had probably died. "But you didn't die. Not entirely."

I did die. I succumbed to darkness over and over again. They melded together, and they brought my breath back every moment after. Darthon hadn't been able to kill me, but he thought it was Jessica who was protecting me. That was why he wanted to separate us. But it was the ring.

It was my mother.

But it was more than that. It was the connection Darthon wanted to sever. If Luthicer was right—if the jewelry had kept me alive—then, Jessica's ring was a part of the spell. That meant one thing. If she wasn't wearing her ring, Darthon could kill me.

When I started to leave, Luthicer grabbed my arm. "I know you didn't know your mother, but she loved you very much." His nails dug into my bicep, and I knew he thought I was focused on my mother's death instead of my life. "And I think you need to talk to your father about it."

Darthon had thought the same thing.

I pulled away from Luthicer's grasp. "I'm not sure how to talk to him."

"Just talk," he said, like it was a simple thing. "Parents are supposed to be there for that sort of thing."

I whipped around to face him. "Are you there for Jada?"

His eyes widened, and then softened in seconds. "So, you figured it out."

"Wasn't that hard to guess." Jada was his daughter. "Where's her mother?"

"We divorced when Jada was born," he explained. "Much like Urte's situation."

I tried to picture the elders as young men, the years of marriages, births, divorces, and deaths I had missed. But nothing came.

"It isn't an easy thing," he spoke, "letting someone you love go."

"Are you talking about yourself or me?"

"Love is like coping, Eric." For once, Luthicer smiled. "It's a daily adventure, and some days are easier than others, but," he paused, "there's always another day to do it again."

He began to leave, but I was the one to stop our separation this time. "She took off her ring."

Since I couldn't talk to her, I needed someone else to tell

her to put it back on. I wanted Luthicer to do it, but he laughed. "Even I thought you would have noticed the necklace."

"Necklace?"

He pointed to his neck. "It's new." He had to say Jessica's name for me to understand what I had missed. "I imagine she has something hanging from it."

I stared at the man. "You didn't notice that on your own."

"Someone might have tipped me off."

Who it could've been was beyond me, but that didn't matter. Jessica was still wearing the ring, and that meant our connection wasn't severed like I thought it had been. Darthon couldn't kill me. Not as long as my mother's spell worked.

"That reminds me of others things I heard," he said and began to walk toward the exit. "Abby's portrait."

"I'll return it."

"Keep it." He lingered at the entrance, but I couldn't see his face. He was a silhouette against the bright hallway. Only his white hair glowed. "Remember how many people we've lost for this, Eric," he said. "Don't become the next memorial."

THIRTY

I T ONLY TOOK TWO HOURS TO PACK MY CLOTHES. THE DARK PROM-
ised to get the rest, and my parents had gone out to dinner while I collected my things. Luthicer would meet them
when they came home. He would put an illusion on them and
remove it when the danger was over—whenever that happened. No one could estimate a timeline. I even packed my
summer clothes, but I hadn't expected Bracke to pick me up.

We didn't speak until we walked through four corridors of
the shelter. "Here's your room." He used his shoulder to open
the door, and the wood creaked as if it hadn't been used since
the place was built.

While he lugged in two of my duffel bags, I stood in the
doorway. The room was larger than I was expecting, but it was
also colder. The square space held a desk, wardrobe, and bed.
A queen mattress rested on a black frame, and the headboard
was decorated with ivy etchings. But only one thing caught my
full attention. A painting easel sat by the desk. Pierce. He must
have brought it. I shoved it out of my mind to ask Bracke the
one question on my mind since arriving.

"Where's his room?" I didn't have to clarify who I was
talking about.

"The other side." Bracke placed my bags on my bed.

"How far away is the other side?"

"Far."

I leaned against the wall to prevent myself from stepping into the hallway. Despite all the time I trained in the shelter, it was bigger than I realized. It probably took up half of Hayworth's underground, and I imagined the Dark had shades in the city council that allowed it to happen. The entire town held secrets.

"I know you don't like this, Jess, and I'm sorry." My bed creaked when Bracke sat down on the mattress. "This is my fault, and I hope you don't hate me for it." He laid his forearms on his knees. "I already think of you as a daughter." His words made me bite my lip. "Perhaps that's why I'm selfish when it comes down to protecting you both."

My gaze moved over the man who had once been so cold about Eric. When I met him, he questioned why I would even want to work with his son. I hadn't understood their circumstances then, but I did now. Eric's father wasn't cold at all. He was the opposite. He was protective.

When I didn't speak, Bracke stood up. "I made sure your parents get the best treatment possible—"

"Did you know my parents?" I interrupted before he could consider leaving.

Bracke's eyes widened. "Your biological ones?"

I nodded.

He leaned against the bedposts. "You must know by now—"

"They were in the Light," I confirmed without telling him Fudicia's parents had been the murderers.

Bracke's brow furrowed. "But we were the ones to save you that day."

It was everything I suspected, but hearing it out loud was different. My back slid against the wall as I sat on the floor next to the bags I had carried. "I want to know everything."

"Originally, we thought they were attacking our own," he said without hesitation. The elders meant it when they agreed to tell us the truth now. "When we realized they were attacking lights." He sighed. "We figured out who you were."

"How?" As a baby, I wouldn't have had a Name. "You

wouldn't have known until Shoman was Named—"

"Instincts," he interrupted. "We think the mothers knew when the children were born." His expression twisted. "When Eric was born, we reminded Kim it wasn't for certain." Kim was Eric's mother. "But that wasn't enough for her."

It wasn't enough for my parents either. I knew that was why they ran. It was also the reason they were killed. But I didn't have a reason for the Dark's final decision.

"Why didn't you keep me?" I asked.

Bracke's wrinkles stiffened into hard lines. "My wife," he paused. "She—she struggled. A lot." He didn't have to remind me of her death.

Everyone in Hayworth knew she killed herself on Independence Day. It was the reason I didn't understand Eric's love for the holiday, but perhaps, it was his only connection to the woman who gave him life.

My hand snaked up to my shirt, and I grabbed her ring through my shirt. "Did she want me gone?"

Bracke whipped his face toward me before he shook his head. "Quite the opposite, Jess," he said. "She wanted to adopt you herself." When he steadied his head, a frown broke his expression. "I wanted you gone."

My heart slammed into my chest.

"My wife's struggles, they didn't begin with Eric or you," he paused to take a breath. "She was a good woman. Perhaps, too good of a person." He rubbed his forehead. "She didn't want you two to go through the pain of the prophecy, and I—" His voice shook. "I've made mistakes thinking I could control it, thinking I could control Eric."

When Bracke stood, I saw a man who had only tried to protect his family.

"You should know Eric made sure we wouldn't hurt you before he told us anything," he said and straightened his shirt. "He's on your side, and so are we." He took two steps toward me before he looked at me. "I'm only sorry you thought we might not be, but I cannot blame you." He laid out his hand, and I took it before he helped me stand up. "I can't blame him either."

His grasp dropped from mine. "I see her in him."

"What was she like?" I asked.

"She was beautiful." A smile broke his lips, but it twitched. "But even the most beautiful people can have ugly insides," he said. "I love her anyway."

Love. He hadn't stopped loving her, and he had always loved Eric.

"I suppose that's why I left him to Camille." He spoke about his son as if he had lost him, too. "I didn't want to find out if he didn't just look like her."

"I think you should talk to Eric before you talk to me about this," I stopped him before he could continue. Her ugly insides—whatever they were—weren't something for me to know before her son knew about them.

Bracke's bottom lip hung open before he snapped it shut. He nodded and laid his palm on top of my head in the same way Eric touched me. "You saved him from me," he said and dropped his touch. "Thank you."

He turned toward the door, but I called after him, "You're a good father."

When he froze in the doorway, he laid his hand on the doorframe. "I appreciate that, Jess," he said toward the hallway, "but I have a lot to fix before I can believe that." He only glanced over his shoulder once. "Please, let me know if you need anything at all."

His voice trailed over the room as he left, swerving to the side. I didn't know why until Pierce ducked by. "Hey, Bracke."

The elder walked away, ignoring my guard and disappearing into the corridors of the shelter I had yet to explore.

Pierce leaned into the hallway to watch him before he leaned back into my new room. He ran a hand through his black hair. "What's with him?"

"I don't know." I dragged my bags over to the wardrobe.

Pierce followed me, but for other reasons. He leapt onto my bed and bounced up and down like a child. "This hotel gets five stars."

I cracked a smile. "What are you doing here?" Unlike Eric

and me, he had to go to school. If he was here, it was only because after-school activities had released. He normally stayed after to paint in art club, but only when Urte didn't have training planned.

"Thought I'd welcome you to the lair."

I chuckled, but gestured toward the painting easel. "You've done enough."

Pierce didn't follow my movements. Instead, he pointed to the doorway. "Plus, he wanted to see you, too."

"Hey, Jess!" Brenthan stumbled over himself as he ran into the room. If it weren't for their age gap, the brothers could've been twins.

"Hey," I said as Pierce's little brother leapt onto my bed, too.

"Yep," he agreed. "Five stars." He grabbed a pillow and pretended to fluff it. "Maybe four."

Pierce laid a hand on Brenthan's head. "That's enough, kid," he spoke through a smile. "You do have training."

"Fine," he grumbled and ducked away from Pierce's touch. "You're really going to live here, though?"

I nodded. "But you're not supposed to know that."

"Like anyone could hide it from me." His scrawny chest poked out. "Don't you know? I'm a warrior now."

Pierce leaned forward and pushed his brother's back. "And warriors train," he said. "Go beat someone up."

"I'll win," he declared before running off. "See you later, Jess," he called over his shoulder before disappearing into the same hallway as Bracke.

Pierce stared at the doorway like his brother stood there. "He still acts like a kid sometimes."

I sat down next to my guard. "You say that like you aren't one." Like me, he had a summer birthday. We wouldn't be eighteen until after graduation.

"Eh," Pierce brushed off my words, but his face fell into an expression he rarely held. He was about to be serious. "Why didn't you tell me about the realm?"

I looked at the floor. Showing my powers hadn't just shocked the elders. "I should've," I admitted. "I know that."

"Just overwhelmed?"

I nodded.

"You'll be fine." He bumped my arm with his. "You know, Camille struggled with her powers, too." He stumbled over her name. "But she got through it, and I know you will, too."

I had to brush my hair back to see him. "Why do you say that?"

He cocked a grin. "Because you're a badass."

I hit his arm.

"Come on." He laughed, and didn't speak again until his laughter died. "I saw you fight in battle. You did better than I did." He leaned back on his hands. "I'm sort of jealous." When he looked up at the ceiling, he shook his head. "You even broke Darthon's neck once."

The memory of our first battle was clouded with the fact that Darthon had stood back up afterward. Only Eric could kill him. Unless someone killed me. Then, Darthon would die. Darthon had been telling the truth back then, and he was still telling the truth. Through Eric, he was telling more than the truth. The illusion wouldn't stop us from figuring it out.

"Do you think Darthon is trying to break us up?" I asked.

"I know he is." Pierce leaned forward, but his face twisted. "He probably thought you'd go running back to him once Eric left you."

I huffed. "I'm not that desperate."

"He seems to think so."

My hands curled against my knees.

"I know you're hiding something from me," Pierce's words sounded far away, even though his thigh touched mine. "But you can tell me when you're ready." When I looked up, he smiled. "I won't force you like Luthicer did."

My next breath felt lighter than the previous ones. "Thanks, Pierce." Despite everything, I couldn't tell them about the suicide attempt, especially after I spoke to Bracke. Eric's mother had been a loss to everyone, and confessing that I had tried to mirror her movements wouldn't be easy for anyone to hear. The Dark had done enough by accepting the fact that I was also a light.

Pierce stood up as if our conversation was over, but I grabbed his forearm. "Wait."

He looked back. "Yeah?"

"Thanks for the easel." I pointed to the home-warming gift. "It helped."

Pierce looked up, but his eyebrows shot up like he hadn't seen it before. "I didn't get that for you, Jess," he spoke through a grin that practically split his expression in half. "But I could guess who did it."

When he gestured to the desk, I saw the other gift I had overlooked before. A Picasso book. Eric was the one who had welcomed me home.

THIRTY-ONE

T HE MORNING CLOUDS BUMPED OVER THE HORIZON AND LEFT Hayworth High in a hazy mist. Overnight, February had arrived as silent as my illusion, as present as my nerves. When my Charger's engine rumbled beneath me, I squeezed the stick shift. I didn't want to be at school. I wanted the Dark to order us to stay away—that it wasn't worth the risk—but my father had forced me. Even then, I could drive away. I had that much freewill. But it meant abandoning Jessica at school, and I couldn't do that.

I searched the parking lot for Crystal's car, knowing she would probably be with Jessica, but it wasn't present. It was too early. The only car I recognized was the one that pulled up next to mine.

Robb's Suburban.

He didn't meet my eyes until he got out of his car. I locked my doors, but he knocked on the window. His knuckles smeared the glass. Even then, I didn't unlock my doors.

The air sparked as he disappeared, only to reappear in my passenger seat. A blast of hot air burst through my vehicle, and I sucked in a breath as his powers died down. Unlike shades, lights could use their abilities whenever they wanted to.

"I don't remember inviting you in," I grumbled, facing forward.

"I'm not a vampire, Welborn." He blew air into his hands.

It was cold outside. "Where were you two yesterday?"

"I don't have to tell you—"

Before I ever saw it coming, his fist smacked across my face. "Answer me."

I grabbed my chin as the pain radiated up my jaw. Blood dripped off my lip and onto my lap. "If you get blood on my car—"

"What? Your daddy will get you a new one?" Robb growled as his seat leaned back. He stared at the ceiling. "You'll heal in five minutes anyway."

"Not as a human," I managed to gain the feeling back in my face. "Or don't you know how shades' powers work?"

He glanced over, but his neutral expression didn't shift. "I know they're not working like before."

I stared at the boy I had once considered a friend. His face hadn't changed much in three years. The skin below his eyes had deepened, but I imagined mine had, too. It was from the lack of sleep, the training, the death. If he had killed his parents, I hadn't heard of their deaths, but I was with him when his dog died. It was the only time I had seen him cry. Now that I knew he was the one to do it, I didn't know how to accept the memory. It seemed just as impossible as his identity as Darthon—but he was. He was the boy I was destined to kill. He had killed Camille.

I had to tear my eyes away to speak. "My powers are just fine."

"Mine, too."

"So are Jessica's."

Robb sat up, and the chair snapped into place with a crunch. "And?"

"And you wanted to know about us," I pointed out, knowing it was my best move—for once—to follow his orders. "The Dark is forcing us to live in the shelter."

He couldn't attack us all to get to her, but he chuckled. "Wait. Wait. Wait." He laid his hand on his chest. "I'm controlling your speech, and they're controlling your actions?" His laughter was louder this time. "Don't you just love being a pawn?"

"They're forcing Jessica, too."

My words stopped him. His face hardened.

I made my next move. "She told them."

"Told who what?"

"Don't act stupid," I said. "The Dark knows she can be a light, too."

His skin drained of color, and for a moment, his complexion mimicked a shade's. "She wouldn't tell them that."

"She did." He might have been able to silence me, but he couldn't force me to tell the entire truth. I was the one who told the Dark, but he wouldn't know that. He would only know what I told him. "And they aren't going to hurt her, so give up, Robb."

When I said his human name, he flinched, but leaned back like he could cover it up. "If they won't push her away, you will."

"I already broke up with her."

"And you transferred out of homeroom," he finished. "Nice touch."

I grinned. "So, Fudicia told you."

A light shattered throughout my car, only to dissolve into the backseat. The blonde girl appeared as she slowly melted into her human form. Her soft face was nothing like her bony appearance as a light, but her smile was just as threatening. "I'd prefer if you call me Linda."

Her powers wavered enough for me to know the Light was struggling, too. "Using your powers so openly?" I chuckled at Robb. "You are getting desperate." The Dark was winning.

"Call it what you want," Robb muttered. "I don't care." He reached into his sweater pocket and pulled out a cigarette. "You mind?"

"I do."

He took out his lighter and lit it anyway. The orange end burned as he dragged and pushed out the smoke in my direction. "Have you spoken to your father yet?"

My fist tightened, but I held back the urge to hit him. I

wasn't allowed, and I couldn't win if I attacked him during the day. If I were going to kill him, I would have to wait for an opportunity at night.

I reached for the door handle to leave, but the metal burned my palm. Air hissed out of my mouth as I let go. My flesh was red.

"It's rude to leave in the middle of a conversation," Robb spoke at my back.

"We haven't talked yet," I snapped and twisted toward him. "What else do you want?"

"I want you to get a new girlfriend."

I huffed. "That's not happening."

Robb's eyebrow rose. "You have to follow my orders."

"I'm done, Robb." I hovered my fingertips over the handle, but the metal radiated with heat. Darthon wasn't done yet. "You can't kill me," I added, "and once I find you at night— alone—I will kill you." It was only a matter of time before I found a way, but he wouldn't find out what was protecting me. His pride was too blinding.

Linda leaned forward and laid a hand on Robb's shoulder. "He knows what's protecting him."

She was the one I should've been worrying about. Apparently, my pride had blinded me, too.

My gut twisted.

Robb stared at me like he was seeing me for the first time, and I wondered if he saw the boy I was when we were friends. "You know how she's protecting you," he said.

He still thought it was Jessica, and I needed him to believe that. As long as he believed that, he would leave her alone.

"You can't hurt her," I played into his suspicions. "You know you won't."

"No." Robb took another drag, and smoke filled my car. "But she won't let you go until you prove you don't love her anymore."

I dropped my left hand between the seats. If he ordered me to take off the ring, I would have to find a way around it. I would just wear a necklace, too.

"Date Linda," Robb ordered the last thing I expected.

I glanced over at the blonde. Her eyes widened as if she hadn't been expecting it either. "Robb—"

He raised his hand, and her bottom lip snapped shut. I wasn't the only one under orders.

"We'd rather not," I said.

"You'll do it," Robb spoke, but I wasn't sure if he was ordering her or me. Probably both of us.

"Or what?" I tested. "You'll punch me again? Kill me? I'll come back to life—"

"Jonathon Stone won't."

My sternum squeezed in my chest.

"I know he's Pierce." Robb ashed his cigarette on the floor. "I saw him with Jess."

"They just have a class together—"

"Outside of class," he clarified. "And I imagine Jonathon's not a very good fighter as a human." Robb's eyes darkened. "I have Zac following him."

The half-breed. Linda's brother. I glanced at her, expecting a reaction, but she was staring out the window.

"Maybe I won't let Zac kill him," Robb continued. "Maybe I'll do it myself." He chuckled, and smoke bounced out of his mouth. "Maybe I won't even kill him. Maybe I'll just put my cigarette out on his good eye."

"Fine," I growled, thinking of my best friend. I had punched him myself, and I couldn't protect him either. "But only if you leave him out."

Robb opened his door, speaking as he ducked out, "I think we have a deal, then." He slammed the door as if it were equal to a handshake.

"See you around, honey," Linda said and mirrored Robb's movements.

I watched their exposed backs as they walked toward the school. If I waited five more minutes, Jessica would arrive and see Robb's car parked next to mine. If I got close to her, she would smell his smoke on me. But if she were with Crystal, there was a high chance Crystal would tell Robb. It was too big of a risk. Either way, I had to make another move. And fast.

My foot slammed on the gas pedal, and my tires squealed as I drove out of the parking lot. I wanted Robb to hear my disobedience. I wanted him to know I was leaving and fighting back. I wanted him to know I was going to the shelter to train. My hands would end his life. When I looked in my rearview mirror, he was staring.

I only wondered what look he would give me as he died.

The training room was colder when I was a human, but I didn't want to strain myself by transforming before sunset. Although it was possible to transform in the shelter, the powers were weaker. It was one of the reasons Luthicer was generally the only elder on staff most of the time, but I felt another one as he entered the room.

"What do you want?" I asked, keeping my back to him.

"For one," Urte responded, "I'd like you to look at me."

I turned around. Unlike me, Urte was transformed. His black hair hung against his neck, as wild as his eyes, but the rest of him was tamed into forced stillness.

I raised my arms only to drop them at my sides. "Better?"

Urte leaned against the wall as his eyes skimmed my face. "Did you get in another fight?"

I didn't have to touch my face to remember the mark that was there. Robb had split my lip open. I could taste the raw skin that was healing. I wanted it that way. It was just another reason not to transform. Everyone could see it now.

"Who was it this time?" Urte asked.

It was impossible to speak Darthon's name, so I didn't even try.

Urte stepped toward the control panel. "If you're going to train as a human, be careful."

He thought my injury was from the disks. The setting was one I generally used as a shade when I could shoot them down with my powers. I was enjoying the challenge as a human today. But I didn't want Urte to think my injury was from the clay. When I opened my mouth to correct his assumption, he spoke, "It doesn't take a wise man to know you're fighting more than disks."

As he said it, a disk shot out of the wall and missed my face by inches. My bangs shifted from the wind before the disk broke against the far wall, shattering into pieces.

Urte cursed and slammed his hand against the panel. The room buzzed as it flipped off. "Eric—"

"I'm fine," I said, stopping him and grabbing my water. I took a drink and wiped my mouth before I spoke again. "Go ahead. Talk about what you really came here for."

"Darthon." Urte didn't hesitate.

"What about him?" I didn't either.

"He tortured you in there."

I dropped my water so I could stretch my arm over my head. "I've had practice with torture."

My trainer didn't flinch at the reminder. "That's precisely why I know it isn't the reason you broke up with Jess." His words lingered. "I also know that isn't why you punched my son."

Jonathon. I remembered Darthon's threat, even though I didn't want to. "Watch over Pierce," my voice was quiet, but Urte paled, and I knew he heard me.

"What does that mean, Shoman?"

I hated to hear my Dark name when I was a human.

When I didn't respond, Urte marched across the room and grabbed both of my shoulders. He was shorter than I was, but—somehow—his stare pushed down on me. "Eric, you have to fight through this," he said. "You need to find a way."

"I'm trying." My voice cracked. "There's nothing I can do right now."

"Why not?" Urte's eyes flickered over my face. "Jonathon and you are best friends—"

"Not anymore."

Urte's hands fell away, but he didn't step back. "You're breaking up with him, too?"

The question forced a chuckle out of me, but it wasn't light laughter. It stung my insides.

Urte shook his head, and his hair waved. "You can't break up with everyone, Eric."

"Not when you're forcing me to stay here," I agreed.

Urte choked.

I forced a smile. "Thank you for that."

He kept his gaze on me as his feet shifted backward, slowly making his way to the exit. "We'll find a way."

"I know."

He spun around and walked toward the door like he was on a mission to solve it all, but he froze in the doorway. "Eric?"

"Yeah?"

"Whatever happens," his voice wavered as he opened the door. "Whenever you resolve this, I won't judge you," he promised before walking out.

I didn't try to stop him. I couldn't. This was my battle—just like the prophecy dictated—and I focused on that as I walked to the control panel and flipped it back on.

THIRTY-TWO

Jessica

EVEN THOUGH HE WAS SUPPOSED TO, ERIC NEVER SHOWED UP FOR school. His absence was suffocating. I barely made it through the day, and my concern only increased when I arrived at the shelter. The elders were in a meeting, Jonathon was training Jada, and I was alone.

I sat in my room, living through my paints. The Picasso book sat on my lap, and a splatter of blue paint landed on the open picture I was using as inspiration. I stared at the edge of the liquid as it hardened and crusted onto the page. The color was three shades off. Ever since my powers became red, I hadn't been able to see blue the same way. I slammed the book closed.

When I stood, my feet moved as if they weren't attached to me. I walked across the room and placed the book on my pillow. The heavy weight of the paper caused it to slide down, only to land against the wrapped present I had kept for over a month.

Eric's birthday present. I still hadn't given it to him.

After his father had bought him another car, it felt useless to give him something so trivial, but the pale wrapping paper gleamed in the dim room. My fingertips skimmed it before I picked the gift up and held it against my chest.

I knew what I had to do.

I marched out of my room and made my way through

the halls. In art class, Jonathon had already told me the one thing I wanted to know. Eric's room rested on the east side, right between the library and the nurse's quarters. It took me eight minutes to get there, but I was sure when I saw the door. The thick wood gave it away. It was the same door I had on my room. What they had once been used for was the only mystery.

I knocked three times, and every knock sounded louder than the first, but the silence that followed was deafening.

I knocked again, even pressing my ear against the wood, but no one came.

"I know you're in there, Eric," I said, loud enough that my voice echoed down the hallway, but he didn't respond.

"I just wanted to thank you for the easel." I laid my forehead against the door. "I started painting, but—" I couldn't tell him I was struggling with the color blue. It was the color of his powers. It was his eyes as Shoman. It was everything he was. I forced a breath out to gain my composure. "I know I'm a little late, but I never gave you your birthday present." I placed the package on the ground. "I bought it a long time ago—with Crystal, actually."

The memory seemed years away, but it had only been six weeks.

"I know it's not as good as the other gift you got," I added, "but I thought you should have it."

I waited. For what, I didn't know, because I knew he wouldn't come. I patted the door instead of knocking one last time. "Okay, then," I said. "Goodnight."

I forced myself to walk away without looking back, but it took me fifteen minutes to return to my room—double the time it took me to get to his. I stared at the clock on my dresser as I fell asleep, pretending we had all the time in the world to figure out what had happened to him, and I let the time take me.

———◆———

When I woke up the next morning, I was late for school.

My alarm hadn't gone off, and I rushed through my morning routine in a foggy haze. It was my job to get back home before Crystal picked me up, but today, someone else would have to take me. Luthicer was my only bet, and I was thinking about him when I ran out of my bedroom and tripped.

I fell onto my knees, but my feet hurt more. I had kicked something and spun around to see what I had tripped on.

A model car.

It was a build-it-yourself Charger, near the same year Eric's original car had been, and Crystal had found it in an antique store at the mall. I had only bought it because Eric had just lost his in a car wreck. I hadn't given it to him until last night.

The estimate on the box stated it would take a week to assemble and another week to paint, but this one was finished. I grabbed it, unsure it was real, but the metal was cold in my hands. The paint wasn't even damp, and the decoration on the hood was all too familiar.

Eric's willow tree pendant—the one Camille had made for him—was sketched onto the hood in red. Eric had used that color for a reason. My new powers were not a problem for him. They were not a problem for the Dark either. It was only me who was struggling, and I touched the symbol like I could absorb it instead of having it absorb me.

THIRTY-THREE

Jessica

"MAYBE IT'S NOT OVER," I FINISHED TELLING CRYSTAL ABOUT the car without mentioning how Eric and I lived together in the shelter. I couldn't even mention the willow tree symbol he had painted, but I hoped she would see the significance.

"Maybe he was just returning it, Jess." Her voice was a whisper among our fellow students.

Our homeroom was about to end, and then we would go to lunch, but Eric wasn't with us. He had a different schedule now, but he had come to school. I already planned on running into him between lunches. As his lunch ended, ours began, and it would be the perfect time to confront him. I only had to hurry.

"I don't think so," I responded, even though I was focused on the clock. I only had a few minutes to get to him before he went back to his new homeroom.

"Jess," Crystal kept repeating my name. "I really think you should let him go."

I grabbed my necklace through my shirt. "I can't—"

"For God's sake, Jess," Robb interrupted from his seat next to Crystal. I had almost forgotten he was there. "He has a new girlfriend."

Crystal smacked his arm. "I told you not to tell."

"It's for her own good," he grumbled, only glancing at me

for a moment. "At this rate, you're never going to move on."

Move on. His last two words were the only reason I heard what he had originally said. "Eric has a new girlfriend?" My hands were already curling into fists. "That's impossible—"

"He does," Crystal confirmed, but she didn't have her usual pen marks on her fingers. Even she didn't want to write about it for her student gossip column.

"Who?" I asked.

Crystal gestured to Robb. "He's taking that one."

I stared at Robb as I repeated the question. He shrugged like it was nothing. "Linda."

Her name was the last one I thought I would hear. She was Robb's ex-girlfriend, and she had just transferred into our school. Despite the day we all sat together at lunch, I didn't even know they had officially met or how Eric would decide to date her. She was tall, blonde, and quiet. The opposite of me.

I felt sick.

"Come on," Robb spoke over the ringing bell. "We're better off without them anyway."

I ignored him and stood up. "I'll see you at lunch," I said to Crystal before grabbing my bag and rushing out of the room. My plan hadn't changed. I would see Eric and confront him. The news hadn't changed anything, because it couldn't be true. Eric still wore his ring, after all.

When I pushed through the shifting crowds, I searched their faces for the only person I wanted to see. I didn't see him until I made my way outside. I lost my breath when I realized he was walking with Linda, and I blocked the door before either of them could go back to class.

"I need to talk to you," I blurted.

Eric's green eyes widened, but only for a millisecond. After that, they were slits. "I'm busy."

When he tried to brush past me, I moved in front of him again.

Linda folded her arms. "What do you want?" she asked.

"I wasn't talking to you," I retorted, refusing to take my eyes off Eric even though he had stopped looking at me. "Is it true?"

"So, what if it is?" Eric didn't even ask for clarification. He knew what I had heard.

"We're dating now," Linda clarified by grabbing Eric's hand. He didn't even pull away, but I stared. She held his left hand, the one with his ring—the same ring that said he was my fiancé, not her boyfriend.

Chills ran up my spine as the door behind me opened and wind rushed past us. "Why'd you run out so fast?" Crystal stopped speaking as she stepped out to stand next to me. Her bleached hair gleamed in the gray, winter light. "Oh, hey, guys."

"Hey." Linda smiled at her. "I was just looking for you," she said. "Eric and I were thinking about going on a date, and I wanted to see if Zac and you wanted to double."

Zac. Her half-brother.

My emotions had taken over, but they were clearing now. I could see Eric and focus on Linda. If Darthon was controlling him, Linda was involved. She had to be Fudicia, and Zac—her brother—had to be my enemy.

"We can't," Crystal said as she laid her arm on my shoulder. "We're already doubling with Robb and Jess."

My heart slammed into my chest as I glanced at my friend. She was grinning, and I recognized the light in her eyes. She wore the same expression when she discovered a new story for the paper. She was up to no good.

She pushed her weight against me. "Right, Jess?"

I only glanced at Eric with my peripheral vision. He had paled. Something was definitely wrong, and that something was Darthon. If he knew who Darthon was, then he knew I would be with him. Zac. I was right. I had always been right.

"Yeah," I confirmed before I could overthink it. The date would be the perfect opportunity to get Zac out at night— when the Dark had powers, too. It would be a night we could expose him. I would only have to find a way to protect Crystal from it. "We're going out."

Eric opened his mouth, and then snapped it shut. His jaw locked, and he glared at the brick wall to the right.

I shifted, wanting him to confirm it somehow, but I knew he couldn't. Linda was next to him.

"Too bad," she cooed. "Maybe next time."

"Maybe," Crystal agreed.

"Come on, honey." Eric was the one to say it, yet it sounded nothing like him. He never used pet names. Not once when he was with me. Yet he did with Linda, and when he brushed past me, his arm skimmed mine. Even through his jacket, I could feel his body heat.

I wrapped my arms around my torso when the cold air was all that was left.

"Did you see the look on his face?" Crystal bounced in front of me, her cheeks rosy. "He looked like you punched him in the gut." She giggled like she enjoyed it.

I leaned against the wall to keep myself standing. My knees were shaking. If Zac was Darthon, then my best friend was dating him, and I had no way of telling her. "Yeah," was all I could manage.

"You don't have to worry about the date either," she said. "I just thought you could use some help back there—"

"Actually," I interrupted her as Robb walked out, a sandwich in his hand. "I want to go."

Robb took a bite and stared at us. "What just happened?"

"What?" Crystal ignored him as she questioned me. "You're serious?"

I nodded, but this time it was to Robb. "You want to go on a double date?"

His mouth hung open and food fell out. I tried not to cringe as he brushed off his shirt. "With you?"

"And Zac and Crystal," I added.

He glanced from Crystal to me before nodding too many times. "That would be cool."

"Great," I said and grabbed Crystal's arm. "You two can make it, right?"

It would be pointless if Zac wasn't there.

"I think so," she said, but her words were drawn out. I had never seen her hesitate about Zac before. "Tonight?"

"At eight," I clarified. "Meet you at your place?"

"Sure."

"See you then," I said and started to walk away. I had to talk to Jonathon about my plan before I carried it out, and if I had to drag him out of class again, I would.

As I made my way through the lunchroom, Crystal called after me, "Wait."

When I faced her, she stopped an inch away from me. Her boots touched mine, but she didn't speak.

"What's wrong?" I asked.

"Are you sure about this, Jess?" Her eyes moved over my face. "I didn't mean to pressure you—"

"You didn't," I promised, knowing it was time to push myself forward. "It'll be fun." It would also be the next step to end it all.

THIRTY-FOUR

"I DON'T HAVE TO LOVE YOU," I GROWLED AND SCOOTED AWAY FROM Linda. She had attempted to snuggle up next to me throughout lunch, and I wasn't about to let it happen.

She blew her bangs out of her face. "You have to at least act like it."

The rest of the student body wasn't even looking, but I knew they had seen. Ever since she had stood by my locker in the morning, the rumor was spreading. It was only a matter of time before Jessica heard, if she hadn't already, and I didn't want to be around when she did.

I only had thirty more minutes before I could leave. Due to my new schedule, I had a different lunch, which forced me to go back to class for fifteen minutes while the last lunch took place—the one Jessica was in. If I didn't hurry to get back to class, she would see me.

I glanced at my watch, but Linda smacked her hand over the time. "She has to see us eventually."

I yanked my hand away. "So, that's your plan."

She smiled to confirm it. "That's what you want."

"That's what Darthon wants," I spat, "and the minute I'm out of this, you're falling right next to him."

Her brown eyes widened, and her breath fogged out in front of her. She didn't speak as she inched away me. She leaned back against the wall, and her blonde hair stuck to the

196

bricks when she shook her head. What she was shaking her head at I didn't know, but I did know one thing. She was a teenager just like the rest of us.

"You don't have to die," I said, changing my stance.

She peeked at me through her hair. "Do you know why the powers are weakening?"

My esophagus squeezed. "No."

"Because they're dying," she answered. "If one of you doesn't die, the powers will die in your place." Her face turned back toward the sky. "We'll all just be humans again. Mad humans."

Whenever we lost our powers, we went mad. I knew that. It had happened to too many for us to deny it.

"We'll only kill each other in madness anyway—"

"You hate humans that much?" I interrupted.

She didn't respond immediately. Her eyes stayed on me when she finally spoke. "No," she paused, "but I don't want to be one."

"You talk like one," I retorted.

Her eyebrows shot up. "What's that supposed to mean?"

"I saw the look on your face when Robb ordered you to date me," I said, refusing to stop fighting back. If I had to break Linda, then I would. I wasn't even going against my orders. "You don't want this anymore than I do."

She snatched my hand up as if she was proving a point, but her fingers were shaking.

For once, I didn't pull away. "You love him, don't you?"

Linda's nails dug into the back of my hand, and strangely, it reminded me of Jessica's touch. "Why do you care?"

She did. It wasn't hard to guess. She had dated Robb on and off for years, after all. Even if it was a cover for her position as a guard, she had fallen into the illusion as if she had used her own powers against herself. She was still a child.

"You're blind," I managed.

Linda glared at me as if to prove she could see. "I'm not like Jonathon."

Just the reminder of their threat was enough to make me

hesitate, but it wasn't enough to stop me. I would have to trust in Jonathon's abilities as much as I trusted in Jessica's. "Darthon doesn't love you."

She exhaled a breath, and it blew out in a visible stream of hot air against the February cold. "You think I don't know that?" She let me go. "He isn't capable of loving. The elders beat it out of him." When she glanced at me, I knew what she would say, "Didn't they do the same to you?"

They had. They had taught me not to care, showed me how to shut everything out. Even mourning had escaped me. It was one of the only reasons I hadn't dealt with Camille's death until now. It was the only reason I hadn't confronted my father about my mother's suicide. But I had overcome it, and I had dealt with Abby's death.

"You killed Hannah, didn't you?"

Linda's soft face twisted, and for a moment, I could imagine the sharpness of her cheekbones—the ones she had as Fudicia, the ones I had seen when she poked her head into the car wreck. She nodded.

"Did you know who I was when you saw me?" I asked, knowing our eyes had met that afternoon. She knew I had lived, and she had left me alive. She could've ended it all years ago, but she didn't. "Didn't you consider killing me?"

"No." Her lips thinned into a white line before she licked them. "I didn't want to know it was you."

My stomach twisted. "Why not?"

She yanked her red jacket around her as if she could tighten the coat. It only brought out the flush of her cheeks more. Linda—Darthon's guard—was just as broken as the rest of us.

I grabbed her arm. "Why not, Linda?"

She pulled away from me. "Because Robb doesn't want to kill you," she practically cried. "That's why."

My face heated up. "Bullshit."

She leapt to her feet, and her hair spiked out like she was going to transform in the middle of the school day. "I'm done talking to you, Welborn."

I grabbed her again, only to pull her back to the wall.

"We're supposed to stay together," I reminded her of her orders. "Or do you want to get in trouble?"

She squirmed, and for a moment, I considered letting her leave. It would've been nice to be alone, but it wouldn't get me any closer to killing him. Forcing her to talk was the only way I could learn more information. It was the only way I could win.

"You can get out of this," I said.

"I'll tell him you said that," she threatened.

"Go ahead," I retorted. "If he doesn't want to kill me, he shouldn't have a problem with it."

"You don't get it, do you?" She wiggled out of my grasp. "He's just as forced into this as you are, and when he found out it was you—" When she stopped speaking, she dug her hands into her jacket pocket. "You're the only one who showed him kindness," she finished, but she didn't look at me. Of all the things she could look at, she stared at the willow tree. "Don't you remember when his dog died?"

I did. We were kids then. Crystal was there, too, but her mom picked her up. Robb's parents hadn't even come out to say goodbye. It wasn't unusual for them, and I knew we had that in common. My dad didn't care about my emotions either. When I told Robb that, he cried.

"He's the one who did it," I pointed out what he told me.

"He tried to run." Linda's words brought back the memory.

Robb had run. He had stayed at my house for a week, and no one even called to ask if he was there. When my father finally kicked him out, it was the first time my father and I had fought. He didn't want me to have friends, but I yelled back. I had Crystal, Robb, and Hannah. Later that year, I was Named and found out why I couldn't have any of them.

"He killed his parents shortly after that," Linda finished.

My feet dug into the ground. All the snow had melted, but the surface was hardened from the cold. Somewhere in Hayworth, Robb's parents might be buried in the ground, but I never heard of their deaths. No one had. According to the town, they were alive, but I knew better now. Everything was an illusion.

"How did the Light cover it up?" I asked.

"Various members watched him." She didn't have to clarify they used their powers of illusion to look like Robb's parents. "It was an honor if you were chosen." She tore her eyes away from the tree. "Everyone celebrated it. He hasn't been the same since."

The bell shattered the air between us.

"But that's that." She brushed her hair out of her face. "You still have a lot to learn about yourself, don't you?"

My mother. I nodded, knowing I would ask my dad about her death tonight. After that, I could concentrate on breaking the illusion further.

"Let's go back to class, then," Linda said, picking up her giant purse.

She walked next to me and didn't feel like an enemy, but she was. It took everything in me to remind myself of that when I asked her, "Are you going to tell him?"

"No." Her brown eyes glanced at me. "Are you?"

"No."

"Looks like we're in something together," she mentioned, but her soft expression fell. It wasn't until I followed her eyes that I realized why.

Among the crowd, Jessica had appeared, and she hadn't just appeared. She stood right in front of us, and her blue eyes were focused on me. The piercing glare was the same one she had when she blocked the doorway in the shelter. She wasn't about to let me walk right past her.

"I need to talk to you." Her voice was sharp.

"I'm busy," I replied faster than I thought I could, but my orders allowed me to. I wasn't supposed to talk to Jessica. If Robb saw it, he could hurt her or Jonathon, and I didn't want either situation to happen.

When I ducked toward another door, Jessica leapt in front of me. Before I could tell her to move, Linda stepped to my side and asked, "What do you want?"

"I wasn't talking to you," Jessica snapped, but I stared at the blonde. She was trying to get Jessica to leave, too.

"Is it true?" Jessica's voice was the only reason I could concentrate again. I could hear everything in her tone. She had used it once before. That time, she had thrown her prom dress at me, and ten minutes later, she told me she hated me. Back then, she didn't have a memory, but today, her voice held anger. She knew I was dating Linda.

"So, what if it is?" I asked, hoping she had recognized the painting on the model car I had left outside of her room, and she knew what it meant. It was the only way to tell her I was still with her. I knew she would find out about my relationship with Linda today.

"We're dating now," Linda said and confirmed everything I couldn't say aloud. She grabbed my hand to prove it.

Jessica's eyes fell to our hands, and her bottom lip quivered. If Linda hadn't been holding my hand, I wouldn't have been able to stop myself from reaching out to touch her.

"Why'd you run out so fast?" Crystal said as she opened the door behind Jessica, but she stopped speaking when she saw us. Her shoulders rose as her face flushed. "Oh, hey, guys."

With everything that Linda had reminded me of, I thought of our childhood and how Crystal had black hair as a child. It was shortly after Abby died when she pierced her face and started changing her hair color. Back then, I wanted to ask Crystal if she was okay. Today, I wanted Crystal to ask Jessica if she was okay.

"Hey," Linda was the one to speak for both of us. "I was just looking for you. Eric and I were thinking about going on a date, and I wanted to see if Zac and you wanted to double."

My stomach was twisting, and my grip on Linda tightened. Right when I thought she was on my side, she betrayed me. She was trying to hurt Jessica, but Jessica acted like she hadn't even heard. Her expression hadn't budged at all. For once, I couldn't read her, and I wondered how far I had actually pushed her away—if Darthon was right and she would go back to him.

"We can't," Crystal dismissed the idea as she leaned against Jessica. They were both so small. "We're already doubling with

Robb and Jess."

Jessica's eyes widened at her friend.

Crystal smirked at us instead of looking at Jessica. "Right, Jess?"

My lungs felt like they had collapsed. Despite everything that had happened with Robb, she was going back to him. Darthon was right all along.

"Yeah," Jessica said. "We're going out."

I opened my mouth to yell at her, to tell her about the danger she was in, but my neck burned. I would've grabbed it, too, but the powers sizzled out as it traveled down my arm. Linda had taken the pain away. I snapped my mouth shut and forced myself to look away. If I had to see Jessica for one more moment, I would lose it.

"Too bad," Linda said as she started dragging me away. "Maybe next time."

"Maybe," Crystal agreed.

As we walked past Jessica, I found the strength to talk to Linda, so that Jessica could hear, "Come on, honey." My arm skimmed Jessica's, and her touch radiated through me before the heat from inside blasted against my face. I didn't look back to see if Jessica was watching us leave because it didn't matter. I only hoped she heard what I called Linda and knew something was wrong—that everything was wrong—that the date was the last thing that needed to happen.

But Linda smiled like everything was perfect. "That was interesting."

I searched the lunchroom for Robb, knowing he had to be close by, but I never saw him. "You helped me," I said, referencing to how she took the pain of the illusion away, but she shushed me.

Robb was close. She didn't want him to hear, and I didn't know what to think about it. I didn't know if Linda was on my side or not, but I knew one thing. Robb was getting closer to Jessica, and I had to find a way to stop it, even if that meant betraying the bit of trust I had gained from Darthon's guard.

THIRTY-FIVE

Jessica

"**I** AGREED TO IT BEFORE I THOUGHT ABOUT IT," I SAID TO PIERCE while searching my wardrobe. I had already told him about what happened at school, but he grew quiet when I told him why I wanted to do it. "Zac has to be Darthon."

"I don't know about this, Jess." Pierce laid his chin on his hands. "It's not safe."

"Nothing is," I retorted and spun around. I held up two sweaters. "Green or blue?"

His eyes flickered over them. "Blue." He gestured to my face. "It brings the color out in your eyes."

My face flushed, and I was glad he couldn't see it as I pulled the sweater over my tank top. "Thanks."

"No problem," he muttered, "but don't get too comfortable with my advice. I'm only doing this because I'm your guard."

I flashed a grin at him. "And my friend." I gestured to my easel. "You can use it while I'm gone if you want."

"Like I'm staying here." He stood up. "I'm not letting this happen unless you let me follow you."

I bit my lip.

"Don't tell me you thought I'd let you do this alone." His shoulders slumped. "We're a team."

"It's dangerous." I wasn't denying it. Whether Zac was Darthon or not, I knew it was a risk, but it was my risk.

"Exactly why we need to go together," he said, "especially

since you're not telling the elders."

I raised my brow. "I could've already told them." I had gotten permission to leave from Bracke, after all. It was the first thing I did after returning from school. Talking to Pierce was the second.

"I know you didn't," he pointed out, "or Bracke wouldn't have agreed."

"Which is why I didn't tell him." I folded my arms. "We can't sit back and wait for Darthon to attack. That's what got us into trouble in the first place. We have to attack him first, catch him off-guard, and—"

"You are not attacking him tonight," Pierce interrupted.

"And why not?"

"Jess." He grabbed his hair like he was going to tear his brain out. "Just be patient. We don't even know for sure if Zac is involved."

He sounded like Eric.

I had to sit down on my bed to calm down. "I—" I stopped myself and stared at my hands. All I could see was how Eric had held Linda's hand. "He wouldn't be with her unless she was involved, and Zac is her brother."

"Half-brother," Pierce added.

"It has to be a cover," I argued. "They're the same age, and they don't look anything alike."

"Linda's dad had an affair, and his mistress died from cancer," Pierce spoke as he sat next to me. "They took Zac in."

"How do you know that?"

He shrugged. "Jada." The new breed of shade was proving to be more useful than anyone. "She's on the case, too, you know."

I couldn't even picture her looking into everyone's lives. She knew who Eric and I were. Everyone did. But she couldn't know anything beyond that. No one did, and because of that, I knew she had looked into my friends like the elders had.

"Why did she suspect Zac?" I asked, wanting to hear the truth.

"She didn't. You did," Pierce said. "I told her."

That was the last thing I thought he would say. Back when I realized my friends' memories were erased, I explained to Pierce how Zac was the only one who remembered. Eric and I had argued about it, and Pierce had listened to both sides. He hadn't argued with either one of us, but he had been on my side all along. He had looked into Zac, too, but he also sided with Eric on some parts. Pierce still didn't want me to hurt Zac.

"He's a jerk, for sure," Pierce spoke up, "but we don't need to hurt any more innocent people."

I stared at him. "You're sure they're related?"

Pierce nodded. "I trust Jada as much as the elders do," he said. "She wouldn't have told me that if it weren't true." He pushed his arm against mine. "But that doesn't mean we've ruled him out. He could still be Darthon, and you could still be in danger."

My hands curled into fists when I thought about the black-haired boy. "He's hated Eric from the beginning."

"So does half the school, Jess."

I straightened my fingers. Pierce was right. My desperation had taken over, and my lack of training had me making a quick decision. I needed direction—a lot of direction—and I would listen if it meant helping the Dark.

"You can cancel the date, Jess."

"Do you want me to?" I asked.

"No."

My neck snapped when I looked up. My guard was smiling. "I think you're onto something. You did good," he said, taking a moment to run a hand through his hair. "I'm actually surprised you didn't focus on the fact that Eric's dating someone new."

The reminder twisted my gut. "I haven't forgotten," I admitted, "but it doesn't matter." Not when his life was being controlled. "He called her honey."

Pierce chuckled before apologizing for his laughter. "That's ridiculous," he managed. "I almost would've liked to be there just so I could've heard it."

I laughed, too, and for once, the laughter didn't feel

strange. Pierce and I knew Eric well enough to understand how much he wouldn't have done it on his own. It was all we needed to confirm that our plan was worth it.

"Then, I'll try to find out if Zac is involved somehow," I promised as I stood up.

Pierce stood up with me. "Try to find out without tipping him off."

I wiggled my fingers. "I already have a plan."

"Better be a good one." He walked across the room toward my door.

I followed him. "It's better now that you have my back."

"Always."

He opened the door, but we were stopped from walking into the hallway. Eric stood in front of us, his hand half-raised to knock.

"Eric?" I said. "What are you doing here?" As far as I knew, he should've been on a date with Linda.

"I'm—" He stopped speaking when his eyes moved over my clothes. "Where are you going?"

My heart skipped. "Out."

His green eyes were as bright as Pierce's shade ones. "I'm staying in for the night." He wasn't going out with Linda. "You two should, too."

"Why?" Pierce asked. "You going to hang out with us?"

Eric's jaw locked. Of course he wasn't going to. According to him, neither one of us were his friends anymore. Not while he was under an illusion. It was the exact reason Pierce and I had to leave. We had to fight for him.

"Have a good night," I said and ducked under his arm.

I didn't take two steps before Eric grabbed my hand. "Don't." His voice shook.

Pierce was silent as I turned around to face Eric. Worry lines appeared on his face, and I imagined they would be wrinkles one day when he was old, but until then, they were temporary.

"I'll stay if you give me one reason why I shouldn't go," I said, squeezing his hand back. I didn't want to let him go.

Eric was the one to drop my hand, but he also dropped his head.

My palm was cold. "I know they're involved, Eric."

He didn't look up. "Don't do this because of me." He didn't deny it. Linda was one of them. Zac must have been, too.

"It's not just for you," I whispered, but my whisper was loud in the echoing hallway. "We're doing it for the Dark."

"So, let them handle it."

"They can't," I snapped, "and you can't either." My voice strained against my throat.

Pierce laid a hand on my shoulder. "Let us help you, Eric."

He didn't respond.

"Tell us you need help or tell us you don't," I pressed. "Just say something."

But he didn't respond.

Pierce pulled me away. "Come on, Jess."

I ducked out of Pierce's grasp, and I walked up to Eric. Instead of touching him, I knelt down and looked up, meeting his eyes under the shadow of his hair. They were covered in a tearing mist.

"We love you." A choke escaped me. "We love you even if you can't say it back, but I wish you would." And for a moment, I wished he would stop me, but I tore the wish into pieces by ducking away.

When I walked toward Pierce, I focused on the end of the hallway. "We'll be back tonight," I called over my shoulder. "Don't wait up for us."

THIRTY-SIX

I couldn't do it. I couldn't stop her, and it wasn't for her, or Pierce, or the Dark at all. It was for the opposite. It was for Linda. It was for my fight. If I had to beat Darthon, then I had to get him alone, and tearing up his relationship with Linda was more important than making sure my own relationships were fine. Jessica had to go on a date, and I had to let her. She was fighting, too. I knew that. But she was fighting the wrong person, and she had no way of knowing. I could already tell she was focused on Linda, which meant she was focused on Zac instead of Robb. But I had to focus on my own troubles first.

"Why did Mom kill herself?" The question left my lungs as I burst into my father's office at the shelter. I knew he was there, but I didn't realize he wasn't alone.

Jada and Luthicer stood by his desk, and they stepped back as if they hadn't sensed my approach. I had to remind myself I was still in my human form—unlike them—and humans weren't traceable. Humans were only traceable if they came in contact with my sword, and I hadn't used it in months. With Darthon controlling me, it seemed pointless. While under Darthon's orders, my question seemed pointless, too.

My father stood up, but his palm stayed on top of his paperwork. "What?"

The adrenaline coursing through my veins had taken control of my every move. I hadn't even hesitated to come and ask him my last question before I fought Darthon. I needed to know about my mom.

"Why did she kill herself?" I repeated, but my voice rumbled.

My father's shade skin, somehow, paled further. Even then, he didn't respond.

Luthicer cleared his throat. "We should be leaving," he said and grabbed his daughter, the only new breed of shade I had met so far. The others were forbidden to join us until we understood everything. We couldn't risk new members working as double spies.

Jada's multicolored eyes met mine as she walked out of the room, but Luthicer never glanced my way. As the door shut behind me, I leaned back against it, hoping the steady frame would calm my beating heart. If I could talk to my dad, it would prevent me from chasing Pierce and Jessica.

My father gave no indication he knew they were gone as he transitioned into his human form. His black hair shifted to brown and gray, revealing his receding hairline. He didn't speak until he picked up his glasses from the table. "Sit down, Eric."

I did. My entire life was following orders, but for once, I was obeying instead of rebelling.

He mirrored my movements from behind his desk, and we were face-to-face. "I knew we'd have to talk about this eventually—"

"Is it true?" I wasted no time.

"Is what true?" He, apparently, had all the time in the world to avoid the truth.

I swallowed Darthon's confession. "Was she the bloodline?"

His shoulders rose. "Who told you that?"

"Darthon."

He didn't move. His face didn't budge, his shoulders didn't slump, and his wrinkles didn't deepen. Nothing about him seemed to be alive. He was frozen, but it told me everything

I needed to know. When my expression didn't move, it was because I didn't want someone to be able to read my thoughts.

I gripped the table. "Why didn't you tell me?"

"That." He paused. "That isn't what I thought you wanted to talk about."

"It's what I want to know," I said, expecting a response, but the ticking clock was the single sound I heard.

His expression hardened, and he placed his elbows on the desk before removing his glasses. The dim lighting cast shadows over his cheekbones, and they shifted when he nodded. "She was," he admitted, "but I don't know how Darthon could know that." His fingers curled against the glasses in his palm, and I expected them to break. "Only the elders knew that."

Urte. Luthicer. Eu. Only they had known. It was a secret. My mother was the bloodline. It was never my father. I had inherited everything from someone I barely remembered.

"The Light," he struggled to continue his speech, "they must have had a spy among us."

The other elders—the ones I had never met—had died long before I was born. Each generation had ten. There were only three left, and Luthicer had actually replaced one of the originals. Out of the eight originals that were gone, one had been an enemy. One had told the Light about my mother's bloodline, but out of everyone who knew, it was my enemy who had told me.

"Why didn't you tell me?" I repeated.

My father stared back, but he didn't look like my father. His softened eyes weren't the ones I remembered from my childhood. "What else did Darthon tell you?"

"Answer my question first—"

"I'm trying," he promised, "but I need you to answer me first."

My neck burned, but not from Darthon's spell. It was from my own hesitations. I didn't want to speak anymore. I had done it on a whim, and the sudden actions didn't have a plan behind them. I kept my mouth shut.

"She was young when I first met her," he began. "She was

210

fourteen, just starting high school, and her father called on me to be her guard." His throat moved as he coughed into his hand. "I had dropped out of college. It wasn't for me. I was only really good at one thing—"

"A guard?" I interrupted him. My father had always been a leader, not a protector. Imagining him in Urte's spot was unfathomable. Guards didn't have guards. It was unheard of, but my father nodded.

"The ancient ones knew the bloodline had returned because our powers had grown stronger, and they told the elders she was the carrier," he explained, "but she was a child, and I was their best fighter."

"So, they asked you to protect her?"

He shook his head. "Your grandfather—her father—asked me to take her place." When he leaned back, he folded his hands in his lap. "My powers were strong enough that the Dark knew the other shades would believe it, and your grandfather didn't want his daughter to be in danger," he said. "That's when the lies began."

My insides twisted. "And they continued until now?"

He didn't have to nod. "It was for her protection," he said. "It was for your protection," he added. "If the Light figured out who I was, and they killed me, the bloodline could continue." He was a fake target. "I gladly accepted. At the time, it was an honor. It was everything I was raised for. It was—"

"I don't understand," I stopped him. "You never lied about me, and I'm the descendant."

"I know."

I gripped the table. "That makes no sense."

"Eric," his voice was sharp. "Things changed when she died."

"When she killed herself," I corrected, "after she lost her powers."

My dad's eyebrows shot up.

"Darthon told me that, too." And he was right about it all. My enemy knew my life better than I did. I hit the table. "Start talking more. Tell me everything—"

"I will when you calm down," he snapped.

"I don't have time to calm down," I said back, but my voice dropped. "If I'm going to kill him, I need to know why she died. I need to know who I am. I need to know why you had me anyway, why you did this—" A gasp escaped me, but my words kept tumbling out, "Why would she have me if she knew who I would be?"

My heartbeat was the loudest echo I heard.

"Why would she kill herself if she knew I got my powers from her?" I rambled. "I know it was me. I know—"

"She wasn't going to kill herself, Eric."

His words made me stop.

I blinked at my father, but he was the clearest image I saw. His lips bent into a frown, but they shook. "Do you remember that night? The night she took you out to the forest?"

The bats. It was the only time I could see her eyes.

"She was going to kill you."

I couldn't breathe, but my chest moved up and down. My blood coursed through my veins. My mind remained in the eternal race it had always been in. The memories were clearing. She had the gun with her. I remembered seeing its silhouette against the sky, how it was black like the bats.

I leapt to my feet, but my father stayed in his seat. As he looked up at me, he croaked, "That's why I didn't tell you."

My mother—the woman who had given me life—had almost taken mine, and I had left the light on for her. Back at my bedroom, my nightlight was probably on.

"She loved you, Eric, but—"

"Don't."

"Eric." My father stood. "Please." He gestured to my seat. "You need to hear everything. All of it. You're old enough now—"

"I'm eighteen," I spat.

"And I was eighteen when I met your mother," he said it like it meant something, "and she had problems, even back then, and I protected her anyway just like I tried to protect you."

"Protect?" I growled.

"She was only trying to protect you, too." He nodded as if he could ignore my tone and his words at the same time. "She didn't want you to go through the same pain she went through. She—"

"She had me," I pointed out. "That was a choice."

"You weren't planned."

My legs collapsed beneath me, and I fell into my seat. My knees bounced up and down, and my hands shook on top of them. "This is just getting better," I muttered and gripped my hair.

My father's chair squeaked when he sat down. He was her guard, someone who was supposed to protect the bloodline, yet he had been with her. It didn't make sense.

"Are you even my father?" I managed.

"Of course I am." His voice was calm, but it wasn't emotionless. He sounded nothing like the man I used to know. "But we shouldn't have dated. I know that. That was my fault."

Guards were forbidden from dating their warriors. It was a strict rule, as strict as keeping our identities a secret. My father had broken it.

"We didn't date immediately," he added after a moment. "It happened over time. We both fought it, and then, we hid it."

"Until you couldn't," I guessed.

"We used protection." The information was almost too much. "But fate had other things in mind."

My fingers squeezed into fists, but nothing stopped the shaking motion.

"That's why she was sure you would be Shoman," his voice sounded far away, but I listened to every word. "She only kept you because I asked her to."

I covered my ears, and they burned beneath my grasp. My breath had to come and go for minutes before I could remove my hold. "Why?" I asked. "Why keep me?"

"There was no guarantee you would be Shoman."

I glanced up. "Is that how you convinced her?"

"Yes," he spoke without hesitation, "and we were very happy for a while."

I tried to imagine what they were like—sneaking away to have alone time, laughing at one another's jokes, training together for the future—but I could only see the bats. Nothing before that. Nothing after that. I didn't even recall if she took me into the forest where she killed herself, or how she gave me her rings, or if she had cried. I barely heard her voice, but I knew she called me beautiful. How she could say that while planning to kill me was beyond my comprehension.

"Even after she lost her powers, she was happy to have you," he said. "Her father had lost his, and she wasn't the descendant, so she knew there was a chance you might not be—"

"So, what changed?" I interrupted.

His lips pressed into a thin line. The gesture ordered me to think, and it only took me a second to remember all of the events Luthicer had explained.

"Jessica," I whispered her name.

My dad leaned forward. "Your mother wanted to take her in after the car wreck," he paused, "but I was afraid for Jess. I thought—" he paused. "The way your mother looked at her. It was the same look she had when she found out she was pregnant."

"You thought she'd kill her."

"Not exactly," he said, "but I didn't want to risk anything." My dad's brown eyes flickered over his desk as if he wanted to drown himself in his paperwork. "Even after I placed Jess in a home, the look never left her." He drew in a breath. "So, I took you from her. I stopped letting her watch you."

"Why?" The question had been asked so many times that it was beginning to lose meaning, but it continued to fall out of me.

"She had problems before you," he said. "Too many of them to count. When she was fifteen, she tried—" He choked instead of elaborating. "I saved her a few times, but I knew I couldn't save her from herself forever." Her suicide hadn't been her first attempt. "Her childhood wasn't easy."

"Neither was mine."

"Just because your situation is different than hers doesn't

mean she didn't have a reason to struggle, Eric." His tone was taut, filled with a line he was drawing between us. "But you should be glad you don't have the same problems."

Feeling any form of happiness seemed like a wide order for him to give, but I locked my jaw to prevent myself from arguing.

He stared at my mouth like he knew. "She was just as beautiful of a person as she was ugly," he said. "She had many friends, and she didn't hold back, even though she knew they could be in the Light. She loved, and she laughed, and she taught other shades how to understand parts of their powers they couldn't control otherwise." His bottom lip trembled. "She helped them because she couldn't help herself, and I imagine she took her own life because of that."

"Because she couldn't help me," I added the piece left unsaid in his speech.

"It doesn't mean she was right," he spoke so quickly his words melted together. "None of it was right, and I am sorry for that. We made mistakes. We are just as human as we are shades, and—"

"Who are you trying to comfort right now?"

My dad stopped speaking.

I dropped my face. I didn't want to look at him anymore. "I'm sorry."

"You," he paused. "I don't want you to apologize to me anymore."

I stared at the ground. It was speckled with dust, tracked in from the outside world, from the very forest my mother had died in, from the same ground where I had met Jessica.

"I don't remember her killing herself," I said, searching for the next part of the memory, but my father tapped the table to break my concentration.

"She never took you into the forest, Eric," he said. "We found you by the river."

"You were looking for me?"

He repeated how he didn't let her watch me, but explained how he couldn't watch me while pretending to be the leader of the Dark. "The night before, I left you in Urte's care," he said. "When I went to pick you up that morning, he told me she had gotten you already. She had done it before, but since she hadn't arrived at the shelter, we knew something was wrong."

My gut twisted.

"I went straight to the bats." He knew about the nocturnal creatures that had been so important to me. "She always went there when she was in one of her moods."

"She showed them to me."

"I know. She showed them to me, too." His lip pulled up in a shaky smile as he gestured to my ring. "But when I saw you were holding her ring, I knew." Even in the lighting, his eyes reflected the mist covering his irises. "I think I knew before that. I sensed it when she took it off." His hand rose to his face, and he rubbed his eyes. "I only hoped she left you alone, and while I found you—" He stopped. "Urte found your mother."

My trainer had been more involved than I ever realized.

"I didn't sleep that night," he continued. "I think that's why I can't stand the fireworks." She had killed herself on Independence Day. "But I also think that's why you love them so much."

He didn't have to remind me of how much I had begged to sit on top of the hill during the holiday. Every year he took me, and every year, he ended up leaving me there.

"You stayed up with me all night," he explained. "We sat on the front porch, and you just couldn't take your eyes off of them." He fiddled with his shirt before touching his paperwork, before fiddling with his shirt again. "You had the same look on your face when we found you that morning, and you showed me the bats. You loved everything you saw, and I—"

"Dad."

A tear escaped him, and he rubbed it off his cheek. "I am sorry, Eric," he said. "I am so sorry."

"Can you stop apologizing to me?" I repeated the same thing he said to me, but he acted like he hadn't heard. I had to say it again, but this time, I forced a smile. "We aren't going to get anywhere if we keep doing this."

His cheeks sank in, and his lips pressed together, but he

nodded.

I stood up, but my knees weren't shaking anymore. "Thanks for telling me," I formed the words I never thought I would say, "even if it is a little late."

He stared up at me. "A child shouldn't know these things about a parent."

"I'm not a kid anymore," I said, even though I wanted to be. I was only eighteen, but I didn't have the luxury of a normal childhood, and for once, I didn't want it. I wanted to live my own life. "I think—" I paused and tried to find the words I logically had, but had yet to emotionally feel. "I have a lot to think about," I managed, "but you did what you could."

"Let me do more," he insisted and stood up. "Let me help you now."

"You can't," I said, knowing I had to fight Darthon on my own. "But I will let you know if you can," I added before he could argue. "I'm going home for a bit."

He closed his mouth only to open it again. "Mindy and Noah will like that."

"I won't be late."

"Stay out as late as you want," he said. "Just come back in one piece."

THIRTY-SEVEN

Jessica

"THAT'S IT." I POINTED TO CRYSTAL'S HOUSE, AND JONATHON parked two houses down. We were both humans—for now.

He killed the lights, but kept the engine on. "Are you sure about this, Jess?"

"How many times are you going to ask me that?" I unbuckled my seatbelt before turning to him. In the dark, his eyes were green. He had to use his shade sight while driving. "You saw Eric's face. They're involved."

"What if Crystal is too?"

I dropped eye contact. "I'll text you if anything goes wrong," I said as I stepped out of the vehicle. I shut the door before he could repeat the question.

As much as she was a gossiping punk, Crystal was my best friend. She showed me around Hayworth, even before Eric did. While Eric showed me my shade identity, Crystal helped me find one as a human. She never spread rumors about me, she always confided in me, and when I thought about our friendship, I smiled. Even though she didn't remember it, she stood up for me when Robb attacked me, and she would again when her memories returned. Until then, I had to push my personal life aside. The prophecy was bigger than my problems, and it had to be dealt with first.

I stayed focused as I walked up to Crystal's house, stopping at the end of her driveway. She already stood on her front porch, and her eyes gazed down the street. "Who's that?" she asked, even though she wasn't stupid. She knew whose car it was. She always knew everything.

"A friend dropped me off," I said, waiting for her to question the fact that Jonathon Stone and I knew each other outside of school, but she didn't.

She pointed her head toward her car. "Ready?"

Her voice wasn't bouncing as it usually was. It was tight and strained. She almost sounded like someone else entirely.

"Yeah." My grip tightened on my bag when she didn't walk toward the car. Zac and Robb must have already been waiting. "Are you?"

She nodded as she stepped off the porch, but she didn't speak as she walked toward the car. It was only then that I was able to see her stride. She was marching like a warrior headed into battle.

Perhaps she was involved, after all.

———◆———

Zac's clothes matched his pitch-black hair. He blended into the darkness as he picked a table on the patio. Robb, on the other hand, glowed in his red coat, but neither of the boys sat down as we took our places at the coffee shop. Even though it was cold, it was nice enough to sit outside, and we were all desperate for fresh air—except for Robb. I half-expected him to smoke later on.

Robb pulled his wallet out of his back pocket. "What do you two want?"

"Macchiato for me," Crystal answered. "Black coffee for Jess."

I stared at her, and she shot me a grin. "Am I right?"

She was, so I nodded.

"We'll be back," Zac said before the two ducked inside the building.

The coffee shop lit up the only shopping street Hayworth

had, but I couldn't see Jonathon's car parked anywhere. I had to trust him when he said he would be watching. This place set my nerves on edge. Even though the coffee shop was only one year old, I was familiar with it. Too familiar. In my first semester at Hayworth High, Eric had ditched me here during our project, and this was the last place I ever saw Camille as Teresa alive. Crystal had been with me that night, too, and staring at my friend was an eerie reminder of the time she left me alone, oblivious to what I would later face. I couldn't blame her, but I wished we had picked somewhere else to go.

"You okay?" Crystal broke through my thoughts as she spoke.

I nodded.

"You seem tense." Her brown eyes dragged over my face. "Just the date?"

"Yeah."

Her right cheek lifted with a half-smile. "I didn't mean for this to happen, you know," she started and stared at the street. "I just hated to see Eric acting so calm about it all."

Eric. She had only recently begun using his first name. When I first met her, she called him Welborn like everyone else, but she eased into it better than I had. I knew it was because she used to call him Eric before, when they were kids.

"Why did you two stop being friends?" I asked.

Crystal's back pressed into her chair. "After Hannah died, he started getting in fights, and I didn't like it." She made a squeaking noise in-between her sentences. "It reminded me of my dad."

A fog crossed her gaze, but everything was clear to me. She hardly spoke of her father. All I knew of the man was how early he had left her life. I didn't know why he divorced her mom or stayed out of her life, but I imagined the reason wasn't good.

"He wasn't the nicest man," she said, glancing over her shoulder to look into the coffee shop. "But he's still my dad, you know?"

I did understand. I didn't have a single memory of my

birth parents, but they remained in my heart as much as my adoptive parents. Even after everything I learned, I loved them both.

"Do you talk at all?" I managed, wondering what it was like to actually have the opportunity to speak to someone who gave you life.

"No." Her single word was harsh. "It's weird, I know, but I don't want to," she stumbled over her words. "Not anymore."

I didn't have a chance to ask her why or question why she was telling me tonight because the door chimed behind me. I knew the boys had returned before they even announced their presence, and I wasn't about to continue our conversation in front of them. It was something Crystal and I shared. She was my only friend who knew I was born and adopted out of Hayworth, and a part of me knew I was the only friend she talked about her dad with.

Zac laid a drink in front of her as he sat between us. "One macchiato for the lady."

"And one black coffee," Robb used Zac's sentence to create his own as he sat on the opposite side of me. The boys were in-between us, and the round table had never seemed so large.

I grabbed the hot mug to stop my fingers from shaking, and I took a sip even though I knew it would burn. I wanted my insides to be warmed up.

"It's kind of hot—" Robb started.

"It's fine," I promised after I consumed the sizzling liquid.

Robb chuckled. "You're tougher than I am."

"She's a tough chick," Crystal said, but it didn't sound friendly. It sounded like a threat, but she quickly covered her tone with a large grin. "I've seen this girl run a hundred miles an hour before." But she hadn't. "You should've joined track."

My face burned. "When have you seen me running?"

"You go jogging all the time." Crystal waved my question away. "It's a small town. I've driven by you before."

"I have, too," Zac mentioned as he raised his cup up. "You are a fast one."

The memory was one I could never forget. While I was

having nightmares, I ran after one. It was the only way I felt like I had any control, and Zac was the one to pull up in Robb's car. Even though Robb had explained it, I didn't believe their excuse, but our conversation only deepened my confusion. I couldn't figure out which memories my friends had and which ones they didn't.

"Maybe we can go running sometime," Robb said. "I go jogging on Saturday mornings."

"I didn't know," I mumbled into my cup as I avoided his offer. I didn't want to spend more time with him. I wanted to spend time with Zac, and I needed to find a way to get him alone if I were going to test him.

"I used to play basketball in middle school," Robb continued, "and Zac and I were on a soccer team as kids."

"Don't remind me," Zac muttered.

"What?" Crystal beamed. "I didn't know that."

"There's a reason for that," Zac said.

"Our parents were close, so they wanted us to be," Robb continued anyway. "It was a soccer league outside of school since we went to separate schools. What were we? Five?"

"Six."

"He could barely kick the ball." Robb laughed as he leaned over the table to hit Zac's arm. "You're better now."

"I don't play now." Zac formed a smile when he looked at Crystal. "It was a long time ago."

A long history hung between everyone at the table but me, and I wished I had taken notes over everything I had learned from them. If what Jonathon had told me was true, Zac's mother had died when he was a kid. In fact, it would've happened around the same time Eric's mom died, but the two boys couldn't have reacted more differently. Zac didn't seem bothered by it at all. It fit Darthon's personality perfectly.

I gulped down the rest of my coffee. "I'm going to get another one." I stood up before Robb could offer. "Want to get Crystal another one?" I asked Zac.

He stared up at me, but didn't move. "She isn't finished."

"Yes, I am." Crystal slammed her cup down like she had

downed a beer.

Zac glanced from her to me, and I waited for him to ask what was going on, but he didn't have a chance.

"It's okay," Robb said and slid his chair away from the table. "I'll grab you one."

A silent curse took over my heart.

"Thanks, man," Zac dismissed his friend, and I knew what had happened. Robb was giving his friend the chance to be alone with his girlfriend. I had lost my chance for now.

I walked into the coffee shop without waiting for Robb, but he caught up with me. "Let me get yours, too," he said before ordering the same drinks.

"Thanks," I muttered, even though I wanted to say the opposite. It wasn't Robb's fault. He didn't know.

I went to the pick-up counter to wait and kept my eyes on Crystal and Zac through the window. The murky glass made it hard to see him, but I could make out Crystal's white hair. If he attacked her, I would know.

Robb appeared next to me after he paid. "I hope I didn't ruin something."

I glanced over. "Why would you say that?"

He fiddled with his shirt. "You seemed like you wanted to talk to Zac."

I shrugged. "Valentine's Day is next week." The lie slipped out easily. "I was going to see if he needed help picking out a present."

Robb leaned against the counter, inches away from me, and caught my stare. His brown eyes were as warm as the coffee we drank. "You're a really good friend, Jess."

I tried to shift away without him noticing. "Thanks," I managed, even though it wasn't the truth.

I was putting Crystal in danger by allowing her to be around them, but she was dating Zac, and there was nothing I could do about it. Asking Zac out alone wasn't a possibility, not without a potential fight breaking out. In the end, if he were Darthon, the Dark would kill him. We would have to kill Crystal's boyfriend, and when she mourned, I would have to comfort her. How I would face her was beyond me. I would lose her, too, and I knew that was why Jonathon had brought it up in the car. He didn't want to say it out loud because he knew I would realize it.

Everything was getting more complicated by the second.

"Are you okay, Jess?"

"What?"

Robb leaned closer, and his finger skimmed my cheek. "Your face is all red."

I pulled away and stumbled into a trashcan. It fell over, and half of the coffee shop stood up. Everyone's eyes were on me.

"Sorry," I muttered and bent down to pick it up.

"Relax." Robb touched my shoulder as he knelt down. I straightened up to get away, but he didn't look at me as he cleaned up my mess.

I had to shove my hands in my pockets to keep them from shaking. I had lost my concentration.

"Robb." The barista called his name as she placed two cups of coffee on the counter. He grabbed the drinks and apologized for the mess. "Don't worry about it," she said. "Happens all the time."

He shifted toward the exit. "Let's go outside."

"I'm going to use the restroom," I dismissed myself so I didn't have to follow him. Before he could question me again, I said, "I'll be out in a minute."

I concentrated on my walking so I didn't run. Every step felt lighter than the first one, and every part of me wanted to run just like I had so many times before. If I lost control now, everyone would be in danger, and I wouldn't even have the chance to learn anything.

When I got into the bathroom, I locked the door behind me. *"Jonathon."* Our connection buzzed, and I had to take two breaths before I felt it solidify. *"Jonathon."*

"You okay?" His voice was already high.

"Fine," I promised. *"Are you close?"*

"I'm in the alleyway."

That explained why the car was out of sight. He had parked out of view.

"*Give me ten more minutes,*" I said.

"*I don't know if you have the time.*"

My heart pounded. "*What do you mean?*"

"*Zac and Crystal just walked past me.*"

I grabbed the doorknob and ran out of the bathroom. Zac was taking Crystal away, and I couldn't let that happen. I practically broke down the exit door to get outside, and the cold air slammed into me like it wanted to push me back.

Jonathon wasn't wrong. Crystal and Zac were walking down the street, and Robb was sitting at our table by himself.

"Where are they going?" I asked and started to walk toward them.

Robb stood up and grabbed my arm. "They just wanted to talk," he said, dropping his hand. "I think they wanted more time alone."

I stared at their backs as their bodies melted into silhouettes against the street lamps. "Are they fighting?"

"Not at all." Robb pulled out my chair. "They're fine."

I looked at him before glancing at Crystal. If I followed her, it would look suspicious. "*Keep your eyes on them,*" I spoke to Jonathon, and he confirmed my order.

She would be safe for now. I would have to wait until they returned.

I plopped down in my seat, and a sigh escaped me. I covered my mouth as if I could take it back, but I knew it was too late. Robb had heard me. I glanced at him. "Sorry."

He shook his head. "It's okay." A smile spread across his lips. "I know you don't like me like that."

My throat tightened so I couldn't speak.

He didn't talk either. He simply pulled out his cigarettes, packed them against the palm of his hand, and pulled one out. He put it up to his lips before he asked if I minded.

"I don't care," I said, even though a part of me did. The smoke bothered me, but the expression that had crossed his face bothered me more.

Fine lines had appeared beneath his eyes, but his gaze deepened as he lit it. The orange end lit up as he dragged in, and his shoulders relaxed as he breathed out. "I know you only agreed to this to get back at Eric."

"It's not like that—"

"I did it to get back at Linda," he said it so simply, like he wasn't afraid of exposing his darker side, like he wanted me to see all sides of him. He took another drag before he spoke again, "But I don't mind that we both agreed to it." He squinted through the cloud of smoke. "It means we have something in common."

I wanted to argue with him, to tell him I had other reasons, but I couldn't explain I was after Darthon. Robb thought I was crazy enough after I told him about my nightmares. I knew him well enough not to confide in him. Plus, the subject matter wasn't exactly acceptable.

"I guess," I finally agreed as I leaned over and picked up my second coffee.

"They're good for one another, aren't they?" Robb's voice sounded far away.

I wasn't sure if he was talking about Crystal and Zac or Eric and Linda until I studied him. His gaze was locked on Crystal and Zac. When I glanced over my shoulder, they were near the end of the street. They would have to come back soon.

"I guess."

"Do you like Zac?"

My neck snapped as I turned to Robb. "What?"

He shrugged. "You seem," he paused, "focused."

"I don't like him," I practically snarled, but the dramatic tone took the opposite effect I wanted to get across.

Robb tilted his head. "He liked you for the longest time," he said. "I always thought you two would end up together, especially after prom." He took another drag, but he blew his smoke away from the table. "I think he thought that, too."

"Then, why'd he date Crystal?"

"Zac likes her, too."

"You can't like two people at the same time," I said.

"Why not?"

"Because," I paused because I didn't have an argument. I had never liked two people at the same time. I had only liked Eric, but I wasn't everyone. I didn't have the right to discount other people's feelings. Still, the concept was beyond me. "I guess I just don't feel that way," I finally managed.

"You still like Eric?"

My face heated up, but it cooled the second Robb's chair scraped across the ground. He had moved closer. His cigarette smoke burned my nostrils.

"I don't like the smoking," I choked.

He leaned over and put his cigarette out on the table. "I know."

The end sizzled out in a light stream of gray. I watched it until it disappeared. Every part of it reminded me of transporting as a shade, and every piece of me wanted to transport back to the shelter, to the place Eric told me not to leave. I was failing—again—and figuring out if Zac was Darthon seemed to be getting further out of my reach.

"What's this?" Robb's fingers grazed my neck.

I shivered and pulled back. "What?"

Robb didn't try to touch me again. He stayed in his chair and pointed to my collarbone. "You're wearing a necklace."

My hand landed on my chest where the ring laid against my sternum. "It's just jewelry—"

His eyebrows lowered, settling right above his eyes. They were golden in the dim light. "You're still wearing it, aren't you?"

My grip tightened. "So, what?"

"So?" He placed his elbows on the table. "You guys aren't together anymore. He treated you like crap, Jess."

"You don't know him," I snapped, but my voice came out as a whisper.

"I know how he treated you," he emphasized. "From the beginning, that guy pushed you away." He scooted his chair closer, and every part of me was paralyzed. "How hard does he have to shove you before you realize you've already fallen down?"

Eric's ring. It burned my palm through my shirt, and my hand dropped to my lap. I stared at my hand as it shook, but it only shook more when I saw my skin. It was red. I hadn't imagined it. The ring had physically burned me.

"Trust me for a minute?" Robb spoke, but his voice sounded like it was underwater. I barely felt him as his fingers skimmed the necklace, but his cold touch was strangely soothing. It curled through my veins as he dragged his hand to the nape of my neck. When he unclipped the jewelry, he pulled the necklace up, and the ring burned my skin as he pulled it up.

I breathed when he finally took it away, and the cold comfort dug against my gut. The feeling was one I felt before. It reminded me of the red rain, the chilling river where I had been reborn. My powers sizzled somewhere deep inside of me.

"See? It's not that hard," he spoke.

His voice broke the sickening sensation.

"Don't you feel better?"

I did, but I wouldn't admit it. The Light's power felt stronger, closer, and it tempted every part of me to succumb to it. Even then, a second heartbeat had left me. Eric's. It was gone. As Robb dropped the jewelry on the table, it pinged with the last beats I had felt. The blue jewelry was no longer glowing. It looked like something I had never seen before, and I knew it was the jewelry that had held me together all along. The Light would not take me over.

I reached for it, but Robb put his hand over it. "You don't need him."

"Give it back." This time, my voice was loud.

Robb didn't budge. "You'll get used to it—"

I ignored his words, wrapped my hands around his wrist, and yanked his hand away. The force was strong enough to rock the table, and my ring dropped through a hole. I dove to the ground and snatched it up before it stayed away for too long. I didn't even care about the necklace. I shoved the ring back onto my finger. The metal burned, but the burn sizzled into my veins, and my insides heated up. I was warm again. I could breathe again.

"Jess?"

I spun around, nearly hitting my head on the table, and Crystal stepped back when we met eyes. She looked from Robb to me, but she stayed focused on me as she walked over to me. "Are you okay?"

"Yeah," I muttered and stood up. Zac was by her side. "I can't do this." The words left me.

Crystal's arm threaded with mine in an instant. "Want me to take you home?"

I nodded back. "Right now." I didn't even look at Robb as I started to walk. Crystal had to call over her shoulder to let them know we were leaving, and her words were the best ones I had heard all night.

The worst ones came from Robb, but so did the worst realization. The jewelry was more than jewelry. It didn't just connect Eric to me. It connected the Dark to my powers, and if I took it off, I didn't know what would happen, but I did know one thing.

Eric was alive because of his mother's jewelry.

THIRTY-EIGHT

"IT'S GOOD TO SEE YOU," MINDY SAID FOR THE UMPTEENTH TIME AS she heated up the oven. I had only been home for fifteen minutes, and she was already baking lemon cakes. Even though I told her not to, she didn't listen. A part of me was glad she hadn't.

"It's good to be home," I breathed and leaned my chair on the back legs.

"Noah will be happy to see you," she said, even though we both knew the truth.

Her son was under an illusion. Noah wouldn't know I was even gone. He probably had false memories of me living right next to him. My presence would be nothing unusual to him.

"How is he doing?" I asked, knowing he was at a friend's house. I would only get to see him for a minute before I had to return to the shelter.

Mindy's low hum made me look her way. When a red curl fell from her bun, she blew it out of her face. "He's a little different," she admitted, "but it won't be long."

I sat all four legs of my chair on the floor. "You didn't have to agree."

"Yes, I did." She picked up a tray and slid it into the oven. "It'll be fifteen minutes," she said. "Think you can stay that long?"

"Sure."

She beamed as she walked around the kitchen counter and came into the dining room. She brought tea with her, and she slid a mug toward me before sitting next to me. There were six chairs at our table, mainly because we always had Urte over, but she sat in the chair closest to me. Mindy didn't even hesitate to put her hand on my shoulder.

"I am glad you're home."

"You can stop saying that," I chuckled.

"Sorry." Her face was as bright as her hair. "It gets lonely here sometimes."

My dad was practically gone, too. He rarely left the shelter. I doubted they had seen one another much at all, and the house was too big for two people. After my mother died, it had echoed from my father's silence. It hadn't been loud again until my stepfamily moved in.

"I know I don't say this a lot—if ever," I hesitated and had to stare at the table to continue, "but I'm glad you married my father. He's happy now."

Mindy didn't talk until I looked up. "He's happier when you're safe."

My jaw locked, and then popped as I shifted it around to speak again, "I'm sorry your son isn't." It was all because of me that Noah had to be under an illusion.

"He's safe because of you," Mindy said, and her squeaky voice had never sounded so comforting. "I know you didn't know him before, but he was really quiet until the marriage."

"He loves my dad—"

"Noah loves you," she emphasized. "Really. The boy doesn't stop talking about you." She took a sip of her tea, and her bangs became frizzy in the steam. "He toughened up a lot after he started spending time with you."

"He's a tough kid."

She agreed. "And if Jess' parents can go through it, then my son can."

My chest sank. Noah wasn't the only human affected by my life or Jessica's existence. The entirety of Hayworth had succumbed to the danger, even if they were oblivious to it.

231

"I'd like to meet them one day," Mindy continued. "I bet Jess' parents are as sweet as she is."

"We broke up—"

"Please," she interrupted. "I know better than that."

I couldn't fight a smile, but the smile did fight me. It felt wrong to be grinning in such a time over such a topic. "I'm sure you'll get to meet them," I finally agreed.

"I'll have to make lasagna." Her face glowed as she dreamt of the day we could be together. "I'm known for that meal, you know." She winked. "I think it's why your father married me."

Before I could respond, the door burst open. "I'm home." Noah's shout traveled over us as he ran up the stairs.

"I'm making lemon cakes," Mindy announced as she stood up. "I should check on them."

"Why?" Noah asked as he stopped at the top of the stairs and saw me. "It's not your birthday."

A chuckle escaped me. "That's a good thing."

Noah's face twisted. "You're weird," he said, but he walked to the table. He dropped his bag on the furthest chair, and just like his mother, he sat in a chair right next to me.

I stared at him. His face hadn't changed much, but he had gotten a haircut. Even then, his short hair was a mess.

"You got a haircut," I said.

He rolled his eyes. "Where have you been?"

Dishes clattered together in the kitchen, and Mindy apologized. She had dropped something, and I imagined it was from Noah's question. It was perfectly natural, but in the situation, it felt uncomfortable.

"School," I spoke up anyway.

Noah's brow furrowed like he didn't believe me. "I thought you might have been with Jess."

My face went hot. "We aren't together," I reminded him.

"Yeah. Yeah." He stood up from the table. "I'm going to my room."

"Good to see you," I called after him as he started walking away.

Right when I thought he would disappear into his room,

he spun around. "Good to see you, too." And then, he was gone.

Mindy leaned on the counter. "He's had an attitude recently."

"The spell will wear off."

She smiled. "It's not the spell," she said and reclipped her hair. "He's almost a teenager now."

I stared at the hallway like my stepbrother was standing there. "Yeah," I breathed. "I guess he is." Noah, somewhere along the way, had a birthday. He was eleven. I had completely forgotten the date.

Before I could speak again, a chill ran over my skin, and nausea consumed my insides. My heart slammed into my chest, but it didn't beat. It froze.

I fell over, and the ground spun as I hit the floor. Pain seethed down my spine, but the pain in my chest was worse. Much worse. Everything burned. Everything squeezed. I couldn't breathe. I couldn't move.

"Eric!" Mindy's scream shattered through the fog. I clung to the noise to prevent myself from losing consciousness.

My vision was blurry, but I could see her red hair through my misty vision. "Eric—"

I was going to die.

The darkness was creeping over the sides of my vision, and my chest was caving in. The only thing I could feel was the cold, and it was a cold I had only felt once before. In the Light realm, I had died, but this time, I wasn't there. I was in the human world, and nothing was here to bring me back.

Right when I thought the darkness would win, everything brightened. The world buzzed, and my mind spun, and the ringlets around Mindy's face solidified. Her face was pale.

"Eric."

I wheezed, but my heart raced, beating against my ribs as if it had been shocked into living again. I coughed as air rushed down my esophagus. I was alive.

"What's going on?" Noah. He was walking toward us.

"It's fine," Mindy called over her shoulder, but she never took her eyes off of me. She placed the back of her hand on my forehead. "Do you need me to call an ambulance?"

"No. No." That was the last thing we needed. "I'm okay."

I laid my head against the ground as it thundered with blood returning. I hadn't been wrong. My life had almost left me.

"Is Eric okay?" Noah peered over his mother's shoulder.

"I'm all right," I promised again and shoved my arms under me. I took a breath before pushing myself up. "I just got dizzy," I said, even though my thoughts were consuming me.

My ring kept me alive in the Light realm, but I hadn't considered that it kept me alive in the human world, too. Jessica. She must have taken hers off.

"I have to go," I said, but when I stood up, I fell into my seat. My strength wasn't returning as quickly as I wanted it to.

"Just sit for a minute," Mindy said. As she rushed into the kitchen, she told Noah to watch me. He sat down, but not as close as he had sat before.

"Are you—"

I shushed him. I didn't want to, but I had to concentrate. I unlocked the block I placed on Jonathon's telepathic thread to my mind. *"Pierce—"*

My mind burned before I could even finish my sentence. I didn't have the strength. I had one last resort. I yanked my phone out of my pocket and dialed his number. It rang and rang and rang again, and then it clicked.

"Jonathon," I spoke before he could. "Where's Jessica?"

He was silent for a millisecond too long. "Eric?"

"It's me," I ranted. "Where is she? Is she okay?" If her date had taken a bad turn, I needed to know.

"She's fine."

"Where is she?" I growled through my pain.

"I—um—Crystal is driving her right now." I could hear his car's engine in the background. He was following them. "She's fine. They both are."

I didn't care about Crystal. "Are you sure Jessica is okay?"

"Positive," he answered, but his voice moved into his next sentence without a breath. "Why are you calling? Are you all

234

right?"

"I'm fine," I said right before I hung up. I dropped my phone on the table, and all the muscles in my hands tingled. I had to draw in a breath to prevent them from shaking, but the pause allowed me to see what was in front of me.

Noah and Mindy were staring.

"I have to go," I said as I stood up. My legs didn't fall beneath me this time. I would be okay in minutes, and I had to meet Jessica back at the shelter. I had to see her for myself.

"But Mom made cake—" Noah started, but Mindy interrupted.

"Go," she said. "Do what you need to do."

I nodded. "I'll come back for cake soon," I said, but as I started to walk away, Mindy cut me off for a hug. She wrapped her arms around me almost as quickly as she stepped away.

"I can always cook more," she said. "Stay safe."

"I will," I promised before I raced down the stairs toward the darkness that had almost taken me minutes before.

THIRTY-NINE

Jessica

CRYSTAL DROVE ME TO MY HOUSE, BUT I NEVER WENT INSIDE. I waited on the front porch until she left. I had to tell Jonathon what she told me in the car, and every second that passed seemed too long to bear. It only took two minutes for Jonathon to appear. I jumped in the passenger side, but he didn't take off like I expected him to.

"Is everything okay?" his voice rushed in the same way I wanted his car to do.

"I don't know," I admitted before I corrected myself. "No. Something is wrong."

Jonathon reached up to put his car in park, but I grabbed his hand. "Not here," I said. "We need to go to the shelter."

He blinked, but obeyed. When he rotated his wheel, the front tires squeaked, and the small car lurched as he stepped on the gas. "I don't drive a lot."

"Doesn't matter," I said, collecting my thoughts. "The jewelry. It—" I couldn't fathom what I was thinking. "We need to make sure Eric is okay."

Jonathon gripped the wheel, but he didn't increase his speed. "He's fine."

"But—"

"He called me, Jess."

My heart was beating faster than normal, and my hand curled into a fist. My ring was back on my finger. It no longer burned, but it did glow. The sapphire was bright, and I wasn't imagining it.

"Does that happen a lot?" Jonathon asked.

"You can see it?"

He nodded, even though he had kept his eyes on the road. It was that bright. "Why is it back on your hand?"

"I took it off," I admitted. "Robb—" I thought I would lose my breath. "He took it off, and I felt it. I felt Eric leave, and—"

Jonathon's breath was sharp as he pulled his car over.

"What are you doing?" I nearly screeched.

He put his car in park and switched off his headlights. "You need to calm down," he said it like his father did—as a trainer instead of a guard. "Acting on emotions won't get us anywhere. It's dangerous."

I only stared back.

"Take a breath."

His voice was the only thing I heard, so I obeyed, and every racing part of me simmered down. Every part of me but my heart. It thundered.

"Feel better?" he asked.

"A little."

"You and Eric both," he chuckled. "You're both so hot-tempered."

"It's kind of a tense situation," I started, but Jonathon shushed me.

"Just breathe."

I did.

"Eric called me," he spoke while I calmed down. "He's fine. He sounded fine. He was just worried about you because you went out on a date. That's it. Okay?"

He waited for a response, but I kept my mouth shut. I was sure my nerves would heighten again.

"Did you get a chance to test him?"

I shook my head because I knew he was talking about Zac. "He walked away."

"And you left when he came back," he finished. "I thought something might have happened." His tone dropped, and it was only then that I noticed the sweat on the side of his face. He had been worried about me, too.

"Something happened," I confessed. "I took off the ring."

Jonathon's eyes shot down to my hand. "You said Robb did."

My nod almost hurt my neck. "He wanted to be alone with me," I explained. "He told me that Zac and Crystal wanted to be alone, but Crystal told me it was the other way around in the car." I told him everything that happened—how Crystal had rushed us to the car, how she thought Robb was acting strange, how he had asked them if he could have a minute with me. She had cursed at herself in the car when I told her about the ring, and an apology had escaped her before she drove off. She was in a hurry.

"I think the ring kept Eric alive in the Light realm," I said without telling Jonathon the other part. It had kept me alive, too. When I had tried to kill myself, I hadn't died. If there was any explanation, it existed in a tiny piece of metal a mother had left behind. "Darthon can't kill him, and that's why." I even told Jonathon about what I learned in the realm, how I had accused Darthon of being unable to kill Eric and how he had confirmed it. "Eric can't die."

Jonathon didn't move, but his face paled. "But you took it off."

"Only for a minute," I promised, but I grabbed Jonathon's arm like I needed to hear more from him. "Are you sure he is okay?"

Jonathon pulled away from me so he could start the car. "He said he was all right before he hung up on me," he confessed. My blood ran cold. "We should check on him."

He took off without waiting for my confirmation. The shelter was only ten minutes away, but it was long enough for me to ask the one question I could manage, "Do you think—"

"That Robb could be Darthon?" Jonathon knew what I was thinking. "Definitely."

My palms were sweating, but I brought them up to my pounding forehead. "Oh, God." Robb had been so close. All along. Both of them had been. But I hadn't considered Robb as much as I had thought about Zac. Even though Robb had hit me at the bar, Zac was the only one who remembered it—that we knew of—and Zac had threatened Eric from the beginning. Zac had also left prom when I had. Robb had stayed behind with Linda, so it made sense for Zac to be able to be Darthon that night. Zac also didn't seem to care about his parents, but Robb hadn't mentioned his in depth. Still, Linda was around both of them. So was Crystal. Either of them could be Fudicia. Either of the boys could be Darthon. And both Zac and Robb had used force against me at some point. Even then, it was Robb who had taken my ring. He was also the one trying to get closer to me. And yet, at the beginning of our friendship, he had encouraged me to get closer to Eric. None of it made sense.

"I don't know anymore," I said before I cursed.

"Calm down," Jonathon reminded me.

"I didn't even get a chance to test them," I admitted, knowing my plan failed. I was sure I could use my powers to feel his. If I had the chance to touch him, I was positive I would feel it if I concentrated, but I had lost all concentration. When I had the opportunity to touch Robb, I was too busy trying to get my ring back. I had lost my chance. "I didn't get a chance to test him," I repeated.

"Maybe he was testing you."

I couldn't breathe.

"Relax," Jonathon kept repeating the same phrase like it could change our circumstances. "You figured out something, right?" His voice raced as fast as his car took the last corner. "That's enough. That got us a step further, so stop questioning it."

I stared at Jonathon. The scrawny boy who was so built as a shade seemed more powerful than he ever had before. His squinted eyes were focused, and he wasn't even using his shade vision. Even though he was telling me to concentrate, he couldn't either. What we had learned was deadly. The problem rested in the fact that Darthon could've learned it, too.

239

FORTY

I WAS ONLY FIVE YARDS AWAY FROM THE SHELTER WHEN I SAW HIM.
Darthon was standing by the edge of the river—next to the
railing where I had first met Jessica—but he wasn't in his
light form. He was Robb, and I was Eric. We were both humans, and I knew why. The Dark could sense him if he were a
light. As Robb, he wouldn't even hit their radar.

I froze, but his stare was already on me. He even knew
what direction I would be coming from. He was waiting. "Eric."

Every part of me told me to run, but I didn't. I stood my
ground. The forest was my territory. Not his. He could take a
part of my freewill away, but he wouldn't take everything. Not
Jessica. Not my place. Not my life. I wouldn't die as long as we
had our rings on.

"Go ahead and scream," he said. "Call for your elders. Call
for your guard."

His words were empty because they were dead. He had
killed Camille, his people had killed Eu, and he was here to kill
me, even though he couldn't.

"I guess your date didn't go well," I said.

He walked toward me, and right when I thought he would
hit me, he threw something at me. It hit me in the face before I
realized what it was. Jessica's necklace. The chain that held her
ring no longer hung on her neck.

"Why is she wearing it?" he growled. "I told you to stay

240

away from her—"

"I have been," I snapped. As I picked it up off the ground, my fingers shook. If it wasn't on her, she had taken it off. The reason I had almost succumbed to darkness was clearing. In the human realm, the spell wasn't as strong. I would die if she simply took off her ring. Darthon didn't even have to try to kill me.

I slid the chain into my pocket. Knowing she must have put it back on was my only comfort, but my biggest worry stood right in front of me. Whether Robb had figured it out or not was still a mystery.

"Take your ring off," he barked.

"No."

He punched me, and I stumbled back. Even though he was a human, he was fast. Just as fast as me. He had trained in both forms, too.

"Take it off, Welborn."

I rubbed my face, but I kept stepping back. He followed me. "I gave you an order."

"You can't force me," I growled.

"I own you."

"You control my voice," I said back. "Not my physical movements." My hands rose in front of my chest. I would fight him. Unlike me, he could die, and all I needed was a moment like this—clouded in darkness, we could both have powers. "You sure you're not the one who should be calling your elders?"

He didn't step toward me. "I came on my own."

If he had brought lights with him, the Dark would've sensed it, but I didn't believe him. There had to be others waiting nearby. Other humans waiting to transform.

"Where are Linda and Zac?" I asked, but I didn't dare search the trees with my eyes. If I didn't look at him, he would attack. "You don't fight alone. Not in this world."

Robb didn't argue.

"You can take me back to your realm," I suggested. "Go ahead. See if anything changes."

"I'll figure it out," he snapped, "and if I don't, I'll just kill her instead."

His words were the opposite of what they should've been. He wanted to threaten me when he had told me everything I needed to know. He still didn't know the jewelry kept me alive. He only thought it kept Jessica's powers tied to the Dark.

"I felt it," he said. "She took it off, and I felt it." He took a step toward me. "Her powers. They shifted when it was off. It's stopping her from coming to me—"

"She's never going to come to you," I interrupted.

When I took a step toward him, he froze. "You can't fight me."

"I can," I said because I knew he wouldn't kill Jessica. "And I will."

"I gave you orders—"

"And I haven't broken them yet," I pointed out, never dropping my hands. Every part of me wanted to transform, but the smallest slice of my soul held me back. If I transformed, he would, and it would be war. The shelter wouldn't even have time to prepare. More people would die. I needed to get Darthon alone, and I needed him to be as far away from the shelter as possible.

"Let's go somewhere else," I suggested. "Battle this out for good."

He smiled, but the corners of his mouth shook. When a breeze passed between us, he actually looked away from me—toward the woods, toward the place I was sure his comrades were hiding. "Have you spoken to your father yet?"

"Yes."

"And?"

"And I don't care."

His face was as red as his jacket. "They lied to you."

"People lie for a reason." In all the years I thought my dad had hated my existence, I now knew my dad had tried to protect me, even though he couldn't. "I stand by their decisions."

His fists curled as he raised them, and his shoulders broadened. I half-expected him to transform, but he didn't. "I'm not going to lose this, Welborn."

"You need Jessica to win," I pointed out, "and she's figuring you out on her own, Robb." I used his name to emphasize his identity. "She only went out with you to test you guys."

It was the last sentence that did it. He shot forward, and punches were thrown. When he hit me, a pain seethed down my neck, but my fist landed on his jaw. We stumbled back, only to move forward again. In seconds, we were on the ground, and a tangy liquid filled my mouth.

Blood.

I didn't bother to breathe as I hit his ribs, and he reacted by kicking my shin. We scrambled against the cold grass, and dirt flew up as we stood, only to fall again. It was the fall he took advantage of.

His fingers wrapped through my hair, and he slammed my face into the ground. His foot was on my back before I could even fight back. "Why you?" he screamed at the back of my head. "What's so great about you?"

My cheek burned as I squirmed beneath him.

"You're pathetic."

Robb had trained more as a human than I had. I knew that now. My spine stung as he twisted my head. He was attempting to break my neck, but it didn't work. I swung my arm up and held my head in place. Urte had taught me more defense than anything.

Robb's breathing was all I could hear as he tried again. Every part of me hurt.

"You can't kill me," I seethed, and blood escaped my mouth. It mixed with the dirt.

"Go ahead. Transform." His voice was ear splitting. "Declare war."

He wanted the blood to be on my hands.

I squirmed under his foot, unable to gain control again, but I wouldn't do what he said. I wouldn't allow any more of my people to die, but for once, I didn't want more of his people to die either. If Jessica was one of them, if Luthicer and Camille had been a part of the Light, then I didn't want anyone to die. I only wanted Robb to see it, too.

"Why don't you do it?" He let go of my head, only to kick me in the back of it. "Do it, Welborn. Just do it."

"Why don't you?" I formed a response before he slammed his foot into my ribs. I braced for another, but he didn't kick me again. The ground shifted as he stepped away.

Thinking it was my only chance to gain control, I rolled over, but Robb wasn't in a fighting stance. He was walking away.

"That's it?" I called after him as I stumbled to my feet. Even my knees were weak. "You're giving up?"

"Far from it," he said and continued toward the trees. "You have company."

Before I could chase him, a beam of light—brighter than the sun—shot out of him, and he transported away. Robb used his powers, and his force vibrated through the trees. The Dark would know he was here, and he wasn't even trying to hide it.

That's when I heard it.

"Eric!" Jessica's voice.

She was running toward me, but she was too far away to see what had happened. Darthon wasn't giving up. He still wanted her, and he wanted me to know it.

FORTY-ONE

ERIC WAS BLEEDING, AND HE SPAT OUT MORE BLOOD WHEN HE SAT up on the ground. He didn't even look at me when I called his name. He simply laid his forearms on his knees and hung his head between his limbs.

"Eric." I landed next to him and grabbed his arm like it would make him see me, but he never moved. "What happened? Eric?"

When Jonathon screamed for help, his voice was deeper, and I knew he had shifted into his shade form. Even over his shouts, I heard Eric grumble, "I'm fine." He stood up like he actually was, but limped when he started to walk. Someone had hurt him, but I didn't understand how it was possible.

"I was with them," I ranted as I followed him. "I was with Zac and Robb. How did he do it?"

Eric stopped walking and finally looked at me. His right eye was already bruising.

"It was Darthon," I spoke for him because I knew he couldn't. "Wasn't it?"

Eric never responded. Bracke and Luthicer were already outside. They hadn't even bothered to run outside. They had transported together, and Pierce was next to them.

"What's going on?" Bracke started to speak before he really looked at his son, and then, he sucked in a breath. "Eric—"

"I'm fine," he repeated his promise, but he never stopped

245

limping toward the shelter.

"You're not fine." Bracke grabbed him, and Eric didn't fight it. He stopped walking. "Who did this?"

"It was Darthon," I said.

"Jess," Eric spoke my name like it was a curse. "Jessica." His voice softened. "Wait until we're inside."

It was then that I felt it. The air was hot. The trees were shaking. Everything reeked of fire. Darthon had been here—briefly, but here. Everyone else must have sensed it, too, because Bracke wrapped his arm around Eric's torso, and he helped his son walk to the shelter. Everyone else rushed ahead of them.

"Lock the place down," Luthicer barked as we entered, and a group of shades scattered.

"You can do that?" Pierce asked.

Luthicer shot him a glare, but the moment was clear. The shelter had security that was beyond what we had previously believed. Within minutes, the ground was shaking, and Bracke sat Eric on a bench as if he couldn't hold them both up during it.

"Looks like we'll have an earthquake on the news tomorrow," Pierce muttered.

Even in the darkest times, my guard joked, but his face didn't cock his usual grin. His expression was one I had seen on Urte. The squinting eyes gave away Pierce's true feelings. If we had rushed, we might have been able to prevent it. We might have been able to help Eric. He had been in trouble all along.

Eric stretched his arm in front of him like he had simply been training, but his face was swelling. Even when he winced, his cheek moved unnaturally. He only became a shade when his father put up a silence barrier. All of his injuries began to melt away, but not as quickly as they usually did. His jaw even made a noise, but he rocked it like it was nothing. His blue eyes were burning.

"What happened?" Bracke repeated, but his voice hadn't calmed. It shook with his fingertips, and small shadows spiraled out of his skin. Apparently, Eric inherited his emotions from his father. "Is it true? Was it Darthon?"

Eric opened his mouth, but only a squeak came out. He shook his head.

Darthon still controlled his speech.

"It was Darthon," Luthicer agreed with me. "We all felt it."

"But not until we were outside," Bracke argued. "We should've sensed it before—"

"Unless he was human," I interrupted, keeping my eyes on Eric.

He looked up at me as if to confirm it. Eric—all along—knew who Darthon was. He knew if Darthon was Zac or Robb, or someone else entirely. He knew everything, and he couldn't tell us.

"That's impossible," Bracke said, but his tone was quiet. "Right?"

Eric didn't respond.

Before anyone saw the elder move, Bracke grabbed Eric's shoulders. "Why wouldn't you kill him if you know? Why wouldn't you tell—"

Luthicer pulled Eric's father back. "Don't."

"Don't tell me how to raise my son," Bracke argued, inches from Luthicer's face.

Luthicer never looked away from Bracke. "You won't have a son if you keep acting like that."

Bracke's chest caved in as if the man had slapped him, but I tore my eyes away from the two men. I only looked at Eric, who had yet to move, yet to speak, yet to explain. He couldn't tell us anything.

It was Pierce that changed everything. "There's going to be another war, Shoman," he said, calling Eric the name I hadn't heard anyone use in weeks, the name of the first descendant. "You can't stop that. It has to happen again."

Shoman disappeared back into Eric almost as quickly as he had shifted before. He cringed as his angular face shifted and squinted as his black hair sprang up into brown waves. Shifting quickly was painful. Everyone knew it, but Eric did it anyway. He wasn't even completely healed. His lip was bleeding.

"I'll handle it," he finally spoke, and all of the tension in the room dissipated.

Pierce was right. Eric hadn't shifted for one reason. He knew Darthon, and they would've fought, but Eric knew it would've declared war. He knew people would die, and he knew he couldn't die, and—now—I did too. The elders, for once, were the oblivious ones.

"Darthon was here," I spoke to Bracke and Luthicer. "He's either Zac or Robb."

"We aren't sure," Pierce agreed, "but we are sure it's one of them."

Eric was on his feet like he could stop us from speaking, but he hung back because it was too late.

Bracke's gaze flickered from his son to Pierce to me. "I thought you were going out with friends."

"I did," I said and stepped to Pierce's other side. I didn't want Eric to stop me. I explained what I knew. I told them everything—how the bar fight had happened, how Zac had threatened Eric in the beginning, how Zac remembered everything, how Robb took off my ring, how they wanted me to leave Eric behind. I even mentioned Linda and Crystal. "So, we know they're involved."

"We just aren't sure which ones they are," Pierce finished.

Eric never budged.

"We can't kill them all," Luthicer spoke directly to Bracke. "Not without knowing."

"We know one of them," he said.

My breath caught in my throat. "What?"

"This isn't your responsibility," Luthicer was clear. I was not to question him.

"The elders said no more lies. You guys promised—"

"And you promised to fight with us, and you went behind our backs to do something alone." As Luthicer argued, his white hair spiked up. "Look where that got us. You could've been killed. All of you."

I was silenced.

Bracke laid a hand on Luthicer's shoulder. "Calm down." This time, Bracke was holding Luthicer back. "Go find Jada."

Luthicer lingered, staring only at me, before he disappeared without a word.

"What does Jada have to do with this?" Pierce asked. While Eric and I didn't speak, Pierce never let anyone silence him. "She didn't come with us. She—"

"Pierce." Bracke was loud.

"We did what we had to do," Pierce spoke over the elder. "If you guys had done something, we wouldn't have had to do it."

Bracke stared him, and Pierce looked directly back.

"No one died," Pierce said, "and we got closer to winning." He unfolded his arms as if he were prepared to put himself in a fighting stance.

I grabbed him, and his arm shook beneath my touch. *"Breathe,"* I reminded him of everything he had told me in the car. Emotions wouldn't get us anywhere. We were only turning on one another.

Pierce took a sharp breath as if he realized the same thing, and Bracke did, too.

We were a team. We couldn't fight one another if we were going to win.

"I'll accept any punishment you give," I spoke up for my guard and me. "We both will."

Bracke nodded, but his blue eyes flicked over my shoulder. I knew he was looking at Eric, but I didn't know what he saw. "No punishment," he said, "but no one leaves. Not even for school. Not now."

"That'll just give us away," Pierce started.

"We've already been given away."

Pierce stopped speaking.

"We understand," I said again only because I knew the order couldn't stick. In the morning, things would calm. We would miss two days at most, and a lot could happen in two days. War could happen. The elders wanted to prepare. I could tell that much.

Bracke looked at his son. "Get yourself checked out."

Eric stood up to go to the nurse's quarters. When he started walking, Bracke walked in the opposite direction. I waited until the elder was gone before I chased after Eric. Pierce's footsteps echoed behind me. Both of us were following the only person we wanted to help.

"Wait," I spoke up, but Eric had already stopped.

He had heard us coming. "What?"

I searched his face, expecting to see a glare, but his eyes were heavy. I had to use all of my energy to say what I had held back before, "It's the rings."

Eric's lip twitched, and the movement caused his injury to burn brighter. The blood reminded me of the blood he had on his face in the Light realm where he had been tortured, where we had both been tortured in different ways.

I had to close my eyes to speak again, "It kept you alive, didn't it?"

His hand was heavy when he laid it on top of my head. I opened my eyes to see a small smile escape him. "Just," he whispered as he dropped his hand. "Just don't take it off again."

He knew. He had felt it just as I had. His heartbeat almost stopped. He started walking away like it was nothing, like his life had always meant nothing.

"I felt you leave," I called after him, and he froze in the hallway. "I took it off, and I felt you leave." My voice cracked. "It's my fault he attacked you. I'm sorry—"

Eric crossed the hallway. Before I could finish my apology, his arms wrapped around me. His tight hold was suffocating, but it was the deepest breath I had felt.

"Don't," he spoke against my ear. "You did the right thing." As his fingers moved across my spine, shivers traveled over my body. It was the warmest I had ever felt, warmer than any power the Dark had given me, warmer than any slice of Light energy, and when he pulled away, his words kept the warmth on my skin, "He's losing because of you."

He walked away without saying another word, but this

time, he didn't limp. He marched, and I knew I was seeing Shoman—the first descendant that trained me in the beginning. I had done well because he had taught me, but it had never occurred to me that I was the same strength for him.

Darthon wasn't getting me on his side any more than he was defeating Eric, and it was because we couldn't be broken. We were together even when we were apart.

FORTY-TWO

Jessica

I WAS RIGHT ABOUT TWO THINGS. ERIC KNEW WHO DARTHON WAS, and the elders couldn't keep us away from our enemy. After today, the Dark had to let us go to school, and if I had to make another guess, they had protection in place. Even then, we had missed one day, but it had dragged on longer than the February day should've been. I hadn't even been allowed to step outside. The only reason I knew it was dark out was the sizzling in my veins. Nighttime always brought on the urge to shift into my shade form, but below that feeling was another desire. After I had taken off my ring, transforming into a light had never felt so close. I painted to distract myself, and for the first time in months, I used the color blue.

It flew across the canvas, and it spiraled down in swirls. A mask of black drew across it, hitting the hues I had created by mixing colors together, and everything took over me. I didn't think. I didn't even feel. The brush was the only part of me that existed. I didn't even realize the amount of time that had passed until knocking broke through the blockade my passion had built.

Before I turned around, the person spoke, "Hey, Jess."

It wasn't Jonathon, and it wasn't Eric or the elders. "Brenthan." I expected to see my guard's little brother by himself, but he wasn't alone.

A middle-aged woman stood by his side, and a young

girl stood behind her. The child's thick, brown hair sprang up around her face. She never looked at me, but Brenthan did.

He pointed back at the girl. "This is Raquel."

"And I'm her mother," the woman spoke, but she didn't offer up a name.

"They wanted to meet you," Brenthan explained.

I forced a smile at the two. "I would shake your hand, but—" I raised my hands to show the splattered paint.

The woman didn't laugh. "That's okay." Her voice was soft, but her face wasn't. Her sharp cheekbones made the rest of her expression sink in, and her blue eyes defined her as a warrior, but her daughter had swirling eyes, remnants of a preteen that hadn't gone through the Naming yet. It wouldn't be long. She might have one year left.

"Why don't you two go train?" the mother suggested, but she never looked back at her kid. Her eyes were locked on my painting.

I fought the urge to cover it.

"I can't train yet—"

"Go, Raquel."

The girl straightened up, but she left. Brenthan ran after her, but I only heard his voice as they disappeared down the hallway. My door stayed open, and the entryway remained empty. I half-expected Pierce to walk in. He was always chasing his brother around, but today, he was training, and rumor had it that he was training with Eric. The two were talking again.

"Do you know who I am?" The woman's question tore my concentration apart.

I searched her face, but she was unfamiliar to me. "No. Should I?"

"My name is Ida."

Her identity made my heart sink. Eu's wife was standing right in front of me, but now, she was a widow, and Raquel didn't have her father anymore. He had died in the Marking of Change, and Ida had lied about her identity to the Light. To them, she was Eric's mother, but the lie had died over the winter.

"I didn't know Eu very well." I stood up. "But he seemed like a really good man."

Ida's eyes finally landed on me, but her stare was cold. "Do you know why I lied that day?"

My mouth was dry. It was her tone, sharp, but low, a momentary growl.

"I only lied to protect my family," she finished when I didn't ask. "Shoman was supposed to win, and now—" Her fingers curled against her hips until they disappeared beneath her jacket. "I hear he's being controlled."

I didn't have to confirm it. She was practically an elder herself. The others would've told her.

"He's not here." I stepped away from the canvas, so I could gesture to the door. "If you want to talk to him—"

"I want to talk to you."

Her eyes brightened, but the rest of her face lingered in the dim light. Even though her hair was short, the blackness blended over her, and her powers heightened.

Every nerve in my body spiked. "Are you okay?"

"Is it true Shoman left you?"

I stepped back, but she stepped toward me like she was my second shadow.

"Is it true your death causes Darthon's?"

"I don't think we should talk about this," I snapped, trying to focus on her abnormal movements.

She lunged at me. When she tore her arm out of her jacket, a blade caught the lamplight and gleamed as it streaked through the air. I didn't have time to breathe.

I lifted my arm, and her forearm slammed against mine. A sickening noise snapped through the room, but I wasn't hurt. She screamed, but it wasn't out of pain. She kept lunging at me, and her cheeks burned red below her widening eyes.

"Stop!" I shouted as we fell to the floor.

Ida—Eu's wife—was trying to kill me, and her body was on top of mine. When she brought her hand down, I barely moved in time. The knife hit the floor.

I screamed.

She was a shade, and I was still a human, but in that instance, I transformed. Every piece of my human skin shattered into the form I hadn't taken in weeks, and my powers rushed through my veins.

When she tried again, I was faster.

I grabbed her wrist, but she twisted, and my wrist was in her hand instead. My lack of training was at fault. Her knees slammed into my sides, and I gasped as she restrained my other hand. She could hold me down with one grip.

"I'm sorry about this," her voice tore out of her as her eyes glistened. It was the same glisten her knife had as she brought it down.

My adrenaline took over.

Power rippled through my veins, and my descendant sword split out of my hands. It tore right through her torso.

The knife fell from her hand and sliced my cheek before it clanged against the floor. It was the only noise I heard. She didn't even let out another breath. Her blue eyes slid to brown, and her shade's complexion disappeared into a human's right before all the color left her cheeks.

My sword zipped back into me before she fell on top of me, and warm liquid soaked through my shirt.

Ida was dead, and all I could do was scream.

Forty-three

As Pierce and I trained, three hours passed, but we didn't talk, even when the machine was off. The stifling room took another ten minutes to cool down, and we sat drinking our water with our backs against the wall.

Pierce was the first to speak. "Too bad we can't go for a flight."

"It's been a while."

"Too long." He tipped his water toward me, and we hit the bottles together like we were having beers instead.

Even though we had fought, both of us understood the circumstances now. It was beyond us, but we could still be friends. As far as I was concerned, everything had been forgiven, and things felt normal for once.

After he took another sip, Pierce cleared his throat. "I should probably get going. I told Jess I would see her."

Just the mention of her took all normalcy away. It wasn't her fault that things had changed so much. In fact, she was the only reason Darthon didn't have as much control as he thought. I hated to admit it, but her actions had helped. If she could figure out who he was without me telling her, then we could all fight back. We could find a way to win, and I wouldn't have to do it alone. I didn't want to anymore. For once, I wasn't alone, and I was comfortable with it. She had changed that about me, and when I could tell her, I would explain everything. It was only a matter of days. I could see it in Darthon's desperation. He would snap soon. Robb would have to die.

Pierce stood up and brushed his clothes off, but he didn't say goodbye. He asked the last thing I expected to hear, "You really know who he is?"

I wanted to nod, to speak, but my neck burned. The spell, imbedded deep inside of me, hurt, but the pain was succumbing to repetition. I didn't even flinch anymore.

Pierce chuckled. "I guess it's useless to ask." Unlike Jessica, he was just now accepting the circumstances. "I should get going." The words left him before the air split.

The surge of power was both deafening and energizing. It filled the entire room, and it made my own abilities increase inside of my veins. My fingers twitched with temptation. It was unmistakable. Jessica had used her sword.

Pierce's green eyes widened. "What was that?"

He shouldn't have had to ask, but it was impossible. There was no reason she would use it, let alone outside of the training room.

I leapt to my feet and raced to the exit. Pierce was right behind me when I opened the door. Shades of all shapes and sizes rushed through the corridors in a black stream, but Pierce was the first to step into it. Someone running by bumped into him.

He tried to ask what was going on, but everyone acted like they didn't hear him. Luthicer's voice bellowed over the hallway, but his orders went unheard. His voice was drowned out by the shouts.

Jada was the first to break through the crowd, and she gripped Pierce's arm to gain his attention. "You need to go to the nurse's quarters," she breathed. "Now."

Pierce didn't move. "Where's Brenthan?"

His younger brother had stopped by earlier, but the shelter was on lockdown. No one but shades could get in and out. For once, Pierce had let the boy explore by himself.

"He's fine," Jada said, but her strained voice sounded like she was saying the opposite. "It was Jess."

Every part of me froze.

In an instant, Pierce took off, disappearing into the river of shades before I could even comprehend what Jada had said.

Jess was in the nurse's quarters. She had used her sword for a reason. Someone had attacked her, and she was hurt.

I sprang toward the crowd, but Jada whipped around and grabbed the back of my shirt. Before I could tear away from her, she lunged forward and dug her nails into my arm. "Don't."

"Let me go," I growled. I didn't care if she was Luthicer's daughter or not. She would not stop me from seeing Jessica.

"Jess is okay—"

I grabbed her hand and pulled it off me. Right when I was about to run, Jada's shout stopped me.

"It was Ida." Eu's wife flashed in my memory. The woman who had pretended to be my mother had tried to hurt the only girl I loved.

I whipped around. "What?"

"She did it for you," Jada hissed as her multicolored eyes flickered over the crowed. She clearly wasn't supposed to talk about it, but I didn't care.

"I have to go—"

"Ida's dead, Eric," she snapped. "Jess killed her."

Her words sounded as far away as Jessica felt, and in reality, that was too close for comfort. Jessica's heartbeat thundered inside my veins. It was Jada's words that allowed me to feel it. Jessica was alive, but someone else had died by her hands. I didn't understand.

Jada lifted a hand to grab me again, but she stopped at the last moment. "The elders want you to stay away for now."

It was a phrase I had heard before. When Abby died, when I met Jessica, when I crashed my car, when I returned from the Light realm. Everyone always wanted me to stay away.

"Who cares?" I cursed and turned away from the girl. Urte was standing right behind me. His hands landed on my shoulders before I could dodge him.

"Eric." His fingers dug into my skin, but other than that, he was perfectly still against the backdrop of rushing people. "Stay here."

"Why?"

Urte didn't answer, but his darkened expression said it all.

My sternum was crushing inside of me. "You think I had something to do with this?"

"It's not that," he said, even though it was. If Jessica died, Darthon died, and I wasn't with either one of them to the Dark's knowledge.

I brushed my trainer off and stepped back. "I can't believe this."

Urte didn't try to touch me again. "She's okay," he confirmed what Jada said. "Scrape on her cheek, but that's it. Luthicer is checking her out right now."

I kept stepping back, trying to get away from them, but I had stepped back into my training room right where they wanted me. They followed like I had obeyed.

"Just stay here," Urte repeated before leaving.

My knees shook until I sat on the ground. I couldn't do anything. Knowing the elders, they had someone standing outside the room. Jessica was right. We were just as much prisoners in the shelter as we had been in the Light realm. We were never going to be free again.

I cursed.

"They don't suspect you." Jada's whisper was loud in the silent room. The chaos outside couldn't even be heard.

"Yes, they do." My breath was rigid. "That's why they want me to stay away."

"No, it isn't," she interrupted. When I looked at her, I could see Luthicer's genes in her white hair. "Jess asked for Pierce," she spoke as sternly as he did, too. "She didn't want you to come."

Jessica even wanted me to stay away.

FORTY-FOUR

Jessica

THE BLOOD WAS NO LONGER ON MY HANDS, BUT I STARED AT MY fingers as if I could still see it. The color was the same as my Light powers, and it was the color of murder. My sword had even been red. Even though I had transformed into a shade, it wasn't my Dark powers that saved me. It was the Light. Above all, it was me. I had killed someone—a mother—a widow—a person.

"You did what you had to do," Luthicer said from the corner of his room.

I had managed to tell him what had happened, but the words seemed beyond me now. The scrape on my cheek had even healed, and the nurse had found a change of clothes. Warrior clothes. It was all they kept around, but the dark cloth hid the scar Luthicer had seen while checking on me. Other than Darthon, he was the only person to see it, but he had yet to say anything.

He spun around in his chair with his clipboard in his hand. His fingernails tapped across it as his black eyes searched my face. I knew what he would say before he asked, "Where did it come from?"

My hands shook. "I can't—"

"Jess." His sharp voice somehow softened in a single syllable. "I know it's from the Light realm. I can sense these things." It was that reason I hadn't let them check me out in the first place.

My chest felt like it was being torn open all over again.

"I need to know why you hid this from us."

I couldn't look at him. "I want Pierce." I could tell him. I could manage that. I had to. I just couldn't see. My tears were clouding my vision, and I closed my eyes to prevent them from falling.

"He's coming." The chair squeaked, but I hadn't realized Luthicer had stood until he laid a hand on my shoulder. I leapt up, and he leapt back.

"I—" My voice croaked. I lifted a hand to my face only to drop it again. My touch was hot. "I'm sorry."

"Don't be," he sounded like my father.

I had never missed my dad so much. I just wanted to see him reading in his chair, hear his laughter when he teased my mother about her hair. Anything. I wanted my family.

"Just try to relax," he said it like it was an easy thing. "You're okay now."

"But Ida—"

"Don't," his voice was harsh again. "Don't worry about her."

I nodded, but I didn't have a chance to speak.

Pierce burst in, his green eyes wild. "I'm here." As soon as he saw me, he rushed across the room, and his hands landed on both of my arms. "Are you okay?"

Nodding, I didn't speak. I didn't want to cry. I just took a breath and then, I took another one—one after the other. I had never killed anyone before. I had tried to with Darthon, but he had stood back up. A part of me wondered if I would've been bothered if he hadn't. I would never know. I would only know Ida's death. Darthon was for Eric.

"What happened?" Pierce asked Luthicer.

The elder looked at me, and I nodded. He told Pierce everything, but he only paused right before he told him about what the nurse found. My scar. I had to explain it, and Luthicer knew I wanted to explain it to Pierce alone.

When the elder left the room, I finally sat down, but Pierce stayed standing. He shifted from foot to foot as he ran a hand through his hair. The black spikes melted into brown fuzz. He flipped back into a human as if he knew I would rather face Jonathon than my guard. We were both human now, and I was sure we were alone in that. The noise around my room told me of the chaos that had happened.

After Ida had died, my scream was heard. A shade I had never met found us. Other shades responded, and no one knew who the enemy was. I thought I would have to kill another before Bracke stepped in. He had barked orders, but I couldn't even remember them. Everything was a blur after that.

"You sure you don't want Eric here?" Jonathon's voice squeaked just like the chair did as he sat down.

"I—" I didn't know how I would confess my suicide attempt to Eric. Not when his mother had died that way. "I can't tell him."

A moment passed before Jonathon took another breath. "Okay, then."

He waited.

"Aren't you going to ask?" I spoke up.

"I'm just going to listen."

I stared at the boy I barely knew as a human. We only talked about art when we were together, and even then, his face hid behind glasses. Tonight, he hadn't picked them up. His blind eye was completely visible, a fog of a gaze. His other eye was brown. It looked just like his mother's eyes in the portrait he had painted so long ago, and I wondered how she would've felt if she knew where her sons were—how Brenthan had been detained with Ida's daughter.

"Is Brenthan okay?" I asked.

"My dad is talking to him now." Apparently, Jonathon had spoken to others before being allowed in my room.

"It wasn't his fault," I started to speak, but he raised his palm to stop me.

"Worry about yourself for once."

I swallowed my words as they attempted to form. I had to concentrate again, but my thoughts scattered. I saw Ida's face again. I saw my sword. My powers were bubbling. I curled my hands into fists out of the fear that my sword would form on its own again.

"I didn't mean to," I managed.

"No one thinks you did."

I stared at the ground, and Jonathon's feet suddenly appeared in my vision. As soon as he had gotten up, he was sitting next to me. His arm pressed against mine. "Close your eyes."

I did, understanding why he said it. The position was the same we had taken so many days ago in the shelter. It reminded me of every time we had spoken in my room. It felt normal. My heartbeat slowed, but Eric's remained—racing. He was worried, and even with the distance, I knew he wanted to be the one that was next to me.

"I'll tell him, too," I said first, knowing Jonathon would understand.

"What happened to you?" he finally asked, and I finally answered.

"The reason Darthon tortured Eric—" I choked on my words, and every passing millisecond burned. "Is this how Eric feels?" He couldn't speak, and now, I couldn't either.

Jonathon didn't respond. Oddly enough, a chuckle escaped me, and I hung my head in my hands. My eyes even opened. The stone ground was starting to become the most familiar sight I owned.

"Darthon can't kill him," I continued, even though the others already knew that part. "But Darthon doesn't care about that. He just wants me on his side, but I couldn't—I wouldn't—and Eric suffered because of that, and—"

"Breathe."

I did.

"Eric lived," Jonathon spoke when I couldn't. "You both did."

"I almost didn't."

Jonathon's hand landed on my arm, and when he pulled me back, I was forced to look at him. His complexion was drained of color. It looked like Ida's. "What are you saying?" I couldn't breathe until his cheeks filled with color. "Did Darthon try to kill you?"

"No."

Jonathon's hand dropped from my arm. The space he had once touched chilled against the sudden rush of air.

"I tried to kill myself." The words. They finally left. They escaped before I could stop them.

"What?" Jonathon's single word came out in a whisper.

My voice was much louder. "I thought we'd never get out, that he'd figure out a way to kill Eric, that he'd kill the Dark if he didn't die, and I wanted the Dark to win." Even my stutter was comprehensible. "I thought if I died, Darthon would, and everyone would be okay—Eric, you, Bracke, Luthicer—"

Jonathon hugged me, and my voice smothered against his shoulder. His fingertips dug against my back, but they were shaking. For once, I knew I was the still one.

"I won't do it again," I tried to comfort him. "It's wasn't out of depression—"

He leaned back, but his hands landed on top of my shoulders. "It's not your fault," he said.

"I know that—"

"Darthon tortured you, too," he interrupted, and his voice suddenly seemed closer, even though he hadn't moved. It was louder, clearer, something I couldn't ignore. "He hurt you, too. He did this to you. Do you understand that?"

My face burned, and I tried to close my eyes, but it was too late. The tears escaped. They cascaded down my cheeks, and the salty water filled my mouth. I nearly choked on them. "I'm sorry." I hiccupped. "I thought it was the only way to protect everyone, and I—"

I couldn't breathe. I couldn't speak anymore. The pain took over, and I succumbed to it. The moment I had almost died had been a panicked one, one that I didn't want to relive, but one that kept coming back to me over and over. I hadn't dealt with it because I hadn't had the time, but time was forcing it on me. It felt like Darthon had all the control again. I couldn't help but cry.

"You're okay now," Jonathon's voice sounded like we were underwater—all foggy and far away—but his thumb moved over my bicep, and it reminded me of how close he was. "Just cry if you want to."

"I don't want to," I stopped the tears by wiping them away, but my body felt like it had been crushed. My ribs hurt. My sides stung. My skin was cold. I shivered, and my reflexes reacted. I grabbed my ringed hand, hoping to feel the burn, but the only warmth that filled me was Eric's heartbeat—calmer now, but still racing.

"I can tell him if you want me to," Jonathon said.

I finally looked at my guard, the boy I had met as a warrior, then, as a painter. He was more than a guard. He was a friend, and he was Eric's best friend. Of course he understood why I couldn't tell Eric. His mother had died that way. Confessing to it to him would feel cruel.

"I was hoping I never had to tell him," I admitted, but it was no longer a possibility. The elders would know in minutes, and asking them to hide it was just as cruel. "It isn't fair."

Jonathon agreed. "But keeping it in isn't fair to you either." A small smile pulled at the right side of his lip. "I think Eric will understand more than you think."

"But—"

He held up his hand again, but he took a breath before he spoke, "Sometimes we hurt the ones we love, but hurting ourselves to avoid it doesn't make it better."

My bottom lip trembled. "You say that like you've been in love."

"I have."

I couldn't tear my eyes from him. Even though his face was one I saw every day, he was someone I barely knew. Jonathon Stone held secrets, too.

"Maybe I'll introduce you to her sometime," he added.

My mind raced. "You have a girlfriend?" The thought hadn't even occurred to me.

"Not exactly." His face reddened. "It's rather complicated," he paused, "but I think friendship is the foundation of love."

He turned away from me for the first time all night. "And if that's the case, I very much love Eric, and you, and Jada." It was also the first time I heard him stumble over his words. "The girl has grown on me."

Jonathon had a crush on Luthicer's daughter.

"I cannot believe that." A giggle escaped me, and the lightness that took over my body felt foreign. My giggle died, but Jonathon kept laughing.

"I told you it was complicated."

I stared at the wall, trying to imagine Jonathon's life when he wasn't around me, but nothing came. My nerves were shaking, and the emotional turmoil of the day made it impossible to daydream. "I didn't even know you two spent time together."

"More than you'd like to know," he admitted. "Pretty much anytime I'm not with you." He scratched his head. "I was supposed to be training her." He glanced over, and his eyes were brighter, even his blind one. "I guess that's how Eric and you fell in love, too. Huh?"

My stomach fluttered at the reminder. When I had seen Eric for the first time, he was Shoman, and I had been terrified of him. It was only when I escaped his radar that I realized I had to go back, and when I did, I fell slowly. I wasn't sure if it had happened when we were flying, or talking, or training, but it had happened somewhere along the way. I remembered every moment between us, and every moment felt more precious as time passed. One year seemed so long ago.

"I'll tell him," I promised.

Jonathon patted my leg. "That's a good idea."

"Is everything okay in here?" Bracke entered the room. He looked between us, but didn't step closer. "It got quiet," he explained and straightened. "I thought something was wrong."

I wiped my face again, even though the tears were long gone. "Everything's fine," I said, "but there's something I should tell you, too."

Bracke didn't speak, and neither did Jonathon as I explained it again. This time, it was easier. My voice shook at certain parts, but I didn't cry, and I didn't feel like biting back the truth. I only felt tired when it was over. Bracke's fallen expression made him look the same as I felt.

After a moment of silence, he asked, "Is there anything I can do for you?" He never even mentioned his late wife, or Eric, or any of the repercussions I had always worried about. The Dark was there from the beginning, and they would continue to be until the end.

There was one thing I wanted the most. "I want to see my family."

Bracke's eyebrows lifted and fell. "You can go." He didn't even hesitate.

"What?" I had expected an argument. "But we aren't allowed to leave—"

"We can't protect you here. It would be wrong to keep you any longer," he interrupted, but his tone wasn't the one he had as a leader of the Dark. It was the one he used as Eric's father when he spoke to me about Eric's mother. "I'll drive you myself."

"Thank you." I stood up, only to glance at Jonathon once more. "Thank you for listening."

He nodded. "I'll keep my eye on your house," he said, "but I have something I have to do first." He looked past me to Bracke. "Can you watch the place until I get there?" I would still have protection.

Bracke agreed. "Let's go."

I practically ran past them. As much as they were my family, I wanted to see my real family, my parents who had been with me since I was a baby. I wanted to hug them first, but most of all, I wanted to be home.

FORTY-FIVE

Eric

THE SHELTER CALMED DOWN IN TWO HOURS, BUT EVERY MINUTE felt like an entire night. Jada came and went, keeping me informed as much as she could. She even snuck me out. It was only then that I realized how much she was involved, how much time she had spent in the shelter to understand the movements of the elders. I went straight to Jessica's room, but it was empty.

Almost all of her belongings were gone, and the blood had been cleaned from the floor, but the room showed signs of the struggle. Her easel was flipped over, and a canvas was on the ground, facing down.

I had snuck the gift into her room a few minutes before she moved in, but I never admitted to it. The car she had bought me was sitting on her desk. I stared at it—at the design I had painted on top—and I wondered if she had understood the meaning I attempted to convey. Either way, she now knew the jewelry kept me alive, and Darthon was still oblivious.

Even then, he wasn't Jessica's only enemy. Ida, our own kind, had tried to murder her, and I had been right down the hallway, unable to do anything.

I walked across the room, half-expecting the recent death to be in the air, but the only eerie part was the echo of my footsteps. I grabbed the painting without a single chill running up my spine, but every part of me went cold when I flipped the canvas over.

The blue streaks were the same hue of my powers, and they melted across the trees. Even the leaves were a shade of cobalt midnight only we knew. It was the night we met, but it was from her perspective, and I was the centerpiece. My black hair blended into the shadows behind me, but small wisps clouded off my skin. The only bright part was my eyes, ice-blue stars in the blackness.

"Thought I'd find you here."

I spun around to face Pierce, but he was in his human form. My grip tightened on the painting when I realized no one was behind him. Jonathon and I were alone.

"Why aren't you with her?" I asked.

"Relax." He leaned against the doorframe like relaxation was possible. "She's okay," he said, but his expression said something else. It was twisted. "She went home."

"What?" We weren't supposed to leave.

"Bracke let her." My father. "He's watching her now," he explained, "but you should go see her."

I wasn't supposed to. On top of Darthon's orders to stay away, I had received the same ones from her. Neither wanted me in her life, and for once, I worried that she would go back to him. I had two hours to think about it. She had hid her Light powers from the Dark for a reason. She was afraid we would hurt her, and we had promised we wouldn't. Now, the promise was broken.

"You need to talk to her," Jonathon continued.

"She didn't want me."

"She does," he argued. "She just didn't know it at the time."

I stared at my best friend. Only a few hours ago, we were laughing. The memory was now a mirage, but his fallen expression deepened my fear. Something had gone terribly wrong, something beyond Ida's death.

"You know something." The words slipped out of me.

"You need to hear it from her," he confirmed as he started transporting away. "Come on."

FORTY-SIX

Jessica

WHEN I MADE IT HOME, MY PARENTS DIDN'T EVEN REALIZE I had been missing, but a part of them must have. I recognized the confusion in my mother when she started cooking my favorite dinner—chicken Alfredo—and I saw it in my father when he put his book down to talk to me. They could sense it.

I watched them laugh and eat in-between more laughs. I didn't talk a lot, even when they asked me to, because I just wanted to listen. I never wanted to forget what either of their voices sounded like, what they looked like, how they loved one another.

The only time I did speak, I asked them where they met, and my mother blushed. I couldn't remember the last time I had seen her face flushed, and my father's mirrored hers when they met eyes.

"A rafting trip," my dad explained as he draped his arm over her shoulders.

She leaned against him like he was her favorite place in the world. "On a little river east of here."

A river. Just like Eric and me.

"We should all take a trip there this summer," my dad added. "It would be fun to get out."

"That old place?" My mother giggled—actually giggled—and she flipped her blonde hair over her shoulder.

"Why not?" My father moved the only strand she missed out of her face, and I stared at them as if I were seeing them as teenagers, young, in love, completely oblivious that they would, in fact, end up together. "It'd be fun. Right, Jessie?"

"Yeah," I agreed and stood up. Four months would pass between now and the summer, but making the plans made the possibility seem attainable. "That would be fun."

My mother's brown eyes moved across me as she stepped away from my dad. "Are you going to bed?"

I didn't want to, but my sleepiness was taking over. "Yeah."

"Don't stay up too late on the phone," my dad joked. Even he knew I almost never used it. In fact, I wasn't even sure where it was.

"I won't," I promised before I crossed the kitchen. I wrapped my arms around both of them, barely able to hold onto them together, but they hugged me back. "I love you."

"Oh, Jessie." My mother patted my head before I broke away from them. Her frown lines, for once, were defined by a small smile. "You okay?"

I nodded. "I will be after I sleep." It wasn't a complete lie, but it was half of one, and I knew that was just as bad. I wanted to sleep and dream of a day I could tell them what I was. A shade. A light. Whatever I was, I wanted them to know.

"Then, get some rest." My dad pushed my shoulder lightly, something he had done since I was a kid. He always did it when I hesitated, and I always stopped hesitating afterwards. "You have school in the morning."

"I know." I didn't want to think about it. Seeing Zac or Robb, or the others, was beyond me. "I'll see you guys in the morning."

"Good night."

I called it back at them as I rushed out of the kitchen and ran up the stairs. I didn't stop running until I reached my bedroom, and I froze in the doorway when I opened it.

Eric—in his human form—was standing right in front of me, but his powers lingered in the air. He had transported inside, and the sparks of the Dark energy flooded my veins. No matter how tired I had been, the powers rejuvenated me.

We locked eyes, but we didn't speak as I shut the door behind me. I locked it before I pressed my back against the wall. Even though my bedroom didn't have a single light on, I could see him. My eyes adjusted. His human complexion was unlike his shade one. It was tan and alive, and his cheeks reddened as he fiddled with his shirt.

"Sorry for intruding," he whispered. "Jonathon knows I'm here." His voice leapt up an octave. "And I wanted to see you. I had to see you," he choked on the last word.

My guard was back in place. Even though I was home, I was being watched. Eric, too. None of us would be free until it was over. Until another person died. Until Eric killed someone just as I had. I knew that now, but I didn't want to know it. I didn't want him to know what it was like.

"Are you okay?" he asked.

I nodded. "Sorry for asking for Jonathon."

Eric took one step, and I watched his feet as he took another one, inching closer and closer to me. I was motionless until he was right in front of me. I moved to him, and his arms were around my torso before I took another breath.

"It's okay." His hand curled and uncurled against my spine. "I'm just glad you're okay." His words were right against my ear.

My forehead pressed into his shoulder. "Did Jonathon tell you?"

Eric paused to move back, and I half-expected him to confess to it, but he didn't. "Not a word." He never looked away from me. "He said I should ask you myself."

Jonathon had kept his promise, even though the promise was to keep a secret from his best friend.

I grabbed his hand, and I pulled him across the room to sit on my bed. I didn't want my knees to shake when I told him. I didn't want to find an excuse to keep it inside anymore, and Eric sat down next to me like he understood.

We sat beside each other, facing the wide window, and I stared at the sky as he leaned against me. Sitting next to Eric was different than sitting with Jonathon. Eric held my hand.

His thumb moved across my skin, and when goose bumps traveled up my arm, Eric stopped holding my hand so he could rub them away.

I told him.

I explained every little moment, from the second Fudicia entered my room, to the confessions she gave, to the dinner, to Darthon torturing him in front of me. He already knew most of it, but I didn't stop at the torture this time. I explained how I saw the knife at the last second, how it felt when I stabbed myself, how it was worse when I woke up.

"I thought the Dark had lost," I confessed.

Eric never spoke.

"When he let us go, I thought it was because he didn't want me to die, because he would die," I voiced the only reason I had come up with. "But I never thought he had control over you. I never thought he continued to torture you—" I took a shaky breath. "I'm—I'm sorry."

"For what?" The two words were the only two he had said since I started speaking, but they weren't harsh or strained. They were low, a barely audible construction of two syllables.

I searched his face for something, a small indication of anger, but his eyes were half-closed, tiny squints of green beneath his bangs. Eric Welborn was looking at me. He didn't take his eyes off me once. He never let go of my hand. His heartbeat was the same rhythm as mine, and we breathed together.

"For not being able to save you, or the Dark, or anyone." My fingers twitched in his grasp, and as I thought of his late mother, I had to drop all eye contact. Our ringed hands had never glowed so brightly. "For doing what I did."

"Jessica." My name left his lips. "Jessica, look at me."

I did.

"None of this is your fault," he said. "Don't you dare think that." He squeezed my hand. "And don't hide things from me because you're scared." A small smile pulled at his lips, but he looked down at our hands. "I am, too."

I stared at the side of his face as his jaw popped. As familiar as the gesture was, I hadn't seen it happen so closely. The way his eyes clouded over reminded me of the time we had worked on a science project together. It was the first time he opened up as a human, and it was before either one of us knew who the other actually was. I knew he would talk again when his mouth opened, "I have something I have to tell you, too."

My breath caught in my throat, so I nodded.

Even though he didn't look at me, he started speaking, and his confession took over the room.

He had spoken to his father about his mother's suicide, how she was the bloodline, how she took in Camille, how she had almost killed him, how she had taken her own life instead. He didn't stop talking until he lifted our hands. "She gave these to me for a reason." The rings that kept him alive. "I don't think she ever wanted me to die. I don't think she wanted anyone to."

In that moment, I saw Jim Welborn in his son. Their expressions were identical. The twist of their upper lip was unmistakable. They even shared a line on the side of their face, but Eric's wasn't a wrinkle yet. It would be one day. I wanted to be there when it was.

"I didn't know," I said after a moment of silence.

"There's a lot we didn't know," Eric agreed as he leaned back, "but that's over now." His bangs brushed in front of his eyes, but his glare burned through the shadows. "I'm not listening anymore."

The four words came out in a strangled stutter, and I wondered if it was the illusion, the one Darthon controlled him with. Even though Eric couldn't control his voice, he was fighting back again. We both had to.

He straightened up, and his face hovered inches away from mine. "Can I kiss you?"

I didn't think I had to nod, but I did before he let go of my hand. With the freedom, he touched my face, and his touch lingered before he kissed me. It had been weeks, but it felt like months were melting away between us, months that we wouldn't have if we didn't live, and I knew why love was always described with eternity. A single minute stretched out for lifetimes.

When he shifted back, I was reminded of our actual timeline. Before I could break away, he pressed something cold into my palm, and our kiss ended.

I glanced down and couldn't believe what I was seeing. Eric had returned my necklace, the one that kept his ring against my sternum, the same one Robb had removed from my collarbone.

I gripped the chain Crystal had gifted me. "I left this at the coffee shop." But it was in my hand, and Eric was the one to return it. Not Robb. Not Zac. "How did you get it?"

Eric's face tilted to the side. "You don't need to ask that."

Darthon. Eric may not have been able to speak, but he had control of his actions, and Darthon had attacked Eric that night. The necklace had somehow been exchanged. It was undeniable now. Darthon had to be Robb, but my stomach twisted at the reminder that Zac had been present. Both of them had to be involved. Even if I knew Darthon was Robb, I was unable to kill him. Only Eric could. Only Eric could get Darthon's blood on his hands.

"I get it now," I said, "why you stopped me from hurting Zac." I thought back to the day in the parking lot. "Killing isn't something to take lightly, not for yourself or your enemy."

"It has to be done—"

"You've never even killed anyone, Eric," I interrupted without realizing what words had left me. A gasp followed, and I covered my mouth like I could take it back, but it was too late.

Eric paled.

"I—" My head dropped to my hands. "I didn't mean that."

Eric pulled my hands away from my face. While I expected to meet his glare, I was met with a smile. "You did," he said, "and you're right." He dropped my hands, and they landed on his knee. "I don't expect it to be easy, and I don't expect this to be easy for you either."

He laid a hand on top of my head as he stood up. "You need to take care of yourself right now," he said it like he was actually saying goodbye. "I can't do that anymore."

Before he could transport away, I grabbed the back of his

shirt. "You never had to take care of me, Eric."

When he exhaled, his shoulders fell. "Yes, I did." I only let go of him because he turned around to face me. He knelt down to my height. "And you took care of me," he said before kissing me again. This time, it was intense.

He didn't breathe. I couldn't breathe, and I didn't want to.

His fingers curled through my hair, slightly pulling the strands as he kneeled on either side of my legs. My bed creaked as his torso leaned against mine. We laid back, continuing to kiss. We only stopped to breathe, but he didn't roll off me. His chest pushed against mine as his face pressed into my neck. Every breath he took glided down my skin. He wasn't even kissing me, but they felt like kisses. They were warm shivers.

I threaded my fingers across the nape of his neck, just to hold him there, and then I felt it. The burn. The Light's sizzling power was vibrating, and it wasn't coming from me. It was falling off him. The spell he was under imbedded itself into his neck.

My fingers were cold as I dragged them across his skin, but the electricity moved with me. Eric didn't react. He just kept breathing. Even he couldn't feel what I could, but he was a shade, and I wasn't. Not completely anyway.

"We're going to have to take care of each other after this," he said, but his words were already in the past.

"For a long time," I agreed, knowing how I could take care of him now. I had one thing I had to do first.

I let him go.

When my elbows pushed beneath me, Eric moved off me, and the coldness of my room seeped into my skin. "We're going to win," I said, but he stared at my ceiling.

"I wish—" he stopped. "I don't want to leave."

I held my breath as his face tilted to the side so he could look at me. He smiled before he sat up, and his smile disappeared before he stood up. "But I have something I have to do."

"Me, too."

He spun around. His bottom lip fell open like he was going to question me, but he ran a hand through his hair, and I knew he wouldn't. Not when he couldn't tell me what he was going to do. We were at the point where we just had to trust one another.

"Don't fight without me," I managed.

"Same goes to you." His promise wasn't straightforward, but it lingered in his tone. He walked over to the window, and I expected to see him transport away, but he didn't. He simply laid his hands on the windowsill. "I guess we both had it wrong."

I stood up. "What do you mean?"

"We thought we were fighting my battle," he said with his back facing me. "We're not." He glanced over his shoulder. "We're fighting yours."

His words made my heart pound. "We're still together."

"Always."

"Go."

He only turned around for a second. "Do you trust me, Jessica?"

"I love you," I emphasized every word, knowing trust imbedded itself in every one of them. "Do you trust me?"

As he shifted, he blinked, and in one second, his green eyes were blue. "I love you, too." Eric was Shoman, but both of his sides loved me just as my sides loved him. No matter which one I became.

"Do what you need to," I said. "Just let me do what I need to."

He nodded. "I'll see you soon." As he spoke, a cloud of smoke consumed his place. He was gone, and I was alone.

I only stood when no one else came to check on me. I went straight for my desk, but my calendar caught my attention first. It was Valentine's Day, and it had nearly passed without my knowledge of it. A part of me wished I had known so I could tell Eric, but we had already told one another what mattered most. We did love one another. I knew that. But I wasn't sure we would get another chance to see each other again.

I didn't know what he was doing, but I had to do what I needed to do, and we had to concentrate on ourselves. This time, though, I knew exactly what to concentrate on, and I knew what I had to do to fight back. This time, I could free the Dark, and this time, my words would be the only knife in the room.

I transported away.

FORTY-SEVEN

SCHOOL WAS NORMAL—TOO NORMAL—AND I WAS HALF-TEMPT-
ed to unblock Jessica and Jonathon to check on them. We
were halfway through the day, and I hadn't heard a single
thing. I hadn't even seen Zac or Robb, but I did see Linda.

At lunch, she was sitting in her usual spot, her back
pressed against the brick wall on the edge of the outside tables.
For once, she didn't look at me when I sat down next to her.
She only stared at her nails. They were purple, and as much as
I hated to admit it, they reminded me of Camille's obsession
with nail polish.

"Why purple?" I asked.

"Huh?" She glanced over, but her brown eyes didn't wid-
en. They were heavy, and small bags hung beneath them. She
hadn't slept.

"Your nails," I said. "Why are they purple?"

She fixated back on them, but her fingers curled into a fist
as if she didn't want me to see them anymore. "Why? You want
to borrow my bottle?"

Fudicia was back. Their caustic tones were almost identical, and it was exactly what I wanted. I needed her to be both a
human and a light if we were going to talk.

"Did you know she tried to kill herself?"

Linda's neck whiplashed to face me. This time, her eyes
were wide, and her pupils moved as she searched my face. I

279

kept every part of my expression still.

She huffed. "Who told you?"

"Jonathon." Even he wouldn't mind the lie.

Linda didn't speak immediately, but when she did, her tone was soft, "Did you talk to her?"

"Would my answer make a difference?"

"I guess not."

It was against the rules. We both knew that. But so was hurting Robb, and I had punched him. As far as I was concerned, our rules were over, but the spell still existed. I doubted I would ever be able to speak again, but I could fight, and if Robb wanted to, I knew the Dark had practically surrounded the school. The Light probably had, too. We were on the verge of war, but even the Light wouldn't choose to fight at a high school. It was my only hope anyway.

"It's coming to an end, isn't it?" Linda voiced everything we already knew but had never spoken. She looked at me like I would confirm it, but I kept my face unreadable. "She's going to figure Robb out."

"She's smarter than he thinks."

When Linda nodded, her blonde hair blew into her face. It was one of the reasons I couldn't see her expression, but the other reason was she faced away from me. I followed her gaze to the willow tree, and I wondered what memories she possessed from the Marking of Change. I knew who the Dark had lost, but the Light had just as many members die. Whether or not she had been close to any of them was beyond me, but I knew one life that had to matter to her.

"You don't have to die," I said.

Her back lifted as half of a chuckle escaped her. "Guards protect their warriors to the death," she said it like the Light had taught her how to die. "That's the point of having a guard, isn't it?" Her eyes darkened. "Even Camille knew that."

I ignored her words. "You don't have to guard him anymore," I said, knowing that we needed her help to defeat Darthon. In the end, he could take us back to the realm. In the end, we would need a light, but I hoped Linda needed the Dark in the same way we needed her: for survival. "You can be on our side."

Her lips pressed into a thin line, but they opened as she brushed her hair back. "I can't."

"We have lights on our side already. Luthicer—"

"He's a traitor," she interrupted, "and a half-breed."

"And half-breeds matter to us. My own guard was one." Camille's memory would never leave me. "Zac is one," I spoke his name, even though it was difficult to. Unlike Linda, I never had the opportunity to understand his involvement. "Don't you care about your brother?"

Linda's face hardened, but it was in that expression that I saw myself. It was one I held whenever I didn't want someone to read me. If she did care, she didn't want me to know. "Zac would gladly die for Robb."

"Would Robb die for him?"

Linda's cheeks flushed. "What are you getting at, Welborn?" Her gaze became a glare. "You can't mess with me."

"I'm not trying to." Even I wasn't sure if it was a lie. "I'm trying to help you two."

"And in turn, we help you," she spat. "Right?"

She knew what I ultimately wanted, and I wasn't about to hide it. "It's a way we can all survive."

"Except Robb."

I nodded.

She leapt to her feet. "Forget it."

I grabbed her hand. "The Dark will take lights," my words rushed out of me. "Jessica is going to take over anyway. Help her now, and she'll help you more in the future—"

She yanked her hand out of my grasp. "Jess?" Her tone was tight. "She'll never accept her powers."

"She will."

"She didn't."

"You tried to force her," I argued as I stood up, but I kept my distance by leaning against the brick wall.

Linda's eyes moved to my hands and arms—as if she were waiting for an attack—and she stepped back before looking at my face again. "She tried to kill herself instead of joining us."

"And then, you really wouldn't have a single leader." Robb would've been dead, too. "That's how your Light half will die. Jessica is your only hope."

Linda stopped moving away.

I shoved my hands in my pockets to assure her I wouldn't attack. "Don't you see that Jessica has to live, no matter what?" I chose my words carefully. "Whether I die or Darthon dies, she has to take over the other side, and she will. She's prepared for it."

Linda huffed. "So, let her take over the Dark."

"I can't do that."

Her right eyebrow lifted. "Why not?"

"Because I don't believe Darthon will let the Dark live," my confession escaped me. "I don't think he'll let Jessica live."

"She has to—"

"Not after I'm dead," I interrupted. "I know how the rules change. I've seen it happen." When the prophecy failed, every-thing changed. We even had Jada. New shades meant a new beginning, and it had already started a long time ago. "Her life won't be connected to his anymore. He'll be able to kill her without dying himself." There would be no need for the weak-nesses to exist. "He'll kill her for power."

I expected Linda to argue, to pale, or react with shock, but her frown was frozen. She already knew what I had been thinking all along. Darthon didn't want balance. He never did.

I knew it when I heard how he treated Jessica in the Light realm. Her life didn't matter to him, not beyond keeping him-self alive. Once I was dead, she would be his next target.

"The sects should've never fought for themselves," I con-tinued when she was silent. "We should've been fighting for one another this entire time, and I can't take back the past, but I can fight for the future, and—"

"Shut up, Welborn."

My mouth snapped shut.

"Seriously. You're a walking headache." Her fingers rubbed her forehead. "The Dark won't let the Light live either."

"That's not true."

"What part of 'shut up' do you not understand?"

The rebel inside of me always ignored the rules. "The Dark proved they won't destroy the Light," I spoke anyway.

Her sneer crinkled her nose. "How?"

"Jessica's alive, isn't she?" Even Linda knew the Dark was aware of both of Jessica's sides, but I hoped Linda was oblivious about Ida. "What has the Light done to prove they'll keep the Dark alive?"

"Why should I care about the Dark?"

"I'm not asking you to," I said. "I'm asking you to care about your own life."

Linda's head didn't move, but her eyes met mine from the corners. Her upper lip twitched.

"I care about your life," I said, knowing it was true. As little as I knew her, she had helped me. She had taken the pain of the illusion off me, and by doing that, she had protected my relationship with Jessica. Even if she didn't admit it, she had to have cared about me to do any of it. When she started caring was the question, but if I had to guess, it was during our time in the Light realm—it happened when she was watching Darthon treat Jessica the way he had. Fighting for someone so cavalier had to be impossible, but Linda never responded.

"The Dark will care about your life," I added. "Jessica, too."

Linda's hand finally dropped from her forehead, but she didn't look at me. "You trust her so much, and you've only known her a year."

"A year and two months."

Her eyes met mine. "You can't love that quickly."

"We have one word for love." I smiled when I thought of Jessica. "But we have no words for how it grows over time." Every moment we had meant more, and as time passed, each moment grew into another. "Does your love for Darthon still grow?"

Linda froze.

"I think you should consider that," I said and stepped away from the wall. It was time for me to leave. I had done the last thing I needed to do before the Dark went into battle, and now, all I had left to do was prepare to fight. This time, I would win, and I wouldn't hesitate, but I didn't take two steps before Linda grabbed my arm.

"Why?" She let me go almost as quickly as she had touched me. "Why help me?"

Instead of facing her, I stared at the willow tree I hadn't sat under in weeks. "I learned one thing from Robb." The tree was the same place where I had almost died. "We were all born into this." I couldn't help but remember all the times I spent with Robb, too. The way our childhoods melted together was a cruel reminder of our fate. "But we still have choices to make."

I stepped away before I said anything else. I couldn't risk showing my emotions about Robb to her, the girl I was trying to get on my side, the girl who was supposed to be on his side. If she saw my face, she would know how I felt. In all of my suffering, I had my friends and family, but Darthon only valued his violence. Robb had been alone more than I had ever been, and I couldn't bring myself to tell her I needed him to be alone when he died. It was a horrible decision, a selfish one, something I would live with for the rest of my life, simply because I would live and he would die, but I had no other choice to make. He had to die so I could live, but—more importantly—he had to die so the Light and the Dark could live in peace. Harmony would only come with destruction.

"Not anymore." Linda's shout flew over me.

I spun around, but kept walking backward, away from her, toward my family. "What?"

"It stopped growing a long time ago," she shouted louder.

Her love for Darthon. It had stopped growing, and in my mind, that meant she had stopped loving him.

"You're going to have to prove that," I shouted back.

She did the last thing I expected her to do. She jogged toward me, and she kept walking by my side as I increased my speed. "Then, you'll believe me when I tell you the truth." Her words came out as fast as our strides.

"Try me."

"She went back today," Linda's voice dropped. "Jessica is in the Light realm."

FORTY-EIGHT

Jessica

"I KNEW YOU'D COME BACK," DARTHON'S VOICE MET MINE MILLI-seconds after I transported into the realm. It wasn't difficult. In fact, it was easier than I had anticipated. All I had to do was think about it, and I was there. Even then, I hadn't transformed. I had remained human, but Darthon wasn't.

His golden hair was the first thing I saw, but I forced myself to stare at the pits he had for eyes. "I'm sort of predictable, aren't I?"

His elongated arms folded in front of his chest, but he towered over me. Every part of his stance told me that he was expecting the unpredictable. Even he knew my arrival wasn't as simple as he wished.

I wasn't on his side yet.

After all, I was remaining a human, and both of my powers simmered deep inside of me. I had come for a reason, though, and I wasn't leaving without completing my last mission.

"There's something I have to know."

"And what would that be?" His shoulder pressed against the stone wall, and I searched for familiarity in his movements. Would Zac lean, or would Robb? I thought both of them would, but they should've been in school, too. If it came down to it, Jonathon would be able to tell me who was missing that day, and we would know. No matter what, I had to know for certain.

"Who are you?"

His lips stretched into a smile, but the right corner twitched. "Why would I tell you that?"

"Eric would."

Darthon's mouth opened. Then, his lips flipped into a grin. All of his teeth were spikes. "I'm not Eric."

Eric's name on his lips caused my nerves to race, but I curled my fingers into a fist. When I felt his heartbeat in my palm, I could breathe again. "I know you're Zac or Robb."

Darthon's eyes slid over me. "And?" Not even a denial.

"And you've wondered why I haven't taken your side," I clarified. "Eric would sacrifice his identity for his people." I waited, and waited, and waited some more, but Darthon didn't budge.

"I will gladly tell you when you're on our side," he spoke slowly enough that every word dragged out like a sentence. "I would bet Eric didn't even tell you his name in the beginning."

It was true. I had figured it out on my own, over months of time spent together. With Darthon, I only had days. Horrible, drowning days.

"Is that what you wanted?" Darthon asked as he pushed himself off the wall. He took two steps toward me before he stopped. "Is that all you want to know?"

"I want to know how to use my powers fully." I forced myself to stand my ground. I couldn't step away from him. I wouldn't. Not until I got what I wanted. "I want to know everything about the Light."

"Both of those are pretty simple," he stated. As he walked, his back muscles shifted his shirt. "Come with me."

I followed him, but not for long. The entire realm shifted, and the floor melted into wooden ground. Bookshelves surrounded us, and every spine was marked with golden thread. The titles glittered in the dim light. The dust made me sneeze. We were in a library.

Darthon waved his hand over the nearest shelf. "This is every text we've ever written, anything we've ever collected." Hundreds of books circled us. Hundreds of texts I never even knew existed. The Dark had a library, too, but Darthon's collection made the Dark's room look like a simple stack. "You can learn everything here whenever you want to."

I stared at the array of papers until my eyes landed on the single desk that sat in the corner. It was covered in books, and I wondered how much time Darthon had spent studying every single word. An entire lifetime wouldn't be sufficient, yet he had already tried.

Darthon sat on the desk, and his torso blocked me from seeing his latest read. "Once you're a light," he spoke, "you can manipulate this realm just like I do."

I stepped toward the nearest shelf and touched a leather-bound book. I half-expected it to disappear beneath my fingertips, but it didn't. The bumpy ridges rubbed my skin. "Do these explain what we are? Where shades and lights come from?"

"Of course."

I only looked away from the books to stare at him.

He placed his hands on either side of his hips. "We come from the Highland, another realm much like this one."

I had never heard the word before. Not once. I hadn't even heard Eric mention it, and I knew why.

"The Dark doesn't know this," I guessed.

"Not anymore," he said, confirming the amount of history that had been lost over the hundreds of years the bloodlines had lain dormant. "We keep them out of here."

I pulled my hand away from the book to prevent my temptation to take it. "Why?"

"They followed us here from the Highland," he said. The Dark and the Light were more alike than I knew. "The Light broke through, and they came here to learn, to explore the humans' abilities, but the Dark—" A growl escaped him. "They tried to stop it all."

"Why?"

Darthon's eyes slanted into a glare. "So many questions."

My ears burned beneath my curls. "Do you want me to take your side or not?"

He stared, and for a moment, his chest didn't even move.

He didn't breathe or budge. "The Dark thought we destroyed the Highland when we broke through." Darthon was telling me everything I wanted to know. "They didn't want us to destroy the humans, too."

I knew enough about the Dark's past to know how many wars had erupted. Thousands of people had died, but it was impossible to know which wars were caused by the Light, by the Dark, or just the humans. I had to bet the books around us would explain it, but I hardly had the time to read. Not yet.

"Did you destroy them?" I asked. "The humans, I mean."

"Not intentionally. They did as all good creatures do," he said. "They fought for a better cause, and we created that cause, and we will continue our cause when the Dark is gone."

I had to bite my lip to keep myself from screaming at him. Not only had he admitted to his agenda, he had told me the one thing that stayed with me ever since I had left the first time. Darthon would kill me, too. He may not have even realized it, but he would in the future. If I were left to govern the Dark, I wouldn't let him affect the humans. The war would never end. If it meant gaining knowledge, Darthon would rip the Earth apart. He would kill the humans, too. He was too desperate to win to see my true intentions. Or, worse, he simply didn't care. I was his weakness, too, just as I was Eric's, but I was starting to realize mine—the people—and I knew humans were the reason my bloodline was created.

I took a breath so my voice wouldn't shake. "What about the people?"

He blinked, but it was almost as if his eyes never closed. His elongated eyelashes drew a thick shadow over his eyelids. "What about them?"

"What are you planning on doing to them?"

"With them," he corrected and locked his eyes with mine. "We will teach them."

I didn't respond because I didn't want to know what he planned on teaching them. In the end, it would only kill them just as it had others in the past. Either way, I had lessons of my own to learn.

"Jess," he sighed my name as he slid off the desk. When he straightened, his height caused his glowing hair to appear as a beacon. "What did the original voyagers gain by sailing across the ocean? What did Lewis and Clark gain by mapping the West? What did astronauts gain from space?" He pointed to his scalp. "Expansion is gain. Deepening knowledge is a necessity."

I swallowed my nerves. "Even if it causes war?"

"Even if people die."

"Even if it destroys their world?" I asked.

"It won't."

"Then, what happened to the Highland?"

A rumble escaped his throat as he rubbed his forehead. "How do I explain this?" he muttered. "This is sort of a myth, Jess. It's based on faith, and it's an intricate part of our culture." His hand dropped from his face. "No one has actually been there," he said. "No one that I know of anyway."

"Because it was destroyed," I pointed out the singular fact he had yet to explain.

"You sound like a shade." His eyes shifted into onyx slits. "You speak as if we're monsters."

"Because monsters destroy," I interrupted, "and your legend says you did."

"Destruction happens everywhere," he argued, his voice slowly rising. "The humans had war before we arrived. We didn't cause that." His fingers shook at his sides. "There will be death no matter what."

"And there's no glory in that."

He leaned his lower back against his desk as a smile crept over his face. "You say that like you know what it's like to execute someone."

"I do."

The smile fell off his lips.

I didn't give him a chance to speak. I would be in control of our conversation. "I want to prevent as much death as possible," I said. "And joining your side seems like the best way to do that."

My insides were pounding, but we were both frozen. In our silence, I wondered what he was feeling. When he crossed his arms, I knew he was reading me.

"Why should I believe you?" he asked.

"Because they tried to kill me." The truthful words were the easiest to say.

Darthon didn't look surprised. We were connected, after all. Even though my cheek had healed, I had to bet his cheek had slit open when mine had.

"So, that's why you're here," he said under his breath as if he were speaking to himself, but his eyes explained the opposite. "Do you want to know how to be a full-light?"

I nodded, knowing that complete absorption was the key, but not knowing what it entailed. No matter what, I had to do it.

Darthon unfolded his arms, stretched one out, and curled his forefinger. "Come here."

I did. My legs moved forward, and I crossed the room in four steps. I counted every single one, every breath I took, and hoped it wouldn't be my last.

He never moved, even when my toes pressed against his. I was close enough to feel his warmth radiating off his chest, and every part of me wanted to know how his scar looked, stabbed into his flesh.

I had to tear my eyes away from his shirt to prevent my temptation. He smiled when I looked up at him.

"You were never Named by the Dark for a reason, Jess," he said. "You didn't pick a side, but if you pick ours, we can give you one."

"Is that absorption?"

He nodded.

"Then, do it."

His hands wrapped around my arms, and his fingertips pressed against me. The pressure felt as if he would break my skin, but I didn't move away. The electricity held me there like gravity.

"Iris." My name was so close to Ida. "It was your mother's

Light name, and you can carry it now."

The Light power filled my veins just as it had before, but this time, the sizzle was liquefied. The hovering wisp was the strength of a warrior that held it carefully, something that laid dormant until it needed to be used fully. It filled every inch of me.

I stepped back, and my hair flew in front of my face. My brown curls were white strands of snow. The ends glittered like silver, and I touched them to make sure they were real. Just like the books, it didn't disappear. My physical appearance had changed. I imagined my eyes were just as hollow as Darthon's. The way he stared at me was anything but hollow. He grinned, and it lit like a hundred stars.

For the first time in my life, Darthon looked magnificent. My powers even changed my emotions. All of my hate for the lights began to simmer away, but I turned back into a human before it could consume me.

A gasp broke from my lungs, and I stumbled back. I had to grab the bookshelf to keep myself from falling over.

"So quickly yourself again," his voice was as warm as the aftermath of the powers.

"It's overwhelming," I dismissed. "I'll turn back when I'm needed."

"Good." Darthon didn't step toward me. "Being a light suits you." His low whistle broke his sentence apart. "Of course that will change when Eric dies." The words were lined with delight. "You'll be a full shade again."

"Can I still be a shade now?" I asked, hoping I had the ability to shift until the end came.

"Yes," he answered, but it sounded like a threat. "Why would you want that?"

"Don't you think I should lure Eric out?" My lips curled in a sneer.

Darthon didn't squint at me this time, but his eyes moved to my hand. "It hurts you, doesn't it?"

My ring. I didn't have to ask him for clarification. The jewelry was already burning my skin.

"You can take it off," he suggested, "and it'll all be over."

I stared at him, but gritted my teeth. When my fingers curled, the pain wasn't as bad. I kept my hands fisted to stand the feeling. I would not take it off.

"It will kill him," Darthon confirmed. "I figured out how he stayed alive." But he didn't know that I was well aware.

I stepped back, slowly inching away from Darthon, but the room moved. The walls bent toward me, and the floors lifted where I stood. Darthon's section squeaked as it moved backward.

He stared at the movements. "You can change it now." I had caused it all. "But I don't know why you would put more distance between us."

I saw him coming even before he made the decision. Like a vision, his movements flickered before they even happened, and I jumped to the side as he lunged at me. He never got the chance to touch me. The bookshelf fell, and he slammed against it.

Even as a human, I moved everything. My powers were beyond his, just like they were beyond Eric's.

As he stood up, I raised my hand, and a glass wall shot up from the floor. Darthon hit it, but the wall didn't shatter. It pulled and pushed like liquid plastic, and it clung to his skin like chains.

His face reddened as he shouted, "You picked me."

"I didn't pick anyone." My fingers parted, searching the air for the electricity that brought me power. My red rain was already falling. "I didn't pick you or Eric, or anyone." My voice rumbled out of me. "I picked both of the sects."

Darthon froze as if I had ordered the realm to hold him in place. His face didn't twitch or shift, but I searched one last time for any sign of his human side. I saw nothing in his eyes.

"I will teach your people everything you didn't when you're gone," I promised as I left him behind, knowing he would find a way to fight in the realm I would eventually call my home.

FORTY-NINE

I LEFT LINDA BEHIND. EVEN THOUGH I HAD PROMISED HER SAFETY, the Dark's safety had ended. Jessica went back to the Light realm, and it was confirmed when I arrived at the shelter. The elders were already suiting up, and fellow shades were dressing in war gear.

"Eric," Pierce was the only one who saw me among the crowd. "Did you hear from her?"

I stared at his attire. Unlike the others, he was dressed in normal clothes. "No," I managed. "What happened?"

Pierce's shoulders fell as his gaze dropped. "I was hoping—" He shook his head. "I refuse to get dressed. I won't until I see her."

My best friend—Jessica's guard—would not give up on her, and I wouldn't either. She asked me to trust her, and I did. I had to.

"She did it for a reason," I agreed, searching the crowd. "Where's my father?"

"Right here." Somehow, in all the chaos, my dad had found me, too. "You two need to prepare—"

"Dad," I said and latched onto his arm before he could walk away. "She isn't on their side."

He pulled away from me, but his eyes closed. "Just get dressed, Shoman."

"I won't," I called after him. "I'm not fighting her."

The entire crowd stopped, and for a millisecond, I thought it was because of me, but their eyes were nowhere near me. They stared behind my shoulder. Even Pierce was frozen.

I spun around and knew what they saw even before I saw it for myself. The energy had consumed the air—Light energy—and Jessica wasn't herself. She had white hair.

"Listen to me," she started, but it was too late.

The shades lunged forward. I was the only one who fought them. I transformed, and the shelter succumbed to the power I shot out. It blasted everyone away, everyone but Jessica.

She stood her ground, completely untouched.

"I trust you," I managed, knowing I couldn't hold everyone off for long. They were already beating against the barrier I had put up. "I do."

She didn't waste any time. She transported the few feet between us and grabbed my shoulder. "It's going to hurt," she whispered. Despite her transformation, her voice was the same as her shade one. It was delicate, and so was her touch as it rose to my neck.

Her fingers clasped the nape of my neck, and I screamed. I had felt the pain before. It was Darthon's. He had placed an illusion inside of me, imbedding it in my flesh. Jessica was touching that exact flesh, and the spot moved like a metal plate had been screwed into my spine.

It shattered, breaking into pieces around my bones, and I collapsed. My barrier did, too.

I couldn't breathe until Jessica let me go, and it was only then that I realized my transformation had been torn apart in the pain. I was human again, and so was Jessica.

"He can't control you anymore," she said right before Luthicer grabbed her by the hair.

"Wait," I shouted, but no one listened.

Luthicer was already plunging a blade toward her, but he wasn't fast enough. She shoved his chest, and a burst of light exploded between them. The elder fell to the ground, and I stood up before anyone else could fight Jessica.

"She's on our side," I screamed and felt her hands dig into

my back. "Darthon," I managed to speak his name before I felt the last burn of his illusion burn away. "I know who Darthon is."

I could speak again. I was free, and everyone finally stopped fighting Jessica. They only stared at us, and I moved my hand behind my back to hold her hand.

"It's Robb McLain," I said. "Darthon is Robb."

FIFTY

"I'M SORRY FOR HURTING YOU," JESSICA SPOKE TO LUTHICER AS HE bandaged himself. His chest was covered in a blue bruise. "I should be the one apologizing." He didn't look at her as he finished the wrap. "I shouldn't have attacked you."

Jessica fell into the nearest seat. "I didn't want to attack you either."

"Let it go, Jess," he said, finally looking at her for a moment. "We all make mistakes."

She nodded, but put her head in her hands. Every bit of her was shaking. I laid my hand on her back, but she didn't stop. She just grabbed my hand. "So, it's Robb."

"Yeah." The ability to confirm it was foreign, even though I had already explained it all. Jessica had, too.

After I shouted out Darthon's identity, the entire collection of shades stopped attacking. My father ordered them to hold back, but he also told them to keep their gear on. The war was going to happen tonight. It was undeniable. The heavy air proved it, but we sat in the elder's room as if we had the luxury of time to talk about it.

"He will come," Urte was the only one willing to speak the truth.

"He can't come here," I said. "Kids are here." Almost every member was. Even the untrained ones had been dragged in by their parents. When Jessica had gone back, everyone had felt it, and panic controlled the crowd.

"I should've warned everyone," Jessica said, only lifting her face to lay her chin on her hands, "but I knew you wouldn't let me go." She wasn't wrong. I wouldn't have allowed it. "We couldn't win if Eric was under his control."

"It was just his voice," Luthicer scoffed.

"And he couldn't tell us who he was," Jessica argued. "Now, we can use it against him."

"How?" Luthicer growled, but his growl died out. "We can't set him up. Not now."

"We can," she argued. "He doesn't know everyone is prepared for war. He doesn't even know that Eric can talk—"

"Enough."

"No." Jessica stood up. "I went back so we could fight back." She practically screamed. "And we can now, but we have to move quickly."

Luthicer opened his mouth, but my father laid a hand on his shoulder, and the half-breed silenced.

"Do you have a plan, Jess?" Every part of my dad's tone told me what I had seen in his face before. He never gave up on her either.

"Not exactly," she admitted, "but if we can get him to meet us away from the shelter, the others won't get hurt."

"She's right," I said. "Even if he suspects it's a setup, Darthon's desperate for a chance to win. He'll go somewhere else." I had to take a long breath before I could continue, "He would meet me."

"He won't meet you at night," Pierce pointed out the time.

"He will if it means he can check the spell," I said. "He will if it gives him a chance to kill me alone."

Everyone was quiet, but Jada's foot tapped against the ground. My attention was on her before she even spoke, "They might be right." She leaned over to brush Luthicer's arm. "Especially if they're talking about Robb."

I glanced at Jessica, half-expecting to see dread on her face, but nothing crossed it. She might not have known his identity for certain, but a part of her had been prepared for the truth all along.

"I can't risk this," my father said and shook his head.

"You either risk this or risk everyone in this shelter," I said back.

My dad stared at me. "Darthon will know it's a setup."

"So, send some warriors with me," I said, "but let's keep the Light away from here as long as we can. At least until you can get the kids out."

"It would give us enough time," Urte said. Everyone knew Brenthan was among the children at the shelter. Even though he had his full powers, he wasn't strong enough to fight. He would definitely be among the casualties.

"We don't exactly have a lot of time to debate this," Jessica said.

My dad blew out a rigid breath, but his stare was unreadable as he turned from Jessica to look at me. "Do you want this?"

"It's the only choice I want," I said. Both of the options would result in death, but preventing more was my only goal, and I knew it was Jessica's, too. She wouldn't have gone back if that weren't the case.

"Then, go," my father decided before his attention averted to Urte. "Prepare the others, and get the kids out. You, too, Luthicer."

The half-breed didn't argue, but he did linger by Jada's side. "And you? Where are you going?"

She straightened up. "With Eric."

Luthicer nodded. "I will see you later, then." He left without another word, and Urte followed my father. The only ones left made up my team—Pierce, Jessica, Jada, and I.

Pierce laid his forearm on Jada's shoulder. "I knew you'd come in handy."

Jada brushed him off. "Don't get excited at a time like this."

Every part of her reminded me of Camille.

"Let's do this, then," I said, but Jessica grabbed my arm.

"There's something else you need to know," she said. "Darthon knows about the rings."

I glanced at her hand, the one that held the jewelry, the piece of metal that kept me alive. "It's too late for him to take it off again."

"Why do your rings matter?" Pierce asked.

I told him what I knew. "We think it's imbedded with a spell."

"An immortality spell?" Jada was the one to give it a name, but she crossed the room so she could see the jewelry herself. "That's wicked."

"What are you talking about?" Jessica asked.

Jada stared at us. "You two don't know?"

We shook our heads in unison.

"Immortality spells exist," she said, "but they're practically legends. They're almost impossible to make." A blush ran across her cheeks. "I've been doing a lot of reading in the library."

"My mother made them," I said.

Jada's blush paled into a grimace. "That makes sense," she said, "but she couldn't have been the only one to do it."

"How do you know?" Jessica asked.

"Because," Jada drew out the single word, "two people have to die for them to work, one from each side."

Camille's death may not have been a plan, but it was always a possibility considering her position as my guard. It made sense to create something just in case. And her relationship with my mother wasn't a coincidence. It was my mother's suicide that destroyed me. It was never out of depression, after all.

I had to sit down. Jessica sat right next to me.

When we didn't speak, Jada continued, "How did you think the ancient ones kept both of the sects' powers alive?" She took the moment to look at each of us. "The elders at the time killed themselves."

"Well," Pierce leaned against the wall. He didn't make a joke.

"It's a legend," Jada repeated, but her voice lowered when she looked at me, "but I guess I should've kept that to myself."

"No, no," I found the words, but I had to grab Jessica's hand to speak. "Thank you, Jada."

She beamed. "So, are we going to set up Robb or not?"

"You seem entirely too eager for this," Pierce noted.

"I've been following the guy for a decade," she said. "It's about time the story breaks."

"Crystal?"

Jessica said it, and her question changed everything.

Jada met her eyes. "I told you I was the best reporter Hayworth would ever see."

I couldn't believe it. Jada—the new breed of shade with multicolored eyes—was Jessica's best friend, and she was going to fight with us. I was numb to it. The only memories I had of Crystal were ones that included Robb. She had been by my side just as much as he had been, and I had deserted her when she never left me at all. She had followed Robb for a reason.

Jessica shot up from her chair and wrapped her arms around Jada. "I can't believe it."

"I would shift out, but it's kind of painful to shift back," she managed to squeeze out the words during their hug. "I thought you would've figured it out when I gave you the necklace."

"I'm sorry," Jessica said. "I thought—"

"It's all right, Jess." Jada pushed herself out of the hug. "Let's get through this, and then we can talk about it."

Jessica nodded, but they kept chatting.

Pierce took Jessica's seat, and he leaned against me. "Crystal, as in Crystal Hutchins, right?"

"Right," I breathed.

"I thought Luthicer was Jada's father."

"He is."

"But Crystal only has a mother," Pierce said.

Lola Hutchins—practically the only reporter in town—was a woman, and Luthicer clearly wasn't.

I shook the contradiction out of my head. "I'm not questioning it," I said. If Jessica believed it, I did, too. "Hand me my phone." It was on the table closest to Pierce, after all, but he didn't reach for it.

"Why do you want your phone?"

I cracked a smile at him. "I have to ask someone out on a date."

FIFTY-ONE

O UT OF ALL THE PLACES IN HAYWORTH, ROBB MCLAIN WANTED
to meet at the coffee shop. He didn't even question why
I wanted to meet, but he agreed to it, and that was all
that mattered.

"What happens when he figures out the illusion was removed?" Crystal's question echoed through the alley we stood
in. We were all humans, and surprisingly, having her with us
didn't seem outlandish at all. Her punk appearance fit in right
between Jessica's focused stare and Jonathon's forced smirk.

"We'll fight," I answered when no one else did. We knew
it would happen. Getting him away from the shelter was the
only thing that mattered, but even Robb wouldn't start a battle
in front of humans. He would find a way out, and the Dark
would clear out the children by then. In a way, we had already
succeeded in the first part of our mission.

"The elders are ready." Jonathon's eyes shifted around as
he used his telepathy to speak to my father. Their adrenaline
was the only reason they could speak, but I was relieved by the
news.

We were in the clear, and a few warriors were near us. I
could sense their energy in the air the way I sensed rain coming. It was heavy.

I straightened my jacket. "I'll let you know if I need you
guys."

"When you need us," Jessica corrected. When I glanced at her, she smiled. "We'll be right here."

I nodded, but didn't respond before walking away. I held my head high. Robb couldn't kill me, after all—not unless he removed my ring—and I wouldn't let that happen. Or rather, I would do my best not to let it happen. Jessica and the others would, too. Unlike Darthon, my people watched my back, and when it came down to it, I believed Linda would have mine, too. It would only be a matter of time before we found out.

The entrance bell chimed as I pushed the door open.

He was sitting at a table in the corner with his back to the wall. He faced me, and his head was held high. His chin was practically pointed to the ceiling. It was just like Robb to overdo everything. I had to fight a grin as I crossed the room.

I sat down across from him without saying a word, but I let my chair do the talking for me. It screeched against the floor.

"Welborn." We were back to my last name.

"McLain." I had never used his before, but it came out easily. "How are you?"

He didn't smile. "Where's Jess?"

"I thought you would know."

He simply stared back, and for a moment, his brown eyes were as hollow as Darthon's black ones were.

"She's with Jonathon," I said. Not a lie.

Robb's eyebrows rose as if they were connected in the middle. "You expect me to believe that?"

"He's her guard." I shrugged. "Is there somewhere else she should be?"

Robb leaned forward, and this time, the table screeched. "She came to see me today."

"I didn't know."

"I don't believe that either," he snarled under his breath.

His eyes never shifted away from me, but I was tempted to look around the shop. For the small size, it was practically full. Even though I glanced at the crowd when I walked in, I knew there was a chance Light members were among them.

Knowing my father, Dark warriors were here, too. Humans as well. It was as much of a comfort as it was disturbing.

"Then, why meet me?" I asked, knowing every reason why we wanted to be away from the shelter.

Robb grinned. "My people need to prepare just as much as yours do."

He had a plan of his own, and somewhere in the silence, war had been declared. Tonight would be the last night for some, but I wouldn't allow it to be written on my gravestone.

"Don't think you're safe anymore, Welborn," he continued. *As if I would.*

"I never thought I was." My life had never been about safety. Neither of ours had been—not even when we were born—but right when I thought he would attack, the entrance bell broke his stare.

It was the only reason I glimpsed over my shoulder, and what I saw made me turn fully around. Jessica and Jonathon had entered. Crystal wasn't with them, but that wasn't important. Their interruption was.

"*What the hell are you doing?*" I asked Jessica telepathically.

She didn't meet my eyes as she sent a message back, "*We watched your back long enough.*" She sat down next to me, but smiled at Robb. "How are you?"

His brown eyes lightened. "Great," he said. "Just catching up with an old friend."

He didn't know she knew his identity—not for certain—but she did, and so did Jonathon.

"Well, does anyone actually want a drink?" Jonathon chirped, but no one responded. He chuckled and stepped toward the counter. "I'll be back."

I could not believe him.

Robb's eyes never left Jessica's. "Some guard you have."

I couldn't believe Robb more. He had confirmed his identity right to Jessica's face. If he wasn't sure before, he was positive now. We no longer had time to play games, and even Robb was making that clear.

Jessica didn't flinch. "You're right," she said. "He's pretty great." She didn't deny it either.

Robb leaned back against his chair. He smiled, but it broke apart as he shook his head. "So," he said, "you chose him, after all." He spoke as if I weren't even there, as if I were already dead.

"Do you really want to keep talking?" Jessica spoke for all of us. "You just gave away everything I wanted last time."

He flinched. "And I thought you were the type of girl to care."

"I do," she growled. "That's why it's over, Darthon."

Robb's face stilled, but his hand landed on the table, and each one of his fingers tapped the top in a wave. "I'm your friend," he started, but she interrupted.

"Was," she corrected. "What happened to everyone's memories anyway?" Crystal, as far as she had told us, didn't remember the bar. "Did you just erase them to play a game this whole time?"

Robb didn't answer.

"Erasing your own people's memory," Jessica paused, but she nodded. "That's pretty low."

Linda and Zac had fallen victim to him, too, but Robb still argued, "The Dark did it to you."

"I did it to myself."

Right when I thought Jessica would leap across the table and start the fight, Jonathon interrupted—again. "Coffees and crumpets." He laid a plate of pastries on the table before he juggled mugs out of his grasp. "I've always wanted to say that." If I hadn't known myself, I would've thought Jonathon had experience in the service industry. "All on me."

Jonathon sat down right next to Robb.

Our enemy had to stare. "A little close, aren't you, Stone?"

Jonathon shrugged. "I don't mind."

Robb shifted away, but Jonathon shifted toward him. "Want a pastry?" he asked. "They had cherry ones." He grabbed the plate, but Robb met his offer with a glare. Jonathon shrugged before pushing the plate to me. "I guess I bought them for you guys."

Jessica didn't even react. Jonathon was being too cocky.

I had to grip the table to keep myself from speaking to him out loud. *"What. Are. You. Thinking?"*

"Just take it," he said right before shutting off our connection. It felt like he had punched a migraine into my skull, and it only melted away when I grabbed the plate.

Jonathon—in all of our years together—had never blocked me, and he had done it now for a reason. It was the only way I would accept his orders.

My fingers wrapped around the plate, and I pulled it across the table before I realized what sat on the corner. A single knife—just a butter knife—but a weapon, nonetheless.

Jonathon had one near him, too.

My skin prickled with sweat as their reasoning for coming in cleared. A war had already begun. My concentration on Robb had blocked everything else. The Dark's cloud of power was sparking with the electricity of the Light. Everyone was battling. It would be seconds before Robb made a move, even if it were at the coffee shop.

The humans didn't matter to him.

I hesitated and looked at the window. It reflected all the people around us—the old couples, the teenagers, the families—all the possible witnesses were also possible victims. Innocent victims. But I saw Jessica's reflection the clearest. My fiancée, the only girl I wanted to spend the rest of my life with, could die, too. So could Jonathon. So could I. But we could no longer take away our possibilities. We could only fight.

I grabbed the knife without looking back.

FIFTY-TWO

Jessica

A S SOON AS ERIC PICKED UP THE KNIFE, EVERYTHING CHANGED. The coffee shop spun into a chaotic blur as all four of us leapt up. Eric's chair fell backward, and the wood smacked against the floor with an ear-splitting shotgun blast. The heat followed, but it dispersed as Robb transformed into the man I never wished to see again.

Darthon stood in front of us, and he had a weapon.

Instead of Jonathon reaching the knife, Darthon had, and he held it against Jonathon's throat. My guard didn't even have the time to transform, but now, he didn't bother. He stood there with a grin on his face. "Aren't I the damsel in distress?"

"Shut up," Darthon growled.

"If you say so, boss," Jonathon practically laughed, and I didn't realize why until I took a step back.

The rest of the coffee shop was acting normal. The customers continued to chat, drink, and chat some more. Not a single person looked our way. No one was moving. No one was reacting to the fact that Robb had transformed into a superhuman. Not even the people I thought might have been lights. Robb was alone, but so were we. The shades couldn't sense the illusion he covered us with. Only we could see the truth.

"Let him go," Eric started slowly, but Robb only tightened his hold.

Jonathon wheezed as his glasses fell off of his face. "It's all right." He finally transformed, but the transformation was slow. It crept over his skin, and he winced with every inch. Being so close to Darthon affected him more than I knew. "I'm quite comfortable here."

Robb nicked his neck. "I told you to shut up."

A bit of blood popped over the edge of the blade. This time, Jonathon didn't joke, but he didn't flinch either. He was Pierce now. Pierce could handle the pain.

"You're trying to mock me." As Darthon screamed at Eric, his hair glowed. "All of you are."

"I think that was me," Pierce spoke up.

More blood trickled out as Darthon pressed down, but he didn't have time to slit his throat. I transformed, and the powers shifted from the Light to the Dark. Even I couldn't breathe, but the moment extended the second Pierce needed.

I was a shade, and Pierce was free. He had slammed Darthon against the window and gotten away as if we had planned the movements together. In a way, we had. We were all a team. It was in our blood. We reacted as one, and Pierce stood by our sides like we could melt into one person.

Darthon stared at us like we actually had and dropped his knife. Right when I thought he would pull out his sword, he stared at me. "I don't want to hurt the humans."

He had put up an illusion, after all, but I stood my ground. "You can't change your mind now," I spat. "We're finishing this. Right now."

"Not here," Eric spoke up, and it was only then that I realized he was the only human among us. Even then, his moss-colored eyes burned. "Not with the people around."

Darthon shifted from foot to foot, and his illusion shifted with him. I could feel it move just like the realm moved, but it never fell. He only contemplated it. As much as I was one with Eric and Pierce, I was one with Darthon, too. I was sure of it, and I was positive about what end I wanted to slice off me.

"We can fight like we were supposed to," Darthon spoke only to Eric. "Alone."

"Deal," Eric said before I could stop him.

The room erupted into flame. The reddish pull flew over the walls and drowned the floors with electricity. My shade flesh sizzled, and I fell out of myself just as Pierce fell into Jonathon. We were human again just in time.

Darthon was gone, so was his illusion, and Eric was nowhere to be seen.

They had gone back to the Light realm—the one place Eric had no power—the one place where only I could get him out.

I started to rip myself into a light, but Jonathon grabbed my arm. "Don't," he hissed. "Not here."

The coffee shop was staring.

A gasp escaped me as I forced my molecules to remain in place. My human skin had never felt so suffocating before.

"He's not doing this alone," I managed, knowing Eric would die.

Jonathon never dropped his grasp. "Of course he isn't," he said and dragged me toward the exit. "Have a nice night," he shouted over his shoulder as we ran outside. The cold air blasted us apart, but Jonathon grabbed both of my arms to face me. "He expected that."

I knew it before he said it. Eric had practically asked for it. Why was beyond me.

We only had seconds.

"Go after him," Jonathon spoke as he looked over his shoulder. Crystal must have been hiding in the alleyway. "We'll meet you at the shelter." The same shelter that was probably under attack already.

Before he could run for the war, I latched onto him. "Pierce." His shade name was the only one I could use.

He froze as if it controlled him. "Yeah?"

"Protect Crystal."

"Like she needs it," he joked, but his face flinched. "Stop worrying about us." He finally broke away from me, and the world was cold again. "Just go."

FIFTY-THREE

I WAS STARING AT MYSELF. IT WAS THE LAST THING I THOUGHT I would see in the Light realm. I was human, and so was the Eric standing in front of me. He looked exactly like me, down to the frayed bits of brown hair. Even his eyes were green. Darthon—with an illusion—could be me, and we were both in the Light realm. Even with my sudden pain, my shock took over.

"What…" I couldn't fathom the words. "What are you doing?"

His smile was even like mine. "You really think she'll leave us to fight alone?"

It was then that the realm erupted. If there had been heat before, it was now burning. Jessica appeared in a beam of light, and her hair flickered from white to brown to white again. She had to be a light to enter the realm, but she fell out of her transformation the second her eyes saw us—two Erics.

She was human again. We all were. At least, we appeared to be. Darthon was still using his powers. He was only using an illusion, and I hoped Jessica could decipher it, but her eyes darted between us. Her powers weren't beating his this time. She only saw me.

"Jessica," I started to speak, but so did Darthon.

"Jessica." He mimicked me. He even used her full name.

She took a step back.

He pointed to me. "It's him. That's Darthon."

I couldn't defend myself against Jessica, but neither could Darthon. She was more powerful than both of us were, and Darthon was using the only weapon he had against her—me—but it didn't work. She kept her distance. She never lifted a finger. Only her eyes moved, darting between the two of us, searching for flaws in one of us. The biggest downside was obvious. I had spent hardly any time with her over the past two months, and Darthon had spent every other day following me around. He probably knew me better than I wanted to admit, but I didn't have time to think about it.

While Jessica remained still, Darthon attacked me.

I didn't even see him coming. Not as a human in the Light realm. I was already in pain, but the pain vibrated when I smacked the ground. My vision spun, but that didn't stop me from swinging at him.

My knuckles collided with his face, and his fist cracked against my jaw. We weren't two minutes into our battle, and I already tasted blood. I was already losing, and the circumstances were only getting worse.

I couldn't breathe.

The air was hot, and my skin burned. Right as I thought the Light realm was taking ahold of my body, Darthon leapt off me. "What are you doing?" he screamed, and his scream sounded like my voice in the same way he appeared as me, but it was his actions.

Fire had erupted in the room, crawling up a wall, and Jessica pointed her fingers toward it like it didn't burn at all. Only a thread of her hair was white. She had set the place on fire.

The black smoke cascaded over the floors, but I saw every movement.

Jessica didn't speak. She shot forward and punched Darthon in the gut. He didn't budge, but the floor did. It shook as she kicked him—not once, but twice—and this time, he fell. He never even tried to hit her back.

She ran to my side, and her hands pulled me up before I could even register that I was fine. The realm wasn't crushing me like it had the previous time. Jessica was helping. I could feel it when her fingertips touched mine. It was the same relief Linda had given me. She truly was one of them.

"Let's go." Her voice whisked past me as she began to run.

I lingered behind to stare at Darthon. He was lying on his stomach, barely moving. The flames were growing. He was weak. I could kill him, but when I tried to step toward him, Jessica pulled my arm.

"Not now." She continued to tug. "Not here."

Darthon groaned, and his hands landed on the ground in front of him. He was already pushing himself up.

She was right. He was more powerful here, and I was just a human.

I ran, and we fled together.

The hallways twisted on forever, but they didn't move, and they didn't disappear. Jessica wasn't manipulating the realm anymore, and I forced myself to look forward as we sprinted through the place.

"Can you get us out?" I managed between breaths.

"I'm trying." Her high-pitched voice squeaked the last thing I wanted to hear. "It's not working."

Darthon had probably collected himself. My fears were confirmed when the floors creaked. The wood hopped and bolted to either side. We came to a halt as the entire corridor flipped, and there he was. Darthon stood in front of us—inches in front of us—with black soot coating the side of his face, his teeth barred.

Jessica scratched his cheek, and everything changed again.

The floor was the ceiling, and the ceiling was beneath us, but I recognized the room. Every wall was stone, and the dim lighting reminded me of the days I had died beneath Darthon's touch.

"It was the only place I could think of," Jessica muttered, explaining what had happened. She and Darthon were fighting with the realm. So far, she was winning. Another strand of her hair had grown white, but it slowly faded.

I stared at it as I caught my breath. The constant changes

were disorienting. I couldn't understand it. My footing didn't even feel right. It was almost like I was hovering, slightly disconnected to the place, and I wondered if I was.

Jessica looked me up and down. "Are you okay?"

"Nauseous," I admitted. Every word I spoke was difficult.

"We'll find a way out," she promised, but only the lights flickered. She cursed. I didn't ask why, because I didn't have to.

We were stuck, and we had bigger problems.

The door opened, and a silhouette cut through the light. The only good news rested in the fact that it was too small to be Darthon's. When the boy stepped forward, I already knew who to expect.

Zac, in his half-breed form, cracked his knuckles. His multicolored gaze was the only thing I saw as he shot toward me. The movements were beyond my human vision. Everything was a blur. But Zac never reached me.

Jessica leapt in front of me, and her white hair sprayed out as she transformed into a light. A beam exploded out, but they were stilled against it. Jessica's hand wrapped around his throat just in time for everything to rush forward again. She slammed him into the ground, and when he leapt up, she kicked him back to the floor, never allowing him to get near me, but her first mistake was checking on me.

He took advantage of her focus. His foot swung out and kicked her feet out from under her. When she hit the ground, he grabbed her hair and yanked. She screamed as her body dragged against the floor.

I shot forward, but someone else held me back. I didn't even have time to spin around before I heard her voice, "Zac." Fudicia had spoken, and her single word was enough of a speech to freeze the entire room.

Zac stared, but his grasp never left Jessica.

She was the one to tear away, and she had to hit him to do it. Even then, when Jessica leapt away, a few of her white hairs stayed in his hand. He had barely moved.

Jessica, on the other hand, was not hesitating. She came after Fudicia, but this time, I jumped in front of her. "Don't," I managed.

Jessica froze, too. The expression Zac and Jessica had oddly looked related. Both of them searched Fudicia's face. Neither of them looked at me.

"What are you talking about?" Zac cursed as he stood.

Jessica shot to the side so she could face everyone, but her stance was pointed at Fudicia. She was a bigger target.

"You heard me," Fudicia spoke only to her brother. "Stop fighting."

"That's the only thing you've taught me to do," he yelled back before he made his move.

He flew toward Jessica, his hands outstretched, his voice echoing around us, but he never reached her.

In a flash, Fudicia was between them, and in a single movement, she had grabbed both sides of Zac's head. "I'm sorry," she said before snapping his neck.

He fell to the ground. The only sound in the room was his body crumbling against the cement, and the sparks that flew off his skin as he shifted back into his human form. Zac was dead.

I stumbled backward, and Zac's black eyes followed me the entire way.

My back hit the wall before Fudicia spoke again. "He wasn't going to listen." She brushed her hands off on her pants.

"What—" Jessica's skin rushed with color as she fell back into her human form. Even she had stumbled backward. She didn't know about Fudicia. In her mind, Fudicia was our enemy, and in her mind, our enemy had killed their own kind.

"He's better off this way," Fudicia spoke to her. "Are you okay?"

It was only then that I realized Jessica was bleeding. A small slit curled over her brow, and blood trickled down the side of her face. I didn't even know if it was Darthon or Zac. I was completely useless in the Light realm, but I could speak.

"She's on our side," I choked out. Everything was lined with pain.

Jessica didn't look at me, but her chin lifted, and I knew

she heard what I had said. She just didn't believe it. She was focused on Fudicia.

"This isn't an illusion," Fudicia promised.

I took a step forward, and both girls finally faced me. Apparently, I did exist. "It's not."

"She knows," Fudicia said as Jessica positioned herself into a fighting stance. "She just doesn't want to believe it."

"It's true—" I started to speak, but I didn't have to continue.

Fudicia turned her back to Jessica, leaving herself open to be killed—all so she could kneel next to her half-brother. Her fingers ran over his hair as slowly as the frown that took over her lips. Even so, her eyes were wild.

"He didn't have to die," Jessica growled, but she didn't attack.

Fudicia's touch dropped away from Zac. "He would've anyway. At least this way was quick and painless." She stood up, but she never faced us again. "Follow me, or die like him," she said and began walking away. "It's your choice."

FIFTY-FOUR

Jessica

ERIC WAS THE ONLY REASON I FOLLOWED. THAT AND ESCAPING
death. Both were aspects I had to believe in, but Eric
couldn't keep up with Fudicia's lightning-fast walk. I had
to put my arm under his to support him, but I couldn't look
at him. He had clearly spoken to Fudicia more than I knew,
and I definitely didn't know they were on the same side—my
side. It was almost impossible to fathom, even with Zac's death
proving it.

Zac really was the half-breed, and Fudicia truly was Linda,
but that meant she had killed her own blood. I didn't know if I
could trust someone like that. Still, I took one step after another and tightened my hold on Eric as I did so.

My heart thundered as the hairs on the back of my neck
stood on end. Darthon was trying to find us. I could feel his
presence in the walls, but I prevented our discovery by pouring
my own powers into the floors. Air hissed out of Eric's mouth
as if he could feel it, but I kept my hold on him. I didn't know
how much longer I could keep protecting him, but I doubted
it was for long.

"This way." Fudicia instructions were difficult to obey, but
I did.

We made our way down one corridor before meeting an
open doorway. I knew the room well. It was the same one Camille had died in. The heatless fire was too close for comfort. I

316

had brought real flames to the realm, and I was ready to make this room feel it.

I let go of Eric, but Fudicia spun around and glared at me. "Don't let go of him."

"It's okay," he said, but I didn't listen to him.

I grabbed him again. "Now what?"

The edges of Fudicia's darkened eyes illuminated like a claustrophobic eclipse. "I don't know how much time I can buy you two, but—" she paused as her face tilted like an animal listening to the woods. "I can lead him to Zac to distract him, but he'll figure it out."

"What's going to happen to you?" Eric asked like he actually cared.

It took everything in me not to let him go.

"I'll be fine," she said with a smile.

He shot one back. "Thank you, Linda."

Her lip curled downward. "I'd prefer Fudicia at this point."

Eric only nodded in return.

"Wait," I interrupted. They both stared at me, but I only looked at Fudicia. "Save the books."

"What books?" Eric asked, but we ignored him.

A small smile flickered over Fudicia's face. She didn't nod, but it was in her eyes. "Save your people."

I didn't have time to respond. Fudicia opened her mouth as if she planned on speaking again. Instead, the last thing I ever expected happened. Without moving her mouth, a chant of incomprehensible words filled the small room, and each syllable was marked with her voice.

"Close your eyes, and don't let go of each other."

It was the last words I heard.

Even with my eyes closed, I saw the light swirling against my eyelids. It darkened into shadows, and when they twisted, my body did, too. The feeling was too familiar. My molecules split, contracted, and burned. The only movement I could comprehend was Eric's touch—the single motion that remained the same throughout the vortex. If two souls could become one, I was sure it had happened.

Almost instantly, my body slammed back together, and every bone inside of me felt as if it had been crushed and strung out again. I knelt as a gasp escaped me. Breath finally filled me again.

"Jessica." His voice brought me back.

I opened my eyes to a sight that made me close my eyes again. The coffee shop was destroyed. The flipped over remains of the crushed tables were enough to solidify what had happened. Fudicia had returned us to our world, and our world was already crumbling.

Eric touched my arm. "No one's here."

It was the only reason I opened my eyes again. I had expected bodies—all the bodies of the innocent people that had been there—but Eric was right. There wasn't even a spot of blood. Whatever had happened, no one had died. Still, the building was suffocating with the smell of coffee.

"Jonathon," I managed and stepped forward. "Crystal. We have to find them—"

"Wait." Eric's hand wrapped around my wrist.

I tried to pull away, but he tightened his hold. "Jessica."

"What?"

He finally let go, but I didn't move. His emerald eyes clouded over. "Are you okay?"

"We don't have time to worry about that—"

"I always have time to worry about you," he interrupted, "and going into war confused isn't going to help either of us fight."

War. I could feel it in the air. It was worse than the Light realm. The atmosphere was crushing. The swirl of electricity and shadow told us exactly what was going on only a few miles away. The shelter was under attack, people were dying, and someone was going to win tonight.

I took a deep breath, and the rush of oxygen cleared Eric's words. He was right. If my mind was racing, I wouldn't fight well, and we both needed to fight well if he was going to win—if he was going to kill Robb. Darthon was probably already after us.

"He'll go straight for the shelter," I said.

"I know."

My mind reached out as I searched for my connection with Jonathon, but everything sizzled.

"It's too clouded to get through," Eric said. He must have tried the same thing. I knew it by looking at his face. His squinting eyes were blue, and the rest of him melted into his shade form. "Can you be one of us?"

He didn't want me to get attacked by my own people.

I confirmed it by transforming into a shade, but it prickled against my skin. Shifting from one to the other was more difficult than shifting in general, and both were already painful. I had to grab the wall to stay standing, and I took five breaths before I let go of my hold. My powers were slowly filling my veins, and Eric waited out each second.

"Since when has she been on our side anyway?" I asked in our last peaceful moment. I had to know before we succumbed to chaos again. I had to know in case I saw her again.

"For a while," he promised. "I didn't have time to tell you." He reached out and offered me his hand. "Trust her."

"I can't."

Eric's fingers curled only to uncurl. "Then, trust me."

I stared at his palm. I had never hesitated to take it before, but this time, he was asking me to take Linda's, too. She had killed Abby. She had murdered her own brother, and her parents had taken my parents, yet he wanted me to believe in her loyalty. My allegiance had boundaries, and his pushed the limits.

I only grabbed his hand for one reason. "Just don't die."

"Not a chance," he promised as his thumb skimmed the back of my hand. "I promise to see you tomorrow—in daylight—and every day after that." His smile was the only bright part of the darkness we were prepared to face. It was the only daylight I focused on, the only one I could believe in during the moments of war.

"Let's go, then," I said. "Let's win this."

FIFTY-FIVE

THE SMELL OF SWEAT AND BLOOD WAS SUFFOCATING, AND WE were drowning in it. The mixture of the powers from two sects hadn't allowed us to transport directly into the shelter. Instead, we had appeared on the outskirts, so close to the river that I could taste the moisture in the air, but I was sure the blood wasn't helping.

Bodies. Too many of them. All human now that they were dead. It was impossible to assess who had fought on what side, and the soldiers left standing were a blur of white and black. I couldn't breathe until Jessica's hand grasped mine.

"Concentrate." Her single word was all I needed.

We let go of one another and ran across the ground next to each other. While she dodged one attack, I fought back another one. My thundering heart was all I could hear, and the entrance to the shelter was all I could see. Every few seconds, my eyes met it through the thicket of trees, and every few milliseconds, I was fighting off another person.

Being a shade was all I needed to fight, but I needed my ring to feel the confidence of living. I couldn't die—not as long as we kept our jewelry on—but every passing moment seemed like a threat against it.

A claw met my wrist, and the singeing burn cascaded through my right arm. I barely had time to react. The light was fast—like a lightning bolt—and it caught my leg.

I only got a chance to hit them once before I hit the ground. The normally cold grass was warm with blood, and my fingers curled through the soaking mud as the light landed on top of me. Before I could even push them off, they flung off my torso.

Jada was looking down at me. Her multicolored eyes were the only stars I saw among the deathly night. "About time you showed up." Despite her small size, she yanked me up, and all of the sounds broke my eardrums.

Clanging metals, shattering screams, tearing flesh. I thought I heard someone throw up. My vision was blurry, and for a moment, I swore I saw the snowflakes from the night of my first battle, but my vision cleared, and I realized the whiteness was Jada's hair. It looked so much like Jessica's when she was a light.

Jada shouted at me, her mouth moving in frantic movements, her jaw bouncing up and down, but it wasn't her that I heard.

"Why aren't you with Pierce?" It was Jessica. She was next to us, and she had already grabbed both of us. We were running.

"Why isn't Eric thinking?" Jada spat back.

My real name curled through my heavy limbs. I was freezing again. It didn't matter if I were a human or a shade. I always froze. I always remembered the blood—the life Abby lost, both of the car wrecks, every person I would never see again.

"Get it together," Jessica's voice was in my head. It hadn't been in my head for so long, and I wanted it to stay there, to drown out the dying cries of more shades I knew, more students and humans and citizens I had known. But it dissipated.

I could only watch Jessica's black hair—her shade hair—mix with the darkness as she pulled me after her. Jada's white strands were ahead of Jessica. Like a beacon, she guided us through the crowd, broke through the people, and tore across the forest I had crossed too many times to count.

It was the same forest where my mother had killed herself. As we entered the shelter, the amount of black hair increased so much so that the memory of the bats flooded over my vision. There were more shades than lights, but I could not breathe.

"Jada!" Luthicer's voice bellowed as he shot between Jada and Jessica. His hands were on his daughter's shoulders before we could move a single inch forward, but his eyes had locked onto mine. "What are you doing here?"

Apparently, I was in the wrong place.

"We escaped," Jessica breathed. "Where's Pierce?"

Luthicer flipped around only for a second, and in that second, he slit someone's throat. Talking was out of the question, but he managed to shout over his shoulder, "Go to the control room."

The Dark was trying to lockdown again, but time had obviously passed. Lights were in our hallways. Whoever was in charge had failed.

My dad's face flickered through me.

"Eric." Jessica was in front of me. "Eric."

I didn't know how many times she had shouted at me, but she was shaking me. Her nails were dug into my biceps. Her skin burned mine.

I yanked back.

"Where's the control room?" she asked, her voice loud.

I opened my mouth, but nothing came out.

A hand smacked the back of my head. The pain vibrated down my spine, but my reflexes took over. I flipped around, and my hand wrapped around my attacker's throat.

Jada cringed, her face reddening.

I let her go.

She gasped. "At least you're back."

My eyes darted around the room, and every inch of the building zoomed into focus. There were more lights than I originally thought. They had covered themselves in mud, drenching their white locks with brown guck. The dark hair would throw everyone off, and my eyes had to search their faces to see what they really were. Dark pits for eyes were the only difference, and in their eyes, I saw Darthon's.

He would be here any minute. The control room was our only hope.

Breath filled my lungs as I spun around. The air tasted like bile, and I knew what it was. I was breathing slaughter.

"Follow me," I shouted, not knowing if Jessica or Jada had already done so, but as I sprinted around a corner, Jessica shot out in front of me and blocked an attack I hadn't seen.

She was always by my side, and now, I was her shadow, following her through the destruction I would have to end. But—for once—I believed I wasn't alone. We were all together.

We didn't waste any time.

We flew down the hallway, following the only plausible direction I could think of. Changing to another hallway would demand more time, and we were already fighting time. The seconds were ticking into minutes, and the minutes would be someone's last. My blood was cold, but I squeezed my hand into a fist to keep my strength.

I couldn't forget my sword. If I didn't concentrate, it wouldn't work, and I would die. We all would.

Art that had once decorated the hallway was shattered on the ground, and Jada leapt over it, skimming my peripheral vision. It was the next thing she jumped over that caused her to get in front of me. A body.

After we passed, the vision solidified. The person was a boy—a young one—and another body had laid right next to him—an older woman. I wondered what Ida had looked like when she was killed, and I knew Jessica was right. I had never killed anyone. Not a single person. The thought squeezed my lungs into unmovable sacks.

I had to grab the wall to keep myself from falling over, but my hand slipped.

Blood. It was everywhere.

The only reason I didn't fall was because someone had grabbed me. I half-expected it to be Jessica, but the grip was larger than hers.

"Pierce," I breathed as I met his green eyes.

Unlike everyone else, he wasn't glaring at me, but sweat

shone off his brow. "What the hell happened to you?"

"He got hit," Jessica spoke, but it didn't register immediately—not until I tasted the sickening sweetness in my mouth.

My fingertips rose to my face, and my skin met a gash near my hairline. When it had happened was beyond me, but I had to bet it was in the forest. I wiped away what blood I could as I surveyed my surroundings. It was the only part of training I could remember, and it was useless. The hallway was empty—aside from the no longer living.

"I cleared it," Pierce explained as he moved into the nearest room.

I stumbled after him. Even my best friend had killed, and he wasn't even a warrior. He was Jessica's guard, and—in a way—Jada was, too. When I glanced at her clothes, I saw the speckles of red soaking against it. Everyone around me had murdered. I was the only one that hadn't.

"It won't shut down," Pierce rambled and pressed himself against a panel I had only seen on a number of occasions. Only elders were allowed in the room. In fact, elders were supposed to be the only ones who knew the location, but Camille had found it years ago while exploring the secret passageways. She had taken Pierce and me without hesitation, and it had been our secret—a secret the elders must have known we shared since Luthicer told us to go to it.

"Urte and Bracke went back to get you," Pierce was talking to me, but I didn't realize it until I looked at him. "Eric." He wasn't screaming. He was calm. Pierce was never calm.

"I'm here," I managed.

"You're human."

I looked down at my skin, my flushed tone, and it tore apart as I transformed into Shoman again. In all my thoughts, I had lost my concentration.

Pierce turned around like he couldn't face me, but he could face Jessica. "I don't know what to do."

"We'll figure it out," she said and slammed her palm onto the console. Her violet eyes moved over the board of buttons and sticks.

Even in my spying, I had never learned what they were all for. She flicked one anyway, and nothing happened. Her hand curled around a joystick before she yanked it back. All of the lights went off, but they came back on when she flipped it back.

A curse escaped her. "Which one is it?"

"That one." Pierce pointed to a single keyhole, but the key shoved inside was broken. It was always a key. "It didn't work."

"Obviously." Jada pushed past the two. "There's another emergency one anyway." Her mumbling was almost impossible to hear as she yanked open a drawer and shuffled through a pile of objects.

Even elders had a junk drawer.

"I swear—some organization around here would've done some good," she kept talking, and with every word, her husky voice sounded more like Crystal's high-pitched one. She breathed as she pulled a slim bar out. It was longer than anything I thought could be in the drawer. "Here it is."

"That's a stick," Pierce screamed.

"Exactly." Jada didn't hesitate. She started pounding on the electric board. Every thump was louder than the chaos I had heard outside. It split the air with furious smacks, and Jada huffed with every blow.

She only stopped to stare at us. "Are you going to help me or not?"

"You can't break it," Pierce started to grab her stick, but she swatted him away.

"If it breaks, the whole place will lock down." Her voice was as solid as her stare. "Trust me."

Pierce stayed back, but Jessica didn't. Her sword ripped out of her arm—all purple and bright—and she slammed the blade down on the panel. Her power, alone, caused my powers to vibrate through my veins. It drew me to it. It grew somewhere deep inside of me, and my own sword was out. I stepped forward and hit the panel as hard as I could manage.

The piece of equipment didn't stand a chance.

All of the lights shut off, and darkness enveloped us. Aside from the glow of our swords, I couldn't see a thing. The blue and purple blades illuminated the reaction on Pierce's face, and Jada dropped her weapon. The metal clanged against the ground as the emergency lights flickered on, sputtering electricity into the air. In the distance, I could hear the slam of our entrance. The foundation shook, and the vibration sent the first wave of safety through the air.

Pierce let out a sigh. "I cannot believe that worked."

"It didn't," Jada's voice wavered as she spoke, but her widened eyes told us more.

I spun around to face what she saw, and everything in me froze like it did during the Marking of Change.

Darthon was in the doorway—locked inside the secured room with us. His blond hair glowed in the white emergency lights, but his smile was brighter. His sword was worse. It drew out of his arm, inch by inch, and his dark stare never left mine.

"I knew you'd use your sword eventually," he said just as he shot toward me.

FIFTY-SIX

J ESSICA TRIED TO JUMP BETWEEN US, BUT PIERCE WAS FASTER THAN he had ever been before. His grip dug into Jessica's arm, and he yanked her back. A screech escaped her as Darthon reached me.

My back hit the wall before I even realized what had happened. Our swords clanged against one another. Even though I hadn't thought about it, my reflexes had protected me, and my grip tightened as his face solidified in front of me.

This was it.

"How are the injuries?" Darthon glowered as his sword pushed closer to my throat, but he shouldn't have spoken. His cheek was ripped. His right eye was swelling shut. He was as injured as I was. He hadn't gotten into our shelter easily.

I could hear the shouts, but there were too many of them. I didn't know if it was Pierce, Jada, Jessica, or someone from outside the room. I only heard Darthon, but I saw more than him.

An electric bubble surrounded us, shielding us from the others. It was the same one he had used to take me to the Light realm, but this time, even though my molecules pulled, we remained in the Dark's shelter.

"It's destroyed," he screamed. "The entire place is destroyed, and it's your fault." Spit landed on my face, but I knew his blood did, too.

The pressure increased, but I pushed back. My muscles strained with my breath. The heat was too much.

"Zac and Linda are dead." He shoved his knee against mine. "Because of you, everyone's dead. You've had your chance to kill—"

"I'm not dead!" The shout split the bubble.

The barrier keeping us apart from everyone was gone, and everything I saw broke my insides. Pierce and Jada were no longer shades. They were human, bloody and unconscious— possibly dead—but Jessica was standing, and she wasn't alone. Fudicia was at her feet.

As she stood, Darthon's concentration broke. This was my only chance, and I chose to take it.

FIFTY-SEVEN

Jessica

DARTHON'S SWORD MET SHOMAN'S, AND THE TWO SLAMMED into the back wall. A crack split up the stone, and dust spewed out in a suffocating cloud.

I tore away from my guard, but he had grabbed me again. "Jessica—"

It wasn't Pierce's voice at all. It wasn't even his grip.

Fudicia was holding me, and her nails were poison in my veins. "Don't."

I tried to squirm away from her, but it was what I saw that froze me. A bubble of electricity surrounded us, Pierce and Jada on the outside. When they pounded on it, a burst of lightning shattered to the ground. Both of my friends flew backward, hitting the other side of the room like they were nothing but ragdolls. They didn't even fight back. They slumped to the floor, unconscious and bleeding. The attack hadn't even made Fudicia flinch.

"This fight is between Darthon and Shoman," she said it like she was protecting me.

I tore my eyes away from Pierce and Jada before I lost my concentration. "Eric will die."

"Better than you," she growled. Her teeth were spikes.

She was never on our side. I knew it. Deep inside of me, I knew it, and it was that fury that gave me the strength. I yanked my sword at her, and she leapt away from me, but she

329

never tore down her shield.

Her white hair blended in with the bubble. It was the Light's energy that allowed it, the same energy I had in my own veins—if only I had transformed into a light again, if only I let it consume me.

Fudicia's black eyes widened like she could sense what I was thinking. "Don't do this—"

Before I let my veins fill with the fire of the Light, Fudicia jumped toward me again. I latched onto her arm and swung her to the ground. Her body hit the floor in a single thud, and I swung my sword at her. She barely had time to roll away. Her black eyes were on me as I walked over to her, ready to kill another light.

"If you're a light when Darthon dies, you will die, too." She got the words out before I froze. It made sense. Darthon wanted to kill me no matter what, and his encouragement of having me on his side when he won would guarantee it. But Fudicia's voice wasn't the reason I froze. It was another voice entirely.

"Zac and Linda are dead." Darthon was screaming. "Because of you, everyone's dead. You've had your chance to kill—"

"I'm not dead!" Fudicia shouted. "I killed Zac," she said as she stood up, "and I joined the Dark."

She was on our side, and I had almost killed her.

Darthon was staring at Fudicia, but Shoman was staring at him. I saw the flicker of darkness cross his eyes before he did it. Shoman swung his sword at Darthon. The blue blade cut through the air, and Fudicia's screech was the only warning.

Darthon leapt to the side, but not fast enough. Shoman's sword hit Darthon's leg, and Darthon hit the ground. Shoman was on his feet, and before Darthon could ever stand, Shoman kicked him back down. This time, I was the one to freeze.

In movements that seemed too slow for reality, Shoman lifted his sword and brought it down, but it never met Darthon. Fudicia had intercepted it. She had tackled Shoman. The battle wasn't between the two, after all.

My blood began to course again, and I shot toward them. This time, no one held me back. As I neared, Darthon stood up, and I swung my sword at his. Our weapons collided, but sparks never shot out. Instead, the beams blended together, stretching to the ceiling. The smell of fire filled my nostrils.

"You shouldn't have chosen his side," Darthon spat.

I didn't have time to listen to him. I didn't even have time to look at Shoman or Fudicia. I only pushed harder against the blade, allowing his fire to burn my face. I didn't care. As long as I got a chance to kill him, Shoman would get his shot to truly kill him when he came back to life.

Darthon's scowl softened. "I don't want this."

In that single second, Robb's brown irises poked through the black pits Darthon had for eyes, but even then, the stare was one I had seen before. When he had hit me outside the bar, his clouded expression was filled with desperation, but it was lined with evil—the kind of evil no one came back from.

"No one has to die," Fudicia yelled, but I ignored her voice. "The prophecy—"

It was too late.

I swiped my blade through the air and missed when Darthon's leg collided with mine. I hit the ground face first and barely had time to look up as he swung his blade down at me.

"If I die, you die, too."

His voice was in my head—as if I had become a light already—and his sword was the only thing I could see as he brought his blade down. The white light split through the air, burning ablaze as it sizzled through flesh, tearing against bone and muscle. A screech filled my ears, and all of time was frozen in the flickering emergency lights.

Darthon's sword never hit me.

Fudicia crumbled on top of me, a deep slice cutting her torso from her shoulder to her hip. The edges of her skin were black. She spit up blood as she gasped, and in her gasp, she flickered into Linda—the girl I had met on prom night, the one who had already been protective of Robb, the girl who had sacrificed herself for me instead.

No one moved.

"I never left your side," she said, looking up at me. "You

only thought I did." From the Light realm to the shelter, she had used an illusion to follow us. I hadn't felt her because I hadn't thought to check, but she touched my face to prove she wasn't an illusion anymore—that she never had been. "The books are safe."

She died.

Linda was dead, and Darthon screamed.

FIFTY-EIGHT

N O ONE COULD MOVE. THE LINGERING SILENCE WAS DRAINING, and the image before us was worse. Linda—Fudicia—was dead, yet a smile stayed on her face, a smile meant for Jessica, for the Dark, for everyone she had sacrificed herself for, for the people that—apparently—never had to die in the first place.

As the realization of her words hit me, my sword disappeared, zipping into my veins, and energy crept its way into my heart. It was still beating. Only seconds had passed. Two more breaths than Linda would ever have. And her death had caused my sword to deteriorate. It was the only reason I had energy again. It had almost zapped me of everything I had, and by the looks of it, the swords of Darthon and Jessica had done the same to them.

I was the only one who could move. It had sucked nearly all of my energy out. As Darthon screamed, I leapt to my feet. I only had seconds to yank Jessica out from beneath Linda's body. She slid out easily. The blood helped.

I held back my vomit as I stumbled back, pushing Jessica the entire time. She had to grab the console to keep from falling over, and my eyes moved over Jonathon and Crystal for only a minute. They were breathing, I think. I had to concentrate on Darthon.

By the time I faced him, he was standing on shaking

knees, but his eyes were on Fudicia.

"Is it true?" I screamed, refusing to pull my blade back out. It was draining my powers. I had almost nothing left. "Can we both live?"

He was silent, but his glare was his response as he raised his gaze from Linda's body. His growling grimace stretched over his face. "You're dying for this." Even if it were true, he wasn't going to let me live.

I stepped back. "I didn't kill her." Still, I searched for some sign—any sign—that he would give in, that he would stop. "You did."

"I wasn't aiming at her!"

It was the last thing he screamed. He flew toward us, but I wasn't his target. I was never his target. He went straight for Jessica. Their swords collided, but both were weak. Her feet slid backward right as I intervened.

I kicked Darthon's ankles out from beneath him. He hit the ground, but he never got rid of his sword. If he kept it up, I could win, but for once, I didn't want to. I didn't want to kill him—not if he could live, not if he could have another chance—but Darthon squirmed back up.

This time, I kicked him in the face. "Is it true?" My scream scratched against my throat.

Darthon tried to stand. I had to kick him again. "Stop fighting!"

He was practically killing himself.

"We're all going to die anyway," he spat. "All of us. Every last one of us."

His words didn't make sense until his sword disappeared. He had realized what I had. The descendant power was draining, and he was gaining his energy back. A bubble of electricity shot up from the ground, splitting right between Jessica and me, only to ostracize Darthon and me together. From the outside, Jessica yelled something, but her words sounded like I was underwater. It didn't travel through the energy.

I tensed, readying myself to fight Darthon. "I don't want to kill you," I said and meant it.

"You won't have to," he huffed, scrambled to his feet, and straightened. His shoulders broadened, and heat filled the space between us. He had gained his energy back as fast as I had gained mine, but neither of us pulled out our swords. I didn't know how long it would take to drain me again—if it would be instant or over time—and I wasn't about to take the chance.

Jessica shouted again.

I ignored her as I made my decision. It only took me one minute to look over Darthon's face. Robb—Darthon—whoever he was—was already dead on the inside. He had died long ago, sometime in childhood, between his dog and his parents. He had let his tragedies take him, but I would have to be the one to complete his destruction.

I took the first attack, slamming my fist against his face. I hit him again—for Abby—and once more—for Camille—and one more time—for Linda. Each time I hit his face, a lost loved one flickered through my mind, and with every hit that collided with him, he laughed.

Blood sputtered out of him when I stopped. His chuckle was loud, and the blood smeared against his spiked teeth. I hit him again—this time, for him. I wanted him to come back.

When we were kids, we had met by the willow tree. Or so I had been told. I was too young to remember, but we had gone back for Independence Day nearly every year. He had even asked why I hadn't invited him the year after my mother died—the same year Camille was assigned to me—and I hadn't explained a word. He accepted it without another question, but the year Abby died he hadn't been so easy. At her funeral, he confronted me, and I hit him. I hit him for the first time, and I hadn't stopped after one hit either.

Still, he apologized to me. This time, he did nothing of the sort.

"Why are you laughing?" I screamed at him.

"I'm not," he said it at the same time I realized he hadn't been laughing.

His chuckles had morphed into sobs—struggled gasps

of screaming air—but his tears had already stopped. The wet trails left rivers of clean flesh on his grimy face. Still, his eyes were pitch black. He wasn't Robb. He was Darthon, and he looked directly into me as he spoke, "I wish I was sorry."

It was in that second, his hand grasped my wrists, and he yanked my left hand backward. I heard the bone snap before I felt it.

He was on top of me before I knew it, his knees pushed against my ribs. I writhed beneath him, screaming, as his fingers moved up my hands. "This is the only way it's fair," he muttered, his eyes moving over to me and over to my hand.

His warm fingers were wrapped around the jewelry that protected my life.

I tried to move, but it was too late. He pulled it off, and I couldn't breathe.

"You'll never know if it was real," he spoke about the prophecy as I died. "Find peace in that."

FIFTY-NINE

Jessica

I DIDN'T HAVE A CHOICE. WHEN DARTHON SEPARATED SHOMAN from me, I could only watch behind the globe Darthon's Light powers produced. I couldn't become a light to get through. Fudicia said I would die if I did, and I believed her now. Eric looked like he was winning anyway.

Until he wasn't.

In one second, Darthon was on top of him, and Eric was kicking. His screams—somehow—made it through the barrier. I felt his heartbeat leave before I knew what Darthon had done. The rings. Eric's was off.

I didn't hesitate.

I let the fire consume me. Every bit of my insides burned, and I invited them to burn more. My blood boiled, and my teeth seethed, but I only saw my hair as it glowed white.

I was a light, and I would be until the end.

I broke through the barrier, but breaking it wasn't difficult. It simply didn't hold me back. I walked right through it. Darthon's back faced me. He didn't even see it coming.

I broke his neck just like the first time, and just like the first time, I knew he would come back to life. Only Eric could kill Darthon, and right now, Eric was Eric—a human—and he was gasping for air. His green eyes were on me, widened, but I couldn't look back for long. He would live through it, and I knew it, but he didn't know everything.

I picked up his ring and slipped it back on his hand.

A hiss tore out of him as air filled his lungs, and he sat up. His hand landed on my leg. "Thank you."

I didn't look at him. "Do it."

Darthon groaned.

"Fast."

Eric transformed, only tearing his sword out for the kill, but he froze when Darthon spoke, "She'll die if you kill me." His tone was emotionless, and so was his face as he rolled over, chest facing the ceiling. Darthon wasn't even fighting back. "She'll die because she's one of us."

I fell out of my form. At least, I tried to. But it didn't work.

"I can prevent it in here," he half-growled, half-laughed. The bubble was the last bit of strength he was using.

"He's lying," I spoke to Eric, knowing what I had to do before Darthon regained his strength. "Kill him."

Eric—as Shoman—looked from Darthon to me.

"Trust me."

And he did.

Shoman raised his sword, Darthon shouted—like he never thought Eric would believe me—and it was over. The blade met Darthon's throat, but he didn't die immediately. He gurgled, and I closed my eyes as I fell to the floor.

At first, I thought it was from exhaustion, but then, I knew it wasn't. My heart was slowing. My lungs weren't taking in as much oxygen as they needed to. But my body tingled.

"Jessica," Eric was speaking to me, but it was his touch that I concentrated on. The warmth was unlike the Light's warmth. It was solid, as if he had completely embraced me, but it was only his fingertips. "Jessica, are you okay?" His voice rose. "Jessica—"

It was the last thing I heard before I succumbed to darkness.

SIXTY

JESSICA SLUMPED TO THE FLOOR SO FAST THAT I ALMOST DIDN'T catch her head, but that moment changed everything. Her light form was gone. She shifted back into her human form, and her skin paled.

"Jessica." My voice shook as I remembered Darthon's threat. I glanced at him, half-expecting to see Darthon, but he was Robb. He was dead, and Jessica wasn't moving.

"Jessica." I squeezed her arm. It had to be exhaustion. "Jessica."

Her face was getting paler, as pale as a shade's, but she was human.

"Jessica."

She didn't respond, and I pulled her into my lap, repeating her name like it would change something, but it was my hand that caught my attention. My ring—the one she had replaced—was no longer glowing. It wasn't sparkling. It wasn't doing what it was intended to do. It was supposed to keep us alive. It was always supposed to keep us alive.

"Eric."

I startled, staring down at Jessica, but her lips hadn't moved at all. Crystal landed on her knees next to me, her face bruised. "Eric," she repeated my name, but I could only stare back. "Eric, you're bleeding."

She was acting like Jessica wasn't dying in my arms.

"Get back." The voice was Luthicer's, but it was someone else who had grabbed me. I tried to fight it, but I was too weak. I was yanked back like a child, and I looked over my shoulder to see my father. He was alive.

"Jessica—"

"Are you hurt anywhere?" he asked, leaning me against the wall.

I tried to stand, but he pushed me back, lightly at first, rough the second time. He gripped my shoulders. "Eric, listen to me."

I was doing everything but listening to him. I was watching the others—Urte, Jada, Pierce, and Luthicer. They were all alive, and they were surrounding Jessica. Luthicer dug a needle into Jessica's arm. She didn't move.

"You're going to hurt yourself if you keep fighting it," my dad's voice sounded far away.

My mind was racing, and all the muscles in me were tightening, but I kept pushing. I didn't even care about breathing anymore. I just wanted to know if Jessica was alive.

"It was a lie," I screamed, trying to explain what Fudicia had insinuated—the prophecy, the threat, everything—but I didn't have the energy, and I didn't need to, because Luthicer said the only thing I needed to hear.

"She's breathing."

SIXTY-ONE

Jessica

I WOKE UP IN A BURNT WORLD. EVERYTHING WAS COATED IN GRAY ash, and the walls were feathering out into dust. There was no ceiling. The sky was black and starless—like Darthon's eyes. I took a breath. I never knew I could breathe in death.

"You aren't dead."

The voice sent chills up my spine, freezing my head in place. I had to take another breath before I could unlock my muscles and bring my face down to look at the woman.

Camille stood in front of me, and she wasn't alone. A woman with slick, black hair, cropped into a bob, was by Camille's side. The woman's blue eyes were too familiar—like Shoman's. She had to be Eric's mother.

"Well," I said, thinking I couldn't breathe, but I breathed, nonetheless. "I must be dead."

"No." Camille smiled. "Not exactly anyway."

But I remembered what had happened, after all. Eric had finally killed Darthon—Robb McLain—and I had died with my enemy. It had to happen if the Dark would live in safety. It was the right decision.

"I don't understand," I managed.

"That immortality spell was never meant for Eric. Neither was the necklace I gave him," Camille spoke of a time that seemed too long ago to fathom. "Those spells were meant for you. I only wanted to see you one last time."

"How?"

"My spirit has been trapped here," Camille spoke as I realized where we were—the destroyed Light realm. I recognized the burnt horns on the crumbling wall. We weren't in the afterlife at all, but she was still dead, and so was Eric's mother. "She's trapped as long as I am."

Eric's mother never spoke, but she smiled for the first time. She had Eric's smile.

"We won't be trapped anymore," Camille said and stepped forward. She lifted her hands, palms facing me. I couldn't move as her fingers landed on my face, tracing over my cheeks. "Just like before."

She was even dressed in the same clothes she had died in.

I pulled away before she could do what she did before— send me back—but Camille reached out again. "You have to lead the Light, Jess," she said it like I wanted to die, but in truth, I didn't want to leave them behind. "You need to live."

"And my shade side?"

"That no longer exists." A frown escaped her. "When you transform again, you'll officially be a leader, and they need one."

"And you?"

"Tell the others I love them," she said.

I swallowed my nerves. "They'll think I was hallucinating."

Camille's face tilted to the side as her frown flipped into the only sweet smile I had ever seen from her. "Perhaps we all were."

With her words, Eric's mother moved forward, and her hand landed on my arm. She was warm. They both were. And as soon as they had appeared, they were gone.

———— ◆ ————

I gasped as my lungs filled with ice-cold air. My muscles ached as I sat up, and a groan escaped me as I leaned forward, elbows on my legs. I had been lying down on a bed I recognized too well. I was in the nurse's ward of the Dark's shelter, and I was alive.

342

And so many people weren't.

The hum of the chaos caught my ears. The battle wasn't completely over. I only sat up so I could hear more, but what I saw stopped my original decision.

Eric was sitting at the edge of my bed, his upper torso collapsed on the mattress. His brown hair was mangled, matted together with dirt and blood, but his injuries had healed. I must have been out for hours, and now, he was deep asleep, clutching my hand.

"He hasn't let go of you since you were brought in here."

The voice was all too familiar, and it filled my lungs with relieved breath. Jonathon was leaning against the wall, his arms crossed over his chest. Little bags hung from his eyes, but he smiled. He almost looked like he had been sleeping while standing up.

He was alive, too.

Before I could ask, he answered, "Crystal's fine. The remaining elders, too."

No one I knew had died, and as much as I wanted that to be a comfort, I knew others weren't so lucky.

"The battle is still going on," he whispered after a minute. "Just not with us."

I stared back at him. "What happened?"

I could only remember Darthon dying, how his death had brought mine, and what I saw in the burnt Light realm.

Jonathon's eyes moved to my hand that held Eric's. "I think that kept you two alive."

I glanced down, but only for a moment. The jewelry was no longer glowing. Whatever power it had held was gone. It had done the job it was meant to do, and the spell had died with the passing of Eric's mother and Camille, two souls that had been trapped all along. In their death, I had found my own. I could feel it—how my Dark side was gone. My heart was heavy against my ribs, but it was beating. I had another identity to control. The Light side was mine, and it would be in chaos until I accepted it. Once I did, they would stop fighting. My veins tingled with a desire I had never felt before, but with a confidence I knew too well—it felt like the home the Dark had given me so long ago.

I had to tear my eyes away from my guard before I told him what I was thinking. My battle wasn't over yet. My journey wasn't complete. Only theirs was.

"How long have I been out?" I asked.

"A day," he answered. "It's midnight."

I stared at Eric. His breathing was hoarse, but he didn't wake up, even when we spoke. It was unlike him. Too unlike him. "What'd you do to him?"

"Drugged him."

I couldn't help but gape at my guard, but Jonathon only shrugged. "The guy wouldn't sleep until you woke up." He scratched his head, but it didn't prevent the shameful blush from cascading over his cheeks. "We didn't really have a choice. He had to heal."

I bit my lip so I could nod in agreement. Eric had already been through too much, but I squeezed his hand out of reflex. As much as I didn't want him to wake up, I wanted him to wake up. I wanted to hear his voice, to see the light in his eyes, to hug him.

"Darthon's dead, Jessica." Every word Jonathon said came out in struggled pauses. "It's over." The words were the words the Dark had wanted to speak for decades, but it had finally happened, and resulted in the death of a teenager who hadn't chosen it.

In that moment, I remembered Darthon as Robb McLain—the first person I met in Hayworth as a human. It seemed fitting that I had met Eric the night before as a shade. I had been connected to both of them from the beginning, and while Robb started as a friend and Eric as an enemy, it had flipped over a year's time. Now, only one was alive, and I was left to take Robb's place.

I shivered. "Thank you."

"For what?"

"For being there for me—and Eric."

Jonathon didn't speak, but I looked up in time to witness

his nod. Thanking one another over the circumstances seemed cruel. People had died, after all, but at least we hadn't lost one another.

We remained like that—in our silence—for only a moment before the others heard us. One screamed, "She's awake," and then, the room was filled with familiar faces. Urte was in his shade form, and he only stayed for a minute before disappearing to join Luthicer and Jada. They were trying to get the Light under control, a sect that was only fighting itself out of madness, but Bracke stayed.

"How are you feeling, Jess?"

"Better," I managed before I finally found the strength to explain what I saw—his wife and Camille in the realm, protecting us all along.

Bracke returned my words with a smile. "I always was wrong." He had thought his wife was trying to kill Eric when all she had done was guarantee his life if his guard died as well.

"Stop beating yourself up."

The voice came from the last person we expected to hear from.

Eric shuffled around, lifting his head from his sleepy state. "And don't think I'll forgive you for drugging me," he spoke directly to Jonathon, but a smile crept along his lips. His tone said the opposite—he had already forgiven all of us—and his eyes said what he wanted to say. His soft irises were locked directly at me. "Glad you're feeling okay."

I laid my hand on top of his hair, trying not to cringe at the crusty feel. "Are you?"

He nodded, never lifting his face from the mattress. "I will be."

Eric had killed Darthon—finally—and unlike the rest of us, he didn't praise it. Not even his expression did. He only looked groggy, as if a part of him had faded away in the chaos, and I squeezed his hand as if I could pull him back.

He reciprocated the squeeze. He never said a word about his mother, or Camille, or what had happened in the control room, and I imagined it was because a part of him already knew they hadn't truly died. They had lived through us all along. It was the reason he had never dealt with their deaths. I could see it now, even though it was finally over, and because of that, I could breathe again.

He fell asleep again, and no one spoke. Bracke simply nodded and left the room. Jonathon followed, and I was alone with Eric for the first time in what seemed like months. But it wasn't peaceful. The room sizzled with energy from the battle that had happened, and the battle that was continuing to happen outside.

The new breeds of Light and Dark members existed, and the Light had crumbled beneath their leader's death. Until they got a new one, they would fight, and I was the only one who knew how to step in and fix it, but not yet, not now. I was too tired.

My eyes closed, and I fell into a deep sleep once more.

SIXTY-TWO

I DIDN'T KNOW HOW MUCH TIME HAD PASSED, BUT IT HADN'T BEEN as long as I thought. When I found the clock, only a few extra hours had ticked away, but I felt alive again, not drained like I had felt before. I glanced at Jessica—her sleeping face, the calmest expression I had seen on her delicate features in weeks—and I slowly inched away from the bed.

I needed to talk to the others, figure out what was happening, and see if there was a way I could help, but I wanted to do it without waking Jessica. In a way, she had died and come back to life—all in the name of the Dark and the Light—and I had simply killed Darthon.

Simply.

It disgusted me, but I pushed myself away from the bed with a focus on making it right. Still, Jessica woke up. She never let me get away with anything.

"Where are you going?" Her voice was as groggy as her eyes as she rubbed them.

I didn't speak as I looked at her blue eyes. I doubted I would ever see them as violet again. Even though the prophecy could've been a lie, I believed what Darthon had said. Jessica would be a light. It was a matter of time until her eyes would be black.

"I'm going to check on the others," I managed as I stood on shaky knees. My legs were tired, but with every movement, my strength grew.

She sat straight up. "Me, too."

I didn't argue with her, because there was no point in fighting. She would come if she wanted to. That was her right.

I walked out, knowing she was behind me, and when I stopped in the hallway, she stopped next to me.

Everyone was there. Urte, Luthicer, and my father were still in their shade forms, but Crystal and Jonathon were human, and they were the first ones to see us. Crystal even had her lip ring in.

"Jess!" She ran over, and before Jessica could react, Crystal's arms were wrapped around Jessica's torso. "You're awake."

Jessica hugged her friend back before slowly prying Crystal off. "I'm alive."

Crystal's lips formed into a pout. "Don't be so dreary."

Somehow—in some way—I wasn't surprised that Luthicer's daughter, out of all people, was the most callous about everything. He must have raised her that way, gone against the rules and trained her from the beginning. We knew she was tracking Zac, after all, and that was long before she had developed powers. The one elder notorious for following a strict policy was also the one who had broken the most rules.

"You two lovebirds get some alone time?" she joked.

Jessica laughed—actually laughed—before she responded, "We got some nap time."

Crystal cringed. "Boring."

"These two are boring," Jonathon interrupted, sporting his usual grin, but this time, he laid his forearm on Crystal's shoulder. She didn't even move away from him. "And they probably need more time alone."

Before I could argue, Jessica grabbed my arm and pulled me away from the two. Even then, I kept my eyes on my best friend and Jessica's best friend. Her white hair was eerie next to his dark hair—almost as if they hadn't transformed back into humans at all—but they smiled like humans, and they talked like it was any other day.

Jessica and I didn't speak as we leaned against the wall feet away from them, our arms pressed against one another. I no longer sensed her heartbeat in my veins, and I knew she probably didn't sense mine. Our rings were regular pieces of jewelry now, but they still mattered to me. Even then, our touch seemed to be missing something when I watched Jonathon and Crystal interact.

They talked, seemingly in their own world, but the sight relaxed me. "She doesn't seem too heartbroken about Zac."

In my peripheral vision, Jessica cringed. "I'm pretty sure she was only doing that for research."

"That's ethical journalism." I knew Crystal's reason when I spoke, but I wanted to hear Jessica's voice say anything, and a bigger part of me wanted more than that. Even though they were apart, Crystal and Jonathon were standing so close to one another that they were practically hugging. I had never seen Jonathon like that with anyone. It made me realize how far apart Jessica and I were, but I focused on our friends. "They seem awfully close."

"Jonathon has a crush on her," Jessica said.

When I turned to look at her, my neck popped.

She shrugged. "He didn't know she was Crystal at the time." None of us did. Not until it was almost the end, but a part of me wondered when Jonathon had confessed to Jessica. He hadn't said a word to me, but I knew that happened between guards and their warriors. Camille had told me things she had never explained to anyone else—like how she wanted to go to college—but she was dead, and she was finally able to pass.

I looked at Jonathon as if I saw Camille. I wondered if she would've found anyone if she were alive, but I had to push the thought away because it was a useless one, a depressing one that would never be resolved.

Jonathon and Crystal, on the other hand, had a chance, and meeting as shades wasn't rare. "I guess that's how most shades used to start relationships," I said, knowing the old rules the Dark had valued before my birth. My great-grandfather had changed the rule of arranged marriages, and there was still speculation that his law change had caused my birth. A part of me believed the rumors were true.

"You don't think they'll actually date, do you?" Jessica whispered. "They're opposites."

It was true. Crystal was brash and invasive. Jonathon was shy and supportive. But watching them was like watching the sunset and the sunrise, equally beautiful in different ways.

"Maybe they'll balance each other out," I joked.

Jessica nudged my arm. "If you mention balance one more time—"

I couldn't help but laugh. "Relax." My words and my attitude seemed foreign in the dreary moment, but it was starting to feel familiar again—like it truly was over.

Crystal let out a loud giggle.

Jessica's head pressed against my arm. "Did she just giggle?"

I draped my arm around her shoulders. "That was definitely a giggle."

Before Jessica could speak again, the elders finally stepped in. Luthicer was the one to talk first, "All right, break it apart." He stared directly at his daughter. "Now is not the time to be laughing." People were still fighting, after all. Whether or not they were dying was beyond me, but it would only be a matter of time. The Light wouldn't lose their powers immediately, but they would lose them eventually, and the drain would bring them into deeper madness.

"Sorry." Jonathon took a wide step to the left, away from Crystal.

She took a wide step after him, and when they touched each other, they both started laughing again. I had never seen Jonathon laugh so much.

Luthicer's shoulders slumped. "Well, I guess that's that."

I tapped the elder's boot with my own boot to get his attention. There was something I needed to know, and when he looked at me, I spoke, "I thought you said you were Crystal's father."

As far as I knew, Crystal only had her mother in her

350

life, but Luthicer argued that when he said, "I am." Everyone stopped as the man glanced at his daughter. "Sort of."

Before anyone could ask for a better explanation, a light surrounded him and sizzled down his body. He shrank with the beam, and his beard curled up into his face. The long white hair he normally had was replaced with a dark bob, and his sharpened facial features softened. Luthicer wasn't Luthicer at all. He was Lola Hutchins.

"You're—you're a lady," Jonathon stuttered.

Lola crossed her arms as her eyes slit into a glare. "You have a problem with that, Mr. Stone?"

Right when I thought Luthicer couldn't be more terrifying, he proved me wrong. Lola was terrifying.

"Nope." Jonathon waved his hands in front of his chest. "No problems at all, ma'am."

"Good." Lola's legs locked as she brushed off her clothes—a simple pantsuit. "A lot of things can change during transformation." Her words were taut. "But more can happen with a lack of sleep, so I suggest all of you rest." We would have to deal with the fighting lights in the morning. "In separate rooms." Lola wasn't even looking at me. She was looking directly at Jonathon.

He froze. It was Urte—Jonathon's father—who responded. "Everything's already set up." Urte wasn't fazed by Luthicer's transformation at all.

Jonathon's eyes widened when he looked at his father. "You knew about this."

"You didn't?" Urte said like it was obvious, but his tone dropped when he continued to speak, "Brenthan wants to see you." The youngest of the Stones was alive.

Jonathon rolled his eyes like he didn't care, and then grinned because he did. "I'm going. I'm going." He started to walk away, Urte followed, and Crystal left with her mother.

Jessica and I stayed with my father, but it wasn't long before he pointed down the hallway. "That way, you two."

"Yeah. Yeah." Even though I had slept and gained energy, I was drained. I could sleep one hundred years, and I doubted I would ever feel fully rejuvenated.

As I walked down the hallway, the darkness flickered beneath the emergency lights. Shades were already cleaning the walls. I opened my mouth—ready to offer assistance—but my lips snapped shut as if I weren't able to do it. When I closed my eyes, I saw Robb's pale face plastered against my eyelids.

Jessica squeezed my hand, and I jumped. Still, she never let me go. "You okay?"

I didn't nod, but she did. She understood. She was there, after all. She had even killed Ida. I doubted we would ever be the same, but at least we would be together.

The words left me as I came to a stop, "We're okay, right?"

Jessica's eyes—the color of the sky—moved over my face. "Of course." She hadn't taken off her ring, and neither had I.

I didn't want to leave her. Even though I knew we had separate rooms, the separation seemed cruel. I wanted her to stay by my side, to sleep next to me, if we even managed to sleep at all, but she moved toward her door only to stop in-between the rooms.

"Darthon," she stuttered and shook her head as her eyes fell to the floor. "Robb," she corrected, "He Named me."

It didn't surprise me, but I couldn't breathe. The Dark had never offered her a name, but it made sense now. Perhaps the Dark's instincts had known the truth all along—that Jessica would be a light, that her name had to come from them, but I had never suspected that she had gotten one before the end.

"Iris," she said. "It was my mother's."

My shoulder pressed into the wall next to hers. "Are you going to keep it?"

She didn't speak.

I reached over, laid my fingers under her chin, and lifted her face so that she had to look at me. "I think you should." She had wanted a Name from the beginning.

Her bottom lip trembled. "Why?"

I wanted to say it was for her biological parents, for their legacy, but it was beyond that. Robb added to it. "He suffered just as much as we did." Like us, he was born into it. He didn't have a choice. The choices he did have had died a long time ago, when he was a child, when he had no ability to fight for it. As much as my father and I had struggled to have a relationship, we had one. Robb didn't have anyone but fellow murderers.

Jessica nodded like she understood. "But I still hate him," she spoke, "a part of him anyway." Her eyes darted to the wall only to look back at me. "For now."

"Me, too," I agreed, trying to find a place in my heart to understand that our battle was long from over. We had to heal. I cracked a smile like it was the first step. "That's the human side of us."

Jessica hit my arm lightly, but her frown concealed the smile I knew existed beneath it. Her eyes glowed because of it. "Get some sleep," she said, but her voice dropped on the last word.

Before she could walk away, I grabbed her hand. "You don't have to be alone tonight if you don't want to be."

"I know." She stared down at our hands before unlacing her fingers from mine. "But I should be." It was me who didn't want to be alone, but it was worse when I saw the light in her eyes leave right before she turned around. "Goodnight."

Jessica wasn't gone yet, but she was striving to be.

SIXTY-THREE

Jessica

I HAD THE FINAL DECISION TO MAKE, AND I KNEW I HAD TO DO IT ON
my own. While Eric had to kill Darthon, I had to save the
Light. They were still fighting, and the stench of the night
filled the air. It only got worse as I snuck out of the shelter.

It was much easier than I thought it would be. None of the
shades who saw me stopped me, because they trusted me, and
I hoped that trust would remain as I ducked outside.

While I expected to see people running around in their
madness, I saw nothing. I only sensed it. Perhaps they had
gone elsewhere. Perhaps they were all fighting inside their
own minds at home. But I knew they wouldn't be for long. I
would bring them together again.

I walked straight for the only place I wanted to be.

Amazingly, the railing that sat above the river was still intact, and I inhaled a deep breath as I climbed on top of the first
bar. It shook like it had the first time I stood on top of it—the
second I had met Eric—the moment I had realized I was never
alone—and it was for that reason that I turned around.

At first, I thought I was hallucinating, that my memory
had taken over my consciousness and I was losing my mind
with the rest of the lights, but then, he smiled.

Eric was right behind me.

He shoved his hands in his pockets as his emerald eyes
glowed through the dark night. "You really thought I'd fall for

that?"

When I had told him goodnight, I knew he didn't want to be alone, but I didn't know that he was aware of my own feelings. I didn't want to be alone either. I only thought I had to be.

"No," I managed as I stepped down. The rushing river was the only sound that cascaded between us. It roared with every word we hadn't said. "I love you" hadn't seemed appropriate when others had lost their lives. "I want you" seemed just as selfish. Everything did. That's why I wanted to do my last battle on my own. "I thought I'd try anyway."

Eric grabbed my hand, his touch warming me. When he pulled us up onto the railing, we stood on the shaky metal. A cold breeze pushed against us. It smelled like death. "It's dangerous out here," he said exactly what I was thinking.

"It won't be for long."

I knew I had to do it. I had to listen to Camille and Eric's silent mother. I had to transform into a light, I had to let my shade self go, and I had to declare myself their leader. I had to let them know they would live on, too. I had to give them hope, even when all the hope I previously had died. I had to believe in that hope again, and in order to do that, I had to sacrifice my own identity all over again. I had to be Iris—the Light's descendant—and I had to accept everything that came along with it.

"The Dark will support you," he said the only words I wanted to hear. Eric always did that.

I gripped the railing as if it would fall over, but Eric's hand landed on top of mine. He slowly pried my fingers off the metal. "Whatever happens," he said as he leaned over and kissed my cheek. "I'm here."

I nodded, we spread my fingers out together, and I felt our love flow through my veins as they filled with the heat I was all too familiar with.

I let the red rain fall.

SIXTY-FOUR

Four months later

J ESSICA'S PARENTS CAME TO OUR GRADUATION, AND SO DID EVERY-
one else. Everyone who was alive anyway. A huge section of Hayworth High's ceremony was dedicated to the
victims of the cult—the same cult that the sect had created
during the first illusion. Only this time, an illusion wasn't used.
Everyone just accepted it—almost as if they knew about the
Light and the Dark—but still, no one spoke of it out loud.
Even though the new breed of shades and lights added to our
numbers, humans existed. Mindy had proven it to us all, and
for the first time, my father didn't feel guilty for breaking his
own laws.

My family—Mindy, Noah, and my dad—sat on lawn
chairs in the same field the Marking of Change had happened,
but this time, they laughed, and I wondered if they would sit
there when Independence Day came again. It was only two
months away, but it would be the first one I wouldn't make it to.

In the morning, I was driving to Iowa with Jonathon. We
would speak at a council of shades—and lights. It was only
our first stop. There were hubs of lights and shades all over
the states, people Urte had tracked down after the Marking of
Change. Apparently, many of the out-of-towners had bought
his cupcake service. Now, Jonathon and I were in charge of
bringing everyone together with Jessica's message. We were
taking more cupcakes for good measure.

Jessica would stay behind.

It was her plan. After the final battle, she had become a light, and in that power, she had saved the Light. When her red rain fell, dozens of survivors came to us—one by one—and she gave them the strength to stop their insanity. She gave them their powers back, but afterward, she was too exhausted to do much else. Everyone took shifts watching over her until she recovered. It took three weeks, but she was graduating with the rest of us. She was the strongest person I knew.

Because of her, the Light hadn't died. They lived with the Dark, and we were one sect again. Still, there was discrimination, and we had already dealt with two murders over it. At the age of eighteen, Jonathon, Jessica, and I were officially elders. We had seven spots to fill, and Crystal was guaranteed one when she returned from college. Jessica would choose the other ones from the Light.

I leaned my back against the willow tree only to stare up into the leaves. The light that flickered through the spaces looked like tiny stars, and for once, daylight felt like home.

I only tore my eyes away from it to glance down at Jessica. She was sitting at the base of the tree, right at my feet, and her brown curls were tied into a tight ponytail. She didn't want her hair in her face as she read, and she flipped pages faster than what I thought was possible. Jessica hadn't dropped a book since she recovered, and because of it, she already knew more about the sects than I did. Jessica was reading all the ancient texts she could.

Fudicia—or Linda—hadn't lied when she said they were saved. In fact, she had saved them before Jessica had asked, but the location was only revealed to her once she became a light. Out of all the places Fudicia could've put them, the books were finally found in the art room of Hayworth High. Even more surprising was the person who told us where they were.

Ms. Hinkel—our homeroom teacher—was an elder in the Light, and she was Fudicia's trainer. She was also one of Lola's best friends, a friendship that had remained intact even after Lola—as Luthicer—had left the Light in a murderous rampage. Their friendship was the only way Luthicer had gotten us out of school all along, including Crystal. It also proved that Fudicia wasn't the only light to choose the Dark in the end, even though—in reality—they hadn't chosen the Dark at all. Like Jessica, Fudicia and Ms. Hinkel had chosen both sides. But Ms. Hinkel lived, and she named off every graduating senior at the ceremony. She only cried when she got to the end of the list.

Eric Welborn.

My surname fated me to be last, and for once, I found my place in it.

The graduation ceremony was over, but our lives were just beginning, and Jessica was already beating me to the race. Even in her graduation robe, the girl had her nose stuffed in the latest book—one about the Highland, our apparent home—and she rambled off facts as she came across them.

I hadn't known a single one of them—how our powers came from another dimension and how we had grown into a human form over time. The sects had been together once before, but when they crossed into our current world, the Light didn't want a shadow anymore. The Dark refused to accept it, and the elders of both clans decided to take the powers away. Why they gave them back through three eighteen-year-olds was beyond me, but I was sure Jessica would read that fact any moment. Until then, I was satisfied knowing that, for the first time in centuries, we were one sect with our powers intact, and the possibilities were endless. It would take years to understand everything, but right now, I had hours until the morning took me to Iowa.

I leaned over and grabbed Jessica's book. She yelped when I took it away, and I had to put it behind me to stop her from snatching it back.

She pouted. "I was reading that."

"You can read it tomorrow," I said, knowing that I wouldn't see her for a long time. Today was our last moment together for months. "Why don't we enjoy the moment?"

Her pout moved from the left side of her mouth to the

right side, but it eventually subsided in the middle. "Let me put it in my bag, at least." She knew it was one of our last days together. I respected her dedication, but even she needed a break. History would always be there.

I handed her book back, and she placed it in her backpack carefully—like it was made of glass. She zipped her bag closed, leaned against the willow tree, and blew out a sigh. "Can you believe it?" Jessica's voice was a whisper as she laid her head on my shoulder.

I threaded my fingers through her curls. "I can't believe we don't actually get our diploma today." It would be shipped to us in two weeks.

Jessica nudged me, but she laughed. "You know what I mean."

"Sorry." I chuckled. "I can't believe I am even getting one at all."

She hit me again, a light slap on my leg. Before she could lecture me, I grabbed her hand, bent over, and kissed her.

As her hand curled against mine, her lips moved with mine. It was a short, consoling kiss, but it felt deeper than all of the other ones we had shared. Every kiss we had felt like that—better than the first—and every moment that passed between us was another moment I was grateful we had.

When we broke apart, she laid her palm on my chest. "This," she said, "is how I know we're still alive."

I kissed her forehead. "Do you need more proof?"

She pushed herself away, but giggled as we stood up. It wasn't two seconds before Crystal and Jonathon joined us on top of the hill, both dressed in graduation robes that were too long for them.

Crystal hugged Jessica like she hadn't hugged her before, but—in reality—Crystal hadn't stopped hugging Jessica. "That wasn't as painful as I thought it would be." She cracked a smile, but it was her makeup that gave her away. She had cried during the ceremony, and Jonathon had been the one to console her.

I wasn't sure if they were dating, but Jonathon stayed by

her like they were. "I'm surprised you didn't stumble across the stage," he joked at me.

"Coming from you," I started, but he raised a hand.

"Go ahead: make a blind-kid joke."

I cracked a smile. "I was going to make a clumsy joke."

Jonathon chuckled, but his eyes never left Crystal as the two girls began chatting. I leaned against the tree just to get his attention, and when he finally looked at me, he was already talking, "It's going to be weird."

"What is?"

"Being apart." His eyes moved down the hill, and I followed his gaze to the familiar faces—George and Brenthan, Lola and Mindy, my father and Noah. Jonathon and I would be going alone, and we would truly put distance between us and Hayworth for the first time in our lives.

"It won't be for long." The trip would last one year, and Jessica and Crystal would meet up with us in six months. By that time, we hoped to have a large council together—a united front for a better future. It was a task the previous elders had gladly given us. No more secrets. No more fighting. Only talking.

We would leave in the morning.

"I'm going to see my family," Jonathon said before shouting over to Crystal, "Lola wants to see you."

Crystal spun around, her hair now black. She had stopped dying it. "She does?"

Jonathon grinned, but the silent message was clear. He wanted to give Jessica and I more alone time. Crystal bounced over because she understood, but she stopped inches in front of me. "Take care of my girl," she said. As she walked away, she shouted over her shoulder, "I expect to be the maid of honor."

Jessica laughed and walked over to my side. "Get out of here, Crystal."

Her friend winked, running down the hill and following Jonathon like they had been friends for far longer than they had been.

I watched their backs for a minute, but my attention was

quickly drawn to Jessica. She was holding my hand again. It was all I wanted to do, but her other hand was occupied. She waved down the hill, and I followed her gesture to her parents.

They waved back, grins plastered on their faces, before her father made the motion of driving a car. He had already borrowed my Charger four times, and now, they made jokes with my father. They had officially met two weeks ago.

"I love you," Jessica said so suddenly I almost didn't hear her, but I knew she had said it when she shifted from foot to foot. She always did that when she was nervous.

"I love you, too," I responded, wondering what it would be like to be apart again, but this time, the distance wouldn't be forced. It was agreed upon, and the nerves I felt weren't nearly as high as all of the times before.

"Be sure to call me when you get to Iowa," she said as if she was thinking the same thing.

"Be sure to know where your phone is so I can," I joked.

She giggled. It was the best sound I had heard all day.

"And when I get back, I think we should pick a date," I added.

Her blue eyes met mine—widening as a blush blew across her cheeks. "Eric—"

"I'm still marrying you, Jessica." A grin fit itself onto my face. "Only if you want to."

Her blush deepened. "I do."

"You're supposed to save those words for the wedding day."

She laughed. "Leave it to you to keep joking about everything."

I didn't respond because I didn't have to. I only wanted to kiss her, to live in the moment without worrying about what my next day would bring. I only wanted to live, and for once, I felt like I was truly living, but even better, I knew all of Hayworth was finally allowed to live in peace.

In the end, the Light and the Dark came together. In the end, we were the same, and I believed we would remain that way for eternity.

ACKNOWLEDGMENTS

NINE YEARS HAVE PASSED SINCE I WROTE THE FIRST SENTENCE OF The Timely Death Trilogy, and now, the trilogy has come to an end. A countless number of people – including readers and writers and editors and designers – have guided me along the way, but there is no guidance when you meet the end of a road. My emotions range from absolute delight to terrified reluctance, but I am mainly met with the uncanny feeling that Eric and Jessica understand this situation. Their story has explored the light and dark moments of life, and I am honored that I was able to share these characters with the world. My first "thank you" is for all of the readers who have supported this trilogy. I am eternally grateful for your love, and I'm glad I've found so many friends who love the mysterious night as much as I do.

Special thanks also goes out to my team at Clean Teen Publishing—Courtney, and Rebecca, and Marya, and Kelly, and Cynthia—for exploring the Dark with me! (And for helping me find my way through it.)

Between conjuring supernatural beings and cuddling with cats, I promise another story is always in the works.

Stay Dark,

Shannon A. Thompson

ABOUT THE AUTHOR

Shannon A. Thompson is a twenty-three-year-old author, avid reader, and habitual chatterbox. She was merely sixteen when she was first published, and a lot has happened since then. Thompson's work has appeared in numerous poetry collections and anthologies, and her first installment of The Timely Death Trilogy became Goodreads' Book of the Month. As a novelist, poet, and blogger, Thompson spends her free time writing and sharing ideas with her black cat named after her favorite actor, Humphrey Bogart. Between writing and befriending cats, she graduated from the University of Kansas with a bachelor's degree in English, and she travels whenever the road calls her.

Visit her blog for writers and readers at
www.shannonathompson.com

CPSIA information can be obtained at www.ICGtesting.com
Printed in the USA
LVOW10s0657111015

457770LV00003B/15/P